Sweet Eyes

Also by Jonis Agee

Houses

Mercury

Two Poems

Pretend We've Never Met

Bend This Heart

Anthologies edited by Jonis Agee

Stiller's Pond

These Women

Secrets

Border Crossings

Sweet Eyes

by Jonis Agee

For Cathy—
Thanks for your
years of support—
helping me keep my
imaginings alive during
our years of knowing each
other— you've been a voice—
wonderful influence—
My Best—
Jonis Agee
May 2
1991
CSC

Crown Publishers, Inc.
New York

For Brenda, Jackie, Cindy, Laura,
and all my sisters
walking toward the light.

Published by Crown Publishers, Inc., 201 East 50th Street,
New York, New York 10022. Member of the Crown Publishing Group.

CROWN is a trademark of Crown Publishers, Inc.

Manufactured in the United States of America

Library of Congress Cataloging-in-Publication Data

Agee, Jonis.
Sweet eyes / by Jonis Agee.—1st ed.
p. cm.
I. Title.
PS3551.G4S94 1991
813'.54—dc20 90-41617
CIP

ISBN 0-517-57515-9

10 9 8 7 6 5 4 3 2 1

First Edition

Contents

My guide and I came on that hidden road to make our way back into the bright world; and with no care for any rest, we climbed—he first, I following—until I saw, through a round opening, some of those things of beauty Heaven bears. It was from there that we emerged, to see—once more—the stars.

Dante
Divine Comedy,
Inferno

Sweet Eyes

1

My Job at Bowker's

Marylou Jackson, the other girl in the office who lives over Steadman's Drugstore down the street with her two preschoolers, has just left. After the first one, she moved from the country into town. Mike, her drunk husband, was gone so much it took him two weeks to find out where she lived. "Coming to get her back," he yelled at anyone who'd listen. She met him at the door, cool as ice, and told him, "Get your ass upstairs if you don't want to sleep in the street."

Some days I feel like calling the baby-sitter as I watch Marylou getting on her coat, changing her shoes. I want to alert her, "Put away those cigarettes, hide that candy bar." Marylou has her cross in life. That's what Mama would say: "We all got our crosses. You got to understand that, Honey. Don't be so hard on everyone."

Well, if she were alive, she'd see who is being hard. I hope that Baby and Sonny Boy meet up with Mama someday. Just a glimpse on their way down. Like the elevator in Goldstein's Department Store in Des Moines we once got on because Mama couldn't stand escalators. We couldn't decide which floor we wanted, and then Tolson got off in toys and we kept trying to find him again. The next time we'd see him in Boys' Wear on another floor or standing in front of a bunch of sofas in Furniture on another one. We couldn't figure out where to get off, and the operator was snickering at us, burying her snotty nose in her handkerchief like we smelled. Finally Mama marched us off on the main floor and we walked up the others, eight floors, until we'd seen everything and found Tolson.

I hope when Baby and Sonny Boy die, they get on the elevator, see glimpses of Mama up there, floating around tending sheep, and before they can call out to her, zip, they're on their way down.

Today, after we finished the typing, filing, and bookkeeping, Marylou put on her street shoes, flat with no-nonsense square toes. She only wears the three-inch pointy toes for work, to make herself tip around on the carpet. Bowker likes that. That's part of her, trying to please her boss. She always talks about "my boss" like he is the head of the world or something.

Usually Marylou asks me to cover the phone while she's gone, and she'll offer some little excuse so I think she's being the Good Employee. But today she just walked out. Not a word about when she'll be back.

"Hey, wait, wait," I called after her. "When am I—" I wanted to go out for lunch. I was supposed to pick up my friend Twyla, we were going to grab a burger together. "Well, that's that," I said out loud to the door that closed behind Marylou. Then I called Twyla, leaned back, and took a look around me.

Facing Main Street, the north wall is mostly windows that rattle when the wind blows and let in the cold. Bowker's put a lock on the thermostat, too. Marylou and I had to buy little heaters we keep under our desks for warmth when it gets too cold in the winter. I haven't had mine on in a month. It's April, and that's usually okay in Iowa. Unless some damn thing blows down from the Dakotas. One of those Alberta Clipper storms.

Outside I can see the sky starting to gray up like old porch paint, and I can tell it isn't any rain coming. Damn. We're going to have one of those late snows, and all hell's going to break loose for a day or two. Then it'll warm up and melt in a morning, everything underneath fresh and green like yesterday was only your imagination.

That's why Marylou took off. She must have taken her Girl Scout training to heart. Be prepared. She knew it was truth the moment she said it, and since then she had been. (Well, except for the cross, Mike.) Even plain looks hadn't caught her with her attention down. She took it in stride and did the most with it.

Twyla always marvels at Marylou. "You wonder if she sleeps with her makeup on, like women in the movies. What's she like under all that? I can't remember from junior high school, and that's the last time anyone saw her plain self."

"Who knows," I tell Twyla, "maybe she was so prepared not to turn out pretty, she stopped it from happening. You know Marylou." We nod.

Twyla and I agree on most things. Except Sonny Boy, my brother, and we don't talk about him much.

I feel like calling the sitter and saying, "She there yet?" But I don't. I want to keep that distance between Marylou and me. So I spin my swivel chair, making the room a dull whirl. I used to do this as a kid, and whatever I saw when I stopped had to be part of a story I'd invent.

Once I did it with Clinton when we were stoned up in the woods behind Bevington's farm. We laughed so hard we fell all over each other. Clinton was like that. Things changed so quickly around him. Up there in Bevington's woods, a ladybug crawling up his arm while he slowly pumped in and out of me, watching my face, me watching the ladybug, and him whispering, "Look at me, Honey, look in my eyes." When I did, he came and pulled me so far, so deep, inside of him. Clinton gone inside, and me after. I never felt anything so naked in my life. When I was married, I closed my eyes tight when Jake was on top. I squeezed him out, didn't want to see.

The chair stops, and I open my eyes. It's the storage closet. The first thing I think is darkness. I don't know whether I can tell that story. Marylou and I never go in there with Bowker if we can help it. He has this way of forgetting to pull on the light and calling one of us to help. We exchange a look and pretend not to hear him. Then he calls again, impatiently, he has big business to conduct and we'd better get along or find ourselves another job. The one he calls for taps off her typewriter and heaves a big sigh as she climbs out of the chair. The other one looks sympathetic and smiles, grateful it isn't her this time, then ducks her head as if she's busy. The one heading for the closet knows the other one is watching, wishing she had X-ray vision and glad she doesn't. Inside, Bowker's standing in front of the light cord, and you have to be careful not to knock into the shelves of paper and supplies.

I spin the chair again to watch the snow fall in little mincing flakes outside the front window when Jasper Johnson, our town's only black man, walks in. Except for the tan oaky glow of his skin, Jasper looks like the other farmers around here. Big coveralls open at the sides where they've been pulled over his other clothes. Rubber-sheathed boots, tracking the yellow brown grids of manure on Bowker's grass green carpet. And five kinds of old flannel shirts with a denim jacket on top. He lifts his cap with "Reiler's," the local grain elevator, printed across it.

"Bowker in?" His throat rattles with something caught there.

I shake my head. "Won't be in for a couple of days. Maybe not till after Easter. Gone up to Watertown to check on some land. Going to have

Easter with the family, he thinks. Maybe not, though. But he's not in today for sure."

"Marylou Jackson in?"

"No, she's out. I don't know when she'll be back for sure." I try to sound patient, without hinting that I want to get involved. Jasper is looking around the office with that expression you see on animals that've been put in the back of a truck for market, wild and hopeless, wondering what they did to get there.

"I gotta, I gotta get someone up there. Take a look. Vet won't do nothing unless there's someone checking from the office here. Insurance. He made me drive in, said I had to bring someone back. But you can't—"

I can tell he doesn't want to ask me. He's hoping I'll say yes and hoping I'll say no. When Bowker's out of the office, it's Marylou who goes on the accident claims. The vets won't put an animal down now unless there's an agent around, not since the case a couple of years ago when Frank Simpson's agency won a hundred grand off a vet over in Good Earth. They said the vet should've tried to save the animal, but he was trying to collect with the farmer. Since then any bad accident with insured stock meant inspecting the damage and authorizing the terminal shot. It's pretty brutal. Animal lying there suffering for hours sometimes. Bowker's been sickened by it and usually sends Marylou to do the checking. Then we fake the claims and write that he's done it. They never said I should go. Marylou's gone, and Bow-wow is zooming around in his Travelaire motor home, acting like Burt Reynolds on his CB.

Jasper glances at my nameplate on the desk in front of him. "Ms. Parrish, Honey, would you please come out to okay this? It can't wait." I think about trying to call Marylou. Then I decide not to. Let her talk her way out of this one. I'll close up the office, and if Bowker calls, tough luck.

"Wait while I get my coat." I scribble a quick note to Marylou and put it in her typewriter so she'll know what's up, then pull on my coat. Damn, no boots. It's going to be rough hiking around that farm mud in these heels and nylons.

"Jasper, you don't happen to have any boots for me?" I ask as we leave the office. Locking the door, I turn to the truck, which is huge and humming now in front of me, the passenger door flung open. I hitch my skirt a couple of inches and make the long stride. Jasper grabs my frantically waving arm from inside and pulls me the rest of the way up. Settled in, I reach out and grab the door and with a mighty heave pull it to. It doesn't shut completely. Jasper reaches across me, opens the door again, and gives it a jerk. It slams shut with a thud.

As we drive out of town, a little faster than we should, I notice the startled expressions of a couple of people as they spot us. Baby will be on the phone by nightfall. Most people in town have suspicions about blacks or Jews. Lately they haven't been too pleased about the Mexicans, either, the ones that drift through to pick the crops. Used to be they just went unnoticed, like birds that migrate here in summer and leave in fall. They're here, make their noise, live their little bird lives, and then leave. Now, the board of education is putting up a stink because the feds one day want the kids in school, the next day not. Can't make up their mind if they're birds or people, educate them or not. It's probably better to get them in school. Why shouldn't they have to go through the same bullshit we did?

I'm just about to ask Jasper what he thinks when I notice that his breathing is getting rougher. Pretty soon he's driving too fast down Highway 11, tears rolling down his face, dropping into his lap, making a dark place on his shirt. I want to reach over, touch his arm, tell him it's okay, but I don't. I clear my throat, try to look outside, but there's nothing to see. Flat brown and white where the snow is starting to cling. Planting will begin soon as this stuff melts. It doesn't look so bad on a day like this, kind of hopeful, maybe. It reminds me of the farm we had when I was little, before Daddy went broke and we moved to Omaha and then back out here, to Divinity. Things have never been the same since we lost the farm. I know, that's what everyone says. But it's true. Something happened to Daddy, like the anger and hurt inside got taken out on animals or children ever since. He always acts like he's been let down in some big way, more than anybody else around. Like it wasn't supposed to happen to him.

Mama always said to us, "Your father's got his pride, now you remember that." But I can't see why that has to let out everyone else's.

Mama's southern kin are wrong: Daddy isn't so different from them. He sure isn't any Yankee, like they thought. They just never bothered to ask, and him and his pride never bothered to say.

It sure would have helped Mama to have her sisters with her at the end. But they wouldn't come as long as he wouldn't ask them, and he wouldn't ask them as long as he thought they wouldn't come. So thirteen years ago Mama died just looking a bunch of ungratefuls in the face. All of us too embarrassed to grab hold of her and hang on, keep her with us a minute longer. All of us so full of pride that day that we let her go empty of our hands into another place. The thought makes me so sad that I feel the wet streaking down my face, too. The two of us speeding out to this farm, fifteen miles outside town, crying our heads off. And it is snowing, sure as hell, it is snowing, and in a few days it'll be Easter.

It's when we almost get thrown off the road around the curve with the big Monkey Ward's truck coming the other way that Jasper eases his foot on the gas and clears his throat to speak. "Sorry about that. Just forgot myself. Don't want another accident, God knows, not today." He coughs and clears his throat, unwinds the window, spits, then rolls it back up. This time he glances at me. "You got some black stuff on your face. Here." He flips down the visor on my side with a little mirror attached on the back.

"Thanks. Yeah, I was thinking about my mother, she's dead."

"Yeah, I lost my ma about ten years ago. Used the insurance money to put a down payment on the farm. Left Van Dusen's racing stable out in Nebraska. Putting money in mares, prospects, for a while. Waiting for 'em to break down, wash out on the track, then start the real work of having babies. I was building a future that way. Not wasting my money. Now, well . . ." He swallows hard without looking over.

"You see a lot of guys bettin' all their pay. Investing in some gelding. They'll be flat in a couple of months. Geldings break down fast as anything, then what've you got? A lame horse. With a mare, you got a little mama." He stops, pulls out a crumpled red handkerchief, and blows hard.

"I was watching bloodlines. Couldn't afford nothing fancy, but every once in a while I'd spot some honest blood, might throw an honest horse. Nothing Kentucky Derby, you understand, but good enough for Ak-Sar-Ben, Canterbury Downs, places like that. Figured those rich dudes would come around looking for a nice, big, leggy colt to show-jump, too. Saw it on TV. Olympics. I wouldn't have to just supply track meat. Then Ma died."

He's driving slower now, under the speed limit. A funny guy, first he's racing to get back, bawling his head off, then he's trying not to get there until Sunday. But I figure he knows what's waiting for us, so he's reached that point where it isn't going to go away, faster or slower than it's already happening. Maybe talking helps, too. "How'd you get this place? Land was so high around here then, all over Iowa." I'm always curious how folks get farms. I only know about losing them.

"Kingman's my uncle."

Well, that is news. "How, I mean—" He glances over at me with the first sign of amusement in his eyes. A little grin widens his mouth. I wonder how old he is. Could be thirty or forty. Looks either, but looks good, too, handsome with a strong nose, high cheekbones, and large yellow-gold eyes that glitter brightly against his skin. "I'm sorry. I didn't mean that the way, you know." I reach out and squeeze his arm, hard under the layers of clothes. He doesn't jerk away or twitch. He laughs. A throaty chuckle. My face reddens.

He reaches over with his big hand, pats mine, which sits limp on the seat between us. "It's okay." We both pause for a moment, watching the wipers *whoosh*ing the snow away and the land around us whitening up faster as the sky fills with flakes.

"Making beds in heaven, Ma called it. Shaking out pillows, feather mattresses. I believed her for the longest time." He chuckles again, a pleasant throaty sound that makes you want to follow it. "George Kingman married my mother's sister, Marvel, during the Depression." Jasper reaches over and turns up the heater. "Wish I'd known her. Ma said she was a marvel. A marvel to be born and a marvel to live as long as she did. Light-skinned. Lighter than me." He glances over at me and smiles. "I take after my father. He was a mix, a mongrel. Ma always said, 'Be proud of it. Day will come when people won't hide their skin anymore.' She lived to see Miss Rosa Parks on
that bus in Mississippi, lived to see the folks marching in Washington. Made her real happy at the end."

We hit a pothole, and the usual clutter along truck dashboards rattles and jumps around, some of it landing in my lap. Notes and bills and pieces of rubber hose and little metal things, farm stuff. A single old leather glove, the size of a baseball mitt. We gather everything back up, and he plunks the glove on top to hold things down.

I'm curious by now. "What happened to Marvel and Kingman?"

He clears his throat again and goes through the window ritual. Usually I can't stand it when people spit. "Well, you know how it is. They met, fell for each other, got married. Family farm was doing poorly, dry as Hades. Depression. He went to Omaha to work. Marvel was cautious, but George won her over.

"She kept him out of trouble, working; they both worked, of course. She worked for a white family, caring for their kids and helping in the kitchen. Lived on her money, split his money between her parents and his. That's the way it was then. Finally he got on at the railroad and things were okay until the war broke out and George was drafted. Then Marvel died. Took the diphtheria, bad heart. George came back to Iowa, the farm. Ran it. Even after the two brothers ran off and died. Then the parents.

"Then he wrote me 'bout buying it. So I took a run out here and fell in love with the place."

We're almost there, and I want the rest of the story. "How'd he act after all those years? He was a little odd, you know, even for around here."

"Fine. Okay. Treated me like a relative. Teary-eyed. Always wanted a son like me, stuff like that. Things were run-down, and he apologized. He'd been crippled with arthritis, bad heart. Couldn't find help. Practically gave the place to me. I worried maybe he was crazy, but when we went to sign the papers Monday morning, it was okay. I'd take over in six months when he retired.

"Clement Collins set the papers. He looked at us like we were crazy. Kingman for selling land cheap to a 'black' man, and me for raising horses. Surprised he didn't try to stop us. Afterward he said, 'If you have any problems, you know what I mean, call me. But stay out of folks' way. They're not bad people, they're just not so used to seeing colored people. Remember that. And good luck.' Kingman died two months later."

Jasper spins the wheel, and we are suddenly bouncing high along the hard ruts of a dirt road, the turn off to his place. I grab the door handle to anchor myself. "Sorry. Forget to slow down when I'm talking." Now the silence settles in on us, waiting as we are for what is ahead. I look at his big hands and the scarred knuckles showing yellow as they grip the wheel. I can see his jaw muscle coil like a snake, then uncoil.

In another moment we turn into his farmyard. The vet's cream van is nosed into the lilac bushes that are just leafing out, the green blinking at us through the swirl of snow.

Jasper jumps out of the truck without a word and strides for the house, then turns back. I'm still sitting in the truck, trying to decide what to do about my shoes. Without a word he opens my door and holds out his arms. I wish Baby were here, to get a good fright seeing me carried breathlessly up to the porch by a tall, handsome black man. As it is, Roger the vet, silent as ever, barely lifts his eyes to acknowledge us. "Made coffee," he offers.

I brush off the snow, take off my coat, and look around the kitchen. Surprisingly enough, it's neat and clean for a man living alone. Old-fashioned like the house still, but I like it that Jasper has left Kingman's family kitchen. Most young people move in and tear out all the old-fashioned wooden cabinets and counters that stood their parents and grandparents in good stead all those years and replace everything with Formica and particleboard with fake finish on it and some wallpaper that'd kill a chicken to look at.

I like what Jasper's done, just cleaning up the old pine trim and cabinets, letting the natural soft glow of the wood warm up the kitchen. It makes me lonesome for our old farm, or even for the old white frame house in town. The trailer I got in the divorce from Jake isn't bad, it's just so *new*. There's no life rubbed into it. At night when I'm alone, I don't hear the whispers of the old living in the walls, along the ceiling, the way you do in an old house, the way the wind comes in just so along the floor. The trailer is airtight, and only Sonny Boy roaring by in his car late at night disturbs my lonesome peace. They advertise them that way. Soundproof. Why would you want that?

I take another look around as I sit down at the wooden table with Roger, while Jasper is hustling up another coffee cup. "How is she?" he asks the vet.

"I tranqued her. Calm her, kill the pain. Not much of that though, just panic. Doesn't know what's wrong. Just something big, lying there like that." Roger gestures for us to have some coffee before we go out. "She can wait a few minutes more." Jasper winces, and his hands shake as he pours my cup full. I look away to the wall over the table, where two people's faces stare quietly out of their frames. A white man, Kingman, and a woman who might have only a deep tan but for the coarse black hair, Marvel. They make a handsome couple.

Jasper clears his throat again. "Uh, Roger, this is Honey Parrish, works for Bowker. Everyone else's gone today."

Roger gives me a replica of a smile, a tiny thread that seems for a moment to jerk up the corners of an otherwise straight line. "Yeah, I know Honey. How are you?" Then he looks into his cup, embarrassed.

Jasper continues, "Better tell her what's happening, so she'll know what she's looking at when we go out there." Both men pause, looking casually distracted like dogs trying to avoid a confrontation, as if the whole world's more interesting. I take a sip of the coffee. Not bad. A man who can make coffee. It'd be even better if he could make tea.

"What's the injury? It's one of the horses?" I try to sound professional, not like a second-rate secretary or bookkeeper, more like Bowker might in that situation. Jasper looks at me blankly for a moment.

"Oh. Yeah. It's the oldest mare, thoroughbred, Prince Aquillo line, twenty-two, bred, due in June. Late foal, didn't take for a while. Happens in an old mare. Good producer, though. Made a fair amount off her foals. Now, I suppose, well, I guess we'll lose the foal. Too early, and she's been down for, uh, well," Jasper looks at his watch, then the grease-speckled clock over the stove to the left. "Oh, I guess we figure it musta happened sometime in the middle of the night. It was warm, so I left some mares in the paddock with the loafing shed. They could get out of the wind, stretch their legs. Been a long winter. So much time in stalls when the snow was deep. When I came out in the morning to feed, she was just lying there, in the shed. The other horses kept coming up and nosing her. At first I thought she was dead," Jasper's voice breaks for a moment. Roger concentrates on the weather outside the little window over the sink opposite us. I looked at my cup, nice old china, thick with heavy yellowing flowers along the edge.

"Well, when I got down next to her, her sides were heaving, like she was trying to get up, and her hindquarters kept twitching like she was trying but couldn't. When she saw me, I don't think she even recognized me. She twisted her head and flung it around trying to bite the air. Then she laid back down. Her eyes were crazy. First I thought she'd colicked and twisted a gut, but it didn't seem right for that. Then when I hooked a rope to her halter, and tried to pull her up, I realized she couldn't move. There wasn't any use. I'd seen that before. Broken

neck. Don't know how. Took X rays with the portable unit, Roger'll show you."

Jasper, fighting not to cry, gets up and walks into the other room. In a minute I hear water running, a choking sob, and then a toilet flushing. I look at Roger. "Save the X rays for Bowker, in case he has to see them. Maybe we should get this over with. I don't suppose there's anything . . ."

Roger shakes his head. "I know a fellow over at Ames took a young mare with this injury, got her up, and she lived. Twisted neck, of course, but she could be bred. This mare's too old. She's got the foal, too. No, she won't get up. Another hour or so on the ground and the muscles'll atrophy anyway."

Roger stands up, starts pulling on his coat. "Better have Jasper give you some boots. It's snowing like hell out there." As his eyes linger on the scar along my forehead, a strange light comes into them. "Who did that to you, the one I tried to stitch up?"

"My daddy."

His eyes harden. "I thought so." Then he turns and goes out onto the porch. I'd wondered if he'd remember.

When I get my coat on, Jasper comes in with a pair of black galoshes. "Keep your feet dry."

The snow is starting to pile up, and I'm grateful for the galoshes, which clink each time I take a step. I break two nails on the rusty metal fasteners and remember the same struggle as a kid trying to close them.

Fortunately the storm is blowing up mostly from the northwest, so the mare still has protection under the three-sided loafing shed. She seems calmer than I expected, but then I remember the shot Roger gave her. When she hears us coming, she nickers. There is something awfully lonesome in that sound.

Jasper bends down to stroke her neck and jaw. "Hello, little mother, how're you? How's my sweetheart? Feeling better?" He reaches into his coat pocket and brings out a lump of sugar, which he crushes and rubs along her lips; her tongue reaches out and licks his hand. In her eyes, a grateful look replaces the anxiety of before. She seems like a big, gentle cow, content and warm, about to go to sleep for a while in her green summer pasture.

"Honey," Roger begins, pointing to a place two inches behind the mare's ears, "here's where the trauma occurred. She hit something, ran into a wall or fence, with enough force to drive a vertebra out of place. It shows up on the X ray. You can see what happens then. Hindquarters nonfunctional, torso, same. Front legs, a bit of movement, but not enough to get her going. Her thrashing around probably finished the nerves, too. She'll have pneumonia in a short time, then die." Jasper's hand jumps, then goes back to stroking her neck and face, reassuring her.

"What about the baby? I mean, any chance?" I ask.

Roger looks at her stomach; there is a slight shift, something pressing against the inside wall, then pulling back. "Oh, I don't know. If she's got almost two months to go, probably can't save it. It might be, probably is, damaged from the fall and lying here all this time. Not enough movement. That worries me. It should be kicking up a storm. Nooo, I don't *think* we can save it. But the only thing to do, I guess, if Jasper wants to, is to keep her alive, and try to operate, pull it out and see if it's worth saving. Jasper didn't want to do that before."

Roger looks over at Jasper, who keeps his head buried in his coat collar for a minute more, then turns back. "Is it an insurance problem? Is that it?" he asks bitterly.

I don't know anything for sure, but I can bet Bowker would rather pay for one horse than two. "You got foaling insurance?" Jasper nods.

The wind sends a sharp gust of snow over us, powdering the mare's face. He brushes it off.

I think about it for a moment longer, the cold creeping into me. April, screw. No, they better check on the foal. They have to. "You got to try to save the foal. It's still alive. Just see, that's all. But you have to do it, to collect. Is it worth it?" That is the question, obviously. But I figure if Jasper waited this long, he must have a bundle tied up in the mare.

He nods again. "She's spent her life feeding people. No reason to stop now."

Without a word, Roger gets up and goes back to the van. In a moment I can hear the whir of tires trying to navigate in the snow and mud. "Stay with her while I get some blankets and things." Jasper leaves for the barn that butts the shed. I bend down at the mare's head and try to reassure her the way Jasper has. Her eyes go wild for a moment as she watches him leave but calm again as she apparently realizes that I am going to stay. I watch her belly rise in a long ripple, like a tide coming in, then subside again. She seems to feel it, and suddenly I think that she might be sorry for that baby in there. She sighs, and a groan comes out at the end. Maybe animals know, then, when they are dying. Maybe everything knows.

"Here, better go change in the tack room. You'll ruin your dress and coat out here." Jasper gives me a bundle of clothes and starts laying wool horse blankets around the mare.

The tack room has a little heater that Jasper has turned on. As I change and rub myself to get warm, I look at the pictures on the walls. Mostly racehorses, winners, with vacantly smiling people grouped around them. The horses look stretched out, lean and tired, with long funereal strings of flowers draped over their necks. One of them looks like the mare lying outside, but I can't tell for sure. The dates seem right, and the markings; then I notice the name, Brown Marvel.

I take my time dressing because I don't want to watch. I know I will go and look eventually, but I'm scared. Jasper will be saying good-bye. They will have to keep her alive during the operation, then they will inject her. I've seen enough on farms to know this. In the bundle of clothes are a beat-up down jacket, a pair of jeans, a flannel shirt, and a sweater with "Cindy" hand-printed on the label. I try taking my mind off what they are doing out there. Cindy who? Cindy Reiler of the feed mill?

I slip out the tack room door into the barn. There are two aisles, with a row of box stalls along each wall and one down the middle. In the stalls stand horses knee deep in straw. A clean, horsey smell. This must have been the old dairy barn. From the outside it is a giant, old, hip-roofed job set into a hill, but on the inside it is completely modern. Stalls, automatic watering system, feed chute, a real professional-looking place. On the second floor will be the tons of hay and grain he grows and stores for the animals. At the end of the aisle there is a big window that faces a pole barn, probably the indoor arena, so he can work the horses and show them to prospective customers during bad weather.

When I get back, the mare is asleep and Roger is getting ready to cut her open. I turn away, concentrating on the eaves of the shed, where some barn sparrows in a burst of optimism have built nests and are now shivering in them. At least the snow doesn't get to them there. I worry about the robins that have nested in the trees across the road from my trailer. Birds can feel it, this sudden cold. You can see them before a storm blows up, huddled and fat, plumping themselves out to fight off the cold or wet. Some life. Of course, here I am, standing out in the snow-storm in galoshes and tight, borrowed clothes. Better than being at that office, though, better than Bowker and the storage closet. I hear one of the men exhale a big breath, like he is trying to swim underwater, and I turn to look. The foal, encased in its bag, has spilled out onto the clean straw Jasper has laid over the blankets. It is kicking to free itself. A sharp little hoof, a miniature of its mother's, pokes out of the cloudy membrane, then another, and another.

"Look! It's coming out on its own. Here, help it, cut the cord." And then we are all helping wipe away the sack, clear off the eyes, blow out the nostrils. Suddenly in the midst of six hands stands a foal, small, but perfect, wobbling on four strong legs and hungry for its mother's milk.

"Okay. Let's finish with the mare." Jasper is in command now. This is the part I hate—when they fill the big syringe, not with something to help the animal, but with death, a clear liquid that makes the animal look falling-down tired and dreamy, then drop to its knees and finally to its side. Everything collapses inward with this drug. And what is left is skin and rubbery bones. The mare, since she is down and opened up, simply stops. Then it is like she disappears and this big mess sits in front of us—blood and hair and guts all over. The mare has flown beyond, before us. We are left kneeling around what is left.

We sit back on our heels, stunned for a moment until another gust of wind brings a whirl of snow over us. "Here, quick, wrap it in this burlap while I figure out some milk for it." Jasper throws me the sack, while Roger works on the face some more.

"Perfect little bugger, ain't she? Just perfect." Roger is grinning from ear to ear. "God, I thought it was dead or going to die. Just not enough activity. Thought the little bugger was gonna be too early. Mare must have caught before we thought she did. That'd put the foal only a month or less early. Doesn't even seem to be hurt from lying there inside its mama on the ground like that. Not a bit. Legs good. Lungs sound good. Heart good. No problem. Pretty little filly if ever I saw one. On a day like this! Can you *believe* it!" He claps me hard on the shoulder like it's the Fourth of July if he ever saw one. I've never heard him say so much at one time in my whole life. "She's a real honey. In fact, I'm gonna tell Jasper to call her that, A Real Honey. After you. You being here and making him do this. Yessiree, it's good to have something come out of all this, after all."

Roger turns to start getting his instruments together. The foal struggles against the confines of the burlap bag and strikes him in the shoulder with a hoof. "Hang on to that baby. She's gonna be a tough one," he jokes, rubbing his shoulder.

I try to stroke her neck as I'd done to her mama, and she calms for a moment before a shower of snow gets her started again. It's like trying to hold a big catfish, she seems so slippery. "Maybe I'd better take her inside before she gets away," I tell Roger as he stands up to carry his things to the van.

"Sure, Jasper'll be in the tack room, probably, or one of the stalls, getting things ready." As an afterthought he adds, "Can you manage her alone?"

"Yeah, sure." Inside, I almost drop her when I run into Jasper on his way back out. He grabs us both. It doesn't feel bad to be so close to his body. Embarrassed, he drops his arms, and I almost lose the foal again. He catches her from me as she starts slipping and struggling.

"Armful, isn't she?" It is the first time I've seen him happy, his eyes softening to a pale brown.

"Let's take her into the tack room. I got some milk substitute heating and a bottle ready."

An hour later we are all inside the house again, sitting around the kitchen with coffee, trying to warm up and dry off. Jasper is heating up some bran muffins he made yesterday. Both men are in a fine mood, and I guess I am, too. Things sure surprise you sometimes. It's nice to think that "Black Beauty" happens right once in a while. Outside, the snow is piling up pretty good, and the wind is picking up more. A regular blizzard. April, it doesn't even bear talking about. This is Iowa, and we are just going to ignore this mistake from the north. It's Roger that changes the mood for a moment. "Well, Jasper, you want me to call the rendering plant? I doubt they could get out here today, but she'll probably hold till this is through tomorrow."

Jasper sobers, his eyes focusing on something out the white of the kitchen window, but this time his hand doesn't shake. "No. I think I'll get Aronson's back hoe over here and put her in the far pasture. She liked to stand under the trees on hot days, swatting flies, probably dreaming of her big race days, who knows. Anyway, I couldn't turn her into—" He chokes for a moment. "No, she gave me a good life. She deserves to be here on the farm, like I intended. She did her part. I gotta do mine." He gets up and walks into the other room.

Roger starts to say something, "Folk'll think—"

Jasper's voice comes back, harsher than before. "Damn folks and what they think. They can cart their pets and livestock to the rendering plant. Let 'em send their kids and grandmothers too for all I care. People'd do anything for a buck, anything to get more use out of a living creature. Christ, I never saw such a lot." Then he comes back in carrying a scrapbook, which he lays on the table between us. "Look, I did this last winter so I'd always remember what a fine horse she was. Tell my children. 'Course, it doesn't look like that's going to happen. But I wanted her to be part of the foundation, one of the lines I bred for."

After a few minutes looking at the photos and charts, Roger gets a signal on his beeper and has to call in to the office. When he comes back, he announces that he has to leave. "Cow down with something up at Sorenson's dairy. They're worried enough they want me right away. Christ, in this weather I'll be lucky to make it at all." Pulling on his coat, he turns to Jasper. "What're you going to call the new one?"

Jasper shrugs. "Something with Marvel in it, to keep the mare's name alive."

Roger pauses, gives me a look, and says, "How about Marvel's Perfect Honey? Or Real Honey? Or what the hell, Little Honey? I mean, if she hadn't been here, the foal might have died, too."

Both men give me a big smile, and I feel pretty good when Jasper nods his head. "Sure. That'd be fine. Honey, you choose one out of the three names, so we've all had a hand in it. Bring the kid luck. She'll need it to stay alive without a mama. Say, Roger, you know anyone with a goat? I might try to wet-nurse. What do you think? I saw it done in Nebraska."

A blank professional look crosses Roger's face, then he nods his head slowly. "Sure, why not try it. I'll check around, have someone give you a call. Maybe we can find a mare who's lost a foal, too, in the last day or two. I'll get the girls at the office on it. In the meantime, give her those shots I left for you, every four hours. Her immunities are way down, a month early that way, no mother's milk. You might even think about bringing her up here tonight, just so you don't have to keep going through that snow."

It isn't until he is on the porch, getting ready to face the storm, that Roger remembers me. "What're we gonna do about getting you home, Honey?"

I don't know why I don't just jump in the van with Roger, go up to Sorenson's, wait around, and get a ride back to town when he's done. But somehow that doesn't have the right feel to it. I should know better, though. Every time I do things by feel, it leads someplace unexpected, someplace I'm not ready for. I wait a moment, while the three of us stare bleakly out at the snow, so heavy it clings to everything like wet toilet paper. The trees and bushes are starting to sag under the weight. Great, probably lose power lines, too. I wonder if Sonny Boy can drive around when it's this bad. It'll be awfully quiet in the trailer tonight. What if the phone lines go, too? Then I can't even get Baby's call bawling me out for coming out to Jasper's.

"My truck's got four-wheel, I can take her after chores. She doesn't have to wait around while you're at Sorenson's. They'll have you checking every udder in the place before you're through. I'll take her. Of course, if you'd rather go with Roger . . ."

By the time we get it settled, and Roger is spinning and sliding out of the driveway, I've worked up an appetite that Jasper's muffins doesn't quite fill. "Let's eat," I announce. The rest of the afternoon, neither of us mentions driving me back to town. I try calling the office, but there's no answer. From reports on the radio, it sounds like the whole town has closed up. Kids are sent home from school at one, stores are shutting down early, and warnings are out about unnecessary travel. It doesn't make me feel much like getting on the road, and I guess Jasper feels the way I do. We just ignore it and enjoy the good talk and warmth of the house. Every hour he goes out and checks on the foal, feeds her a little more, until finally at five o'clock I tell him to bring her up to the house, where it'll be easier, like Roger said. We block off the spare room next to the kitchen, close the doorways, lay down some canvas, and put straw over that, and she goes fast asleep.

"Makes you sleepy, don't it, watching her?" Jasper yawns and stretches. "I got to do chores, feed horses, but why don't you stretch out on the sofa? I'll wake you when I'm done and we'll have supper. Okay?"

I *am* sleepy. Something about the heavy snow outside is filling me up with a soft heaviness, making me want to let go, too, fall under all that weight, forget about the trailer and everything and everyone. Besides, the living room is just like the one in our old house, with the old sofa you fall into that hugs around you like a pillow and the old afghan he tosses over me that smells of the attic, a good musty *old* smell, and the little lamp on the table across the room that shines dully through the yellowed cardboard shade. Just like home. As I doze off, the snow muffles the world outside and my head and heart inside. For a single moment I try to hang on to the name that floats silently by. Jasper. Then I let go of that, too, and the letters fell into an unrecognizable jumble.

As I wake up, I feel his presence, know he is somewhere near me. I never have that problem other people do in a strange place. I always know where I am. At home I'll wake up in a panic, unable to identify the room, myself even. But I know just where I am now and can smell the warm, horsey scent of Jasper and feel the ache in me death seems to bring.

He is stretched out sleeping on the faded rose carpeted floor a few feet from the sofa, one arm flung over his eyes to shade them from the light, the other by his side, the fingers long and relaxed. It's the hands, the tapered fingers that could so delicately touch a thing, that are making me shiver. I crawl to the floor and watch his chest rise and fall easily with his sleep. I slip my hands inside the buttons of the pale blue workshirt washed soft he now wears and lightly run my fingers into the tangle of hair on his chest. He doesn't startle awake, but the pitch of his breathing changes as I undo the buttons so his skin is bare from stomach to ear, and I can see the dark ring of nipple and the nub of belly button in the middle of the hard ridges of stomach muscles he is tensing now.

It has been so long, nine or ten months, almost a year since I've been with a man, so long that I've forgotten or fooled myself about how it feels. Like skipping the Fourth of July fireworks at the park on the Mercy River for a few years, and when I go again it's all new. I realize I've missed it, though I hadn't known that until the first brilliant burst that shatters the dark above me. So you see, I can't stop myself now, can't turn my eyes from it.

When we kiss, his tongue is a fine instrument, probing me until we know each other two ways, with our hands and mouths. Finally he is on top of me, our skin, such sweet, sweet pain of waiting, and I am looking. Not because he is asking me, but because I have to see, like before with Clinton. And his eyes are turning gray like Spirit Lake just before a storm. This time we go inside together, and it is dark, yes, and it is far away, yes, but it is safe, like the house, held in the body of snow around it, and us, held in the house, muffled from the cold, with a flannel of air and breath, we are inside each other and held, safe. And time is that silence, the occasional stir of straw from the filly in the next room, the electrical click from the kitchen, and the same sweet roar of love inside my head.

"Honey, oh, Honey." And it pours inside me and down my legs and pools so thick and sweet on the rug beneath us.

Baby calls me over the lunch hour the next day at work. "What are you trying to do, riding around town with that Negro? Are you crazy?" she hisses. Like radio static, it is hard to listen to. I twist on my chair, glad the others have gone to lunch. Bowker's left me to mind the office, still mad because I left yesterday. He's treating Marylou to lunch. She must have been in the closet again. He wants to make me take a sick day for going out to Jasper's even though it was business, because I didn't come back to the office afterward. He has his suspicions. Thinks I'm crowding him, taking liberties.

"What Negro, Baby?"

"Don't be stupid. Jasper Johnson—who else? Martin Luther King?" She is running out of breath. At 457 pounds, Baby has her mouth open all the time. Her body is as big as the sofa she rarely moves from in Daddy's house.

I sigh. "Yeah, I know who you mean."

"Listen, are you listening?"

"Yes, Baby." She's in her instructional mode. I'll get a lecture now.

"That's okay, Honey, if you don't care about your name, or *mine,* and God knows that's clear enough after the Jake fiasco, think about Daddy and Sonny Boy. I got three calls last night about this." Baby is panting like a dog in July. But it is the exertion of her anger that makes her teeth chatter, her tongue grow thick.

"Daddy?" I pick up a pencil and use the nub of eraser at the end to draw the scar on my forehead, outline its fat shape. The map of Iowa, Clinton told me when the bandage came off.

"Yes, Daddy *and* Sonny Boy. Family never seems to have much claim on *you,* does it? Not like me. I'm stuck here cleaning, and—" I can hear the snuffling begin, like a big square-snouted hog at the edge of the corn bin.

"I care, Baby." I say it patiently, trying to calm her.

"No, you don't. You run all night with that Jasper, that colored man. My God, Honey, think of Daddy, think of his pride."

Screw him, screw you, screw Sonny Boy, especially screw Sonny Boy, I want to say. But I can't, like always. A picture appears of the tall, spare figure of my father, like an old circuit-riding preacher, his arm raised, and it stops me, like always. Those bitter, disappointed eyes, and hands holding something sharp, something to—

"Are you listening?" Baby's whisper fills the room as if it's on a loudspeaker. As if the entire town can hear, she whispers. "You always let him down, you always do, Honey. Like you hate him. Why can't you just act normal? Just behave."

"Oh, that," I say. "I can't help it, I'm always a disappointment, ask Jake."

Baby laughs harshly. "Ask Jimmy and Brewer? Mama, maybe? *Clinton?*" It's like steel wool being rubbed on my eardrums, my eyeballs.

"His name is Jass, he told me that's what he likes to be called by women, Baby, Jass."

I hang up the phone, quietly, being as gentle as possible, feeling my stomach drop and twist with the memory of Jass the night before, his beautiful hands running my skin like he was gentling a horse. I can't help it if my body always does these things, wanting to be close *before* the talking starts and things get screwed up. There is always some dark clearness in that moment, not knowing each other. Like looking into a lake 150 feet deep, or trying to see through coal.

2

Twyla

Someday I'm going to get a can of shellac and spray their hair—*then* they'll have something to complain about!" Twyla tosses her head so the long blond hair she wears parted on the side and flopping over one eye flips back enough to get the burger to her mouth. With her big pouty lips and green eyes, she looks like a model off a magazine cover instead of Twyla Tooley who does hair at the Curl-Y-Que at the end of Main Street.

"Christ, Marlyss Winchell was in this morning, you know her? Married that guy, what's-his-name—"

"Bobby Brugger?"

She chews quickly and swallows. "Yeah, they were a few years ahead of us in school. Well, she's got four rug rats already, what a breeder, and she says her 'hair ain't holdin' like it used to when Vera did it.' "

Twyla puts down the burger, and I watch the red seep into the center of the plate, tingeing the edges of the chips pink. She always tells Simpy to "breathe it brown, quick flip on each side so its pants don't catch on fire." Today Simpy blushes and drops his pencil when she orders. Twyla has that effect on men.

"So one lousy pin comes out and she's back in for a free style. I swear, I'm outta here, come next year, I'll have a new area code." Twyla eats a limp pink chip, eyeing me suspiciously like I'm one of the old ladies or breeders on her chair. "What's up? You fuck that Jasper dude or what?"

"I don't know. . . ." I push my spoon into the pond of cream soup with clumps of green stuff floating on top like algae. Simpy is our resident gourmet, who experiments on his parents' customers who come in to Bob and Shirley's for burgers and pies.

Twyla hoots. Two farmers at the counter push their caps off their foreheads, shuffle their work boots, and glance our way. Twyla's tight sleeveless T-shirt and skirt will make their tractor wet dreams for plowing this afternoon. She smiles sweetly in their direction and giggles quietly to me with her hand over her mouth when they turn to study the worn wooden counter in front of them. "Some sex, you don't know whether you had it or not."

"How the hell did *you* hear?" I try a spoon of the green. Not bad, though the long strand slips down my throat so easily, it makes me nervous.

"Listen, it's been dropped on me so many times the past few days, I feel like *I* had sex with the guy."

Twyla hears everything in town, and what she misses, Baby gathers. Between them they could put the CIA out of business.

"Oh, screw. You know I did it, and I shouldn't have. You always *tell* me that, but . . ." I can feel my eyes filling. I choke down something that tries to come out and let the spoon slide hopelessly from my fingers into the thick surface of the soup. The tip of the handle is gone in a wink of silver.

"Oh, Honey, come on. What's the big deal?" She leans back against the green vinyl booth darkened with the shape of human sweat and oil over the past thirty years. She brushes the hair off her forehead and folds her arms. "He didn't call!"

I nod, take the napkin, a nice big square white cloth one Simpy insists on now, and I wipe the corners of my eyes carefully. Marylou is selling Mary Kay Cosmetics when Bowker's out, and half the women in town are walking around with surprised wedges of pink on their cheeks and green or blue slices over their eyes. My face feels a little stiff under the powder, but I don't want to ruin it.

"What's it been, four, five days since the snowstorm afternoon?"

I nod. I don't like looking so pathetic, though, so I shake my shoulders to get rid of it. "Fuck it."

"No, listen, Honey. Two things. You *have* to toughen up if you're going to pull this shit with one-night stands. Personally, I like a different approach—making 'em hungry. But that's the difference between us. Who knows, maybe you're right. It's all the same in the end. I married Tom Tooley, and you married Jake."

"It should've been Clinton, I really should be married to Clinton. Then . . ."

Twyla picks up her empty glass and, without looking, waves it over her head for another Coke. She always gets great service. Simpy's hand plucks it and puts a fresh one on the table with ice clinking heavily against the sides the way she likes it.

"Oh, not Clinton, sweetie. He was so bad. What a jerk, Clinton, Christ—"

"You didn't even *know* him, Twyla. Not the way I did." I push the weird soup away from me and lean on the faded red Formica table.

"Oh, yes, I did. We tried it once. He couldn't even keep it up, he was so loaded. Booze and dope. Honey, you'd probably be dead too if you'd hung around with him much longer." Twyla's voice softens, and she reaches to touch my arm. "Honey, he was just bad news. No job, no future, head screwed on sideways. That was fine in 1967 or '68, but now—how could he make it in 1983?"

I should have been mad about Clinton and her, but I wasn't. It was just like both of them to try it. Besides, I never felt possessive of Clinton. Just lucky when he did show up. And Twyla, I wouldn't be surprised if she did Jake, too. It wasn't personal with her. She was just shopping, testing the market.

I look at her. Sometimes she is so damn practical it kills me. "I'm not just talking about sex or jobs. Maybe Clinton'd still be alive, though, that's what gets me, Twyla. Sure, I marry Jake, he decides to become an eighties guy, and where am I? Here, alone. Divorced. Waiting for the other town reject to call, only Jass thinks *he's* even too good for me. Nice, huh? Who do I date now, Bowker? The guys at the feed mill?"

Twyla stares at me like I've got flies on my face. She hates the Mary Kay look, but she has such nice features she doesn't need more than a touch of lipstick. She won't wear the pink polyester uniforms the other girls at the shop wear, either. Everything her way. "Take that shit off your face, Honey. Come in tonight, let me put a color and cellophane on that mouse fur hair, and I'll do your makeup. You have to change something—this is ridiculous. This was a perfectly good lunch." She spreads her long tan arms. She was the first person to try a tanning bed in town. Ordered it off a catalog.

I pick at a lock of curly hair on my shoulder. "Red, think red." She picks up her burger and takes a big bite, chewing it with a slightly open mouth to annoy me, her crooked front tooth like a little hatchet cutting at the red meat.

"Red?"

"Definitely. Red. *And,* call him. *You* call *Jass.* Maybe you've finally met some poor SOB who's worse off than you are. Ever think of it that way?" Her voice is muffled by the food, so I lean forward.

"Call him? I hardly *know* him."

"Well, you know him better'n anyone else around here—except maybe Cindy Reiler. You *had* your hands on his dick, for chrissakes, you don't exactly need to follow Miss Manners at this point, do you?"

I smile and turn around to catch Simpy's attention. As usual he's watching Bob and Shirley, who are acting like a pair of new calves by the coffee machine, bumping and rubbing each other. He always seems left out of things that way. Maybe naming him Simpson was the one thing that made sure of it. When he looks up, I nod and point to my soup. Twyla and I come here so often that he knows the routine. He removes my soup bowl and puts a plate with a mound of red, yellow, and white between us. Then he gives us each a clean fork and spoon. We ignore the forks.

"What've we got here today, Simmy?" Twyla pushes her burger plate to the side and leans in to inspect the new arrival. He loves it that she calls him Simmy. No one else will.

"We start with a butter pound cake, grate fresh ginger over it, then
we add red raspberries, some fresh whipped cream, with a secret ingredient, and drizzle with Chambord." When he speaks of his food, Simpy changes, gains authority and confidence. His Iowa clumsiness disappears. I wish he could see himself this way. I always figure he must be an artist, a real one, like you read about in books, whose lives are so messed up but whose art makes them better, more real to us.

We each take a spoonful. When Simpy leans against the booth, arms folded, that critical, cool look in his eyes, and asks, "How do you like it?" we both push back.

"I'm doing garlic recipes today." He explains the odor without apologizing for it. "Baked whole heads, and—"

"Chocolate-covered?" Twyla takes another big bite.

Simpy ignores her by raising his eyebrows and tightening his lips. "There's a contest, a trip to France for two, and two weeks in a four-star kitchen."

"Will you take me, Simmy?" Twyla smiles, letting the blond hair sweep luxuriously over one eye like Veronica Lake in those old movies. I always feel like Barbara Stanwyck when she does that—the plainer one who's trouble prone.

"Oh, Twyla, do you have the time? I know how *busy* you are."

"Touché. Sure. I'm outta here anyway next year, Simmy, and I'll take *you* with me if you're still here." Twyla scrapes her spoon along her half of the plate, to pick up the swirl of red and white. "Hmm. Good stuff. You come with me, Sim, you do the cookin' and I'll do the hookin'." She laughs when his face registers surprise. "Just kidding about that part. I'm trying to get Honey-pot here to go, too, but she's so enthralled with Divinity's men, I don't know."

Simpy waves his towel at us as he heads back to the kitchen.

"Why do you *do* that, Twyla?" I lean back and watch her.

She shrugs and keeps eating, edging her way over to my side of the plate.

"And what do you mean, Cindy Reiler might know Jass, Jasper?"

Twyla swallows her bite and bangs down the spoon. She sighs and leans forward. "What planet are you on? Last year there was this big deal between old man Reiler, his brothers, and Jasper Johnson over Cindy. She was helping him break horses and things . . . well, *you* should know. Anyway, the Reilers broke it up. We almost had a race riot. 'Course it would only have had four people in it, but still, a first for Divinity. So the old man bought Cindy a new truck and trailer and gave her money to go on the road showing her quarterhorse to get her out of town. She got him good, though, went to the Quarterhorse Congress and bought a two-year-old stallion, cost twenty-five thou, and the old man had to build this big new pen to keep them in. I put the total cost of fucking Jasper Johnson up at about fifty thousand now. Not bad for a poor colored boy from Nebraska, huh?"

We laugh. "You *sure* it's all over between them?"

Twyla eyes me carefully. "Whyn't you ask *him*, not me." She concentrates on scraping every streak and crumb off the plate, disregarding the sound. She eats like a horse and looks great. Doesn't even exercise. "Men give me all the workout I need," she brags. She looks up at me while she uses her index finger to sweep up the last of it. "Call him. You were obviously in such a daze the first time, you can't remember whether you fucked or not."

I smile. "I said we did it."

"What was it like?"

This is the part of Twyla that always makes me uncomfortable. It reminds me of my ex-husband, Jake. He always made me recite scenes, things I did with Clinton, Jimmy, Brewer. And I did it, but somehow it hurt. Twyla tells me everything about the men she's with. Stuff I don't want to know sometimes because I can't get it out of my head when I see them again. Wolfgang, Tom, and my brother, Sonny Boy.

"Come on, is he big? Can he screw?"

"Oh, Twyla, you know I don't like this."

"Stop being such a baby, Honey, grow up. It's just sex, like brushing your teeth. Stop glamorizing it, have some fun. You know, for someone who takes her clothes off as she's shaking hands hello, you're awfully finicky."

"Oh, shut up. You know I don't do that very much."

"In this town, once is enough. I'd say that happened to you with Jimmy or Brewer, and I never did get it straight which one."

I laugh and drop my eyes. "Both. I told them both they were the only one. Then later, oh, forget it, okay? Jasper is bigger than Jake, about the size of Clinton, which you should remember."

"He couldn't keep it hard long enough to measure, but go on."

"Well, it was wonderful, sexy. He has nice hands, fingers . . ."

"Oh, he knows what to do with them."

"No, yes, they're just nice to look at, Twyla. But he was good, sweet. It just, like Clinton was, but you don't know, so . . ."

"How'd you leave it? What did he say?"

"Thank you. He said, 'Thank you.' "

"Jesus, Honey. That's weird. 'Thank you'? Like having sex is a favor? A gift? You'd better call him. I got a feeling. Call him and go out there again. Or have him over for dinner. Then when he shows, you're out of food. You've got some beer, and whammo!"

"Who've you pulled that one on?" I laugh.

Twyla rummages in her bag, and without looking up, she says, "Your brother."

I hate it when she brings him up. "I got this, my turn. I gotta get back to work. Bowker has some big deal meeting Marylou and I have to sit in on. God knows what now. He's actually closing the office for an hour."

Twyla stands up, shakes herself, and grabs her purse, a brown leather Coach bag Wolfgang bought her in Chicago for $250. I wonder if his wife, Faye, has one, too.

"Yeah, it's Monday so you know what my afternoon is like—bluegills." I nod and go to the counter to pay the check. On Mondays the old ladies come to take advantage of the cheap first-of-the-week rates. When I call Twyla at work she'll cradle the phone with her chin while she's putting the perm in or styling. She doesn't care when the old ladies complain out the door, only leaving a quarter tip at her station. "Fucking blue-heads. Bluegills. Even the shoes look cranky, twisting and creaking under their wobbly ankles," she says as we wait for Shirley to leave Bob alone and take our money at the register. Twyla pushes her hair off her face as she spots herself in the 7-Up mirror facing us. She pulls a tube of clear red lipstick out of her pocket and draws it over her lips. Smacking them, she winks at us both in the mirror.

"At least it's not Friday," I remind her.

"Thank God for small favors." She makes a face, wets her forefinger with the tip of her tongue, and runs it over her perfect thick eyebrows.

I don't try to adjust anything as I stare in the mirror. I notice how finished, how complete, Twyla appears, whole, as if she's always been that age, that height and weight, with those looks, never younger or older. Next to her I seem unfinished, only half here. Sometimes I'm skinny, sometimes plump. Sometimes my face sags with dark worried circles around my dark eyes. Other times I seem like this little kid to myself, and when I look in the mirror, I ask, "Where are you? How'd you get here?" Even my eyebrows are incomplete. In contrast with Twyla's just right thick dark arches, mine start and pizzle out just when they should peak.

Twyla throws her arm across my shoulders and leans her head

against mine so we are almost the same height. I've given up being envious of her. She winks and I shrug.

"Whaddya think? Black, blond?" I ask.

" 'Red,' I told ya. You're too pale for other colors. You got that nice milky redhead skin. Lucky you're not coated with freckles, too, like your sister Baby."

"I know." I picture Baby's fat red body, and Sonny Boy's unwanted face intrudes. For some reason he's a blond whose skin tans perfectly. No farmer lines on arms and neck. Maybe because he wouldn't be caught dead in a field, not even the ones his father-in-law, Homer Bevington, gave him when he married Rose. He plays mechanic and bookkeeper for the family farms. I almost hate Twyla sometimes for being with Sonny Boy. She notices but never asks me why, and I can't tell her. It's our secret. I have the scar Sonny watched Daddy give me that burns a little in the hot new sun of spring when Twyla and I step out onto Main Street.

Hands on our hips, Twyla and I survey the action like we're tourists, just passing through.

"Well, just remember what the Chamber of Commerce always says, Honey: 'Divinity is as close to heaven as we can get without dying, so why leave town?' "

She twitches her butt like a big satisfied bird and struts off toward the Curl-Y-Que, two blocks away in the bottom of Marcia Bland's house. She half turns and waves. "Call him—then call me."

I nod and wave back. Twyla's so much larger than life here she seems to dwarf the town. Her long hair swinging back and forth keeps the rhythm like a horse's tail as she walks.

"She's like a goddess from those times when gods walked around and talked to regular people," Clinton remarks. "Can't you see her with a bow and arrow slung over her shoulder, a pack of hounds bursting out of Kappler's Barber Shop to follow her? 'Course, she's no virgin, so I guess the analogy breaks down a little, doesn't it?"

Sixteen years ago Clinton Busee tested the ice on Spirit Lake. A while after the funeral with the open casket his mother insisted on, Clinton started talking to me. I don't think you could call it a haunting. There's nothing scary about it, except maybe the half-assed things he says sometimes. Maybe he just wants company. Maybe he's just lonesome.

"You're a big help, Clinton."

Watching Twyla, I can't be mad. Is it her fault Sonny Boy has done what he's done? Isn't it his fault—that charm that can cover everything *he* does no matter what it costs Tolson, me, or the others?

My scar aches, so I drop my head and shield it with my hand as I cross the street. "Clinton, Jake, Jimmy," it throbs.

3

The Business of Doing Business

I don't see why we hafta have such a big deal. Times are getting hard, prices down. I don't know about the resta you fellas, but my business is off every month so far this year." Ad Feller shakes his bald head, leans back in his chair, and crosses his arms over the pumpkin-orange

shirted belly. He thinks he's a snappy dresser, so he never quit wearing the wide white vinyl belt and matching slip-ons when the rest of the town did.

Bowker leans forward across the little conference table veneered with fake mahogany. The edges are starting to separate and curl so that a tracing of yellow particleboard outlines the perimeter. Reiler from the feed mill has spent the last forty-five minutes sticking his thumbnail under the plastic and running it back and forth. If the meeting lasts much longer, he'll have the whole top peeled.

"That's just why we need the centennial—so folks can get their minds off hard times, let down their hair," Bowker says in his most earnest voice.

"Open their pocketbooks is more like it." Reiler doesn't even look up from his carpentry when he speaks.

Bowker nods overenthusiastically like a teacher with a slow student. "Sure, that's the ticket. We have to get people spending, and they'll work harder, get some town spirit again, raise some money." It's his turn to lean back now, his arms folded. He recrosses his legs, letting his thigh graze Marylou's arm. She's bent over her tablet taking notes on the short wooden chair he's placed close to his but a little behind so no one will get the idea she's equal to the men actually sitting at the table.

I'm positioned halfway between the conference table and our desks because I'm the gofer. Bowker couldn't bring himself to close the office like he promised, so I'm watching the phones and door and getting coffee and soda.

Cal Kruik, the Chevy and implement dealer, clears his throat like he does every time he wants to say something. "Well, Ad, sorry you're doing so poorly. My business is going like a house afire. But I think you can see Bowker here's right. We need some team spirit back in the old homestead. You and I could even run a contest to give away a car, what say? That'd bring folks home. We'll celebrate a hundred years and homecoming. Give those that *need* it a boost. I'd hate to see you go down the tubes; having you around keeps my sales up." He taps excitedly on the table with the new yellow pencil we've put at each place with a little yellow lined tablet from the drugstore.

"Now wait a minute, I'm still in business, going to have a solid year just like always, so don't you—" Ad half rises from his chair.

Bowker spreads his arms and motions for Feller to sit down. "Okay, okay, this here is what I'm talking about. We need to get folks thinking positive again, getting confidence in the town. So we have this big weekend celebration, get TV from Des Moines, get a couple of fellas from Congress out, bring the chickens home to roost." Bowker winks at the men around the table.

"We could have a parade with invites out for drum and bugle and—"

The door opening catches my attention first. By the time Jass is closing it firmly enough to rattle the loose front windows, the men have stopped talking. Marylou looks up with a know-it-all smile tightening her thin lips. I'm up and over to the door before Jass can take more than a step into the office.

"What do you want?" I whisper. I notice he's dressed for town this time in fresh Levi's, polished black cowboy boots, and a red plaid shirt. He pulls off his clean gray cowboy hat as he speaks.

"Why, I came to see you." He says it in a voice that carries across the office. I can hear the men behind me shuffle like people waiting for a movie to start. Marylou's smile burns my back.

"Shhh, *not here.* Why didn't you call?"

"Why should I?" he says in a voice only slightly lowered. "You coulda called *me.*"

Behind me, Cal Kruik clears his throat, and Bowker calls, "Honey," impatiently.

"Let's go outside. They're trying to have a meeting here."

I carefully avoid looking over my shoulder as we leave the office.

Outside, Jass touches my arm. "What's the matter?"

I pull back. "Nothing's the matter. Why should anything be the matter? Fuck and run's fine with me, if that's how you want to play it. But don't show up at my job and get me in trouble then."

His eyes go gold with green flares in them. He looks down, folds his arms, then looks over my head, toward the Curl-Y-Que, and rocks on his heels for a minute.

"You know, for someone who seems pretty smart, you sure are dumb," he begins, clenching and unclenching his hands.

"I don't have to listen to this crap." I reach for Bowker's door, but Jass puts his hand gently on my arm.

"Wait—"

I want to as I feel the warm of his fingers travel my body. You betrayer, I want to say to it, you're getting me in deep here.

"Look, I came to ask you to come out to my place for dinner tonight, okay? I want to thank you for everything." His voice is like a glove sliding over my body, and I fight the feeling.

"Thank me for sleeping with you? Do I look like a sex therapist or something? Florence Nightingale?"

He grins. "You'd be good at it." Before I can pull away he has my other arm in his grasp. "Don't be silly. I wanted to thank you for your help with Marvel—" His voice stumbles. He lets his arms drop. " 'Course, if you don't want to . . ."

I pause, watching his eyes flicker colors. In the warm April sun his skin glows like well-oiled latigo leather, gold glints beneath the tan. I want his hands on me, but not here, on Main Street where everyone can see us. "Okay, sure. What time?"

He smiles. "Seven-thirty. Gives me time to do chores and throw some steaks on the grill. First barbecue of the year, okay?"

"Fine. See you then."

He touches the rim of his hat, turns, and walks off before I am back in the office. There is another pause in the conversation as I resume my place. For a moment I imagine that they can see his fingerprints on my white arms. They all have that look on their faces.

Driving out to Jass's, I watch the dark slide over the hills and trees like someone is standing just behind it, breathing the color away. Then the dark brown of new plowed fields powdered with green and finally the sky itself goes indigo, purple, and blue black. The few warm days have melted the snow and left the new green edging the highway pale and fresh. Among the trees the skunk cabbage glows fluorescent before it disappears. It is that time of year when the night isn't so dark, when the colors seem to soak up the light all day so they can keep lit when the sun goes down. The frogs and crickets start their racket in the ditches where wild pink geraniums, marsh marigolds, and meadow rue grow. Clinton took me through the catechism of plants in the spring and summer that wild year we were together. It was the best and worst time of my life. We'd find the lady's slipper, bloodroot, jack-in-the-pulpit, trillium, and come back month after month to check on their stages. Wild columbine, wild roses, black-eyed Susans. Clinton remembered everything he read. I had to associate anything with an experience to remember it. It didn't seem important then, those names, getting them right, except to please him. Now, it is a way to remember.

"Clinton," I whisper out loud, "I don't care what Twyla says, I still care."

Then I feel sad watching the blacktop turn blue and the yellow line stagger down the middle. "Drunk? Were you drunk? Stoned? I just don't get it, Clinton."

"Rue, rattlesnake plaintain, wild ginger, maidenhair fern," Clinton chants, his will stronger than mine this late April night in Iowa. All the life around me pushes its big living against the car, trying to get in. I slow down for Jass's turnoff, and the image of what's ahead makes me go balloon light and my stomach drop. I squeeze my legs together hard, to trap the feeling there. When Clinton's voice tries to say something, I roll down the window and sing to myself real loud "The Star-Spangled Banner," what I can remember of it.

"So what were all the white guys doing in the office today?" Jass and I have shoved our plates to the center of the kitchen table to give us room to prop our elbows. We're both hog full and try to give discreet burps behind our hands. I've noticed that for Jass certain people have names and the rest are generic categories. The white guys are the men who run things in town, or who think they do, with the exception of Reiler, who gets a name. Twyla must be right about Jass having an affair with Cindy Reiler and the old man going nuts. I explain about the centennial plans for next May.

"Hey, that's not a bad idea. A little news coverage might help me, too." He slips into silence, making his calculations.

For me, it's not so simple. I think of the last big celebration years ago—the Appreciation Day when I met Clinton and someone died. "I don't know, things can really get outta hand at these deals."

"Yeah, well, hey, you wanna go take a look at the filly? Get on the coat and boots you wore last time. They're hanging on the porch there." Cindy Reiler's? I sigh and get up. Why should he be any different from the rest of them? Maybe Twyla is right: once the mystery of sex is solved, what do you really have in common?

"Honey, did you hear what I said?" Jass is still sitting.

I shake my head. He has his beautiful hands wrapped around a coffee mug like I might try to take it.

"I asked why you were looking so down all of a sudden, did I say something?"

"Oh, you just reminded me of some stuff, bad memories. A man I used to, know. Things get crazy when this town has a party. You'll get a chance to see that before long. People end up getting hurt, too. It's hard to talk about." He is watching me, his eyes almost a cool blue in the kitchen light. "You coming?"

"Okay, but you're not off the hook. I don't like mysteries." He is out of his chair with his arms around me before I can answer. His lips are on my neck, but I keep my face buried in the cup of his chest and shoulder. After the first time, I'm not that easy.

"If you don't like mysteries, you're in the wrong town with the wrong woman." Jass laughs and hugs me, then leads the way to the porch.

In the barn the sweet-and-sour smell of horses and straw settles on us like dust as we enter. Jass switches on lights and leads me to a stall rigged with big overhead heat lamps. As I look over the door, I see the bay filly lying on her side asleep next to a big blocky mare with feet the size of salad plates, shaggy yellow coat, and long ragged dirty blond mane, who seems to be standing guard.

"Not much to look at, but she's a good mama. Had twins, both died. She's real happy to have this one." Jass holds out his palm with a piece of carrot in it, and the mare stretches her neck eagerly, sniffs at the treat, then gobbles it between her big gray lips. The happy crunching alerts the other horses, who shift in their stalls; a few even nicker.

When the mare reaches again, Jass rubs her forehead. She seems just as content with the petting as the treat.

After checking on the other horses, Jass leads me into the tack room. He turns on the electric heater and gestures for me to settle back on the sofa covered with soft wool horse coolers.

He sits across from me on an old red vinyl easy chair and props his feet on the edge of the couch. He smiles.

"Why're we sitting in here, Jass? Let's go back to the house."

"I like it here. I can be near the horses. They help me relax. Try it. Just lean back, get comfortable. Stretch out."

I obey, feeling dumb. The light oily smell of harness clings to the air in here, and for the first time I take a deep breath. The wool horse blankets give off a musky smell as I shift around to face Jass, who is watching me casually through half-closed lids. At least it appears that way until I stare at the glittering eyes and discover how they're pushing into me. Oh, no, you don't, I tell them. Oh, yes, I do, they answer. I want to get up, run, but I'm hypnotized almost. This is too close, I want to explain. I only have room for one man in my life. Clinton doesn't like a crowd. Sonny makes sure of it. Let's just have our little fling. Don't do this other thing. Men get dead doing that.

"Why don't you tell me what's going on, Honey?"

"I don't know what—"

"Cut the crap, Honey."

"Screw you, Jass."

He sits for a few minutes watching his hands, turning them this way and that like he's just discovered them at the end of his arms. Finally he says, "What's going on, Honey? Why're you so pissed off all of a sudden?"

I punch the sofa, the dull thud giving me almost no satisfaction. "Oh, screw it, I don't feel like 'life story' time. I hardly know you, Jass."

"You knew me good enough to make love to me."

"Seventeen years ago August I met a guy, and some other stuff happened. It's a very long story. Not my favorite thing to think about. Sonny Boy, my brother? There was some trouble. My dad, Julius, and then . . ." I reach up and touch the scar on my forehead as if he can see it. The room is almost dark except for a safety light at the far end, and the red glow of the heat coils between us.

"I had, an accident." My jaw twitches with the lie. Even now I can't tell it. It's just lucky I don't usually have to.

In the silence, I hear the electrical tick of the heater, the muffled nudge of the wind on the barn, and my own breathing, which won't behave. Finally I take a big breath and am surprised when it comes out as a sigh, long and sad.

"Do you always make that sound when you hold back, or lie?" Jass's voice startles me, and I nod before I have a chance to stop myself. "Why don't you just tell it—get a start, at least."

I watch his face shadowed with red light.

"Step into the car going down," Clinton murmurs.

"His name was Clinton. We met at the Appreciation Day picnic. I guess things were never the same after that. I was never the same."

Jass nods.

"He's dead now; he died." I press down a sigh that rises like a bird in my chest. It hurts, beating there.

Jass waits silently like my ex-husband, Jake, used to.

"So what else do you want?"

"I don't know, Honey, whatever you want to tell me is fine." He closes his eyes and leans his head back tiredly.

I get up and go outside, stopping under the eaves of the turnout shelter where the horse died a few days before. The air is clean the way it is in April, with a rim of winter cold lingering on it. I want to cry but can't. I try to think sad things, but they don't bring tears. I want to slam my face into the cool stone wall of the barn instead.

He arrives so quietly I don't know he's there until he speaks. Don't say anything, please, just grab me and hang on so I can go really crazy, I say in my head as he says, "Come back in, Honey."

"Can't we just screw, Jass, can't we just do that?" I turn to him and

put my arms around his neck, seeking his mouth with mine. "Just keep it simple."

Afterward, lying naked face to face on the sofa, he asks again. When I try to get up, his powerful arms hold me to him. Though this isn't sex, it feels like rape, submitting.

"Okay, you want it, then here it is." His hold relaxes as I begin to tell him the Appreciation Day story, determined to leave nothing out, to hurt him if I can, as the telling is hurting me.

"When Mort came in with Roger at the veterinary clinic, we had a big Appreciation Day for the clinic, and that was when it happened."

"Wait, Honey, I don't understand. . . ." Jass adjusts his body so he's propped against the arm of the sofa and my head is on his chest. It's easier to tell it when I don't have him watching my face.

"See, that's the problem with trying to explain things, Jass. Okay. Let me backtrack.

"It was summer 1967, mid-August, and everyone was hot and bored anyway, so the merchants planned a parade and barbecue at the town park on the Mercy River and gave the veterinarians a plaque saying how much the town liked them. Old Roger beamed but didn't say much, like always. Mort smiled all day. I remember it was hot and dusty that day, in the nineties. All the men were gulping beer like water, and my brother Sonny Boy was swaggering around because he had just finished two years of agri up at Ames and was coming back to work on the big farm Bevington owned, and to marry Rose Bevington the next spring.

"I was in high school, and all us girls were casting about for what we were going to do. A couple like Antha Jensen and Wanda Smith were going up to Ames to school; their daddies must have figured that was the only way to marry them off. There was a saying around Iowa then: 'Send your girls to Iowa City and your hogs to Ames.' We used to sit in the girl's john smoking and laughing about it, secretly knowing *we'd* never even get a chance to go to college. We'd heard the stories about how wild it was getting in Iowa City with hippies and radicals. But we didn't care. We knew that Mitch Rosenberg had been arrested and thrown in jail for selling dope to the police. The dummy. His mama looked past us when she walked downtown, with her son sitting up there in the county jail until he went down to the pen in Kansas. So you see, Iowa City had a kind of attraction for us, too. We wanted the chance to be bad."

Jass laughs and strokes my head, trying to straighten the loops of curl.

"I suppose that's why so much happened on Appreciation Day. We were ready for something. Clinton Busee, the man I mentioned before, had just come back from Vietnam. We didn't know much about the war except students in Iowa City were raising hell over it. Daddy said he'd rather take me out back and put a bullet through my head then and there as send me to Iowa City to become a communist or worse. He'd look over at me, across the dining room table, like he knew and I knew what 'worse' meant.

"It sounded interesting, at least. Better than Divinity. Better than miles of corn and alfalfa, or oats and soybean, better than those red lines across the backs of necks when the boys took off their shirts in the backseats of cars in the summer and you could feel what that sunburn would be like in twenty years, all leathery and worn out like their faces would get. Lines settling in with their minds like furrows they were planting each spring and digging up each fall. We wanted something to happen. We wanted to be in the middle of trouble so we wouldn't end up like our parents."

"Thank God I wasn't raised around here if that's how you feel, Honey." Jass lets his fingers step down the vertebra of my back, pausing to feel each as if he needs to remember its outline. I enjoy the feeling of his hands while I remember what it was like growing up here when no matter how good boys' bodies felt in the backseats, with their muscles laced tight around bone like they'd never come undone, I knew they would. They were all around: the old men crippled up from machinery and animals, parts of hands and feet missing, arms stiffened up in some awkward position, legs like wood that had to be pushed along with a cane or a hand. Wherever you looked, the same fields that took father and son and brother gave back grain that rotted in silos or got sold for less than it cost to make. Sometimes a family got rich, but the livestock and machinery ate up the men.

Even the Fleishers and the Sorensons and the Bevingtons who farm the biggest places get kicked and bitten, stepped on, trampled, and gouged by their animals. Pieces of machinery fall over in their hands, fly off and whir across their faces, or reach out and grab at their fingers, their arms, their legs. It's always been the same, each summer the police car whizzing up to Good Earth with some poor boy in the backseat holding on to what's left of himself. Haying season, harvest, we hear the siren and know. Then back at school you'd see the bandages or the pink skin molded over the nubbin of the wound, larvae fresh.

Jass shifts so our bodies face each other, the wool covering a comfortable rasp on our skin.

"I kept thinking I'd find something different if I got away, got out of here," I tell him. "That I wouldn't have to end up with one of those boys. I didn't mention it to my family. Daddy had lost his farm and been miserable ever since, and Mama just wanted to get back to the country. She kept making him buy little acre lots farther and farther away from town, anytime he got a few dollars ahead, like stepping-stones she could use to walk her way out there again."

"I don't understand, Honey. What does all this have to do with the Appreciation Day?"

"Just be patient. You have to understand my family. It's all hooked together, you'll see.

"The thing was we were too big to live in the little house we owned here in Divinity. Daddy and Baby and Sonny Boy were the biggest. Sonny Boy lost his baby fat and grew up six feet. Baby always waddled around, and still does. Daddy, he's well over six feet, stooped a little like a farmer gets from the hard work, but big boned. Maybe you've seen him around. And Mama, well, she was big the way women used to be, round and heavy. She could wring a chicken's neck just like that with those strong hands. She often went out to help Daddy unload hundred-pound sacks when we lived on the farm. Bearing children hadn't been any problem.

"Tolson and I were the small ones of the lot. 'Runts,' Daddy called us, and laughed when we were little. But later we just seemed to always be in the way of something bigger and solider in that house, the other four taking up all the room, all the food, sometimes all the air. Tolson and I lived in the attic because the other two were really too big to climb that set of stairs and too tall to stand up under the low ceilings if they did get there. It was hard on Tolson, being small. It was okay for a girl, but a boy has to be big and powerful in this part of the country. Everything else is just store clerk, salesman stuff. Tolson never heard the end of it, not until he took off one day and ended up in Oregon. He's never coming home, he told me one day when we talked on the phone. 'Tell them that,' he said. 'I'm never coming home, not till they're all dead and buried, and don't invite me to any funerals, either. I don't want to hear it, except that they're dead and buried.'

" 'Does that include Mama?' I asked. Of course it didn't, and in a while I had to call and tell him that she'd died. He tried to get back in time for the funeral but didn't make it. I could tell that the others thought he was just selfish for not showing up in time. The way they treated him, ignoring him or making their voices sarcastic. Maybe that's what drove him back out again. With Mama gone, there sure wasn't much to hold him. So that's what our family was like then. Not much has changed, I guess."

"Nice family, Honey."

I sit up a little, letting the room air cool my bare chest. We are sitting side by side now, both of us looking out the little window that shows patches of the paddock and house beyond illuminated by the yard light and the moon. I'm trying to figure out how to explain it—my family and this town—it's as if we are all related, nothing can touch one without the other feeling it.

"Honey? I've got to check on the horses, it's time. Will you wait? I want to hear the story so don't go away, okay?" Jass smiles and kisses my forehead, nose, and lips. Our scent is clove and sweat I can smell on his mouth, my skin. He gets up and pulls on his jeans without underwear like Clinton used to do.

"Pretty shy around the horses," I tease.

He looks embarrassed. "Oh, it's just, well . . ."

"Better put on your boots, too—"

By the time he leaves the tack room, he's fully clothed. "You're not really going to tell him that whole thing, are you? Scare him off?" Clinton says.

I lie down on my stomach, trying to warm the hole left by Jass's body against mine. "No, Clinton, don't worry. I won't tell your story. Who else could understand it?" I feel him in the room, watching the memory like I am.

4

The Appreciation Day

There it was, our hot, dry little town all dressed up for Roger and Mort. Everyone sweating right through their light cotton clothes within minutes. There wasn't a breath of air; even the corn leaves seemed to hang like scarves from their stalks as we drove over to where the picnic was to be held after the parade. Little riverside park right in the middle of town there. Thank goodness for the Mercy River. It seems to make things hotter on a day like that in August, but other times it just cools you to hear it sinking and rising over the rocks, bubbling along.

The Mercy is pretty shallow in August, so the kids were already in their trunks and shorts jumping in and splashing around. A few of the older women had hiked their dresses up midthigh and were yelling and laughing at the kids as they waded, too. It was always something to see those rubbery thighs bare like that and the raw white legs like clubs coming out of the knees, poked firmly into the water. Some of the women who had kept a little of their figures put on shorts, but the long kind, Bermudas, which gave us kids a charge, laughing at the way the stomachs pooched out in front like they were always pregnant, and usually one of them was.

Mama never liked to see a woman's legs if she was pregnant. She'd always cluck and shake her head as we drove through town if she saw someone dressed in shorts or a miniskirt when they were pregnant. "It's not right," she'd explain when I asked her. "It's just not right."

Pretty soon the women came climbing back up the little riverbank, the hems of their dresses held dripping in one hand, the other flailing out in midair like an awkward paddle. Then they spread the tablecloths on the few tables the park provides, on card tables, and on the ground. Then the food appeared—magically, it seemed—big platters and roasting pans full of fried chicken. Fresh fried chicken. Killed that morning, cleaned, and fried up fresh. It had flavor, the chickens not four hours before pecking out in the farmyard.

The A&P had donated a truckload of watermelons, which sat in the horse tank cooling in ice water. God, we all wanted to jump in there. The little kids kept grabbing off chips of floating ice whenever they got the chance.

There were big pots of water boiling on the barbecue grills for the corn and fresh juicy tomatoes that some of the women were slicing, and you knew they'd taste like the heat and smell of dark green leaves and dirt when you bit in.

The big attraction was the beer the merchants had supplied. All the men kept hanging around it and the few younger women who were working and not married and therefore felt like they had a right. Some of the newly married and wilder couples stood around it, too, those that still went out to drink in the bars or had parties or even played around with each other when it got real late and boring. Talk drifted down among the town folks about such goings-on, but Mama said to never mind, most of it was an exaggeration and sooner or later the women would all end up pregnant anyway and have to settle down. Some of the men never did, I guess, like Sonny Boy.

Clinton was one of the first back from Vietnam. "Wasn't even wounded," he bragged. He was tanned and good-looking, his hair still short from the army so he kept his hat on. The local boys had already started letting theirs grow out, and you should've heard the parents carrying on about that. Clinton was bragging about his escapades and saying how all the guys should grow up and join. Some of us were a little doubtful, wondering why he didn't stay in if it was so wonderful. The older men loosened up by the third or fourth beers and started telling their own stories about wars, the Korean, World War II, and, for a few of the old geezers, the First. Then they'd get to slapping backs, spilling beer down shirts, laughing like all get-out and end up tripping and wrestling each other. It was just a regular picnic in most respects, the Appreciation Day, like the ones we have on Memorial Day, Fourth of July, and Labor Day.

By early evening everyone was pretty well lit up and the food sat around dismantled looking, like a pack of dogs had run through the place.

A lot of the men and women had coupled back up and had lain down on their blankets, drinking and giggling, while a group from over in Pottersville played their favorite country and western songs. Some of the men kept drinking, and their women sat together on the picnic benches talking and throwing bad looks over at the clumps of too loud men. Daddy was around somewhere. Mama was sitting with Clarise and Marjory, her two best friends, and they were sharing a beer around, too. Mama always seemed at her best with those two. I don't know how she changed, exactly, but she became younger with her friends, especially when they had a drink or two and the men were busy elsewhere. And Daddy was.

Naturally, us kids in high school were trying to avoid our families. A few of us had sneaked some beers for ourselves off down the riverbank a ways. Close enough so we could hear when things started breaking up and we had to go home, but far enough so we could drink and flirt without them catching us. We had finished two of the beers when Clinton came stumbling in on us, almost scaring us to death. We had collapsed back against the bank and were watching the sun go down rubbing the sky red and lovely when Clinton started crawling and cursing over our tangle of legs to squeeze between me and Elvin, a boy I liked. Too tired and too full, we moved over for him. It was only a few minutes before I could feel his beery mouth on my face. I pushed him off.

"Hey, I bet none of you ever tried this." Clinton rolled onto one hip and drew something out of his back pocket. We all looked away, back to the sunset or each other, hoping our lack of interest would get rid of him. "Now," he began, unrolling a cellophane wrapper to uncover some little white cigarettes within. "Am I right?" He snickered and rolled onto the other hip, jostling against me hard as he pulled out a pack of matches. I could feel the outline of his body against mine after he had rolled back. It wasn't pleasant.

"You've been setting down here stealing cans of beer like it's a federal crime or something, how come none of you ever drove over to Iowa City and scored?" He paused, gazed out at the river, a funny look crossing over his face; then he jerked back with a shake of his head. "Yeah, I been out there. And you've been sitting here watching the corn grow. Am I right?" He giggled a little and licked the cigarette all over with his pink, slobbery tongue. It was enough to make you sick. Catching my look, he smiled. "Makes it burn evenly, dumbo."

He took a small drag off the cigarette, and instead of exhaling, he held the smoke in his lungs until I thought his eyes would pop out. Daddy used to have a rooster got that same look on its face, like it'd swallowed a frog or something. Finally, Clinton exhaled and handed me the cigarette. "Now hurry up, don't waste it. The rest of you be ready for your turn, too." He was all business now, so we perked up and got ready. Why not? Naturally I choked on the first puff, and Clinton handed me a beer with a wicked grin on his face. "Tough broad, huh?"

I didn't feel a thing for about what seemed like half an hour. We kept joking, watching the sun go down, taking puffs off more joints that Clinton produced, all a little mashed but carefully rolled, with the ends twisted so the stuff wouldn't fall out.

"You know what I got kicked out for, don't you?" he began.

I was the only one who responded. The rest were too skeptical I guess. "Hell, Clinton, we didn't even know you got kicked out. Your mama know about that?" This shut him up for a few minutes, but then he continued.

"You think it's just having to shoot, am I right? Well, there's the goddamn mud and insects. And the people. They never do anything but shit in the water and drink it. Then we all end up getting sick from it. Turns your stomach, right?"

Here he paused and got another joint lit up, but this time I noticed that his hands were shaking. I could feel the other kids smirking and digging their elbows into each other over the lies Clinton was going to tell us. I wanted to reach out and touch him, but I figured he was still Clinton underneath, still that loudmouth full of beer who'd never amount to anything, not even in our one-horse, one-ass town.

"God. After a while," he continued, "you just forget about everything but getting stoned. One way or another. Stoned the whole time, and everyone around you is stoned, and pretty soon you think *they're* stoned, too—the enemy, the gooks—and that this is the funniest, saddest, sickest thing you ever seen. I remember my dad telling me that only an idiot would get wounded or killed in a war. In World War Two, he was a paratrooper and landed in France. Said they just kept their heads down, put the gun around a corner or over a culvert once in a while, and fired. Never even bothered aiming the damn thing. Just fire to keep your hand in. Only a fool could get hurt that way."

We all shifted around then, uncomfortable with this new Clinton, uncomfortable with pity for such a loudmouth who could even manage to get himself kicked out of the army (if that were true), just the way he got kicked out of every high school and vo-tech in the state (and that *was* true). Then we noticed the sky glowing iridescent like the top of a squash bug, and the smell of that evening, as if all the fields in Iowa were blooming right on top of us.

So when I felt Clinton's arm slide under my head, I let it stay there and even leaned back to enjoy the sky. It was his voice talking again that interrupted us, where we had drifted to.

"But you know, my dad was wrong. There wasn't anywhere a person could be safe in 'Nam. Not even in his own bunk in his own United States barracks on his own airfield. They were everywhere. I *mean* it. They snuck up on you, day or night, and *bam,* they had you! A wire around the neck, knife, poison, grenade, gun, mortar attack, bombs, anything they could do to kill you off. One by one, or whole bunches at a time. They didn't give a shit how long it took. Like we were ants and they just had to keep stomping us out, and we'd be done with sometime or another, move on, build a hill someplace else." I could feel his hand working its way down my chest as he drew me in closer to him.

"Before long, most of the guys I came over with were getting whacked. Killed, wounded, or just crazy, they got sent home when the army couldn't make 'em do anything. The rest of us were real nervous. They kept sending new officers, re-forming platoons. I knew pretty soon they'd just send in someone to replace me, too. Replaced, hell, I didn't want that!"

Clinton paused again and leaned to whisper in my ear, "Why don't I take you out a little later tonight? We could talk some more, you'd like it." And with his hand massaging my breast now, making the nipple hard between his fingers, I felt like saying yes. Though I tried to focus on what a loser Clinton was, I wasn't having much luck remembering.

"There was a lot of LSD, acid, there, and we were taking it on and off. Though we didn't feel much like fighting while we were tripping, it was okay between times. We thought that if we put it in the food, or the water, somehow we'd all be sent home. I'm not sure how it was supposed to work, but we hoped something big would happen. If they could see how much we didn't want to be there, then they would send us home. Stoned thinking, I guess. Stupid. It wouldn't have ever worked."

It was getting real dark by then, and we knew our families would be thinking about home pretty soon. I hoped the other kids couldn't see what Clinton was doing to me, but they were feeling their own way along and didn't care what anyone else was up to. Then Clinton took his other hand and gently pulled my free arm to him, leading my hand down his stomach to the bulge in his pants. It wasn't the first time I'd felt a boy there, but it was the first time that I knew exactly what I wanted it to mean to me. I rubbed my hand back and forth, making the fabric whisper and the bulge grow harder. Clinton almost moaned out loud, then slid my hand off. "Later," he murmured in my ear.

"But what happened?" one of the kids asked, and Clinton started giggling so weirdly that we barely heard the parents calling us to come on, they were going home now. It was standing up that did it. That was when I realized what "getting stoned" meant. The world whirled around, and the ground reached back up for me, until I realized that it was Clinton's arm trying to pull me back down.

I told my friend Mary Jo, "You'd better tell them I went out with some of the kids. I can't see them like this." Mary Jo was in no better shape, but I figured my parents could accept that from her.

Clinton and I hid there under the riverbank for another half hour, waiting for people to pack the cars and trucks and get out of there. Meanwhile he kept touching me all over, making me wet my pants almost, putting my hand over his crotch, but always making me stop. And oh, it felt good that night, like it never had before. The river like music at our feet, the frogs and crickets chirruping away, and the smell of dirt and green things working their way up through my skin until I couldn't tell where they began and where I ended.

"Honey," Clinton whispered finally when it'd been quiet for a while, "Honey, let me do it now, no one's around, I need to do it now, please?" He was the first boy who'd ever *asked,* nice like that, and somehow it didn't seem wrong that night. I don't know why, it seemed natural to let Clinton, who'd touched me all over and made me feel that way, finish it. So I did. I nodded my head, but he didn't jump on me like any of the boys my own age would have. No, he kept going slow, taking his time, making sure I felt good, until finally I couldn't stand it anymore and was asking him, telling him what I wanted him to do, and that was what he did.

I'm so sunk in this memory, I jump when Jass closes the door with a soft click. "Jesus—" Suddenly I feel too naked. I sit up and struggle to pull one of the horse blankets around me. "Shit," I mutter, and tug some more at the blanket so I can stand up and cover myself, too, but it's stuck across the back. "Oh, screw—" I throw off the blanket and jump up. My clothes are scattered around the room where he threw them as they came off. I cross my arms across my chest and try to stand my full five feet four and one-half inches tall, facing his easy six feet plus in boots.

"What's the matter?" Jass asks as he reaches for me.

I shrug him off. A bad feeling covers my skin, rubbing it like the spiny side of Velcro. Jass isn't Clinton. None of them are. I know I shouldn't take it out on him, but I can't help it. Remembering that first time makes everything now seem like skim milk next to cream.

"What's this?" he asks tiredly, and turns to walk across the semidark room. I hear the *whish* of a refrigerator unsticking, a metal click and hiss of a poptop, and a gurgle. In a minute he's back standing in front of me holding out a can of Grain Belt. When I don't take it, he says, "Take the goddamn can of beer."

Although I've never liked the taste of this brand, I take a sip of it and hand the can back. He sits down without taking off his clothes and presses the beer can against his forehead. I stand over him, feeling a little awkward in my bare skin. My feet are getting cold on the linoleum, but I don't want to show it, so I force myself to stand still, flat-footed like Clinton would have.

"God, you're the pissiest woman. What's the matter now?" He says it like he's tired to death of me already.

I turn to start the search for my clothes, but he grabs my arm and pulls me off balance down on the sofa. I shove at him, and he goes down on the floor, spilling the beer.

"What the hell . . ." He gets up slowly, rubbing his elbow, his eyes yellow orange in the odd glow of the heater. This time he sits down carefully, not touching me. "What's the matter with you? Jesus, Honey, you know I have my whole life in these horses. They got to come first. Hell, you don't even act like you like me, always getting pissed."

He puts his arms around me, steadying me into his body. Finally he says, "Are we always going to fight, Honey? I'm sorry I had to leave just when you started to tell me your story, but you have to see how it is with this place."

I realize I'm not really mad at him. It's just this story. I begin to unbutton his shirt. "Take your clothes off, I feel silly being the only one naked."

He sighs and begins to pull off his boots. "Doesn't it matter that you turn me on? You're the sexiest woman I ever met."

I laugh. "Give me a break—what about Cindy Reiler? And I bet there've been others."

"Not many," he says as he stands to unzip his jeans. (I love that sound.) "And Cindy is a kid. A real kid. Nice, but not like you, definitely not like you."

Yeah, Clinton used to say I fucked like a whore with the heart of a poet. I got the whore part all right. I just never understood the other stuff. "So you think I'm old, huh?"

He pauses in the middle of stepping out of his jeans, one beautiful lean leg held up. "What're you, paranoid? I'm not even old at forty-five. You're just not a kid, not old, just right. Thirty? Thirty-five? You're a ripe peach, Honey, fallin' right into my hands, and I'm gonna take a big bite." He kicks off his jeans and lunges for me. We wrestle ourselves close again, side by side on the couch. This time our legs are wound around, our toes touching.

"Go on, sweetie, tell me the story of the scar, and I'll try to be good, I promise." He scooches down farther so his head rests on my chest. I stare at the far wall, the night outside the window, the light puddling the ground. Everything is suddenly so still. Here's the sad part, I want to tell him.

"Clinton, the boy I mentioned before, and I got together, smoked some dope, and made out on the riverbank until everyone left the park. It must've been around eleven when we finally crawled out of that place and were heading back to Clinton's car. Clinton wasn't bragging or talking too loud like he had at first. He was tender, holding me up, sort of, trying to brush the bits of leaves and dirt off my back, and giving me little hugs. We wouldn't have even known they were there if they hadn't laughed out loud just before we got to where they were lying in the grass. I suppose if he hadn't had such a distinctive laugh, we wouldn't have known who it was. We would have kept walking for the car, thinking that it was just another couple like us. But as it was, my dad has that laugh with a crackle around the edges, like fire catching hold of cellophane. Even Clinton knew who it was and pulled me out of the way into some trees because I was stunned and just kept walking, my brain not telling my body yet what was going on.

"Then I heard her say, 'Not there, Julie, not there,' in a whiny, encouraging tone. Everyone around called my dad 'Julie,' because his name was Julius. There wasn't any doubt about it. My dad was down in the bushes with someone, and the other voice wasn't Mama's. Mama'd never let him get away with nonsense like lying around in the bushes. When I started shivering, Clinton held me tighter, then he half shoved, half carried me back the way we came. We walked down the riverbank about half a mile and doubled back around, avoiding the park picnic area completely. Neither of us said a word. I couldn't, and he didn't have to.

When we reached his car, we just got in and started driving around. I didn't get home until one in the morning. It wasn't that we did anything more. Mostly we didn't say much, except when we parked for a while in Munson's field and I had a good cry."

I pause, remembering Clinton's words that night. His voice has always stayed in my head, like it belongs there. When Clinton finally started talking to me, he said, "It happens, you know. Things happen to everyone. Trouble. It's just there, and you got to see your best way around it, no matter what anyone else says about you. Now, your dad, he's got his own trouble, and you got yours. Don't get those two mixed up in your head, like I can see is happening, am I right? He's got to live what he's doing, and you got to live, too."

He paused for a long time, and I remember feeling a kind of comfort there, wrapped in his arms, our legs tangled up around the gearshift on the floor. Clinton had taken all the money he'd made and saved in the war and blown it on the fanciest car in that part of the state. A bright red GTO 400 with a Ram Air engine, nothing power. Too much drag on the engine. Just speed and an AM/FM radio with front and back speakers. "The war wasn't worth shit, and neither will this car be when I'm done with it," he told me. He was right, of course.

"Listen," he drew my face up to his. "I did what I did, now I got to live with it. All of it." He let my face go. "And we did what we did tonight, and your dad, well, he's got to live with himself, too. Don't hold it against him, though. None of it's all his fault. Or yours, or mine, or this car's, or this field's or the moon or the sky. It's just shit, see." But I didn't understand what he was saying. I felt like one of Mama's dish towels, gray and ragged around the edges, and I wanted to go home.

Jass nuzzles his head into my shoulder. I begin again. "It was the day after that we had the fight and my face got cut. When I'd finally made it home that night, the whole house was dark. Everyone asleep. I didn't know or care whether Daddy was in his bed, or Sonny Boy or Baby or Tolson. Somehow all of that had slipped away from me. I crawled up the stairs quiet as possible and didn't wake until noon.

"When I came downstairs, Mama was in the kitchen as usual and gave me one of those vacuum cleaner looks that picks up every little detail, then said coldly, 'Your father wants to talk to you. He's in the garage.'

"I was hungry but didn't dare grab at one of the apples she was peeling. She had the look that let me know she'd as soon poke my hand with the knife as give me a slice of her apple. So I just shrugged to let her see I didn't give a damn what anyone thought about me coming in late or anything and went down the three back steps into the garage. Daddy at the workbench had his back to me, but I could see from the side that he was working on something. It looked like a piece of plywood with nails driven through every two inches or so. He had used thin, sharp-looking nails that came out of the other side like little knives.

" 'What's that for?' I asked.

" 'Damn dog. He's scratching up the door, ruining it, but this should fix him.' As he talked, he was pounding through the remaining nails. I looked at his long narrow back, muscular, powerful, and tried to imagine him brushing leaves and dirt off someone last night. It made me sick.

"The dog was a poor, worrisome kind of animal, afraid it wouldn't get enough to eat, afraid someone was going to give it a licking. He was too well bred for our family. My uncle Cyrus had bred him for hunting, but he'd never made much of a hunting dog. Too nervous out there, too worried. He'd come back from the field every few minutes to check on the men, to make sure they hadn't left him off or something. And the guns going off overhead scared him pee-crazy. 'But he'll hurt himself if he scratches that.'

"I should have remembered about the temper, but something in me didn't care that morning. So when he swung around, the hammer in one hand, the board of nails in the other, I wasn't worried. 'Listen, you, don't you tell me what to do, your hear?' I knew he didn't mean it, but he raised the hand holding the hammer.

" 'Oh, sure, go ahead, the neighbors will know who crippled up the dog. You'll be lucky if they don't tell the sheriff about this when they see that thing on the door.'

"A funny look passed over his face for a moment, then he turned back to the workbench and gave a short, harsh laugh. 'Well, Miss Hotpants, if I was *you,* I wouldn't be casting stones at other people about the neighbors. What do you think they have to say about a little tramp who comes in at one in the morning, crawling up the stairs like a bitch in heat?' He turned and pounded another nail in extra hard and almost split the wood for emphasis.

" 'Well, if I was you'—I paused and drew out his name long and whiny like the woman I'd heard with him had—'*Jooleeee,* I'd be careful myself.' I muttered the rest, thinking he couldn't hear: 'Lying in the grass like a dog sniffing up every dress that walks by. You're no—' I didn't get a chance to finish before something cracked me across the face, and it was all dark, then red, and the blood was pouring down over my eye. I shook my head for a minute, and in slow motion he raised his arms to hit me again, claw of the hammer in one hand and the piece of board with the nails pointing out in the other, accusingly, glittering above him. 'No, don't,' I cried, and he dropped his arms, shook his head, then turned his back.

" 'Get inside. Get your mother to fix that.'

"Of course, Mama takes me up to Roger the vet to get stitches. That's why the scar is there." Clinton sometimes ran his fingers over it when we were lying on the chair watching Johnny Carson at Boardman's in town. It was an absentminded thing to do, trailing his finger along the curve the claw made as it bit in, then lifted the flesh up and out in a little arc. "I don't think Daddy meant to hurt me. At least, that's what I've been telling myself for years."

Jass reaches an arm around my middle and hugs me. He pulls a leg over me as if to wrap my body in his, as if to protect me from the hurt. "I'm sorry," he murmurs.

"The next morning, when I went out to bring the dog in, I found it huddled in the broken-down cardboard box full of smelly rags that was its bed. When I called, it shivered and seemed to sink deeper into the corner of the garage where the box sat.

"It was a couple of weeks before the paws healed enough for the dog to go galloping about again. I knew that nobody would spend money to bring the dog to the vet's to have the cuts cleaned, so I did it myself. What bothered me wasn't pouring the hydrogen peroxide on the cut-up pads, or even having the poor dog pee on me the first time when it was so scared. No. It was the sight of that board, full of those little points that would punish anything that came against it, the idea that no amount of hosing could loosen the bloodstains in long thin scratches down the middle."

After my story, we just lie on the couch in the tack room, listening to whatever the world has to give us. Once there is a loud banging as a horse's legs are momentarily caught against a wall, when it tries to stand up in the stall. "Cast," Jass worries, but then it quickly stops and we know the horse is up and safe. Later there is a tiny scratching of a mouse in the wall. Outside the wind has died down. It's the middle of the night. We doze, waking only to shift ourselves again. At dawn, it is his fingertip on my scar that wakes me; following the edge as if he recognizes something about it. I don't even open my eyes, just let his breathing pull me back to sleep, where just at the bottom I can't help but believe I'm with Clinton, after all.

"The circles of hell," his voice says in my dream.

"Rings?"

"Circles," he says, and smiles. "Passion, appetite."

"Jass?"

"You," Clinton says. "And that's only the beginning. Sonny Boy—you didn't tell that story, did you, Honey? What about *that*?"

I moan and roll tighter into the shelter of Jass's body. "Help me, help me," I call in my dream, but know it's useless, I'm too far away.

5

The Blacksmith Lounge

I swing onto Highway 11 off my road and cruise slowly toward town, excited and scared, not in any hurry to meet Jass for the first time in a public place. What if Sonny Boy or Daddy shows up? I try not to think about that as I drive, because May is the best time in Iowa: the way the grass greens up and the trees burst out with leaves like they're singing on stage or something. The way the big flocks of blackbirds come sweeping along in front of you, then go and build their nests and wake you up at five A.M. with their racket. The way the flowers get so full and heavy, they look good enough to eat. Passing Sorenson's, I notice the cows trotting in their new pastures. Bucking at the slightest noise, like a bunch of deer, they get so graceful all of a sudden. And the horses raise their large, delicate nostrils into the wind for smells, then skim like huge birds across the pastures, their hooves barely touching as I watch. Even the pigs at Mueller's get into the act, bucking like ponies and charging clumps of new weeds, looking for the fresh May mud.

I'm a mile outside of town now and notice the way the landscape starts filling up with dots of failure—trailer homes on cement blocks, three tiny tract houses in a subdivision, all that got built before Marvin, the developer, went broke, the dirt streets still bisecting Hoover's alfalfa field, the gas station that closed once the interstate took all the traffic, and Sleepy's Bar, where we'll no doubt end up after we get sick of Potluck Beer Night at the Blacksmith this afternoon. The second Saturday of every month begins with Potluck Beer Night, at three in the afternoon. We start our Saturday drinking as early as we can here in Divinity.

Clinton used to say that Divinity was the real center of the state of Iowa. It sits alone on Highway 11. Ten miles to the north you hit Pottersville, where Twyla and I go to the movies. To the east and a little below us is Iowa City, where all the trouble comes from. Good Earth sits farther down, and to the west is Des Moines, where the state government is.

Divinity is surrounded by hills that roll like little ocean swells with lots of flatness in between. The only breaks in the farmland are the trees and the limestone quarry. Our resident geologist, Azium Boardman, practically lives out at the quarry. I've spent my share of time there with him and Clinton. I'm thinking of taking Jass out there sometime too if tonight goes all right. He's meeting Twyla and Tom for the first time. I hope they like each other.

I enter Divinity and slow way down like always to avoid the sheriff and so I can loop around a few of the side streets and check on the old neighborhood. No point in rushing to trouble. Jass will be late.

In town people always walk friendlier in May than they have all winter, nodding to each other, speaking to those of us who sit along the margin like extra letters they can't decide how to use.

Most of the yards here have the same big old cottonwoods that grow along the Mercy River and little creeks around us. Right now sentiment is against them. "Cheap trees, dangerous," Bowker says because one fell this spring on a farmhouse and he had to pay the insurance claim. "Wood's too soft, they don't last long enough," I hear him advising clients. But I love the silvery clatter of the leaves all summer and the cottony air in May when the seeds burst. It always seems like a person could gather enough of it for a pillow, the way it collects along the curbs and in the weeds.

We also have lots of box elders and mulberries, the old-fashioned trees. And each fall the black-and-orange-striped box elder bugs gently invade our houses, climbing carefully into windowsills, onto kitchen counters, under dining room tables. They don't eat anything. They don't scramble or fly in your face much. They don't make a sound. We don't even know why they live on the box elder tree. They're like the mulberries—a sweet, unwanted fruit that requires nothing of us. Therefore, we don't understand, don't want them. When I was a kid, Mama said mulberries were filled with tiny white worms, which gave me a special daring in eating them. The only person I know who eats them officially is Boardman, who picks them for his cereal in the morning. I'm a little embarrassed when I think of him eating mulberries as if they're as legitimate, wormless, as the wild strawberries in May.

As I cruise our short neighborhood streets, noticing how big the lots are, how small the houses seem sitting on them, I see that we have the usual maples, oaks, elms all right, but that the weeping willows, sycamores, poplars, cottonwoods, box elders, and mulberries are our true trees in Divinity. And when we have the centennial next May, the trees will be a signal to people coming home that they're in the right place, that things haven't changed, so they can relax and be themselves again.

By the time I reach Highway 11, I'm almost past the commercial area I've avoided. The Blacksmith Lounge sits on the edge of town, with a couple of corn fields between it and the last house like a decent interval. The Blacksmith resembles a rambling barn that begins with two stories and runs out of strength as it dwindles into long, one-story sides. The outside is covered with old barn siding but doesn't produce the effect of style or charm. Instead the place looks like someone's abandoned dairy barn. The weekly fights and drunks trying to get unparked have taken their toll. There's the usual debris of bottles and cans and car parts to be avoided as I pull in and look for a spot. I wonder what Jass is going to think about this. Well, he's driven by plenty of times, and at his age he's no novice to bars. I find a place to park with a moderate amount of glass ground into the crushed rock, take a good look at myself, sigh, and push on the door to get out. In the divorce, Jake left me with the beat-up Valiant with the doughnut on back. It had been sitting for five years during our marriage while we drove his Corvette. For one hundred dollars and some new used tires, I got it running. Now it's almost an antique. Hard to hide myself in.

I look for Jass's truck but don't see it. Twyla's Cutlass Supreme is here, though, and so is her husband Tom's beat-up Chevy Impala. I can already hear Baby's voice clanging in my ears like a loose muffler, but of course, she won't be here. I just hope Sonny Boy doesn't show. He's never liked me, but lately he's taken to doing things that really scare me. He's probably worried I'm going to say something to Twyla. If he keeps hassling me, I just might do that. "Even after keeping quiet all these years?" Clinton asks.

"A lot of good it's done me," I say.

I weave through the jacked-up trucks and motorcycles that have claimed the space by the door propped open for air. Inside only one old box fan in the back window moves the stale smoke. Carpeted in dirty red that goes right up the walls until it meets some dirty brown paint halfway, the place is as dark as a cave. Jones, who owns the place, has hung old tools and harness around on the walls. There's a sign from the original old farmstead the barn belonged to: "Eugene Peltier, Blacksmith." The first and last Frenchman in Divinity, I guess. For all the trucks and cars outside, the bar seems strangely empty. Most of the good ol' boys must be in the back room playing poker or shooting craps. "Women Not Allowed," the sign reads over that door. Don't worry, I always want to tell them, we wouldn't want to go in there anyway. I don't know how many men have lost houses, cars, farms, stores, tractors, animals, in there. It's not a very clean game, not like Larue Carlson's in town.

In the minute it takes my eyes to adjust to the new dark, someone punches up Willie Nelson's "On the Road Again" on the jukebox, and I hear Tom's voice calling me. They're sitting in the corner of the big room, at a booth, which is so dark, I want to light a match to make sure it's them. "Why're you sitting over here? The place's practically empty."

"Sit down, Honey," Twyla says. I notice that Twyla is sitting next to Tom, with her arm around his thin shoulders. This end of the room has big school lunch tables families sit at, or groups of drunks. We are marooned here alone, and when my eyes fully adjust, I look around for the waitress. It is going to be a drag for her, so I grimace apologetically as she uncurls herself from the bar along the back wall facing the front door.

After we order, I lean across the table to get a better look at them. Tom is slumped like a sullen teenager, propping his feet on the bench next to me. I can see the glint of the buckles on his black, oily boots. His black greasy hair is tousled and too long, just the way he likes it. His thin face gleams unnaturally white for a man in farm country. Like Sonny Boy, Tom has avoided farming. He works in town at the garage fixing tractors, trucks, and occasionally cars. I've never understood why Twyla married Tom. His nose and chin look sharp enough to cut yourself on. Now that his pimples have cleared up, that dead white skin is scary. As if to accentuate that, he dresses in black only. His nails are rimmed in little dead moons of black, and his teeth don't even bear speaking about.

The beers come, and we salute each other and take a long pull. There's not enough people here yet to make the potluck fun, so we're waiting on that. When Tom gets up to fetch the popcorn out of the machine by the bar and punch in some music, Twyla leans over. "I figured sitting back here would make Jasper feel more comfortable. This isn't exactly his stomping ground, you know. He could have some trouble."

"He might not even show. You know what he's like; so far, at least." I take a slug of beer and lean back against the wall, stretching my legs along the booth. Tom would just have to sit up for a change. It would be weird to see his head above table level anyway. "How come you're giving Tom the green light again?"

Twyla peers into the beer glass as if she's lost her diamond ring in it, her long hair swinging forward to cover her face. A good trick. "I'm pregnant."

"What?" I sit up and lean forward, grabbing one of her wrists.

She looks up, throws her head so her hair falls back again, and smirks at me, in that big satisfied way she has, like after Wolfgang buys her something or she screws someone we thought unreachable. Or Sonny Boy. She nods happily.

"How long, I mean, how far along?"

"Four and a half months; I was waiting to be sure." She shakes my hand loose and takes a delicate sip of beer, which leaves a little pale line of foam around her mouth, like a second set of lips.

"Well, the tests don't make you wait that long, Twyla, not nowadays."

"I know that, silly. I was waiting to figure out who the father should be." She leans back and pushes her hands against the edge of the table, which doesn't move, of course, because Jones has bolted everything to the floor after fighting broke the place up too often. Suddenly it all clicks. "Not Tom! What about—"

Twyla laughs that tinkly way that makes you think of those little silver and brass bells you hang on the Christmas tree. She has lots of laughs. This one is usually reserved for men, to make them feel like she's giving them a big present, a Christmas sort of present. "Tom is one, sure. We're married, even if he does live at his mom's. And Wolfie, and—" She drops her eyes and fiddles with the edge of napkin under the beer glass. Coyness or shyness? "And Sonny Boy."

"Ohhh."

We sit there in silence while Tom's selections on the jukebox start to come up. Buddy Holly's "Peggy Sue." Every summer Tom makes the pilgrimage to Clear Lake to the crash site, to look at the plaque and feel bad for a weekend about the death of Buddy Holly. Elvis laid him pretty low, too, but nothing like Buddy.

"But Sonny Boy's married, Twyla."

"So what? We're all married, Honey. Wolf is, too. You're the only one who isn't."

There is a kind of logic I hate here. Where is Jass? Why doesn't Tom come back to the table?

"Look, I have to tell you something about Sonny Boy, Twyla. He's not like us, you know. He doesn't—"

Twyla waves her hand. "Thank God he isn't like anybody else. That's what I love about him."

"Love?"

Twyla just smiles uncomfortably and then makes a face at me.

"So it's due—"

"September," Tom says as he slides into the booth, pushing Twyla over. He's more careful than usual, I notice, now that she's pregnant.

As the jukebox runs through its catalog of Buddy Holly, Elvis, and the Doors—Tom's taste seems to run to dead people's music—we sit there, caught in the red glow of the carpet and the hot, stuffy smell of cigarettes and beer, though none of us are smoking. Tom, who's always restless, keeps shifting, like a kid in school sitting in a too small desk, and putting his arm on Twyla's shoulder, only to have her shrug it off in a few minutes. She's always been like that. Sometimes I wonder if Twyla wishes she'd married Wolf instead of Tom. I see Wolf driving by my place almost every day, though, so maybe it doesn't matter. Twyla lives at the other end of my dirt road. We're the only two places on it, so except for Twyla there's nothing he'd want on that road, driving that big black car of his, the antennas whipping in the wind. He even has a telephone in there. Clinton didn't have any use for Wolf, who'd stayed home from the war because his dad's money and connections ran the draft board in town.

I remember he used to rant and rave about it on the way to Iowa City for a protest or party. He knew people all over, so we went to parties and meetings sometimes for days.

Once in a while during the day we'd even walk through the university buildings and step into a classroom like we belonged. They never checked, never called your name off, the way they did in high school. Clinton said that he thought we could go to college for nothing, just showing up every day and listening, and then we wouldn't have to write papers or take tests, just read the books and sit there. Who knows, maybe he was doing that, he was in Iowa City so much. Twyla says, "He was running dope and that was all, the rest was bullshit. Clinton never read a telephone book, let alone a real book. Don't let his BS fool you."

I remember once I cut school and we went over there, just Clinton and me, and he took me right onto campus, walking directly to this big gray stone building, inside, up the stairs and down the hall, and right into the back of this class that was just starting. Up in front there was this guy wearing a plaid shirt and a pair of jeans tucked into hunting boots. I guessed he was the teacher because he was the one talking, but you wouldn't know it from anything else, except maybe the pipe he kept playing with. All the professors I'd seen on TV smoked pipes like that—poking and digging around in them like they'd lost a tooth or something and didn't want to light up till they'd found it. I couldn't get over the way he was dressed, though. Like he was going hunting. It was October all right, but no one in Divinity would walk around like that unless they were seriously leaving any minute. It cracked me up. I was just leaning over to Clinton to ask him where the guy's shotgun was when Clinton whispered, "Listen to this."

The guy was talking about history. History. I hated history. Clinton must have caught my doubt, because he whispered again, "No, *really,* listen to him. He's right. Listen."

The teacher was writing on the board now, with ugly big scrawls. I hoped he could shoot better than he could write. "History is a necessary illusion." All the students in the room bent down, scratching away in their notebooks. It was eerie, that sound. I can hear it today even, every time I think about it. Like a mouse in the wall, working away at the plaster, trying to get through, scratch, scratch, and you lying in bed wondering if you'll be awake when it gets there.

Well, it didn't matter. I didn't know what he meant when he wrote
that on the board. But he kept talking, not about places and wars, or heroes or any of that junk you have to study in high school, but "history theory." After a while I realized Clinton might be right. The teacher was pacing now, puffing on his pipe and stabbing its pointy stem at us, like it could hurt if we didn't pay close attention. He told us the West was going to decline, go right down the tubes, but that we could find some way to save it if we worked at it. "Human beings are worth it." Later Clinton and I talked about Western civilization and Spengler's book he'd get me if I wanted to read it. But we let it go at that.

Maybe I shouldn't have. Maybe Clinton would have liked to talk about that with someone. Spengler. I remember that name now. I even look for it sometimes, when I'm reading the paper or some magazine. Spengler. I'd like to get the book out of the library sometime. Read it. Just like Clinton. Maybe I'll do that.

Anyway, the guy kept talking, writing, and stabbing at us, getting more and more excited. Not like the teachers at our school who shuffled through the hour sleepwalking and couldn't tell the difference between us, from year to year, although we're not very many. I mean, they even confused Baby and me. Wake up, I wanted to tell them, it's 1967 and you'd better be awake. We're starting to get tired of watching you asleep. Instead, we just ignored them. Went about our business. School was time we had to put in to get to eighteen. It was like they didn't know what else to do with kids, and the people who blew it ended up having to be the custodians, the teachers. But this guy didn't act like that. He was awake, and I guess I was, too.

When he turned to the board and wrote, "Carlyle: history = splendid nightmare," I almost fell off my chair. "What's that *mean,* Clinton?" I touched his arm, but he shrugged and pointed to the front of the room where the man was working over his pipe again and getting ready to drop the bomb on us. It was dramatic, you could tell, the way he used this little pick thing in the pipe and took a deep breath and looked up right at me and Clinton and like all this hour he'd saved the best part for last. The best part for *us.* The punch line of the story. Just as he repeated it—"Carlyle, on the other hand, says that history is a splendid nightmare"—the bell rang, and all the mice students jumped up and scurried out. I couldn't believe it. The teacher didn't even look upset. He just shuffled his papers together and left, too. So only Clinton and I were sitting there, in the back of an empty room, staring at the board filled with words and arrows and circles going every direction. Then someone came in with a briefcase and started erasing the whole thing until the board was just a stretch of dusty blue.

Later, when I tried to talk to Clinton about it, he shrugged. "It says what it means. You have to think, Honey, you have to use your mind. I can't explain everything. No one can. So you have to learn to come up with things for yourself."

"How the hell am I supposed to do that when you won't help me?" I asked him.

"I *am* helping you. I brought you here, didn't I? What the hell do you want? Do something for yourself for a change. You got a brain, too." He was getting in one of his moods, first quiet and angry, then wild. That's when things usually happened to him.

Like the night he drove his dad's truck through the window of the A&P in town, and Wolf's dad, Mr. Reese, came down with the sheriff and pulled him out of the truck cab and started beating the crap out of him. Clinton was too drunk and dazed to care much. The sheriff had to pull old man Reese off after a couple of minutes. He was pissed, too, probably for getting him out of a sound sleep. The problem was that people kept forgiving Clinton for everything he did, so he just kept doing it. "It was the war," they said to each other. "At least he *went,* not like some."

I figured it out, afterward. If someone had just stopped forgiving him, he might have lived. Old man Reese even offered him a job in the A&P or the Riverbank Supper Club. Either one. Clinton turned him down. He was living fine off the dope money or whatever it was by then and just paid back his dad for the damage to the truck by making a few extra deals. Reese got insurance money for the store, so everyone was happy. He had his brother-in-law do the repairs at cost, and they split the profit, I heard. Clinton got a charge out of that. He could bring good luck by getting drunk and raising hell.

I don't know. Sitting in the Blacksmith Lounge sipping beer reminds me of Clinton. I want to ask him again what that guy Carlyle meant. "Think it out, you got to think it out," he tells me over and over. I'm trying, I just feel like I don't know the right things. Jake, my ex, seemed to, but not me. After ten years of marriage and no kids, he took a traveling job. I'm still here, in Divinity. I guess that's the problem, isn't it.

"Let's go get some free food," Twyla says.

When Twyla gets up, I inspect her long thin body for telltale lumps, but there's nothing. Where is she hiding it? She catches me looking and smiles, pointing at her stomach. "It's in there all right. Doctor says I'm carrying it high, my hips are wide enough—" She runs her hands over her hips. If anyone else did that, it might be obscene, but on Twyla it looked like a natural, appreciative gesture.

Tom is already loading up his paper plate with potato salad before we're halfway across the room. "Twyla, I gotta tell you something." I touch her arm to slow her down.

"If it's about Sonny Boy, don't bother, I know everything."

"No, you don't. Really, you shouldn't trust him, Twyla."

She stops and looks me in the eye. "I don't have to trust him, Honey, I love him, that's all. I have Tom and Wolf to trust." She strides on ahead of me.

How can I warn her when she keeps putting me off? But then, maybe I shouldn't. I've never told anyone about what Sonny Boy did. I just keep my mouth shut, like Tolson told me before he took off. "He'll kill you if you say anything, Honey," he'd warned, looking through the one eye that wasn't swollen shut on his battered face. Sonny Boy's fists. "Who else knows?" I asked, but Tolson just turned and left, walking swiftly down Highway 11 out of town.

As I load my plate with salad and the cheap hot dogs Jonesy puts out for Potluck Beer Night, I keep looking around at the door for Jass. People are drifting in regularly now. I don't want him to miss us and have to wander through the whole place. If he hit the back room, who knows what would happen? Our waitress brings a big black pan of baked beans and plops them on the buffet table. Tom lunges for the spoon before we have a chance and ladles huge scoops on his soggy plate, the second one. "Tom," Twyla warns.

"*You're* not eating for two," I say, and we all laugh.

By the time we get back to the table with our food, someone has punched in a couple of country and western songs on the jukebox. It's playing just loud enough to make us have to repeat ourselves. "Do you catch a falling star?" the man sings, but it isn't about a star star, it's about some old drunk cowboy singer, like it always is. I listen to this music when I get lonesome, and it helps get me sadder. Everybody is always thinking of running off with someone else, or they're too messed up to live a decent life. Seems like there're almost no second chances in that kind of music. Everyone is worn out from working too hard or from being disappointed with themselves or each other. Today, the songs seem wrong.

"So when's the nig—black dude showing up?" Tom asks between huge mouthfuls. At least Tom and Twyla both eat like pigs, slouched over their plates, elbows on the table, they're taking up three-fourths of the room, on both sides.

"Jasper. Jass. Whichever, Tom." I take a little bite of the soggy hot dog, that limp salmon color kind that turns mushy in your mouth. Tom has four in a little pyramid on plate one, and I can understand it. Mostly bun and pickle relish, the whole thing is gone before you can get a taste. "I don't know, he probably had to do chores before he came, don't you think?"

There must have been some pleading in my voice because Tom nods and swells a little with the attention.

"Hey, Honey," Jass interrupts whatever Tom is going to say. "I got tied up, had to wait for the kid down the road to come and feed for me."

Tom pauses with a hot dog halfway to his mouth, then takes most of it in one bite. Twyla brushes her hair back and just avoids getting mustard on it from her fingers. I move over to let him in and look around the room to see if anyone has noticed Jass. A few faces look our way, but they're mostly curious, like steers when a sheep or goat passes.

Jass looks at the couple across the table and nods. Twyla smiles one of her man smiles, like new sheets, it makes them feel good, I guess. "You're Jass, I'm Twyla." Jass smiles back neutrally. I'm secretly relieved that he isn't falling all over her looks. "This is Tom, my husband." Tom nods, chewing the wads of bun and dog with his mouth cracked. Neither man offers to shake hands. I hope that isn't a bad sign. Tom can't seem to decide whether to watch the food he's cramming or Jass, whose skin seems darker, duskier, in the bar light.

The waitress comes and takes our order, this time asking if we want to go potluck on the beer. We're all too sober to want to get up in front of the whole bar and dig around in a garbage can of ice water and beers with our eyes closed. Or maybe it's Jass's being here.

It's the roar of a racing car that brings us to our feet. It's so loud and close, it sounds like it's coming through the front door. Outside there are men leaning over the engine twiddling with things and lots of young girls standing around admiring the hell out of the men making all that noise. Just as we turn to go back to our table and the beers the waitress has just brought, the baseball team sponsored by the Blacksmith troops in and sits at one of the long tables across from us. The girls that come with them look too young for the guys, who settle right in to their pitchers. A couple of the girls have babies playing on their laps already, while they seem barely old enough to hold a beer glass themselves. They have those thin, slopy shoulders that belong on teenagers. Their faces aren't even lined yet, just soft and thin like the baby fat just rolled off them. They look happy with their husbands and babies, even sitting in the Blacksmith on a late Saturday afternoon. The guys are joshing around, poking each other. Somehow the guys swell up so fast when they marry young. It must be the time in the bars, making sure they haven't lost anything being saddled with a kid and a wife. The women get too thin and the men too swelled. The babies are healthy as weeds, spills of orange food down their fronts, flapping drink straws and napkins in their hands, being told to let go the rims of glasses. Then the mamas give them a little sip of beer to quiet them. Nobody minds.

It makes me sad seeing all those kids together. Daddy never took us out. Mama couldn't stand being in bars anyway. Seems like we just hung around the house growing up or running around the farm when we still had it. And then when I was married, Jake's family didn't want anything to do with me because of Jimmy and Brewer. If they'd known what Sonny Boy had done, even Jake might not have married me.

"What's the matter, Honey? Jass finally made it, and now you're looking like somebody just died on you." Twyla pushes her plate of food away. Tom grabs it and scrapes what is left onto his two plates. "Jesus, Tom," she says, and elbows him.

Jass picks up my plastic fork, which threatens to break as he stabs a baked bean on my plate. Tom is watching with a funny look on his face as Jass eats the bean with my fork. Stop it, I want to tell them both. I try to shift over, leaving a splinter of space between Jass and me so people won't get upset. I wish Jass weren't so dumb about it. He presses closer again.

"Uh, well, I'm okay. Jass, you want me to get you some food?" I say.

"When I need a maid, I'll let you know," he says as he gets up.

"Honey—" Tom begins.

"Mind your own business," Twyla orders. "Oh, look who's here." We all watch the team from the Divinity Volunteer Fire Department come in. They're dusty and grass-stained, like the first group, but you can tell they've had a better time—they're weaving from the beer they've already had during the game.

"Maybe I should join a team," Tom says, wiping his mouth with the back of his hand.

"Maybe we all should," I say.

"Except Twyla, the mommy." Tom pats her nonexistent belly.

As I watch Jass being surrounded by hungry players at the food table, I notice that he quickly becomes an island, as if some invisible moat exists between him and the others. No one steps into that space. Then the group parts, and Larue Carlson comes up to Jass and throws her arms around his neck. Great, another race riot, only this time we might have enough people to make it on the six o'clock news in Cedar Rapids. My earlier excitement turns to worry in my stomach, and the hot dog and beans sit like a wad of paper I'm trying to digest.

"I can't believe she did that," Twyla breathes. Tom just shakes his head as he finishes the last of Twyla's hot dog.

Jass is blushing as he comes back to the table with Larue tangled on his free arm. They've left a wake the size of the *Queen Mary* behind them and enough dropped jaws to catch every fly in Divinity. She's going to get him killed or saved, one of the two.

Jass sets his plate down, then grabs a spare chair from an empty table for Larue. We're all sitting there concentrating on our plates of ugly food for a minute before Larue slaps her hand on the table and laughs. "You all are sure having a wonderful time here, aren't you?" Her hair, bleached platinum and curled short around her head in a soft white halo, bobs lightly. Twyla doesn't like it that Larue goes to Chicago, four hours away, to get her hair done. And her face—Twyla swears Larue's in the running for the Mae West face-lift award. "She's had her face done so often, I bet you could hit it with a hammer and it'd clang like a supper bell."

"Where'd you pick him up, Honey?" Larue asks me. "I been trying to get this man in here for three years."

Jass smiles and drops his head an inch closer to his plate. Pretty soon he can just lick the food up, I figure, and move a couple of inches away.

"We run into each other every now and then, Larue." I take a sip of beer. At least it's Special Export, on tap. The tables around us grow rowdier.

"Well, you got yourself a real sweet one here, Honey. I'd watch out for him, though." Larue laughs and taps Jass on the cheek lightly. "But don't worry, I already tried everything I know to get his attention, but I guess I'm just not the natural kind of woman. The smell of horses makes me want to take another bath, and there's only so much a girl can do to her skin, you know." She rubs her hand up her bare porcelain pink arm. Twyla has to be wrong, her arms are as unmarked and young as her face. "Besides, he doesn't like my business. Says he doesn't gamble." Larue looks at us as if this were the oddest thing she'd ever heard of. "And he's the one raising horses. Hell, I think it'd be cheaper to bet on 'em than raise 'em to make yourself a living."

"I'm just not good at gambling, at cards, Larue. You know that," Jass says, and glances at me.

Don't look at me, buddy, I want to tell him. I don't know anything about this stuff with Larue.

"Well, sweetie, you're so good at other things, it just doesn't matter, does it?" Larue says. Tom shifts his legs, bumping the table and spilling the beers a little. When some lands in Jass's plate, he frowns at Tom, who just smiles his juvenile delinquent way.

I slip my hand around Jass's arm, under the table, and squeeze. Jass's body relaxes, and he shoves the beans around on his plate to soak up the beer.

Suddenly Larue turns her focus. "How are you feeling, Twyla? Is it showing yet?" Her voice becomes slightly distant, losing some of its timbre.

I watch fascinated as Twyla stumbles for an answer. Larue's probably the only person in the world who can do that to Twyla. It's worth the price of admission. Tom, of course, lights up stupidly. "It's in there all right, I can *feel* it." He rubs Twyla's stomach. Twyla twists out of the way.

"Honey, I like your hair red. Good cut, too. Short, curlier, like mine. Keep it that way—you look cute." As Larue runs her hand with long, beautifully curved nails through her hair, mine seems to fade and fail by comparison. No matter how much I dye and cut it, I will never have that kind of beauty. It's like a picture on a cold cream jar Mama used to have. I loved to dip my finger into its whiteness and suck on it, feeling the oil line my teeth, coat my tongue. There was a peculiar perfumy flavor, with that slick lard taste underneath I always associate with women that seem so grown up, like Mama and now Larue, women so far beyond me, I'll never be old enough to be with them as equals. Like they've come from some other universe and are just playing around living here with the rest of us. They are Ladies. Not something like Twyla and me.

"Thanks, Larue," I mumble so low that no one hears me. It's like being blessed by the visiting queen, I decide, as she half turns when she hears Jonesy's voice booming hello from the bar. Dressed in white, with what you might call a full figure, she is both soft and well taken care of,

like there isn't one thing on her whole body she hasn't spent money on.

"Give me a little sugar, Jass." Larue puts her hand on his cheek as her lips touch his. Jones is exactly two strides away when it happens. She winks at me and turns to acknowledge Jonesy's big hands on her shoulders. At two hundred and twenty pounds, the owner of the Blacksmith looks an awful lot like one himself, with his big brown beard, dark brown eyes, and straight hair down to his shoulders. I can see why Larue likes him. They've been together for years, on and off. He must have been tuning on the race car out front, because his hands have that fresh black grease smeared on them. When he lifts them from Larue's shoulders, he leaves black smudges on the white silk as if to say, She's mine. Larue ignores this.

He nods at us, then says to Jass, "First time in a long time you been in here, man." The tables of ball players have gone silent, and a few men at the bar step off their stools, gripping their bottles like weapons.

Jass stiffens and deliberately picks up the beer he's ordered, looks at it, and takes a long pull. "Beer's cold."

Larue rises and waves at us, pulling Jones along by the arm as she heads for the back room. "Gotta see what the competition's up to," she says. The conversation and noise around us slowly picks up again.

"Well, that was pretty calculated," Twyla says, watching Larue's full butt sway ladylike across the room beside Jones.

"She's okay," Jass says between bites.

"You seem to think so." I drain my beer. Tom is concentrating on his plates. Like a dog, he looks ready to lick them, then maybe chew the paper, too, for the flavor.

Jass watches me out of the corner of his eye as he eats. I notice that several of the ball players are watching our table, too. Their faces have those flat expressions that say they haven't made up their minds about you yet, but they're leaning toward dislike. It's a look I've seen for years around here. I'm almost used to it. After the beer I've drunk, I want to give an answer.

"Let's go try the potluck beer," I announce, and push on Jass's shoulder to get him out of the way. He sticks, then moves. The tables grow quiet again. My hands shake a little as I wait.

"Okay," Tom says. He *has* licked the plates, I notice as he picks them up to throw them in the garbage. Twyla and Jass follow us, reluctantly.

There are three garbage cans lined up at the end of the bar and a waitress collecting a dollar each for the chance to pull out a bottled beer.

"Got any imported?" Jass asks as he presses a dollar into her palm.
I think I see his fingers stay too long. She eyes him like he's just another dumb steer she's counting. The men from Reiler's Feed Mill are gathering around the garbage cans, and we have to wait our turn. If you get a beer you don't like, you can pass it down the line and see if someone else will take it—which makes this sort of a group effort. It's supposed to be fun, and everyone is laughing as the bottles get pushed around. It's pretty harmless, until Jass comes up.

Tom gets his beer, Hamms, and Twyla picks a Pabst. They only have to send a couple down the line. When Jass draws a Point Beer from Wisconsin first try and turns to hand it on, the man next to him keeps his hands at his side. Then so does the next and the next. I can see Jass's shoulders rise and stiffen as he stares at the man.

I reach for the beer, and he lets it slip from his fingers. Jones and Larue are crossing the room when the glass breaks with a pop that shoves everyone back in a small circle around the broken bottle. The beer runs a moment, then stops and soaks quickly into the dirty red carpet. Even the jukebox seems to take a breath as the room goes silent.

"Fuck it," Jass says as he starts for the door. A couple of the men start after him, but Jones steps in front of them. Larue stands by the front door with her compact out, checking her makeup in the little mirror and watching the tables of ball players. A few are halfway out of their chairs before being pulled back down.

"Wait," I say to Jass's back. "Let's go to Sleepy's," I call to Twyla and Tom. "All I wanted was a normal date," I'm muttering as I pass Larue.

"You forgot to clear it with the town first," Larue laughs as she lets me by.

6

Sleepy's

Sleepy's is just tuning up for Saturday night as we get there. When the sun sets, the place will be crazy with the C&W band on the little stage and the people taking their one chance of the week for fun.

The evening is going okay now. Tom is doing kid tricks, blowing spit bubbles and wiggling his ears. We're telling jokes and getting the buzz on when Tom says, "Twyla tell you how it happened?" He draws the curve of a pregnant belly with his hand in front of her. She knocks it down and laughs.

"It's all your fault, Honey," she says.

"I'm not sure I like the sounds of this." Jass puts his arm around me and peeks around to see if anyone notices. Everyone's too busy getting their own action, though. "Go ahead and tell it—I better see what I'm in for, I guess."

Tom is excited about being the center of attention, so he sits up more. "It all started the day Honey married Jake. She ever tell you about that?" Twyla nudges him with her elbow, but he continues. "We're standing up for them over at old lady Sorenson's. Justice of the peace? And Twyla here says, 'Wanna bet five bucks he doesn't last three years?' I was freaked. I just couldn't believe she'd say that, so I shook my head." The memory of it makes Tom need a drink of his beer. His face looks like she hurt marriage for all time.

"So then she says, 'Okay, ten years. A dollar a year.' She's saying this while the old lady's telling Jake to put the ring on Honey's finger." Twyla grins, and Jass shifts uncomfortably.

"They made so much noise I almost forgot my words," I say. "I yelled at Twyla later. Then the ring was way too big, and I had to wrap a Band-Aid around it to keep it on like we used to do with boys' class rings in high school. I never wanted to get it sized down, though. Wouldn't take it off." I'm struck by my Pollyanna tone.

"Jake bought a one-size-fits-all band. I bet the new girl has it now," Twyla says.

"Screw you, Twyla." It hurts to have her be so cold about my marriage. Or is it that she saw what Jake was like from the start and just didn't say anything? That bothers me more. Don't we have any responsibility for each other—as friends? Family, I figure, is a different matter. Sonny Boy and Daddy proved that.

Jass hugs me, and Twyla smiles. "Come on, Honey," she says.

"So that's the story?" Jass asks as he signals for another round.

" 'Course not." Tom slouches in the corner and folds his arms. "So a few months ago, *four,* to be exact, I run into Twyla at the Blacksmith. 'Ready to pay up?' she asks me. Well, I hadn't been working, and your divorce wasn't *final* final yet, so I tried to argue her out of it." Tom grinned and sat up when the waitress brought the beers.

"But Twyla always gets what she came for, you know, so she pulls out a ten and says, 'Okay, here's a ten says it'll be over by May first.' I shoulda figured out she'd know, but I was a little tuned, so I said, 'What the hell,' and took the bet."

"That's 'cause you were flat—I even had to buy the beers that night, Tom."

"Yeah, but it was worth it, wasn't it, honey?" Tom puts his arm around Twyla and nuzzles her neck. She looks across the table almost apologetically.

Jass looks over at me, then across at them. "I don't understand."

Tom giggles like a boy with a dirty joke while Twyla continues. "Well, before long we ended up in the back of his car, parked under the trees at the far edge of the parking lot. We figured on a busy night someone'd probably notice the car rocking like a boat, but it was midweek slow, so we had the lot to ourselves.

"When we climbed out to untangle our clothes"—Twyla glances at Jass—"in the tree shadows, I noticed that the T'N'T in foot-high fluorescent pink letters across the trunk were getting ragged. 'Why don't you clean up this shit,' I asked, and started picking at a loose edge with my fingernail."

Tom's face gets all screwed up at the memory. "That almost busted me, it did. 'Don't,' I told her. 'I did that for us, for you, now you won't even let me stay with you.' And damned if I didn't start bawling. Hardest I ever cried." Tom pauses, thinking about this remarkable thing he's discovered about himself.

"Too much beer," Twyla says. "I had to sit both of us down right there in the dirt and gravel to try to calm him down. Tom cries, it does something to me. He's the only one who's ever done that, though. He always gets me that way, I realized as I unbuttoned my blouse and pulled his face to me. I was digging gravel out of my elbows and ass for a week."

Now it's Twyla's turn to stare out across the dance floor, thinking about herself as a character in a movie doing something the audience is surprised at. I'm embarrassed that they've told this story in front of Jass. Nobody says anything for a few minutes as the story settles in around us.

Sleepy's wife ran off with Jack Masters from Pottersville a few years ago, so Sleepy is death on women, won't hardly speak to one except for business. He doesn't put up with messing around, either, so women feel safe here. Men don't hit on us as much. Unlike the Blacksmith, which is big, dark, and cavelike, Sleepy's was built out of an old cafe and gas station. There are lots of windows, a pale green linoleum floor, and knotty pine walls aged down to gold. Sleepy left the counter and signs up advertising Meadow Gold Ice Cream and Red Chief Snuff.

When Sonny Boy walks in, he makes the other guys look shabby next to him. He's so good-looking in that all-American way that Twyla keeps trying to get him to pose for the Curl-Y-Que hair album, but he says no, it'd be too faggoty. Twyla hasn't seen him yet, so I keep signaling her, but she ignores me. Jass glances at me. "What do you need, Honey?"

I wave him off as Sonny Boy circles the room. Someone puts on "Heartbreak Hotel," and Sonny Boy arrives at our table to the tune, just like in a movie. I press tighter against Jass. Tom all but slides under the table. Sonny Boy and Twyla are the only ones standing their ground.

"Howdy," he addresses the whole table, but looks at Twyla. "How're you folks tonight?" Again, he's smiling just for her. I know he hasn't realized I'm here with Jass, or he would have freaked.

Since everyone else is space-warped, Twyla smiles back and says, "Fine, how're you?" They're like a couple of old people at church.

Sonny Boy nods and opens his mouth to say something, but out come my words instead.

"Where's Rose?"

"Home. She don't like going out much, misses her house and kids. Want to dance, Twyla?" He holds out his hand, and she takes it.

She doesn't look back at us until the fourth song. By that time Tom has moved over to my side and Jass to the other. Three empty shooters of tequila stand next to the half-empty beer glass in front of Tom, who is half lying on me, his head resting heavily on my chest. Under the music I hear Tom moan, "Just hold me, Honey. God, I feel so bad."

I know Twyla isn't coming back. The music keeps playing, and Sonny Boy smells of the expensive after-shave he likes, nothing you can get here at the drugstore or Reese's A&P. He's left a layer of it in the air over our table. He's a good dancer, and the thrust of his pelvis as they slow-dance is sending the music up between Twyla's legs, I can tell. There isn't anything can stop what they're going to do. I know that.

A while later she comes back for her purse. Tom is gone. When she doesn't ask about him, I say, "He passed out. We put him in my car. You ready to go?" We've come to Sleepy's in one car, left the others at the Blacksmith.

Twyla avoids my eyes, picks up her bag, and says, "No. You go on, drop Tom at his mother's. I'll catch a ride later."

"Twyla," I start, but Jass interrupts.

"Never mind, Honey. We're going. Later, Twyla." He nods in her direction and pulls me out of the booth behind him. She won't look at me, so I just wave at her back and mutter, "Bye."

Then Sonny Boy puts his arms around her from behind and says, "Ready?"

I think about Sleepy's wife, Annie, telling me how she and Jack Masters rode double on her Appaloosa mare, naked. She was in front facing him, and they were making it.

After we drop Tom at his mother's in town, I drive Jass to pick up his truck at the Blacksmith. I pull up beside it and turn off the ignition. "What now?" I ask, facing him.

Jass's big body is cramped on my front seat. Half of him seems to be hanging out the window. He focuses on something far away as he speaks. "I gotta get home, Honey. Check on things." Then he adds, "Thanks for, uh, the night," and fumbles for the door handle.

"Would you like to come over, see my place?" I feel humiliated having to spell it out, but the spring air, the beer, and the music all make me lonesome, deep inside. It's a want, like being so thirsty, so awfully, awfully thirsty, that just a sip of plain old warm tap water is wonderful. Not that

Jass is tap water. Definitely not. He's growing a mustache now; the blackness makes his white teeth shine brighter. His lips, with a violet cast to them in the parking lot light, seem fuller, more vulnerable, than before.

He clears his throat. "No, I've had enough excitement for one night. Thanks anyway." When he just squeezes my hand and doesn't even try to kiss me, I get upset.

"What's the matter?" I ask.

"It's pretty simple. I don't much like your friends, I definitely don't like your brother, and I don't like the places you hang out." He turns to me. "You're okay, though."

"What's wrong with the bars?"

"I almost got punched at least three times at the Blacksmith. It wasn't a very relaxing evening. And I got the evil eye from Sonny Boy and a couple of his buddies at Sleepy's. Okay? I'm just not up to the social life in Divinity, I guess. I don't fuck other men's wives. I don't fit in. I don't even want to."

"Wait." I grab his arm.

"No, I gotta get outta here. Talk to you later." He's gone before I can think of anything else to say, like "What about Larue Carlson?" and "What about me?"

"What are you doing here, Honey?" Clinton's voice asks. "Look around you." The parking lot is alive with action: trucks and cars pulling out so fast they spray gravel all over, two separate fights, each with its own little group of supporters, a couple of drunks throwing up and a few more passed out, draped over cars or beside them, like heaps of clothes abandoned on the interstate, and the endless negotiations of men and women arguing, kissing, or debating where to sleep. Not a single person seems aware of the big full moon hanging awkward and hopeful overhead, almost close enough to touch the new-sown fields of Divinity. No one seems to notice how the moon makes them small and eternal like people locked on a painting or a vase.

I'm sitting in my Valiant feeling like a split seam, like my bare shoulder is poking out suddenly, and I can feel all the wrongness of that public view of my skin. After a while I start the car and drive home. Highway 11 glitters like the Teflon lining of a new frying pan in the moonlight.

When I finally fall asleep, I keep dreaming about Clinton, about him leaving and coming back and finding other people than me to be with. We aren't exactly together, and then every time the scene gets to where I'm going to ask him why, he gets a strange look on his face and walks over to the nearest window—and there are plenty of them in the dream—and puts his fist through the glass. Just like that, and rips it back through so it cuts his hand up good. Then he turns to me, an "is that what you want, are you satisfied?" look on his face. It keeps scaring me so bad, and sometimes I cry and beg him not to do it. Other times I just watch all numb, like it's happening in a movie, and think, he can't live with so much blood pouring out of him.

I wake up at four in the morning. Outside there's just that last surge of real blackness, but I can feel how in a little bit things will start stirring. I get dressed and go out to drive around for a while. The trailer seems so tight, like an envelope someone has put me into and is trying to seal up when I'm not watching.

When I drive through town, there isn't a soul out. Even the dogs are trying to catch the last bit of sleep before morning. I drive slowly down Main Street, looking in all the stores and offices. Past Bowker's. I'm sick of him. I'd probably kill Bow-wow if he laid a hand on me today. Maybe I'd throw him out of the big front plate-glass window. The image pleases me as I drive by: his head surfacing through all that gold paint like a swimmer after a deep dive. I play it over and over in my mind, just for the pleasure of it. I drive by Steadman's Drugstore and Shirley and Bob's Cafe.

Simpy is developing a paunchy, wet look from working in the cafe, and it isn't hard to see that he won't be leaving at all if he waits much longer. Clinton, he's gone, went and killed himself, and I don't really know why. That part is driving me crazy. Twyla, it's easy to see she could be something—she's so beautiful, but she's married to that twerp Tom, who really *does* belong here. And whose baby is she carrying? And Baby and Sonny Boy, I don't know about them, where they belong. Since we were little kids, they've kept their distance from me with dislike they wear like an extra shirt on a hot day. Why bother with me? I want to ask them. Go out and start your own disasters. And Daddy . . .

At Bedford Avenue I turn left and drive slowly by the old house. The sprinkler is out there turned on its side in the front yard, and in the dim haze of dawn breaking through, the house glows dully white and distant, but if I listen hard, I might be able to hear Baby turning over in her bed, creak creak like so many years of my life there. I see Daddy's Ford, a little dented from bad judgment and beer, squatting in the driveway. And I know that if I get out and walk the driveway around back, Mama's flowers will be thick with weeds, the roses peeking their baby heads just above the wild grasses and thistle. Baby hates the garden, and Daddy couldn't care less, with Mama gone and his girlfriend around.

If I step into the little attached garage, I'll see the board with the rusty nails poking out, and the streaks of red staining the wood still, but the dog is gone, so only our human legs catch against the sharpness now. And outside, as I roll down the car window, everywhere, the smells of morning, corn, and alfalfa come rolling in from the fields that surround the town, and tinting it, the faint scent of manure from the distant farms where it rises up from the waiting cattle and pigs and catches on the wind.

I roll up the window and step on the gas, uncertain where I am going. But I have to figure some things out. Why *did* Clinton kill himself? What does Clinton want from me? Why didn't I stop Jake from going? Or Tolson? Or Brewer or Jimmy? Is Jass going to go, too? Is there something I should be doing different? Should I be leaving, too? Can I stay here and keep Sonny Boy's secret forever? And why bother—since he hates me anyway?

This is May, and the Iowa morning opens its eyes and breathes me slowly down the road. There are answers ahead, though I don't know them yet. And things that will make me more afraid than I can ever believe possible on this morning. When the light spills across the fields onto the road like an overturned can of shellac, it just makes the world glitter clean and clear. It's days like this that make me visit Azium Boardman to talk about Clinton, to try to understand how he could leave. I'll drive around until seven, pick some flowers, then stop at his place for breakfast. He's an early riser, doesn't stay out half the night drinking like the rest of us.

I don't hear him behind me at first. When I begin to slow down by Bevington's cow pasture where the wild flowers are blooming, and look in my rearview mirror out of habit, I'm startled by the dark shape of Sonny Boy's car filling the back window of the Valiant. I speed up and watch his car creep closer anyway. His face is a mask of concentration. His eyes fix the back of my head as if it's a target. Maybe he has a gun. Does he know Tolson told me? Maybe he just wants to pound on me, like he did when we were kids. I speed up, hitting fifty-five, sixty, sixty-five. The Valiant begins to struggle. The pedal is on the floor, and the car is starting to bottom out. I'm squealing on the curves, turning too late because I'm scared stiff. Sonny Boy's powerful Trans-Am muscles my back end effortlessly as it edges closer. I begin to pant and swear. A black-and-white cat scurries across the road in front of me. I just miss it. Whizzing past Aronson's apple orchard, I honk at a flock of sparrows splashing the road ahead. They wait and scatter only at the last minute. One thunks the front grill. "Shit," I say as Jimmy and Brewer flash like hazard lights in front of me. At sixty-nine the Valiant starts to shimmy, and that's when Sonny Boy edges up to ride my bumper. There's a light tap as he touches, then a weightlessness as he starts pushing. As if one of the tires hits ice, the car shivers and threatens to skid but recovers so quickly, there's nothing to do.

At seventy-five the car is wobbling so much that my teeth chatter from my hands on the steering wheel. If he keeps this up, the Valiant will disintegrate. There's a strange roar and whine from the engine. I'm praying no one's taking their cows to pasture across the road ahead of us, but I know it's just a matter of time. I pound the horn at the idea of no seat belts. "Damn, Damn, Damn," I begin to chant. Maybe he's going to push me off the road into the ditch when we get to a deep, water-filled one. The image makes my chest ache. I hate water. I'll drown. I can't let go of the wheel to open the other window for escape. Why does he hate me? I've kept my mouth shut.

Jasper, he must hate Jasper. "Oh, God . . ." The road rises ahead, and the shoulders fall away beside Adcock's fields. I remember Sonny pacing in front of the TV as pictures of riots and demonstrations in Omaha, Chicago, and Detroit rolled slowly into our living room after

Martin Luther King was shot. "I'd like to see them come *here* and try that," he'd said. That was years ago, but what's changed? I must be crazy thinking they'll ignore Jasper Johnson and me. Besides that, now he has an excuse to come after me openly.

My hands are so sweaty as we crest the hill, and Sonny gives me one last accelerated shove, I almost lose the wheel. I hang on, though, and instead the Valiant sails light as a dandelion seed down the hill, slowing gracefully as my foot seeks the brake at the bottom, when I realize that Sonny's car has disappeared.

There is a faint burning smell leaking into the car as I pull onto the shoulder. "Jesus. He was trying to kill me."

"No, he wasn't, Honey. Just scare the piss out of you. Worked, huh?" Clinton says.

"Why?"

"Because he's a scary dude. Even when I hung out with him. He should've been in Vietnam. He'd have religion now, instead of hassling women with his bullshit.

7

At Boardman's

I sit rigid for a few minutes, beside the road, gripping the wheel like a life preserver. Shivers keep running the length of my body, though the sun has warmed the car to a comfortable place. My teeth are clicking together, and I can't seem to really catch my breath. The Valiant engine stumbles and putters unevenly as if its effort at speed has done permanent damage. I release the right side of the wheel and pat the dashboard. "Good Prince." Letting go of the left side, I lean back cautiously, as if I've been in the wreck Sonny tried to give me just now.

What's wrong with my brother? Does he know Tolson told me? He must suspect. Maybe he's worried I'm going to tell Twyla. But really, it's probably Jass. That has to be it. Although, as a kid he never needed much of an excuse to come after Tolson or me. Like he was the family prince and we were the servants. Daddy and Mama felt happier every time he came in the house, you could tell. He was the only one had a chance at college. "He needs it," Mama said. As if the rest of us were such poor pickings we were beyond help. "He deserves it," Daddy said. As if Sonny had done something special, beyond being the handsome first son who kept the younger kids on the run. We accepted it, too. I still have a hard time, even this morning, trying to think of some excuse, some reason, that will justify Sonny Boy's peculiar meanness. Disliking-hating me seems too flat, too little. I must have *done* something, I argue. Jasper *has* to be it.

I wrap my arms around me and alternately squeeze hard and relax to get rid of the shivering. I try to let the fear drain out of my jaw, which is harder to do. He could have killed me! I try to think of who to tell—Daddy? Baby? No, Sonny would just lie to them, like he used to when he did something to Tolson or me when we were kids. In the unspoken code of growing up together, we couldn't tell when we knew Sonny had done something. So his stealing, breaking, and hitting were always blamed on us, not him.

Suddenly I'm pissed off, as if all the outrage of the past comes seeping under the door and fills the Valiant. I hit the seat next to me with my fist, and a poof of dust comes out. "Goddamn you, Sonny Boy, just go to hell!" I'll call Rose, his wife. I'll tell Twyla. Someone is going to know about him for a change. I'm tired of covering for Sonny Boy. The rest of the family, too. "Never wash your dirty linen in public," Mama always said. Maybe she wasn't so right after all. Is it worth dying just so the family keeps its secrets?

I grab the wheel again and punch the button for drive, carefully steering back onto the highway. I'm going to tell Boardman. I take a deep breath, letting it out slowly, trying to relax and take my mind off what's just happened. And on my way there I begin to get that sense of hopefulness and dread summer's coming always gives me. My pale green Valiant struggles up a hill, the engine *ping*ing lightly as if it's counting the telephone poles that march beside us. In the little valleys between the rolling hills, the mist lays smooth and white as a lady's chiffon scarf. My stomach drops a little looking at the mist and remembering what it was like when I would sneak out to meet Clinton at four or five A.M., running barefoot through the yard, across the cool asphalt, trying to avoid the pebbles that hurt so when I didn't land just right. But I was light then, running to him, I hardly touched the ground. By the time I crossed the last yard that met the woods and fields the town gave out to, my pajamas were soaked to my crotch, and Clinton would be standing there watching me—his long dark hair and eyes a dark place I was running to. Sometimes we'd keep going, chasing each other along the bottomland, where the mist cut us in half, magically, painlessly, beside the Mercy River. Later his heat took the chill off my body. Every inch of it. And how strange to lie below the mist and watch his head slice away as he reared back or to be the one on top and see the world as half there, leveled and white with green treetops while below I could feel the unseen working at me, pulling me back to him.

Ours is a summer story, then, though Clinton died in winter. Every summer I try to pretend that he doesn't leave. I'm like Prince, my car, struggling to get up one side of the year's feelings so I can slide down the other side.

"It just needs a quart of oil, Honey."

"Okay, Clinton."

As I enter town, I notice that Shirley and Bob's Cafe has opened. A few dusty pickups are parked in front, the farmers collecting for first coffee after first chores. The rest of the town is still conked out. It's Sunday, so they'll get up later and go to eleven o'clock church, then home for Sunday dinner.

Azium Boardman's Gems and Rocks is on Ashland, a few streets off Main. Signs on Highway 11 and along the interstate draw people from all over to visit the shop, though no one here can figure out why.

When I pull in the driveway beside the narrow two-story frame house, painted barn red with white trim, Azium is sitting on the porch. As I turn it off, my car farts embarrassingly as if it's struggling to keep alive. "All right, all right," I tell it, and it shivers once more, then stops. I wait a moment before opening the door. Sometimes Boardman's in a mood, but he waves his arm, so I get out. Going around the back, I check the bumper. It looks like he only nudged it, but it felt so mean, like Sonny wanted to smash my car, send us off the road.

"C'mon in. I got something for you," Azium calls. I climb the scuffed red steps whose wood has been worn into little troughs by the years of traffic. Watching his big body in front of me, clothed in the matching dark green khaki workshirt and trousers he orders from the Ward's catalog, I know why no one in town can tell there's world-famous expert blood underneath his lizardy skin. He looks like the janitor over at the high school. When Clinton first brought me here, I thought he was kidding. This guy? The town nut case? "You can live in one place all your life, Honey, and always be surprised. Just keep your eyes open and your ass down." He was right, of course.

Azium Boardman does have some odd ways. I never know when I pass his place whether he's going to be friendly and wave me in or just scowl like an old hen from her perch, protecting her nest. And after I've been there for a while, I remember why I only visit occasionally.

"I got something for you," he repeats from the next room. He has a big, thick, not fat body that moves clumsily without actually knocking into anything. It has a kind of instinct about weaving through the showroom crowded with display cases. His thin pale hair sprinkled with gray hangs in a greasy banged cut around his head with a split down the middle. His facial features, like his body, are big, almost coarse, with a wide, full-lipped mouth and big white teeth. His complexion is ruddy from years in the sun. I've always wondered if he was so busy climbing after rocks, he forgot to get married, the way you'd forget to pick up your dry cleaning or get the car gassed up.

"Can I help?" I call to him, but the only answer is the sound of heavy boxes scraping on wood.

"Here." He appears suddenly, his hand outstretched.

I recognize the big chunk of jade.

"No, I don't want it. I can't—" With its fake bright outlook, the jade seems to carry some kind of bad luck that chased Clinton all the way back from Vietnam where he bought it.

Azium pulls his hand back, looks down, and coughs. I try to focus on the trilobite in the case next to my elbow.

"Quite rare, you know, this particular shade and depth."

I shake my head again and feel a twinge as I notice his hand shaking, a tremor passing through him like a tiny earthquake. It's hard to imagine Boardman is in his seventies. He still rides a bicycle, the only man around here over sixteen who rides one, in fact.

"He gave it to you as a present, Mr. Boardman. He meant for you to keep it. But how did Clinton ever get hold of something that valuable? Did he ever talk about Vietnam with you? I mean, you two talked a lot when I wasn't around and everything. Did he ever—"

Boardman nods and turns around, heading out of the showroom again.

"Sonny Boy just tried to run me off the road." The sentence surprises me as much as Boardman, who stops, stares at the floor for a minute, shakes his head, and goes to the kitchen with me behind him.

"Your car okay?" he asks as he puts the jade on the table, turns on the water, and washes his hands. As usual, he avoids the question of me, like the old days when I came over with Clinton.

I nod.

"You going to tell the sheriff?"

"No, of course not."

"Then he'll feel free to do it again."

"Yeah. Isn't that a weird thing to do, though? It scared the pee out of me. I don't know, maybe he was just being silly or—"

"I wouldn't count on it."

"Yeah, I know." I sigh and sit down at the table. "I know."

"Clinton had no use for your brother, Honey. He said there was something not right about Sonny Boy, and you'd always have to be careful around him. Any idea what set him off?"

I watch Boardman shuffle around, his shoulders a little slumped, sloping off the one side like he got tilted one day and couldn't right himself again. He was a lot taller than me in the old days, but now I feel like I tower when I'm near him. I hate that feeling of being too big. In all the fairy tales I remember, the giant is mean, bloodthirsty, and deserves the death it gets. It seems better to be smaller, more in scale with furniture and things.

"Well?"

"Oh, I don't know. My friend Twyla's pregnant, and I was trying to warn her about Sonny Boy. I suppose he could've found out."

Azium shakes his head. "What about that black fella?"

"Jasper Johnson?"

He laughs. "We don't have a lot of others, do we?"

My fingers begin to follow the perfect dark circles left by years of hot cups on the little maple table. Some of them Clinton's, some mine. "I guess I did take him to the bars last night."

"You *guess*?" Boardman reaches up into the yellowed white cabinet for the dark blue tin of loose tea he special orders from England. He's the only person I know who makes real tea, not that tea bag stuff. He gets out the tea infuser. "Would you rather have something cold? I made grape juice this week."

"No, tea's fine." Tea is always so comforting for some reason. Maybe I should switch. I don't even like the taste of coffee much. It was just a way of saying I was grown up in high school, when I started drinking it.

"Honey, you should know your family, and most of this town, by now. It's okay to adopt a starving orphan from Korea or India. And most folks like Bill Cosby here, but you have to understand they don't know what to think about a black man with a white woman. The men probably wonder if you're insulting them—saying they're not good enough—and the women probably figure you're flaunting what you have and they don't."

"Everybody just assumes it's for sex, don't they? What about friendship? He's nice to me, for chrissakes."

"A lot of people, white and black, figure it's sex when you mix the races. Friendship between men and women doesn't happen in most people's lives, so why should that be an option?"

"They're just worried because it's something different. They just hate to have to put up with things changing." I lean my head on my arms, the night's trouble beginning to swell in my brain. I could be asleep in a minute.

"No, you're wrong. They like the excitement, don't you get it? They're going to make as much of this as they can. Cheers them up to have the diversion. You're the one who'll suffer, not them."

Like always, I want to say.

When he tries to pinch the loose tea into the infuser, his hand shakes so much, tea spills in a little circle around it on the scarred red linoleum countertop. "Damn it," he growls. He picks up the aluminum canister marked Sugar, pries off the lid, and slams it down again so sugar jumps onto the counter, too. "Goddamn it to hell." He reaches for the dishrag and spills some water around on the mess he's made as he tries to sweep tea and sugar off into the sink. Finally he throws the rag down in disgust. "Well, son of a bitch, I forgot to put the kettle on. Why don't you get up and do something for a change, instead of sitting there watching me make such an ass out of myself?" When he gets like this, the only thing I can do is leave or help. I get up and put the kettle on and clean up the mess while he goes off to the living room for something. I can hear him banging and cursing.

When he comes back in, he's carrying a magazine. "Doctor says it's normal. Hands shaking and forgetting. I think they like watching you fall apart." He sits down, placing the magazine off to one side while I pour the hot water and bring the cups over to the table. His hands look steady now. "Comes and goes. Hate to be such an old trembler that I slit my throat shaving some morning." He gives me a tight little smile to show he's over his temper.

"Well, if it gets that bad, Mr. Boardman, you can call me up and I'll come over to shave you, how's that?"

We laugh, then he adds, "As long as you don't bring Jasper, we're in business. I probably wouldn't make it through another one of your courtships. Clinton finished me."

My silence makes him uncomfortable, and he hands me the magazine he's been carrying around, *Natural History*. "Look on page fifty-nine. I have an article in there about the fossils Clinton—and you—hunted with me." Then he's up shuffling around the refrigerator. "Strawberries?" he asks, interrupting my reading. I nod my head. "Cream?"

"Sure. Say, why don't I take this magazine with me and read this at home. It feels funny to be reading in front of someone else."

He hesitates. "Okay. Just don't lose it. Have to go to Des Moines to get another copy." He plunks a bowl heaped with strawberries in front of me and starts pouring the thick cream out of the little pitcher he keeps in the fridge. I love his cream. You can't find it that way at the store anymore. Have to go to a dairy, not Sorenson's. They're too big. You can still go to one of the smaller places, and although they sell their bulk milk to Sorenson's pickup tanks, they're still friendly enough to let you have some cream in your pint jar. That's what Boardman does.

"It seems good to be living alone, like you do." He nods, watches the berries bob in the cream, turning it pale pink. "You can have things the way you like, not worry about someone else jumping all over you for some petty thing like buying butter and cream or wasting all their hard-earned money. My ex-husband, Jake, always made us eat margarine. 'Better for you,' he told me.

" 'Doesn't taste as good,' I always argued under my breath. When he started being gone for long stretches, I bought butter again. Kept it stuffed in the freezer back behind some old hamburger that'd paled with burn. He wouldn't look there. If he came home unexpected, I'd say I just bought a quarter. If it was out on the butter tray in the door of the fridge, I'd swear it was margarine. I would, no matter what he said. Let him think he was the one going crazy."

Boardman concentrates on his berries, but he's such a slow eater that we finish at the same time. I take a sip of tea and let the flavors mingle in my mouth. When I look up, Boardman's staring at me. "Why don't you ever call me by my first name?" I shrug. "Azium. Same as my uncle who died in South America. Botanist. Has a species named after him. More than I can say."

He pauses, then gives me one of his hard scientist looks, like he's staring through the skull of a rock. "Why aren't you at home asleep?" Boardman always reminds me of Clinton, how he can zero right in on what I'm feeling, not like Jake, who wanted to be left alone and just have a cool beer and a hug when I was around.

"Oh, I don't know. . . ." I don't mean to feel sorry for myself, I don't want Boardman to get that idea of me, that I'm a crybaby or something. When I look across the table at him, he's holding his cup between his chin and chest, pressed in like he's hugging something he doesn't want to let go of, and looking out the window in the far room that he can see from his chair. Every once in a while his fingers shiver. He's the one person I can trust here in Divinity, I guess, though that's not saying much. The one person who knew Clinton more like the way I did.

"I don't know, Mr. Boardman, Azium, I'm just feeling so crazy these days. Like something's going to happen, or is, or has. See, it's so mixed up. I just hate it. I feel like crying half the time, and I know I can't give in to it. Did you ever read Dante? Clinton told me—"

I catch myself and take a gulp of tea. Boardman looks at me curiously.

"He told you what?"

"Oh, nothing. It's just this business of time—I can't stand it. For years I've just let things happen, go with the flow. I figure Clinton tried to stop it, change or block it or something, and look what happened to him. I didn't much care, anyway, after Clinton, I mean."

"Is that what's been going on? I wondered. I never thought your marriage was, well, much of a marriage." Boardman's eyes turn back to the window. "Of course, I tried not to judge."

"You're the only one, then. I guess when Jake came along, there wasn't much reason not to do it." That's a lie, though. When Jake came along, there wasn't a soul in town who would marry me. It was sheer luck, him coming home from the war and spotting me that night in Sleepy's. There were a lot prettier girls around, even the one in Pottersville he'd gone with before he left. But when he got back, it was like some big change came over him, and he made a beeline for me. Naturally everyone blamed it on the war, how it disoriented people.

"Baby said he married me because he felt sorry for me. I just told her she must be jealous." Talking about Jake makes me feel a little hopeless and sad, like you do in grade school when you realize the teacher doesn't like you and you can't see one good reason why except maybe your clothes aren't cute and your hair and ribbons don't match like the girls she does like.

"I married him in three weeks. I'd just turned twenty-three and he was already thirty-five. What'd he want with a girl like me? I was always afraid to ask."

Boardman gets up and takes the empty strawberry bowls away. Then he pours more tea in each of our cups.

"If Clinton had lived—" he begins.

"Oh, sure, the big IF. He'd have left just like Jake. By the time I married Jake, I figured just stay on a straight line. If you see things that move out of the corner of your eye, don't turn around. There's nothing there. And if there were, what would you do, anyway? So I practiced. I didn't look. I didn't open my eyes to anything. I tried doing what I thought Jake wanted—keeping cold beer in the ice box, the TV in good repair, and the trailer clean. I thought those were the rules. After Clinton died, I wanted things simple. Now it looks like I was wrong. I put off everything for all those years. Jake's family hated me. I was a disgrace. And my family thought there was something bad about Jake just because he married me. But things went along okay until one day he took a traveling sales job. Then the only thing he came home for was clean clothes and complaining about the money I spent. He didn't even want sex. I felt like an army supply depot. If I'd wanted to live like that, I wouldn't have bothered getting married."

I am lying, of course. He dumped me and ran. I can see that. And I am grateful for those years his name covered me like a plastic sheet from the spattering of town gossip.

"Didn't you ever, um, 'love' him?" I can feel Boardman's disapproval. I am supposed to be faithful to Clinton—a nun in the church of Clinton.

I look at the jade on the table between us. The sweetest green, like Stiller's pond in June. "I don't know. I really don't. I always *said* I did, of course. I was so lonely. It was like a piece, half of me, wasn't there, after Clinton. I've always loved *him*. I've just given up trying to get rid of that feeling, I guess. Anything else has to fit in alongside him."

Boardman is sitting again, staring at me. I try to make his eyes into obsidian "Apache tears," like the ones in the display out front. Oblong, shiny, opaque, but they're too brown, too full of understanding. I look away.

"I can't help it. I don't see why he left me. If he loved me, why did he leave?"

"Jake?"

"No, Clinton."

"Maybe it wasn't about you."

"What difference does that make? I'm the one stuck with all these feelings. He's free, now."

"Is he? Is he really?"

"No. At least that's what he says. But who can trust him, after what he did?"

"You *talk* to him? Is that what you're saying?" Boardman leans forward as if he's suddenly hard of hearing.

"No. Well, yes." A banging at the showroom door interrupts us. Boardman gets up to answer it. When I hear my father's voice, I stand up to go out there, then I stop. I could just as easily slip out the side door into the backyard. Come back for my car later. I sigh, take a last sip of tea, and head for the murmur of their voices. I can't leave Boardman hanging that way. I'm not Clinton, after all.

My father's six feet three inches seems almost wrongfully tall next to Boardman. He's remained thin and unwrinkled despite years of hard work and hard feelings. It is the thin-lipped mouth I watch now as it rolls tightly against his teeth.

"Sonny Boy called me," he says as if that explains why he is here.

"Oh," is all I can think of to say. I'm always speechless before my father, although I often practice conversations in which I finally stand up and explain myself in a way he can understand, maybe even accept.

Daddy looks around at the carefully dusted bins and display cases of rocks, sighs, and crosses his arms. His jaw clenches as if he is grinding something with his molars. He fixes his pale blue eyes on me, as if I'm a stranger he's going to have to run off the property.

Boardman clears his throat. "I'll just . . ." He gestures to the kitchen, and I nod. No reason he should have to see this. His shoulders drop another inch as he shuffles past us, as if my father's appearance has aged him.

I try to hold Daddy's stare but look away quickly, defeated.

"What's the matter with you?" he begins. It's not a real question. I know this style from years ago. "How long is your family supposed to take this? Are you fucking stupid? Crazy? Or what?"

I take a chance and look at him. He shakes his head, his terrible eyes like a poisonous snake's, unreadable, not of the same species. I flinch despite the fact that he hasn't moved.

"Your life is a mess, Honey. You're a two-bit bookkeeper earning minimum wage, your husband dumped you, you drive a twenty-year-old beater, your best friend's a whore, a pregnant whore at that, so you dye your hair whore red and start dressing like her, and God knows what you're doing at this loony's house at seven A.M., maybe you're doing him, too." He stops, shakes his head again, and reaches for an uncut geode from a box next to him. The size of a hardball, its surface like a rough gray planet, Daddy tosses it from hand to hand. I don't know if he realizes the lightness comes from its hollow, crystal center. I want to warn him to be careful, but I'm mesmerized by the rock moving back and forth between his two big hands.

"But that's okay, Honey, I always figured you'd never amount to anything. Your mama and I, well, we'd look at you some days and ask ourselves if there was a mix-up at the hospital or something. Maybe our baby died. You never seemed to have the same sense of right or wrong as the rest of us, did you?"

I'm fighting my body now. It wants to erupt, go crazy, run away. My nose gets that salty tingle that happens just before I cry, and I couldn't talk now if I had to because my throat's swelling as if I've already swallowed the rock. Daddy, on the other hand, appears to be relaxing. He leans against the dark oak door frame. The scaled varnish seems another shade of his dark red hair. But I remind myself: Pay attention, don't let your mind wander, watch the rock.

"This new thing now, this colored boy, what's his name? Jasper Johnson?" He pauses, waiting for me to acknowledge the name, making me participate. I try to hold out, but his eyes have the power of God, and like Boardman, I slump and nod.

"I know trying to talk to you on most levels wouldn't do any good, would it? I mean, you don't even think like most people—that we don't even know who his people are, aside from slaves, genetic inferiors, thousands of years behind us white people. I won't bother pointing out how they choose to live and breed like animals, Honey, they'll kill their young and each other over a bottle of Coca-Cola. I've had dogs with higher IQs—but I won't bother pointing things like that out to you, Honey. You'd probably think those were benefits or something."

Daddy stops gripping the rock in one hand and straightens his body. He raises his free hand, and I flinch again. It is almost a relief when his index finger finds the center of my chest and begins stabbing it. "But don't you think for one minute I'm going to tolerate this. They only want one thing from a white girl, and no girl of mine is going to be caught giving it to 'em. You hear me?" His finger feels like a chisel, bruising, trying to break its way through the bone, into me. "You stay away from him or—"

He raises his other arm and throws the rock as hard as he can against the opposite wall. I duck and look in time to see gray rock fragments explode across the room, and a shower of crystal splinters sprinkle the display cases beneath like the moon's exploded.

"Get it?"

I nod. His finger has left a steady, accusing ache on my chest. He hasn't laid a hand on me since that summer with Clinton, and the outrage, the humiliation, of it now seems more awful than it ever has before. By the time the screen door hisses shut behind him, I am shaking with anger. I want to run outside, chase his car down the street, heaving rocks at him, pocking the metal, watching them *thunk* into the windows, taking the top off his head.

"Goddamn it all to fucking goddamn hell—fucking, fucking Christ shit." I can't swear hard enough. Don't know words mean enough. I gingerly touch the place he's poked with his finger. It feels like fangs sank in there. I want it to bleed, to show what he's done. Tomorrow there won't even be a dark spot, but I know that I'll feel it on my body for years. The scar on my forehead suddenly tingles as if the appearance of Daddy raises its fleshy memory. I touch the edges gently with my fingertips, trying to seal them again. Daddy and Clinton. Somewhere within me, the throb of Jimmy and Brewer. Now Jass. Would he be part of it, too? Sonny Boy's gun poking from the car window—an accident? The image of his bumper rising like an alien spaceship in my rearview mirror, then the impact and the Valiant shivering out of control all comes back to me, and I start to shake. When I reach out to steady myself, my fingers touch the rough hide of another geode, and I jerk them back as if they've found a snake instead.

"Honey?" Boardman calls anxiously from the kitchen.

8

Clinton

Back in the kitchen I lean against the door frame, covering my face with my hand. I don't want him to see the look of shame Daddy has brought me to wear. In high school we read about a woman who had to wear a red "A" for sleeping with a man, getting pregnant. My family wants to give me a letter, too—probably a "D" for dying, dead, death, desperate, delinquent, don't get close.

The house is suddenly so quiet. The rocks don't make any noise. The wind is still outside. Even the birds seem to pause so the only sound is the small catching breath of a person crying. For a moment I am so outside myself, have so taken the family view, I don't even realize it's me. When I do, I stop.

"You okay?" Boardman asks gruffly. "I heard a crash."

"He smashed one of your geodes. I'll pay for—"

Boardman waves a hand tiredly and gets to his feet. "More tea?" When I nod, he goes to the cabinet for his ritual. This time he reaches down a bottle of brandy, too. As I watch, he pours an inch in the bottom of our cups. I'm still standing when he hands me the hot liquid. I don't question the Sunday morning brandy.

"Well, what about Jasper?" he asks finally.

"What do you mean?"

"I mean, what about him? Do you care for him? Is this all worth it? For him, I mean." Boardman is watching me. I know my face is puffy from crying, and my Mary Kay makeup still on from last night must be streaked and blotchy. The scar on my forehead will be dark the way it gets when I'm upset.

"God, I don't know. I mean, I hardly know him. We got close real quick, and then, I don't know." Suddenly I'm so sleepy, I have to sit down. "He doesn't like my life—my life doesn't like him. Great, huh?" The brandy is making a smoky path through me now. I try to stay close to its safe edge.

"The question is, is it worth all this trouble for either one of you? Why cause trouble if it's just a thing of the moment? Neither one of you needs that, do you?"

I watch the tiny bubbles circle the top of the tea for a moment, thinking, he wants to know if it's going to be like last time with Clinton. He doesn't want to get involved, either.

"I care about Jass, of course I do. I just don't know what it means yet. It's too soon. Anyway, he probably won't want the hassle now." And if I care about *him,* I should leave him alone.

"Hard to say. If he has any character, he will."

"Oh, like Clinton?" I'm surprised by the bitterness in my voice.

"Want to fight with me, too?" Boardman gets up and retrieves the bottle of brandy from the counter. "If we're going to go at it, might as well get in the mood." He tops the cups off.

After we each have a drink, he says, "Maybe you ought to warn Jasper about your family. Give them a few days to cool off."

"Should I call him?"

Boardman nods. The brandy path has widened and smoothed in my head. Everything feels clearer and simpler. Of course. Call him.

I go to the phone, which is in the showroom. Carefully setting down my tea, I dial and wait for Jass. When it takes a while, I'm convinced he's doing chores or dead. Daddy and Sonny Boy. Then I shake my head at how easy it is for me to imagine that.

"Hello?" Jass says.

"Hi. It's me." My voice sounds a little fuzzy, boozy already.

"What's up?" Jass sounds so businesslike in comparison.

"Oh, I just, I had a couple of, uh, run-ins with my brother and dad this morning."

"Yeah?"

"I think you'd better, well, see if you can avoid them for a few days till they cool off, okay?"

"This is exactly the bullshit I was talking about, Honey. See you around."

The click of the receiver startles me into spilling a little tea down the front of my T-shirt. I want to heave the cup at the wall, but I figure our family has already done enough to Boardman's shop for one day.

Boardman's hesitant hand on my back, pushing me to a folding chair he's placed at the end of the counter, makes me stop crying. He leaves the room, then reappears with the teapot in one hand and the bottle of brandy in the other. He sets them down on the floor and pulls up another chair a little too close to mine.

"Didn't go so well, huh?" He leans toward me. I can smell his old-man breath.

"No, he doesn't like the complication of me, I guess. He didn't even give me a chance to explain or apologize."

"Well, he's probably heard it enough times already from white people." Boardman sighs, leans back, and takes a sip of tea.

"I keep forgetting he's not like us. I mean, not white, you know. He just seems like another man, like Clinton, maybe, the way I feel when I'm with him. He doesn't talk like those black or Spanish men on TV or in movies. He just seems like a person, like our experiences aren't so different, or something." The folding chair is so uncomfortable, I shift to the floor, giving myself a couple of extra feet away from him.

"You'll get dirty there."

"I don't care, I'm dirty already. Just ask my family." I open the brandy and pour a big slug in the cup, topping it with tea. The alcohol is burning everything away. My veins feel like circuits of fire now. The path in my head is shiny, metallic, electric. I can make decisions again. Daddy and Sonny Boy are tiny, helpless figures waving their arms as they slowly shrink away.

"Maybe your experiences *aren't* so different. Your family . . ."

"I know." I wave my hand. I don't want sympathy now. I need to get tough, I need to force the metal skin over my head again. I look at the fossils and rocks around us. Each selected by Boardman, chosen and placed here with purpose. How did he know to do that? Was it the bright blues, citron yellows, algae greens of some, neon sparkle of others? What drove him in his life, to do such a thing, anything? This was the part I could never figure out about people, about life. When does life start getting spelled with a capital letter? When does the pronoun *your* get attached to life? Why does everyone else have so much to say about it? Like they give you a deed to a house. It's yours, you just can't lock the doors, and there's all these people living there already who won't move out, and you never get rid of the landlord. You have the deed, but you owe back rent. "I can't figure it out. I'm always out of sync. I hate time. I keep coming to that—I hate time."

"How can you hate something as abstract as time?" he asks, smiling at my ignorance like in the old days.

"Easy. Time's a failure, it stinks, nothing good ever comes of it in the end. See what I mean? How can anyone *believe* in time?"

"I don't think it's a question of believing or not."

"I hate it. I'm sick of being tricked by it, I won't have it. Looking at all these rocks—'pieces of time,' you told us, Clinton and me. Now look at them—junk for tourists. What does it mean? Clinton's dead, time got him, that's all. You make cheap necklaces out of ten-million-year-old rock, and a person's life can only withstand twenty-five years of planetary shit before he's feeding fish at the bottom of Spirit Lake."

Boardman's hands are shaking again as he raises his cup to drink. "That was his choice, Honey."

"That's what I mean. People can make a decision that wipes out everything in time, that makes time and living useless. What in the hell is the point?" My question, asked in a loud voice, echoes along the hard surfaces of the room.

"What's this about? Jasper? Your family? Your life? Clinton?"

"Pick a subject, Azium, any one will do." I'm surprised at how hostile I sound.

He shrugs and says, "Clinton."

"Your favorite." He's the only person I know more obsessed by him than me. It gives me the creeps sometimes, but in my mood today, I decide to play his game.

I shift to my back, cupping my hands behind my head. "Okay, you tell *me* what this means. One day we were out target shooting with Clinton's guns. The pistol, a .22, and an M-16 he snuck off with from the army. We'd set up targets at the quarry, back there among the gravel mounds so there wouldn't be any stray bullets. We shot until our ears rang. Clinton said I'd be a dead shot if I concentrated for more than a couple of seconds at a time. But what really pissed him off was the way I screwed around while he was adjusting targets or trying to get me to take into account the way a gun is sighted, the way it jerks when fired.

"I was getting sick and tired of his ragging after a while, so once when he went down the line to put up another target, I raised the pistol and called to him. He looked back and got this funny expression on his face, like it was just what he expected somehow. Then he backed up to where the old target hung in tatters. 'Go ahead,' he ordered, 'go ahead and see if you can do this, at least. Go on.' There was a tug, a dare, that caught me, that said, Go ahead, give him what he wants, but that went away pretty fast, and I just dropped the gun and walked back to the car, mad as hell."

I roll over and sit up, leaning against the counter. Boardman looks sad, in that way parents and lovers have of looking sad, as if they see you from years ago, coming to this.

"Clinton thinks I'm gutless. A coward. He's always trying to push me into something, like taking a stand. He's making me just like him. Can't sleep. Hate work. I don't seem to enjoy any of the things ordinary people do."

"What do you mean? Now? He's doing it *now*? Present tense?" Boardman leans forward, resting his hands on his knees. Too close again.

I ignore his question. No point getting into Clinton's little visits now. Besides, I don't feel like it. "You know when you asked me why I wasn't asleep? It reminds me of Clinton; he could never sleep at night, either. Used to wander all over town at three or four in the morning. 'Making sure things are running smoothly,' he used to say. If they'd made him a deputy sheriff and put him on night shift, he might still be alive. Some days I'd go to school and there he'd be—parked in front, his head lopped over to rest on the door, looking for all the world dead until I woke him up by knocking on the window. I don't think he slept in his bed at home more than five times that whole year."

"I know, he'd come and see me some nights when I was having a bout of it, too. He'd rap on the window. Used to scare the bejesus out of me. Never used the door unless it was freezing out. Liked to come through a window. He—" Boardman runs a shaky hand into his thin hair, his fingers catching a tangle and unknotting it.

I get an uncomfortable feeling at this vision. What *were* they doing? Boardman was a lot younger then, and Clinton would try anything.

"Remember that time we were at the quarry, and Clinton and I went skinny-dipping?" Right as I say it, I know it's the wrong thing.

Boardman's face flushes, and he looks away to the row of red geraniums blooming like crazy in the windows that front onto the porch. I don't know how he keeps those geraniums so green and bushy. Most of the stores in town have a big pot or two in the window, but the stems grow long, cranky with a couple of droopy leaves and a sickly flower at the top.

"It was the first time I took you with me to look for specimens in the limestone."

"And I found that big plant stem fossil you still have on display over there."

Boardman nods.

"And you were walking around giving us a history lesson on the earth and time. I was surprised. I mean, I thought you were old, an adult like my parents, but there you were, scurrying over those rocks like a kid."

He smiles and looks down into his cup. I hope he doesn't remember the rest. The way I caught Clinton watching me and Boardman. Clinton had this sadness over his face like he needed to hang on to something because he was going away—the look you notice in pictures of people who are determined to make the best of something like taking a vacation, getting married, or going to war. I should have put words to it then, but I didn't. He was just being Clinton, crazy, dumb, the smartest person I ever met. I looked at his body. He'd thrown off his T-shirt, and I could see the dark curve and hollow in his back where he'd been wounded in Vietnam. He never talked about it. Even lied that he'd never been hit. It wasn't until we undressed for the first time in daylight that I found out that he'd even been wounded. He still wouldn't tell me what happened, so I let it go. Just wondering whenever my fingers accidentally dipped into the little valley it formed.

Clinton was built powerful, like so many of the boys around here, from early years of hard work. His muscles remained hard and stringy as if from habit more than work since he mostly just ran around those days. He said he figured he deserved a vacation, and he was by God going to have one. All those years of trouble in school and then the war tired him out. He had to rest up before he could undertake anything else. I sure would have liked to see him sitting on a beach someplace, drinking beer and getting tan, with a dip in the ocean once in a while to cool off. I sure wish he had gone to California instead of staying around here, where the only real stretch of water was Spirit Lake.

While I'd stood looking at him, Clinton gestured at the quarry and pantomimed swimming. I shook my head, nodding over to Azium, who was across the way from us, with his back turned, working up over the cliff.

"You weren't watching us, were you?"

Boardman turns redder. "No . . . well, not exactly. I was trying to track a pattern of something in the limestone, so I wasn't paying attention. I guess I did look back before I went over to the other side."

He's lying, of course. I saw him watching Clinton the whole day. It was not like a parent watching a kid, either. He kept digging things out of rock and handing them to Clinton. Half the time Clinton would be an asshole and heave it into the quarry. Boardman never said a word.

"We would have gotten into all sorts of trouble if someone had come along. Boy, being young makes you take a lot of chances."

It was the middle of a very hot August afternoon, but most kids my age were home or working, and the mothers who drove their little ones out for a swim in the quarry during the week must all have been inside poring over *True Confessions* or *Movieland* while the babies slept off the heat, because no one showed up all afternoon. Once we got our clothes off, we had a great time swimming around in that big old quarry with turquoise water and a bottom you couldn't begin to get to because the cold got you before your breath gave out.

"Remember what a good athlete Clinton always was? He was diving and splashing like a huge water bird around me that day. He could swim good for someone from Iowa. They'd taught him in the army. That was the only way any of us really learn, you know, going away. Most of the farm kids around here just sort of paddle and dive and hang on to their inner tubes. Clinton was a good athlete, though. He could have been something, but he had to show people they were right: had to be no good. Clinton was that way—he tried to do what was expected of him."

A look of pain crosses Boardman's face, making it pale. "Are you all right? Can I get you something?"

He points to the brandy, and I get up and pour him some, topping it with the tea as I've done for myself.

"Maybe we shouldn't talk."

"No, no, it just makes me so damn mad."

You *were* watching us, I want to say. Let's cut the bullshit. You never liked me hanging around when Clinton was alive. You were jealous. I was just too dumb to recognize it then. You wanted him to yourself. Maybe you were even in love with Clinton like Clinton insists. Or maybe it's just another thing I don't understand.

Clinton always made people react, made them feel something. Good or bad. He didn't care. Just as long as *something* happened—that's probably how he got hold of Boardman. Clinton is the only person who ever got his attention for very long. Long enough to break his heart, it seems.

He covers his eyes with a hand for a minute and presses his fingers together as if he can squeeze off his feelings, in an old movie star gesture. "Damn Iowa," he murmurs. "Damn war."

"Mr. Boardman?"

He pulls his hand away from his face, takes a quick drink, and shakes his head. "I'm okay." He presses and rolls his lips together like a woman with fresh lipstick.

I sink back on my heels, watching him. "Sure?"

He nods and takes another drink.

"We don't have to do this."

"Yes, we do."

There's a little *whoosh* of air, like a sigh, and we both look up, startled, to see the last red petals falling from the head of flowers on one of the geraniums.

"We didn't mean to do it." And we didn't know you'd be watching, I add silently. Even then Boardman was weird around Clinton—doing little things for him, buying him things, fixing foods he'd like. I hadn't understood it until later when we both went to the funeral like widows.

It happened while we were playing and swimming. Our bodies kept bumping into each other accidentally, the way naked bodies get clumsy just before they get grace and together. Clinton was giggling, and I started giggling, and we started bumping into each other on purpose, and I could feel Clinton getting harder every time he got close. When I put my head underwater I could see it rising up to a point and swaying rhythmically with each surge of water that our pedaling around to keep afloat made. Suddenly we're in the middle of the quarry hanging on to each other, Clinton holding me up and pushing inside me at the same time. We kept turning in a perfect little circle, and as I leaned back and closed my eyes, I imagined another Clinton there with us, pushing a big cock against my ass and playing with my nipples at the same time. I could feel myself start to cave in from the middle and give over to them, and Clinton was kissing me all over, sucking and kissing on me so I couldn't tell after a while what was water and mouth and hand and fantasy.

"When I came back over the cliff, a little sooner than I should have, I guess, you two were just a dot bobbing on the water. It was hard to tell what. The surface was reflecting the sun, and I could only see one of you—or so it seemed—and you weren't swimming, just floating. At first I was alarmed, thought something had happened. It took me a minute to realize what was—going on."

Clinton and I were just hanging there, suspended in the feeling of it, and we'd be there forever, without effort, if neither of us moved. But Clinton came, and I was so sleepy and full under his hands that a moment later, my head drifting in the water, I felt a big balloon swelling out from between my legs, and as it burst I opened my eyes.

There was Boardman, up on the cliff staring down at us, his big face twisted into something I didn't know, a raw surface of rock, like Daddy or Sonny Boy. I let go, falling out of Clinton's hands, and as I dropped all I could feel was water coming in through me, and I didn't want any of it to stop. I wasn't trying to kill myself. I just wanted to get away from those condemning eyes. I knew they were right—I *was* no good. I wasn't going to amount to anything if I could fuck Clinton in broad daylight. But my head hurt after a while, and I couldn't figure it out and didn't want to open my eyes, and then another stab of pain, and I was rising again, someone was pulling me hard and fast by my hair, and I was on the rocks and Clinton was holding me doubled over while I threw up.

"Honey, why'd you let go?" Boardman asks now, leaning forward.

I can't look at him. "I don't know, maybe just once I wanted to see what would happen if it all stopped, if I gave in, let go, if I let go of everything. I can't explain it." Because I hated time back then, too, and I already knew you had to try to stop it.

"You're lucky he grabbed you before you got too deep. It's a hundred and fifty feet down there. They'd never have recovered your body."

"Maybe that would've been better." Saying this scares me. I don't want to die. I'm just tired of things. Maybe I deserve it, anyway. Me, instead of the men around me.

"Like Clinton?" His voice has a bitter edge to it.

Remembering, I feel a pain, a loss as overwhelming, as awesome, as the day they told me he was gone. It's like sinking into the quarry again, only this time Clinton isn't there to pull me out, and I know I'll always have that thick, suffocating water in my lungs and throat, and when I scream no sound will come out because the water takes everything. No matter how many times I go through it, awake or asleep, it's always the same. Only Clinton gets to die once, in Spirit Lake. I should have known that day at the quarry was just a sample of things to come. Clinton kept thumping me on the back, saying, "Why'd you do that, Honey?" When Boardman told him to stop or he'd collapse a lung, I noticed that Boardman had taken off his shoes and his big feet were white and soft, like a baby's. One little toe had been squeezed so long by shoes that it was all bent under, and the stunted nail was just a frail slice and had caught a piece of lint, which at first I mistook for blood.

Then I looked at Clinton squatting beside me, at how it hung there, all lavender and gray like unripe grapes. It seemed old then, like him, and I got all sad inside and started crying. They both tried to comfort me, but I couldn't tell them what it was that made me feel so bad.

On the way back to town, Boardman had put his hand on my leg, and I left it there for a couple of minutes before I twisted around to look at something out the back. Clinton, he just looked out the side window at the late afternoon fields that hung dusty and full in the heat. After a few minutes he said, "You can't go home again." He was always quoting stuff like that, stuff people in movies or books said. Back then I thought it was original of him, but I was sixteen.

"Remember that?" I ask Boardman.

"What?"

"When Clinton said, 'You can't go home again,' in the car, and you got all excited because you thought he'd read Thomas Wolfe?"

Boardman laughs. "Clinton knew how to get me going. He always tried to pretend he was so ignorant, but I know he read a lot. He had real promise, real intellect; too bad he worked so hard to convince people otherwise." Boardman gets up and walks to a long shelf jammed with pamphlets and books about rocks. "He read through this in a week. Almost total recall, too. He'd come over in the middle of the night, grab a stack, and start in. Usually he'd have some beer or something with him. He was the only person I ever met who could drink liquor and read intelligently at the same time. The alcohol was like caffeine in his system. But the odd thing was the *way* he read—he'd never open a book to page one. He'd always just pick it up, let it flop open, and start in. If he liked it, he might backtrack to the beginning, but he always *knew* what the book was about anyway. Hell, he could quote it to you." Boardman pulls a thick black book from the shelf as if Clinton were about to walk in and take it out of his hands. I feel like we're talking about his dead lover, not mine. It was like that, too. Only I was the one who got to sleep with him.

"Yeah, I remember the two of you fighting about that. You seemed to think it was pretty half-ass then. I know I did. 'The person who wrote that probably had something in mind. First things first,' you'd tell him. But being sarcastic with Clinton never worked."

"He said he wanted 'to find out what the writer *didn't* have in mind, but ended up saying anyway.' " Boardman pauses and taps the book cover. "You know, years later I realized he might have had a point, he just might have been on to something there. Now as I read, I try to imagine Clinton's take on the book—what we'd say about it if we could talk. 'Course I can't go as far as he did. I won't read *everything* in print, cookbooks, car manuals, cheap novels, children's books. I have to limit myself. I'm an intolerant old bastard." He shoves the book back among the others.

"It always seemed like when you two argued it was about books because he wouldn't read what you'd recommended."

"He wouldn't discipline himself."

"No, Clinton had to sneak up on reading, catch it unawares, like it was something to feel guilty about, like he wouldn't want to catch himself at it. He had to pretend he wasn't learning when he was. His mother claimed he was a genius. Teachers hated him."

"Maybe he *was* a genius of sorts." Boardman picks up a handful of small polished stones and lets them drop back into their tray, clicking like nickels. "He was just about the only person around Divinity to have a conversation with, I'll tell you. If I'd had a child, I guess I'd have wanted him to have Clinton's mind, curiosity, life."

"The crazy part, too?" I'm feeling uncomfortable. Boardman's eyes get glassy as a cow's when he's talking about Clinton. I want to shake him, remind him of all the shitty things Clinton did and said.

"Ha! That was the war. Goddamn waste . . ."

"Not really. He was always like that. Maybe it was living here in Divinity and having no one to talk to for the first eighteen years."

"Perhaps. By the time I came into his life, Clinton was probably too far gone. Ruined."

"God, I hope not, or I'm done for, too."

He coughs and heads for the living room. I'm sure getting a tour of the place today. Boardman stretches out on the sofa. "My back," he says as he pulls a throw pillow under his head. I choose the overstuffed chair covered in rusty brown nubbly material that will leave an imprint on the backs of my legs. I know because it's the chair Clinton and I used to make out in while the old man was supposed to be working in the basement or rock shop. I used to love being squeezed so close with Clinton on that chair that his long dark hair swung into my face, and I could catch a strand with the tip of my tongue and pull it like it was my own.

"Now why would you think you were ruined, Honey?"

"Because in a way Daddy's right. I don't—"

"Shut up!"

"What?"

"Don't repeat that ugliness again. I can't stand it."

"But it's true."

"Don't."

"No, *part* of it *is* true. I *don't* have any direction, I don't know where I'm going or what I'm doing exactly."

"Didn't you ever have any dreams when you were growing up, something you wanted to do?"

"No." I pick at a fat brown nub that's beginning to unravel. Maybe Clinton did that, years ago. "As a kid I was too busy keeping out of Daddy's and Sonny Boy's way. First we were losing the farm, then living in Omaha, then back here with Daddy out of work a lot. Everyone was just so mad about things. It was all I could do to just, I don't know, stay alive or something. I never had time to dream. The only time I did, it was about moving back to the farm, and everything being better, growing like it should and nothing being killed, dying. I eliminated the cruel parts in my dreams of living on the farm again. Sometimes I fantasized that my family all got killed in a car wreck, and I got the insurance money, and people who felt real sorry for me helped me buy the farm back. Then I'd be happy living there alone with my plants and animals. Of course, I'd miss them, but I'd get over it with all that peace and quiet. But you see, there's nothing in that dream that could come true. I never saw myself married or having a certain job or kids. I never got that far."

"Then you met Clinton," Boardman says in a voice tinted with sarcasm. I know he disapproved of me then. When Clinton brought me over, Boardman would either ignore me or ask me something to make me look dumb. He was just nice enough so Clinton would come back. After the funeral we came to an uneasy truce.

"When I met Clinton, everything just went into the present. We lived so hard that year. We never talked about the future, like it wasn't going to happen anyway. I was happy to be along for the ride, to get out of the house, to finally be with someone who felt like I did—crazy, like the world was impossible anyway, so why not do what you felt like—as long as you didn't hurt anyone."

"But Clinton *did* hurt people."

"Yeah, I remember that night you two had the big fight about it, too."

"Which time?"

"You were talking about some book, *Crime and Punishment,* maybe, and Clinton kept saying that the main character hadn't suffered enough, that he should have had to die for what he did." I remember it because afterward I tried to read the book, but it was summer and I kept losing track of the characters and having to start over. I always meant to try again.

"Oh, he made me angry that night. He kept laughing at me, taunting. I've never felt so close to hitting a person in my whole adult life." Boardman shakes his head and reaches for his cup of tea and brandy.

Boardman had gotten so mad, he'd paced the kitchen like a panther in a zoo cage, crouching and springing at each point he made. He'd stab the air with his arm, getting it real close to Clinton's face. And Clinton knew he was being mean, pissing off Boardman. I could hear it in his laugh. I tried to stay out of it, hoping they wouldn't end up beating the crap out of each other. What did I know? I figured I'd be in real trouble if Clinton hurt Boardman.

"I never should have said what I did, though."

"What?"

"When I said, 'How can you say that—after what you've done?' I knew it was wrong. I swore I'd never use it, and I did."

"That *did* change things. You could feel the heat and air go out of the kitchen, the two of you just hanging there like old rubber inner tubes in the garage."

"I tried to apologize, but you know Clinton, he just smiled sweetly and patted me, told me it was no big deal. The only problem was he believed I was right about him. He couldn't stand the killing he'd done. He wanted to be punished. That's why Siberia wasn't enough for Raskolnikov. He thought Dostoevski let his character and Western civilization off the hook by not sentencing him to death. Clinton wanted simple justice for himself, and all we could offer him was counseling and the VFW. He wanted to pay for what he'd done. The sad thing was he had to punish himself. He tried with you that day shooting the guns, but you didn't understand, thank God."

I feel sick, not from the brandy, either. "I couldn't *kill* him! I loved him. Why did he pick on me, anyway—a sixteen-, seventeen-year-old kid without any dreams, hopes? I couldn't help him."

"No, but you could be with him. He saw you as his twin, he told me. He saw you as stranded here, like he was. He was in a crazy war, and you were in a crazy family."

Does that mean I have to do what he did then? I wonder what Clinton told Boardman exactly. The old man looks so moony. It's almost like we knew two different people. Or like Clinton was Buddy Holly or Jim Morrison, and we're leftover groupies, star-struck, pathetic. I don't like the old man having possession of Clinton. He's mine, I want to say, keep your fat hands off.

"At least you never killed anyone." Boardman's pale eyes try to intrude, get inside mine. I look away. What's he after? I could mention Brewer, but maybe he's forgotten about that one.

"How do you know he was punishing himself? How do you know it wasn't an accident, his car at the bottom of Spirit Lake? Maybe he was just driving along," I ask the big, clubbed fingers folded on his chest.

"Naked, in January, on a lake?"

"Well, you don't know. Why'd he leave me if we were so alike? Just answer me that." I stand up, suddenly cold, and start rubbing my arms to stop the shivering, as if I'm in the icy lake water, too.

"He wouldn't be able to marry you."

"Who the hell ever said anyone had to marry me? People are always making these goddamn decisions about my life without ever asking me. I hate it. I'm supposed to be like everyone else here. Settle down and have kids, keep house. I already tried that. It was phony—a phony, stupid dream. I got a trailer in a corn field and a husband who, oh, fuck it. And fuck Clinton, too."

When Boardman laughs, I get more pissed off and stop beside the couch, looking down at him. "What's so goddamn funny?"

He waves his hand at me. "Relax. Here, pull me up."

I take his outstretched arm and help him stand up. He straightens his shirtsleeves and hitches up his trousers. "If you don't like the way you let other people run things, run them yourself."

"Okay. That's fair."

"Fairness is beside the point. Don't get hung up on simple ideas like fairness and justice. That's what killed Clinton."

"Maybe. Maybe not." I pick up our cups and head for the kitchen, with Boardman behind me.

"And another thing"—he picks up the chunk of rare jade from the table—"when you want this, ask me. Clinton wanted you to, uh, be taken care of."

I nod and turn to leave. "Bye, thanks."

"Be careful," he calls as I close the screen door.

I pass the last house before open land on Highway 11, and Clinton says, "He's wrong, Honey."

"I know, Clinton."

"It wasn't a simple thing at all. The pain, the hurt, sorriness, was in my body, not just my head. It was stamped in my cells, my skin, I could feel it every time I took a breath, burning in my lungs. The only things that made it go away were booze, drugs, and making love with you."

"God, Clinton."

"No, it's okay now. I just wanted you to know that. I wasn't crazy, it wasn't my head, and I wasn't dumb. I understood how complicated it was, believe me. I needed an exorcism, physical trial, tribulation, my flesh scourged, but I was in the wrong century, the wrong culture. It was too late for me. They just wanted to medicate my head, administer to this bone cave—the smallest part of the problem. I used to wish I could take my skull off like a helmet and leave it with the doctors while I went out and took care of the rest."

"I know, sweetie, I know," I murmur as I pull onto my road. "God, I miss you, Clinton. I really do."

"Watch out for Sonny—he's the enemy. Your father's too self-centered to cause you a lot of trouble."

"What's Sonny gonna do, Clinton? . . . Clinton? Are you there?" I park the car next to the trailer and sit in the silence that answers me.

When I finally go inside, I rummage around for some paper and a Magic Marker. The only way to get this all straight is to begin a list like they advise in those women's magazines. Instead of do's and don'ts, pros and cons, I put good/large and bad/small in columns at the top. Mama always said doing the right thing was large and the wrong thing small. Growing up, I thought the question of "evil" was too hard to think about. I assumed it'd wait until I was older, and it'd matter more. I didn't care about "good," either. To Daddy, it was personal—you did or didn't do what he wanted. To Mama, as I said, the whole thing was in sizes. Baby fooled everyone. Even as a teenager, Baby was so fat, one punch in her doughy middle and she'd collapse like a half-risen loaf of bread. Poof. I remember one time Baby got real mad at Twyla in high school. Baby's revenge happened one late Friday night at a party. While Twyla was downstairs dancing close with some boy, Baby went upstairs and called Twyla's house. When her dad answered the phone, Baby asked for Twyla, and before the old man could have a fit, she said, "Oh, I just heard she was pregnant, and I wanted to congratulate her." Then she hung up.

There was another time. It was on a summer night when I was fourteen. I wanted to borrow back my pillow because it was too hard to sleep on the caved-in little mattress in the attic, with the heat, so I was moving out to the tent in the yard with my younger brother, Tolson. I did have to go in there that night. Baby was always borrowing my pillow. Then she'd forget to give it back.

I wasn't paying much attention, and maybe I was even a little groggy in the night heat, the way it clings to you and sets in your eyes and nose thick and fuzzy, because I didn't notice anything at first, just the usual mound on her specially built bed. I thought she was asleep like always, and I'd just pry the pillow out from under her. She never woke up once she was off, like that weight of flesh pressed her down real hard into sleep, and it took a long uphill climb to come back from it.

I stood for a minute to let my eyes get used to that special dark that seemed to be Baby's room at night. To this day I can't figure out why hers was so inky and the rest of ours regular. Sometimes it seemed like she sucked all the light from the windows, from the moon and the streetlights outside the house. Because of her size, you know, she needed everything she could get, even the light. There wasn't going to be enough. You could tell. She worried the food at the table or in the kitchen. She'd look around as if there weren't going to be enough. I just figured that she ate light, too, like everything else.

And then I could see.

Although it was a big moon, her two windows weren't exactly pouring the light in full volume. There was a trickle, and she was all stretched on the bed—spread, yes, like margarine; I never associated butter with Baby. She was melting and soft in the pale, bruised light, naked, almost like the bones stood out from the flesh that had gotten too hot for the sheets.

I thought she was asleep, but she wasn't. Her hands were moving so slow, though, rubbing herself, down between the legs, fingers caught in the pale tangle of hair. Oh, she's pale where I'm dark, and I realized I hadn't seen Baby's body since we were small, and now she was a woman, though in her clothes you could barely tell where her waist took over from her breasts. Her front rose and just pushed out like a thing glued onto her body. But she did have big breasts, plate-size pancakes with a strawberry in the middle until she pulled them up and stretched them out, and I thought, Let go, don't do that, you'll hurt yourself. I moved, and when my shadow came over her, we made a big X on the bed. Her whiteness beneath my darkness.

I started to ask for the pillow—at least I thought I did, but my voice stuck in my throat. It was the heat, I told myself, and then she was moaning, low and sweet as sugar. Oh, that was where all that candy went, it made her sweet, I thought, not wanting to hear what I heard. Oh, that sweet voice, so low and urgent and mournful, coming back on me like a tide of syrup, it catches me now like then, and I couldn't turn and go like I should—oh, I should've—and her breathing was sucking the light up, and I felt myself getting darker and darker.

Then my voice caught like a car with a hard start, and something I was trying to ask came too suddenly out into the room. As she grabbed the covers wedged against the wall and pulled them over herself, I struggled again to ask for the pillow, that hopeless dumb, little pillow, with all the stuffing beat out of it from too many years of sleep. But it didn't do any good.

"You! You bitch! Get out of here! Don't ever come in here again, or I'll kill you."

The next day I found my pillow upstairs in my attic bed. It had a big yellow stain in the middle of it, and the smell of urine made me gag. There was nothing to do but sneak it out to the trash after that.

That's the problem; even if I say a thing is small, bad, there's something wrong with the description. "You can always be dead," Clinton whispers in the shadows of my trailer.

"Is that what you want, Clinton? Where do you belong?" I draw a middle column with his name at the top. I decide that it's legal to include dead and alive people, past and present times. Just people I know, though—not like Ben Hur or Betsy Ross. My family's the tough part. They've moved around so much, the paper looks like a target blasted by a shotgun.

After staring at it for a while longer, I take a shower, unplug the phone so Baby can't reach me, and go to bed to sleep off the brandy, Clinton, and my family.

9

Cruelty

June passes quietly, the temperature going up so gradually, we don't notice until the Fourth of July that we feel like we're wearing wool long underwear by noon each day. The fields and trees take on that hot green middle of summer look, where everything is so

crowded and sticky with growing. You realize you planted your gardens too close again in July, and you begin to feel the prickle of green forcing itself against you as you step on sidewalks and driveways cracked under the push of green, and you're reminded of how temporary the blacktop of Highway 11 is by the green of wildflowers and grasses pressing its edges. Ditches fill with milkweed, clover, and alfalfa gone wild, with black-eyed Susans, sunflowers, disguising the depths beneath them. In July we abandon our relief, our hope of June, the welcome after the long winter. In July we begin to recognize the angry part of the growing season. We give up trying to kill the invasions of ants and flies. As if something in our spirit, our soul, recedes, pulls inward, we shrink into our lives, trying not to touch another living thing, even if we can hurt it. July. We leave our skin outside, but there is a space now between it and ourselves.

After some negotiation, Jass and I celebrate the Fourth quietly at his place with a few sparklers, a bottle of wine, and fried chicken, the horses watching us curiously from the shade of the lean-to as they swish flies. We haven't made a public appearance together since Potluck Beer Night in May, trying to keep the peace while we get to know each other. Avoiding Sonny Boy.

* * *

A week after the Fourth Bowker's got out-of-town clients coming to look for land. He's just gone to the A&P for Kraft swiss cheese, which he thinks is fancier than American, and Ritz Crackers, which he believes means a party. He's been debating for the last hour about going to the liquor store for a bottle of Scotch. "In Omaha," he brags, "they serve drinks to their customers. In the middle of the day."

Marylou, who is on better terms with Bow-wow than I am, snorts and says, "There's three bars in this town. Let them get their drinks there." Then she adds her personal, cross-to-bear note: "I got all I can handle with this drinking business, don't need it at work, too." Her Mary Kay makeup face cracks along the forehead as she frowns and sighs. She's referring to her husband, of course.

"Maybe pop, then," he says, and leaves in a hurry. The heat from outside curls in along the floor, then shoulders its way upward, splitting the cool in two. Bowker keeps the air-conditioning on low to save money, so we're on the verge of sweating.

I'm going over figures in the books when Marylou says, "Honey," as if she's warning me. I look up in time to see Baby filling the doorway. For a moment I think she's stuck, the way she pauses, then I realize it's the look she always wears entering a room, like she's going to own it soon, so she needs to see what sort of crap she's stuck with this time.

The heat leaks around her until she closes the door. The room seems to be filling with a smell, a humidity, like a Union Pacific tanker car spill. It drifts across us.

Marylou gets up to turn the air conditioner on high. I stand up as if Baby is a visiting general. What the hell does she want? I wonder as she inspects the sketches for the centennial poster taped to the wall next to the door.

"Want to sit down?" I ask her, gesturing next to my oak desk to an old mahogany dining room chair Bowker got at auction. Nothing in the office matches because he buys everything second hand.

Baby fans her face with a hand so small, it looks like a flipper coming out of her huge arms. She's dressed in a floor-length muumuu of faded orange that makes her resemble a giant rutabaga. Her hot red hair has always smelled of scorched ironing for some reason, and her skin looks like skim milk dusted with cinnamon.

When she walks, you can hear the squish and hiss of flesh, but she is surprisingly graceful. If she weren't so afraid or ashamed, Baby would leave the house more and *have* a life beyond the family, I decide for the thousandth time. She sits down carefully so the chair joints only squeak a little. I sit down, too.

Marylou goes to the files in the far corner so we can have some pretense of privacy. If Bowker weren't coming right back, she'd leave, I know. Marylou has a considerate side. Besides, the fall Mary Kay line will be out soon, and she's hoping I'll restock.

I haven't talked to Baby in over a month. I'm surprised by her visit. "Hot, isn't it?" I ask.

"What do you think?" Baby fans herself with her flipper again and pulls her low neckline away from her skin. Sitting down makes her breasts splay and fall to the sides.

"How are you doing, Baby?" I try again.

She pulls her dress off her knees and flops it a couple of times to get the breeze up between her legs. It's a gesture that reminds me of Mama, on the porch after a long day on the farm. "How do you think I am? I'm going into the hospital tomorrow to have my stomach stapled."

"I didn't know that. I'm sorry, Baby, I—"

She flips her dress higher. "Oh, I know. You're so busy with your love life, you don't have time for anybody these days."

"Baby, I—"

"No, it's all right. Putting the staples in isn't so dangerous. It's later. . . ." She lets the skirt drop and wiggles her bottom uncomfortably on the chair.

"God, is there anything I can do?"

Baby examines me carefully. "You can help me with Daddy's wedding." Then she smiles slyly at my reaction.

"His wedding?"

"He's marrying that hairdresser from Pottersville. I guess we can all get free haircuts now. Or dye jobs." She looks at my hair with her nose wrinkled. "Why on God's earth when you didn't get stuck with red hair, you'd—"

I shrug her off. "When is he getting married?"

"August fifteenth. I plan to be at least a hundred pounds lighter, and we all have to be there. Except Tolson, of course. The reception's at the Riverbank Supper Club. Old man Reese is letting Daddy have a room for nothing as a wedding present, because Daddy works for him. And we have to help. His new wife is too busy to do much, she says."

"Daddy married? Seems weird. You sure he wants me to help?"

Baby looks at Marylou, who's only pretending to file. "He didn't say it specifically. That's my idea. We *have* to try to look like a family, Honey. It's the right thing. What will people think if we don't help out?"

I lean back on my chair and cross my arms. "Do you know what he said to me the morning Sonny Boy rammed my car?"

Baby laughs. "Come on, Honey. Sonny was just playing around. That was a joke, and you got all bent out of shape. He told me all about it. Calm down, lighten up, for heaven's sake."

She lifts her hair off the back of her neck. For years Baby has been getting a permanent every two months, trying to get curls like mine, only to have the fuzz drop down to straightness after a week.

"Lighten up? He almost wrecked my car, killed me. Then Daddy comes and calls me every name in the book and threatens me. That was no joke, Baby. I'm not that stupid, so don't insult me."

Baby leans across my desk, dropping her voice. "Calm down. Everyone was just upset about your dating a Negro. Now you've wised up, aren't flaunting it, nobody's said a word, have they? Although how you can let him touch you . . ." She shivers.

"You're an idiot, Baby. I'm not going to sneak around much longer. I like Jass, and I intend to be open about it."

"Well, at least wait until after the wedding, Honey. Let Daddy move to Pottersville where he won't have to *see* it every day. I can handle the disgrace better, I'm younger."

"He's moving? What are you going to do?" Suddenly I have a vision of Baby helpless, penniless, alone. And me having to do something about it.

Baby flops her hands in her lap. "I don't know. I don't know how he can do this to me, really. He knows I can't work. I don't have any money. He says I can just live in the house, but how can I do that alone?"

For some reason, we've always said that Baby can't work. She's not strong enough, as if her fat makes her weak, helpless. I don't believe it, not after growing up with her. But she does, that's why she spends most of her time on the sofa in the living room, surrounded, like an island, by stacks of magazines, telephone, Kleenex, lotions, and food. Her appearance downtown today is a trek she only undertakes once a month.

I want to reach out and take her hand. It's so rare to see Baby like this, in legitimate trouble.

"Oh, something will work out, don't you think? Maybe Sonny Boy can—"

"Him. He's like Daddy—selfish. He has Rose, *and now* that friend of yours, Twyla, is pregnant with his . . . He's no better than the rest of them. *Men.* How could you marry one? They're trash, Honey. I suppose you might as well go with a black one as a white one. You always did like to get down in the gutter. Clinton—he was a real piece of work. Jimmy, Brewer, how many has it been?"

"Baby! Knock it off!" I say it so loudly, Marylou looks over at me curiously, so I know she's been listening. Baby and I don't have the quietest voices around.

"Oh, relax, Honey. I was just teasing."

"You were not. Why do you always bring that up?"

Baby shrugs. "Anyway, you *have* to help, and you *have* to come to the wedding, okay? I have to go pack for the hospital. I'll call you when I get home."

She gets up slowly, as if she's afraid she'll break a piece off if she's not careful.

"Baby, is there anything I can do?" I ask as I get up to see her out the door.

"Find me a way to live after August fifteenth." She pauses in the open door, ignoring Bowker, who now waits outside with his arms full of ice and pop cans. "And *don't* bring Jasper Johnson to the wedding. In fact, don't bring him to town at all until Daddy's safely moved. Then you can be the town pump if you want."

She smiles at Bowker, who must be hating the cold air she's letting out of his office. "Those poster sketches are *really* boring. Better try again if you expect anyone to care about that dumb old centennial." The door snaps shut, leaving Bowker to struggle with his load and the handle.

"Well, fuck you, too," I mutter, anger rising as I turn back to my desk.

Bowker bursts back in then. "Grab the ice, Honey. Put it in the sink in back to keep cool till they get here. It's clouding up, hope it doesn't rain. I hate showing stuff in the rain." I pull the bag from under his arm, and he starts shifting pop cans around, doing a little dance to keep them all from falling. "Goddamn it, Honey, what do you think I am, a juggler?" It shouldn't set me off, but it does, and all of a sudden I'm rushing to the toilet, the bag of ice clutched against my chest like a cold hand.

"Well, wait, I—" Bowker's stunned. Then he turns to Marylou, who is just standing there like she's going to fall asleep from boredom. "Marylou." She takes the cans out of his arms and lets him get his composure back—a grown man running around buying cans of pop, should have made the girls do that.

In a moment he's on his way back to the bathroom, and I quickly shut the door with a bang so he can't crowd in too and give me more grief. "Honey?" He knocks to let me know he's there. "Honey, I didn't mean nothing just now." I don't feel like talking yet.

"Honey, Honey! Answer me!" He sounds more and more like Daddy, like Jake, always wanting something, wanting me to come over to their side of it. Maybe that was why I liked Clinton so much. He just let me be. I could live in the bathroom for all he would have cared.

"Honey, goddamn it, we got people coming any minute. You answer me!" I make a face at myself and Bow-wow in the old scratchy mirror over the little sink where I've dumped the ice.

"Honey, we're gonna need the ice, sweetie, I can't serve these people hot drinks on a day like this. Come on, I didn't mean nothing." It wouldn't do any good to tell old Mr. B. that it doesn't have a thing to do with him, that actually it's my family, my life I'm feeling bad about.

Marylou comes to the door and knocks once with her creamy knuckle, soft with hand lotion she keeps in her desk and applies several times a day. "Honey, can I come in?"

I suppose it's lucky that the out-of-towners arrive then. Although it clearly irritates Bowker that Marylou and I jam into the tiny bathroom together, me snugged up on the toilet seat while Marylou stands in front of the little mirror trying to get enough light to fix her eye makeup. Bow-wow only lets us put a twenty-five watt in there, so just seeing yourself at all in the mirror is a miracle, let alone putting on makeup right. She makes a face at me when we hear him go into his big hearty Chamber of Commerce laugh, and I crack up. Sometimes she isn't so bad. Like now when she asks me if there's trouble between Baby and me, she says it to her image in the mirror so I won't be embarrassed.

"Oh, I don't know." I leave it at that, and she understands, carefully squinting into the mirror as she slowly outlines her lips into a perfect shape with a lipstick brush. You'll never catch Marylou just plowing the stuff on and rubbing her lips together to get it spread out good. I am so taken up watching her do her lips that it startles me when she answers, "Yeah, that's hard. What's Baby gonna do?"

I shrug. "Listen, Marylou, let's stay in here so old Bowker can't get his ice. Want to?" I know she won't. She needs her job to support her kids and no-good husband, and I guess I need my job, too.

In a minute Marylou is out there passing around cups of ice and opening the pop. I wait a minute more, check myself in the mirror, smile so my teeth show, and go out to my desk. Bowker gives me his large-mouth bass grin. I wish I had a pole, he'd be hanging up there sooner than he'd think. As I sit down, he wants to introduce me. It's one big happy family, that's the message. These must be good prospects—we're giving them the down-home routine. In truth, I want to tell them, it'll take a good ten years for folks to start calling them naturally by their first name and another ten for folks to forget that they didn't just move out here last week, and to the day they die, everyone will think of them as the new people down the road.

After the prospects leave with Bowker to look at farms, I tell Marylou I'm taking off, I'm sick. By that time I feel like I am.

When I get outside, I'm hit by the wall of hotness that hangs in the streets this afternoon. My eyes smart with it, and I have to figure somewhere to go, somewhere to think. I feel disorganized all of a sudden, like a big wind has come along and is ripping clothes off the line, dropping the pins every which way. I have a lot of investment in seeing those clothespins neatly lined up, holding things out to dry.

Looking down the street, I notice a truck like Jass's pulling into the parking lot of Reiler's Feed Mill a few blocks away. I begin to walk there, slowly, letting my eyes trail along the store windows, past Miss Ethel's Dress Shop with the yellow shades drawn to guard the merchandise, as if the thirty-year-old mannequin in its button-down-the-front house dress were valuable.

"Baby, Baby," Clinton sings to the old Supremes tune, "Baby, don't you—"

"Cut it out," I order.

"Baby has a point, Honey. Why *are* you going out with Jasper?"

I pause at Steadman's Drugstore to check out the prosthetic devices. They always scare and fascinate me. You can't look at them carefully *on* people. Then I continue on down the block.

"So it's just sex? A black cock?"

"Stop it, Clinton. You're pissing me off."

"A state of mind these days, isn't it? Does anyone *not* piss you off?"

"Yeah, Jass."

"That's not true."

"Well, most of the time. Look, he's a *nice* man, don't you see that? He doesn't hurt things on purpose. Besides, he doesn't expect me to be like everyone else around here. He's not trying to make me into someone else, his version of me. I can just be myself."

"Oh, yeah, and what's that?"

"Screw you, Clinton. I'm figuring it out, you know that."

"Love, my dear girl, is another circle of hell."

"Thanks a lot. Where do you suppose suicides go, buddy?"

"Below murderers, Honey."

At first Clinton's visits filled me with panic. I'd start sweating and couldn't catch my breath. Now I feel maybe relief, maybe just missing him here, physically, his arm around my shoulder, carelessly, like everything else about Clinton.

His voice is better than nothing, though, better than the empty place he left at first. When he died I used to wish so hard for his ghost, but I could see why he didn't want to come to my family's house. It wasn't until Jake and I got married that he showed up, and then it was only his voice, as if he'd been gone too long to make it back with his full body. I was grateful for anything by then.

Clinton's voice appeared one night while I was on my hands and knees on the bed in our trailer with Jake pumping away behind me. He liked it that way. I closed my eyes and groaned to keep him going. When Clinton said, "You never had to pretend with me, did you?" I figured Jake must have heard, too. But he was still humping away, getting ready to come. Then I decided I was going crazy, until it started happening all the time, and I knew Clinton was back.

Now his voice helps me. I'm like a compass seeking a pole, a direction to stabilize it, to swing from, toward, when the world tilts wrongly.

I drag my fingers in the dust coating Jass's red pickup as I walk past. When I stop and look around, I catch a glimpse of two figures beyond the feed mill, back where Cindy Reiler keeps her stud colt.

At first it's hard to see them, they're so close together. Then I can distinguish a tall, slender, brown-skinned man and a small blond girl. He has his hands on her shoulders, she has hers on his hips familiarly. As I watch, they close the small space between them. My heart jumps as if it's trying to break out of my chest, and I suddenly feel like my legs won't stand right. "Oh, fuck—oh, shit, oh, shit." I close my eyes tightly, and when I reopen them Jass is kissing her on the forehead. I look around for a rock, a baseball, anything to throw at them. Stop it, I want to yell, don't do this to me.

As if they've heard me, they suddenly break apart, and in the gap that appears between them I see the stud horse's muzzle reaching over the five-foot fence. When Jass reaches a hand up, the horse's teeth snap at it. "Good for you," I cheer the horse on. The horse is smart, whipping its head out of the way before Jass can slap its nose.

Cindy reaches for Jass's hand and holds on to it, her eyes searching the ground like she dropped something. I can see Jass talking to her, seriously, and her listening the same way. Then there is a sound from the back door I can't see, and Cindy drops her hand and walks back to the mill, leaving Jass at the fence. He turns his attention back to the colt.

I want to run. Go back to the trailer, cross Jass's name off the good column on my list, and move it to the other side. But I'm so angry, I want to confront him, too. Let him know I know. Watch him lie and wriggle like a dog with a chicken in its mouth.

In a moment I'm beside him. His lavender shirt looks fresh out of the laundry, goddamn him. And I can smell the spicy cologne he uses for dates, the one that goes tingling right up my legs. I fight the feeling. He turns, surprised, then smiles. "Hello, Honey. I was just coming to see—"

"Cindy. I know. I saw you." I haven't meant to blurt it out, but I'm so angry, I can't play games. "Screw you, Jass."

Jass frowns. "Now it's not—"

"What it looks like? Sure. If you're lucky, the redneck assholes in the mill didn't see you."

"Honey . . ."

"Then if *I'm* lucky, they did."

I turn to go, but he grabs my arm hard. "You don't know anything about this. She's a kid. I already told you that. It's nothing—"

"Let go of me." I shake my arm, but he just moves his big hand down to my wrist. "I suppose that was a brotherly kiss, too."

He drops my wrist and grins. "Incest?"

"This isn't a joke, goddamn it."

"Well, it isn't a federal crime, either. It was just a good-bye kiss on the forehead."

"Give me a break. I'm not stupid. You two were on each other like a set of clothes. I thought I could trust you, Jass." Fighting the tears crowding my eyes, I turn toward the horse, who is watching us while it paces the fence.

"You *can* trust me, Honey." He leans against the fence, crossing his arms.

The colt pauses in front of me, and I reach through the boards and scratch his chest in big lazy circles. He stretches his neck and nose out, half closing his eyes, curling his lips open.

Jass steps behind me, and I can feel the heat of his body like a stove outlining mine. "Why don't you come out later."

My body keeps saying yes, yes, make love to me right now, here, in the dust beside the paddock. But my head fights him. "Is that all I am to you? I thought you were different, special."

In a few minutes the glow is gone, and when I turn around he's stepping into his truck. Without waving, he drives off.

"That's that," I say to the horse, trying to sound nonchalant. When I stop scratching, the horse reaches down and nuzzles my hair. "I know, I hate it, too." Hate the way everything changes, ends. Just when I think I can trust someone, bam.

Without knowing why, I wander around to the front of the mill and go up the steps into the little store. Maybe I'm looking for Cindy, maybe not. She's just a kid, anyway, though she's at least twenty-one. Her heart got broken a couple of years ago when young Feller married Sharon, her ladylike sister, instead of her. He needed an asset to the car dealership he'd inherit, not a tomboy who trained horses and hefted hundred-pound bags of feed. For some reason Cindy hasn't grown up because of her broken heart. I could tell her a few things about that subject. I'm not really mad at her, though. Jass is right, she's just a kid. It's Jass I better stay away from, or I'll start acting like one of my family after all.

My family? Was Sonny really only joking when he tried to hurt me? He never joked before. Does Daddy really want a family wedding? Why did Baby come to see me like we're actually blood-related? And Jass, the man I thought I could trust *because* he's different, like me, is he just like all the rest?

I go up and down the aisles, letting my fingers trail along the shelves, touching the rawness of sisal on big metal spools and the clean metallic shine of chain sized from dainty for closing the chicken yard gate to thick as a man's wrist for hauling the tractor out of mud. The scenes with Jasper and Baby linger here, following me. Cindy is nowhere in sight.

I hurry past the animal vitamins, medicines, and poisons that are lumped together like a diabolical drugstore along one wall. It scares me that you can cure your chickens and kill the sparrows. It's the sulfury smell I walk quickly past now. The arsenic I remember.

"Impossible," Mama always said when I complained about it. Not possible. A three-year-old waiting in the detached garage, in her wooden playpen with the top bar gnawed, rodent clean, by the teeth as they came in, one, two, three, until I was three and still there, obedient, not climbing out. I remember the spacing of the bars—I could press my face against them and only see with one eye at a time because my head wasn't wide enough yet to span the space and bar and space. I just thought that that was the way the world of looking was to be—a squint, a half view. When the arsenic in the box tumbled from the shelf overhead and thumped into my playpen, spreading itself like dry cream over the faded and stained sheet, my hand was in it, taking its turn before I knew it. The fistful tasted foul and bitter. I don't think much went down.

Now the sick earth smell makes me hurry. I don't remember the ride to the doctor's, the vomiting. Maybe Mama invented that part because I asked, because I wanted to know what they did for a person who received the invitation so unasked for: arsenic falling like flour from the ceiling. They probably did nothing. Wait and see. If the leg falls off, we'll bandage the cut. If she stops breathing, we'll know she ate the arsenic. I want to say, It was just so bitter, so bitter, the smell makes me hurry like little knives. But that afternoon I couldn't climb away from it, in the garage, where it clouded the air of gasoline, old paint, and Daddy's tobacco.

I round the corner and am walking past scissors and anything sharp: hedge shears and scythes, hoes and rakes, that lounge along the walls, hung just high enough to threaten you with their clatter, the new edge of a spade gleaming like the blade of an axe. And it is then that I hear them—bursts of laughing, that way that says something male and something else is happening. It's the sound you get used to growing up around brothers and boys. It has a wildness that hurts, that makes you want to turn around and walk the other direction down the block, that makes you want to stay in front of the house until you hear the yelps, the cries of what they are doing.

I pick up a screwdriver. I want to buy more, but it is only a small, useless one I need today. Not even a Phillips. Something cheap with a clear plastic handle and a rim of red paint around the end, some notion of design, the lettering not grooved in but printed on with black paint that will leave parts of words in your palm the first day you sweat on it. I'm waiting at the checkout stand for help. No one's around, though. We're so good at these useless acts, I'm even thinking that while I look at what's on the counter: the hand-printed poster for a raffle pancake supper for Billy Bond's family.

Their crop got burned out by a bad load of fertilizer and insecticide. The land had to be scraped and loaded and hauled away by the chemical company. They said it'd be fine, promised to do something about topsoil, and were never seen again. Lawyers. It'll be years, and the Bonds have to live somehow. You can see their fields from Highway 11. Yellowy white and bare. The weeds won't even take the invitation.

Looks like Vietnam, the vets are saying over beers at Sleepy's and the Blacksmith. Except there the earth was red. The Bonds are afraid to leave, afraid to stay. They keep their chickens penned up now. The pigs had to be sold. The dog's on a chain, howling because the air smells funny and the water, the well, started turning up cloudy after a rain. Bond trucks his water for the family over from the neighbor's. They aren't too happy, either. I want to yell at all of them: What do you think is going on here? What do you think?

When I hear the bursts of laughter from the back room again, I walk toward the sound, trying to find someone to wait on me. It's the back room you go to in the spring to pick up your chicks and goslings, waiting in boxes under little light bulbs, the warm smell of mash and manure somehow mixed with the fuzzy down of their yellow peeping coats. But back there today, there is something as mean as July. The door is open in front to let the air circulate, and a thin powder of ground oats and corn from the milling has dusted the shelves, and I'm breathing it as I step closer to the back, following the finger of their voices, past the shoulder-high bales of chicken and hog wire, past the rolls of twine for haying, past rounds of electrical cable, more rope, fins of posthole diggers, and finally, the men, in a mean circle. Laughing.

On the floor in their midst is an old snapper turtle the size of a Cadillac hubcap—crusted wet and brown on the dark green diamonds with leeches and weeds, as if it crawled out of time itself. The turtle's neck stretches long, and the jaws are frantically wide—little ragged blades—snapping from one side to the other, while around it lie the legs the men have cut off, with the claws still twitching and clutching at the rough tan planks beneath it. There is surprisingly less blood than you would imagine, the way it trickles from the dark holes in the shell. There's no better light, no nicer side, there's nothing nothing, nothing but it, sitting there—the severed legs clawing to get out of the way, the rim of body waiting while it won't bleed to death.

I want to ask them just before I turn away, shoving the screwdriver in my purse, What do you think you're doing? Just what is it you're doing? Here today, I mean, what is it you think you're doing? I hear one of them say, "Jasper Johnson, that nigger, is next," as I turn and run out.

For some reason I grab a paper bag from the little stack on the counter, and as I run to the car, I am pushing the screwdriver into it, lodging its point into the corner and pushing it through. As I climb in, I throw the bag on the floor next to me and start the Valiant with a vicious push of gas, and it lunges out of the gravel lot.

10

The Dead of July

Jass," I whisper as I speed out of town on Highway 11. What are they going to do to Jass? I have to warn him—have to stop it. I can't sit by this time. I'll go home, call him. He'll listen because he knows how mad I am. I'll tell him what I saw so he'll believe me.

I glance at the bag on the floor. It won't make the transition from the car. I'll let people put their muddy shoes on it until the gray-green Reiler's Feed Store logo is broken and rubbed out, stamped into paper pulp on the black rubber of my Valiant floor mat. I hate that screwdriver.

I try to press Prince forward, willing him to hurry with my shoulders hunched over the steering wheel. Ahead of me the dark clouds are collecting, their shadows moving quickly across the fields. Here comes the rain. Good. I want the wind to howl through here. I want a tornado to twist the tops off Reiler's grain elevators, to pluck the men from their safety and drive them like straw through tree trunks. I want the roofs of town torn off, the blood washed away.

As if answering my wish, the huge bruised clouds roll and tumble toward Divinity. "I can't let them hurt him." I slow down and make the turn onto my gravel road as the first saucer-size drops splat on my windshield. The trees jerk one way, then the other, like heads of shaken children. But the sky doesn't turn that tornado green yellow. It's the dark purple of eggplant and blue black of watermelon rind.

Ahead I can see my trailer squatting lime green and white in the storm. I'm already imagining the phone call as I slow for the left turn into my driveway when Sonny Boy's car appears suddenly. Coming from the opposite direction, Twyla's end of the road, it seems to hesitate, then *whoosh* past me, splattering the Valiant with gravel. "Shit." I can't stop at my place now, what if he circles back? A shiver of fear passes through me. I can't sit here alone, a target for Sonny Boy's mood. What if—no, I shake my head and step on the gas. He's part of it. I'm not going to let them have Jass.

Pulling onto Twyla's driveway, I almost slide into the ditch that runs on either side. The rain is coming so fast, it doesn't have time to soak in. Stepping out of the car, I land feet first in a pool of muddy water.

I push past Twyla to the phone when she answers the door. "Have to call Jass and warn him. Don't ask—I'll explain." It takes a while, and when Jass answers, he is breathless.

"Oh," he says when he hears my voice. "Honey."

The rain pounding on Twyla's trailer makes so much noise that I have to press my ear hard to the phone and talk loud.

"Listen, don't freak out, but those men at the feed mill, I heard them. They're going to—they might be planning something—they took a turtle, it was awful, Jass, and one of them said they're going to get to you, too. You've got to be careful." The static-laced silence on the other end makes me think we've been cut off. A burst of hail sounds like the trailer is being attacked by tennis balls.

"Jass? Are you there?"

"Uh-huh."

"You've got to *do* something—protect yourself or something."

"What would you like me to do?"

"Get a gun—Christ, I don't know. You're a man, you should know."

"Yeah." His voice fades again. Outside, the wind is lifting the metal awning over the kitchen window and letting it bang down again.

"You don't want to hear this, do you? You hate me calling up like this."

"Same old story, Honey."

"God. I can't believe this. You should have seen it, Jass. You wouldn't be feeling so smug, let me tell you—" My voice rises hysterically over the storm noise.

"Look, I've got to get back to my horses. I was bringing in the babies from the storm when you called. Thanks anyway."

I hold the receiver against the impossible click at the other end. How could he do that? Am I supposed to stand, like a good woman, on the sidelines while the men kill each other? "That's it. That's it, really. This time I mean it. Really." I turn to Twyla, who has been waiting on the sofa, one hand resting on her basketball-round stomach. "I need a drink." She motions toward a card table in the corner, loaded with bottles of booze Wolfgang has given her.

After a slug of Cuervo Gold, I tell Twyla about Baby's visit.

"I knew Baby was getting her stomach stapled," she says, chewing on a fingernail.

"What're you doing that for? You always have great nails."

"I can't stop myself, since this," she pats her stomach.

"What about Jass, think he's safe?" I hate asking her, but I can't get that turtle out of my mind.

"I think he's a big boy, Honey. He can take care of himself."

"Yeah, like Clinton."

Twyla snorts and fluffs her hair. "Quit glamorizing him. He was scum, Honey. A drug dealer, a badly dressed one to boot. What a jerk! You and your buddy Boardman would be a lot better off if you'd let that clown die. Dead and buried."

"Well, you're in a mood." I'm not going to get any sympathy from her today.

Twyla looks too hard at her hands, turning them this way and that, like someone else must have chewed off the nails. "Sorry. I'm just feeling

low. Can't get laid because of this—" She flicks her hand toward her belly. "Sonny Boy and I just had a go-round. I can't eat, I started bleeding last night. I'm supposed to be in bed, but it's so boring out here. I'm going nuts. Give me a hit of that—this frigging storm is giving me a headache."

Before I can stop her, she grabs my glass and drains it. "Bombs away." She puts both hands on her stomach and swallows again and again. "Uh-uh."

"What's the matter?"

"Here it comes—" She gets up awkwardly and walks quickly to the bathroom, a hand over her mouth. The sound of her gagging makes my stomach heave. What's the matter with her? I haven't seen her as much since that night when the four of us went out and she ended up with Sonny. Just needed a break from her. It's funny, I ended up feeling sorry for Tom that night. He's lame, but what did he do to deserve Twyla treating him that way? I pour another shot of tequila and sip at it, waiting for it to make that clear enameled place in my head. Her trailer is a wreck, I notice. Not that she was any good at keeping house to begin with. It's hard to judge her.

"You okay?" I ask when Twyla comes back.

She collapses on the dirty orange-and-yellow-flowered sofa, propping her feet up on the coffee table with the melony veneer peeling at the corner. "Doesn't look like, does it? I can't keep anything down. I've lost ten pounds since the heat came on. Wolfie wants to put me in the hospital, but Iowa City . . . Tom would freak out and I couldn't see Sonny."

"Twyla, don't you think you should take care of yourself and the baby first, instead of worrying about the men?"

She brushes her hair off her face, and when it flops back she yanks it. "Look at this"—she holds out the limp strand for me—"ruined. I'm gonna look like a breeder when this baby's born. My whole life's ruined. I want to chop it all off." She pulls at her hair roughly, separating it into three bunches and braiding it together. The dirty white shift she's wearing is so big, the armholes gap open, exposing the side of a swollen, blue-veined breast.

In fact, Twyla's face does look drawn, gray-skinned, hungry. "What's the matter with you? Why didn't you call me when you got sick?"

"*They* don't know. Anemia, some other junk. The baby's fine, of course. They *always* get what *they* want—babies and men. Sonny Boy's *so* excited. It's no big miracle, Honey, let me tell you. Now Sonny wants to name the kid after his dad. Can you believe it? Julius?"

"What do Wolf and Tom say?" She's ignoring my question about calling me, I notice.

Twyla grins. "They don't exactly know about Sonny."

"Twyla . . ." This is the part of her life I don't much like.

"What do you expect? It's every man for himself. That's my motto." She pulls herself up and paces the small room, rubbing her hand in the milky road dust that coats the top of the TV as she passes it. The dirty brown of the cheap walnut paneling on the walls bulges in places, as if something were trying to get in.

"You should get out of here while you still got a chance, Honey. Look at this—thirty-three years old and I'm living in a dump like this." She kicks at a pile of sheets and towels in the corner. It's hard to tell if they're clean or dirty. "Someday they'll find me sitting here watching TV, covered with dust." She pounds her fist on the TV. "Why can't they pave the fucking road? Wolf could do it—at least spread some oil or something. I've been sitting here for days trying to figure it out. Why the hell can't they pave the goddamn road?" She pauses, and the storm bangs on the trailer like it agrees. "Sure, they don't have to choke on this shit. They don't have to watch it cover everything, even my goddamn toothbrush. Do you *know* what it's like to have to brush your teeth with gritty toothpaste? It's because they don't have to dust, keep it clean, keep the windows of their houses shut and watch it come in anyway."

She's scaring me; the look on her face is far away like she sees something I don't, the way a horse or dog will stand still and watch the distance, and when you look, there's nothing there.

"Twyla, honey . . ." I get up and touch her shoulder, shocked by its thinness. I can't speak quietly because of the din. Her trailer's older, less soundproof than mine.

She shrugs me off and laughs a little hysterically. "I'm okay. If I could keep the booze down, I'd be better. There's just no escape. I didn't know it'd be like this, I really didn't. Oh, fuck it. Sorry, Honey. Let me get you something."

I'm about to protest, but she's already a step away from the kitchen. I stare at the brown BarcaLounger in the corner. I wonder if Sonny Boy sits there, tearing the Naugahyde on the arm like he used to do at home.

"Come see what Wolf's done. You won't believe it."

The cracked gray Formica kitchen counters, stove and fridge tops,

and table are crowded with piles of fresh fruits and vegetables, boxes of imported cookies and crackers, candies, cakes, all kinds of food. "Look." She pulls open the freezer, putting up a hand to stop the avalanche of frozen food. "Need some steaks? Prime beef? Lamb, pork, chicken, duck? Insane, isn't it?" She closes the freezer door carefully. "Look at this, then." She opens the lower part of the fridge.

"My God . . ." It's so crammed with food, it's difficult to distinguish any one thing.

"Pretty wild, huh?" She smiles. "Clear a space and sit down. Can I get you anything? Nacho chips and salsa for your tequila?"

"Yeah, okay. How can you find anything, though?"

"It's not easy, but I think I know where that stuff is, that's why I offered. Or you can have some pâté with morels he had flown in from a specialty shop in Minneapolis."

"No, chips are fine. Can't you eat some of this?" I pull out a heavy dinette chair with dented, rust-pocked chrome legs and plastic red seat sprouting stuffing.

Twyla shifts some fruit baskets. "It's funny. The more there is, the less I want. I can't figure it out. It makes me comfortable to have it here, but I can't bring myself to eat any of it. Here's what I eat, when I can." She pulls out a box of Trix sugar cereal.

"You gotta be kidding. You'll starve. You at least use milk on them, don't you?"

"Can't keep it down." She laughs. "Here's your snack." She throws me the bag of chips, which I catch before they crash into a precarious pile of cans. "I'll get the tequila from the other room. The salsa's in front of you there on the table, see it?"

It's depressing after the initial shock—seeing all this food. It's so gross, so out of proportion, there's a wrongness about it. I pick carefully through the stuff on the table. A lot of the fruit has a single bite out of it, opened packages are spilling their contents.

"What does Tom think about this?" I ask as she pulls out a chair and sits down. I notice a trail of tiny sugar ants bisecting the tabletop.

Clearing a space with her forearm, she shrugs. "He doesn't want to rock the boat. He doesn't touch it, though. Avoids looking at it. Hell, I could feed half of Divinity with the contents of this kitchen, don't you think?" There's awe in Twyla's voice, like she's just discovered some big truth. She picks up a box of Scottish shortbread and absentmindedly tears it open, then drops it.

I nod. "Sonny?" Usually I don't discuss my brother, but today is different. It has a new edge to it, like a freshly whetted sickle. A big roll of thunder crashes overhead, making the dishes in the cupboard rattle.

She looks surprised. "Sonny? Oh, Sonny eats himself sick practically, then takes a nap, like it's Thanksgiving or something. He's such a piece of work." She laughs and shakes her head. "That must be why I love him. He's the only person less predictable than me. I always know what men are going to do, except Sonny." She giggles, reaching for a tin of crabmeat with *$5.00* stamped on top.

I pour a shot of tequila and sip at it, letting the spicy burn move my mind one more notch. This is the only booze that feels close to the high I used to get from grass or acid. I save it for very special occasions, like when I catch a man messing around. It puts a special meanness in me that I need today.

Twyla strokes the tin of crab. "You know what he did once?" She has this weird look on her face that should be enough to warn me but isn't. "Here, give me a hit, maybe if I take it slow . . ." She drops the can and puts the bottle to her lips and takes a small amount, letting it roll and coat her mouth before she swallows.

"This is how we first got together. We'd been eyeing each other for a while, you know, but we were each taking our sweet time. After all, it doesn't go away. There's never another first time."

She pauses. "That *did* help me. I guess I'll try a chip." She dips one in the salsa and takes a dainty bite. Hardly the Twyla of old in the eating department. "Can't gulp my food anymore. One good thing, huh?"

I laugh, though this new Twyla is still scaring me. Is she going to be okay? We've been friends by going our own way most of the time. Knowing the other person won't interfere. But this is too much.

"If I could find the cheddar, we could put it on the chips and run them under the broiler. Want to?"

I shrug from the superior place the tequila has put me.

"Yeah, too much trouble." She takes another sip of tequila. "So I brought this guy I'd picked up at Sleepy's home one night. We were both pretty ripped. The guy was a lousy lay, passed out as soon as he unloaded. So I'm in bed there, pissed, I hadn't even had time to get wet. I'm thinking about how to wake this dickhead up to kick his ass out when my closet door sort of creeps open. First I thought it just hadn't been latched, then I saw an arm coming through the clothes. I about shit. Too scared to say a word. Then he steps out, Sonny Boy, naked, not a stitch on, with

this huge hard—" She stops and looks at me. "It looked like a baseball bat, I swear to God. That man's better hung than Jesus Christ."

"Twyla, he's my brother. . . ." I look over her head out the little window over the sink. It's still raining hard enough to drive the water through the crack in the glass. The trickle winds its way down the wall to the sink, which is full of dirty dishes.

"Well, he is. Anyway, he jumps in bed with me, right next to that jerk who'd passed out. After a while, we're humping away. Difference was, I *did* get wet that time. Later he said, 'Sloppy seconds is better than nothing.' "

I pour a shooter and drink it in a large burning gulp. The rain isn't pounding so hard on the metal roof and sides now. We can drop our voices a notch. The wind has settled down. It's cool in here. Twyla has the air conditioner Wolf gave her turned on high.

"Sometimes he's coming through the bedroom window as Wolf is walking out the front door." She pulls her hair out of the braid and examines a strand. The color has dulled to the shade of cornstalks after heavy frost.

"I don't let him get too far out of hand, though. I have to keep the economy here going. Sonny's the entertainment, the icing. If he gets on my nerves, I send him home to Rose. She should thank me." Twyla has a glint in her eye as she says this.

"I'll tell her that." We laugh.

"At least *I* have a program. You've gone with every goofy guy in the county. You need to get a plan, Honey. Decide what you want out of life—and *make* them give it to you." She puts the bottle to her lips again.

"I don't want *anyone* to give me *anything*." I get up for a glass of water.

"Well, there's your problem."

"I didn't know I had one."

"Come on, what are you doing here, then, instead of work? How come the only black man in town hangs up on you? He should feel *lucky* you—"

"Shut up, Twyla. Just *shut up*. You don't know anything about it, really. He's not even black, for one thing."

"Oh, sure."

"He's part Ceylonese, part white, part Indian, and part Negro."

"God, a mongrel."

"Cut it out! He's beautiful. I love the way he looks."

"Never mind. Don't give me the details. That's why he has that straight hair? Blue black. Hard to get that with dye. I've tried. Never looks natural."

"It doesn't matter, anyway. He's through with me, I can tell."

"Those sweet eyes, Honey. I warned you, can't trust 'em. It's all in the eyes. They're the heartbreakers."

"Yeah. What about Sonny Boy's?"

She smiles and looks at her chewed nails. "Bedroom eyes, love. Men with bedroom eyes just fuck you."

"I could tell you something that would blow your mind, Twyla."

"What, that he tapped your car that time? Big deal. A joke."

"Twyla, you don't know what you're talking about."

"Yes, I do. He told me. He's been watching you."

I shift on my chair. Is he still doing that? Suddenly the room is tight with the smell of overripe fruit, dirty dishes, and rotting food.

"That's not all, Twyla."

"*Come on,* Honey. Get real."

"Then what about Jass? I *know* he hates him."

"Just you going out with him."

"He's not the only one." I tell her briefly about the turtle trying to keep the gore down, but she's up and running for the bathroom immediately.

When she comes back, I apologize. "I'm sorry. I just want you to see what's happening. It's not just him going out with me."

"Cindy, too."

"Still?"

"No, silly. Just that he did. Besides, those men are assholes. Sonny isn't like that. He wouldn't—"

"Yes, he would. You don't know him, Twyla. You two connect on one level, but there's a lot more, believe me."

"So what? I told you, I only *need* one thing from Sonny Boy. Anyone who wanted more would be stupid. He's lousy at the rest."

"Yeah, just ask his wife, Rose."

"Or his kids. He hardly remembers their names."

"Poor Rose."

"No, lucky me. Rose is on her own. *She* married him—not exactly smart."

"Twyla, you're *so* cold sometimes."

"Now don't get all pitying about Rose Bevington. She has a house, land, and a father who looks out for her. Sonny Boy leaves? Rose will still be ahead. Everything's in her name. Only thing he owns is his car, and he had to pay for that himself."

"Why shouldn't he?"

"Why should he—married to Rose Bevington?"

"You two *are* alike."

Twyla smiles. "I know."

If she wasn't my friend, I wouldn't be laughing now. She's so honest about her selfishness and games, it's hard not to enjoy her a little. Later it will bother me, like it always does, when I see Rose in town with the little ones, all of them sad-looking like they just stepped off the immigrant boat.

By the time the storm ends an hour later, Twyla is so tired, she has to go to bed. When I go outside, the air has that odd clearness that puts surprising angles and color on everything. It's as if the world really is new, hasn't been spoiled yet. I notice things I've forgotten, like how the aluminum red of Twyla's trailer is the color of geraniums. And the grass isn't one green, it's a whole handful, flattened under pools of water.

Then I feel the heat rising back up out of the ground, off the trees and surfaces of things, as if the rain had only pushed it away, held it down for a while. Now that the rain has stopped, there it is again. It never really went anywhere.

Backing carefully out of Twyla's driveway, I see Wolf's black Riviera coming slowly toward me. He's probably loaded with more food she can't eat. I really am worried about Twyla. I've never seen her sick before. Maybe she *should* go to the hospital. Despite the tequila, I feel sober. The image of the turtle keeps sawing at my world, something I can't do anything about, an action that can't be fixed, repaired, put on my list as just bad, evil, small. Yet I can't escape it. The turtle is marooned in my imagination, in Divinity, in the human world.

"Stop thinking about it," Twyla advised when I told her what I'd seen. "Toughen up. Do something to get rid of it. Think what your mama would say. She was a tough cookie."

"Boys will be boys."

Pulling into my driveway, I decide to do what girls do. At least girls like Twyla and me.

The next day I try it. Control.

I go all day wearing Mama's face. I slide it over mine in that tight rubber glove way as I drive to work. I know it's there the instant I finish talking to someone I haven't met before but disapprove of. Not because of anything they've done or said, but just because. Mama disapproved of something about almost everyone. This gives me power. I can do anything. Nothing surprises me—not even finding myself pulling into the parking lot of the Blacksmith Lounge after work.

I don't ask Terry from Reiler's Feed Mill about the turtle or Jass. What would be the point? We're drinking beer that's barely cool when it comes to the table and that's hot by the time we finish it. The Blacksmith is just right, I tell Mama's face, for doing things we don't approve of. In the little bathroom with walls smeared by lipstick and pencil messages, I look in the mirror and undo two more buttons on my shirt. Back at the table I try to forget his name, his face. I concentrate on the hard July heat coming off his skin like a cheap aluminum pan. I'm hoping it'll burn me when I touch it.

That's why I end up sleeping with Terry, who works at Reiler's Feed Mill. It's easier than going home to my own bed or out to Jass. I just can't face the drive in this heat.

I don't even bother taking Mama's face off before he's on top of me. It doesn't matter. All I remember later is the suck of our chests together, a sound like something breathing in that nun's head, and his hands rolling my nipples like they're balls of beer-soaked napkin on the table back at the Blacksmith. His hair and skin aren't any worse than mine, soaked in smoke and beer and dull conversation, floating on the green breath of July heat.

Later, we lie panting side by side, trying not to touch, in the wet sheets, while the sun finally plops down like a fat lady on a couch and falls backward over the hill. The mosquitoes, almost too lazy to strike, walk deliberately up my arm and with the precision of surgeons begin to sting. I have to debate whether it's worth the effort to slap them.

11

The Wedding

Thanks for nothing," Baby says as I try to pull the box carefully from Prince's backseat without tearing the silver wrapping paper.

"Just a minute, Baby." I close the door, balancing the big box in one hand.

"You could have called." She pouts.

"No, I couldn't." I straighten the silver bow.

She's so surprised that she falls in step with me. Her body seems lighter, and she isn't wheezing today.

"How much have you lost?"

"Eighty-five. I didn't make the hundred."

"But that's a good start. Try to look on the bright side." Though I've discarded Mama's face, I sound like her with this phony advice.

As we approach the front door of the Riverbank Supper Club, Baby smooths the front of her pale pink satin dress and pulls the skirt down around her hips. She orders her clothes from catalogs catering to people her size. She'd do better if she had a chance to try things on. This dress is too snug around the hips and too big in the top. Her breasts peek out of the floppy neckline like Siamese-twin Parker House rolls.

"Do I look okay?"

"You look fine, Baby. Relax."

"You're lucky you didn't go to the ceremony, Honey." She pulls the door so hard, it slaps against the wall and the plate glass shivers. "She was disgusting. Acting like a fourteen-year-old. She's no thirty-eight.

She's forty-five if she's a day. I hate women who lie about their age." She says it loud enough that Daddy and Louverna, standing just inside to greet people, look up. Baby ignores them, taking a sharp left. I follow, hiding behind her bulk. Since I didn't help out with the preparations, I figure I'm about as welcome as the flu. Louverna didn't want us at the ceremony, it turned out, though Baby went anyway. I've been a hermit for the past few weeks, talking only to Twyla, who looks like Mia Farrow in *Rosemary's Baby* just before she gives birth to the devil's son. Something keeps her walking around—I don't know what, though. I scared myself, too, sleeping with that asshole Terry from Reiler's. I've sworn off men now. I can't be trusted around them. I haven't heard from Jass, either. I hurry to catch up with Baby, who is getting ahead of me. She must know where she's going.

The room for the reception is decorated in black and white crepe paper streamers and big fake black and white flowers. The tables are set with black and white candles, favors, and napkins.

"Come here," Baby says, stopping in front of the cake at the far end. "Is this the ugliest thing you've ever seen?"

The cake is five tiers, alternating black and white icing, with black plastic swans stranded on the white and white swans on the black.

"That's awful! *Black* icing? Scary. Whose idea—"

"Hers. She says it's *the* in thing—*decorator* colors. Here's what I want to do. . . ." Baby scoops a finger of black frosting and plasters the face of the white plastic bride on the top of the cake.

"Baby."

"What? She asks for help, then totally ignores me and does this. Looks like a funeral instead of a wedding." She licks her finger thoughtfully. "Yuck, licorice. Funeral's right."

"It is not." I dig a fingertip in and taste the icing, too. "Oh, God, you're right. She's totally nuts. Wait till Daddy . . ." We start giggling. Daddy hates licorice.

"Oh, God, you should see your lips." Baby's lips are rimmed black, and when she puts her tongue out to lick them it's tinted black, too. "Oh, no! Your tongue, mine, too?" I open my mouth, and Baby nods solemnly, then explodes with laughter.

"This is perfect, Honey. *We* couldn't have done it better. Look at your finger," she gasps. Sure enough, the black icing has stained everything it touched.

"Can't you see it?" I say when I catch my breath again. "When they cut the cake and everyone has black teeth and—"

"What did you get them?" Baby asks, wiping her eyes. "Put it over there. So dumb having the ceremony private. I guess it's her third, though."

"I got them a cookbook."

"Cookbook? In that big box?"

"Something Simpy recommended, some gourmet deal. The box is the disguise."

"Daddy will be lucky to get Budget Gourmet frozen dinners, Honey."

"How was the ceremony? Seems weird having him married again."

"It was some hokey deal Louverna made up. Or read about in the same magazine as this. I still can't believe it. Maybe nobody will come. Save us the embarrassment. How do I look?" She turns around slowly. On an ordinary person the loss would show dramatically; still, there is a difference. The indentation of a waistline beginning to show.

"I told you. You look fine. How come you never called?"

Baby stops, hands on hips. "You could pick up the phone, you know. I was the one suffering."

"Oh, come on, Baby."

"Yeah? You don't have a clue, Honey. Not a clue. Did you notice where the bathroom is when we came in?"

"Down the hall to the right."

She nods and sits down at one of the tables. She props her chin awkwardly in her hand. She still has to sit with her legs spread. I wonder how she'll feel the day she loses enough to cross them. I'm about to ask her about the operation when the guests begin filling the room.

Since I still haven't met Louverna, I watch for the newlyweds. Everyone looks surprised by the black and white. When they laugh uncomfortably and inspect the cake with the bride wearing a black icing face, they laugh some more. The bar opens at the back of the room, and the five-piece band comes in, picks up their instruments, and begins to play like they've only been on break. It's Bob and the Bluejays, a local C&W group that also does some rock and folk when the girl singer is on. She thinks she's Joni Mitchell and Tanya Tucker both, and the confusion is obvious—she does the folk like an adolescent sexpot and the C&W like an aging hippie. The rock is just strange.

It's only an instant before couples are dancing the Texas two-step, slow jitterbug, Lindy, waltz, whatever fits their generation. I admire the people of Divinity at this moment—the way they fall into place when a celebration occurs. They know their assigned roles and seem to enjoy filling them. Maybe they could do it at *any* wedding, whether they knew the people or not. And just as easily, I can imagine them crying at the funerals years from now. They're decent people, given a job, a space to fill, some clear demand.

Even Baby is enjoying herself now, gossiping with two other women. They speak behind their hands and giggle as they watch the dancers, who whirl and twist, binding the plain room into a mosaic of color on black and white.

The present table is heaped with gifts. I forgot to ask Baby what she bought them. It'll be good. She never misses an opportunity. Louverna is already her sworn enemy.

The bar is lined with men. I see Terry from the feed mill and quickly look away. We've been avoiding each other since that stupid night in July when I slept with him. He's like a bruised fingernail; I'll just have to let it grow until he disappears.

I'm standing in a corner, so I get the view of the whole room. That's how I see Bowker come in. They invited him? He always imagines he belongs the next step up from my family, but he comes right over to me.

"Honey . . ." He tries to hug me. I keep my arms stiff on his waist and push my cheek at him to be kissed like ladies do. He pecks it obediently.

"Why, I sold Louverna her house *and* her shop," he explains. "Think your daddy will be selling his place?"

I shrug. "Ask Baby." I point to the table where she's sitting.

"Later." Bowker looks at the dancers. "Come on, let's do 'er." He grabs my hand, and before I can resist, I'm in his arms. Too much time being polite in the dark storage closet. I follow his motion, trying to avoid the insistent press of his body. He's wearing so much bay rum, I wonder if he's soaked his underwear in it.

As we spin past Baby's table, I hear someone say, "Flirting with her boss," and I want to drop his heavy body in their laps. Let the harpies pick him clean.

"Hm, you smell good, Honey, like honey." He sniffs my hair and laughs at his joke. Next time I'll use fly spray instead, I decide. But maybe he's just smelling himself and *thinks* it's me.

Circling the room again, I see Sonny Boy's face like a bright new toy among the old ones. He has that kind of effect. You realize his *real* prettiness the more people there are around. You're always able to pick him out, the way the camera follows the leading man in a movie so he stands out, looks better, takes your eye. Maybe if he'd had to work for it like the rest of us, instead of things being tithed to him because he was always so godlike handsome, so athletic, he would be able to care about someone other than himself. Mama always acted like Sonny Boy was the Second Coming. Daddy treated him like he was Daddy-in-training, a pharaoh or king. The rest of us were just the rowers on the boat, down in the hole. We should be grateful to see sunlight.

Sonny looks worried today, I notice. Good. I watch as he goes up to Terry and slaps him on the back, whispering something in his ear, laughing with him as he steps to the bar. I feel sick and try to pull out of Bowker's grip, but he uses the opportunity to slip his hand farther down my back. His fingers tap the music through my light cotton dress as they inch toward my buttocks.

I pray for Bob and the Bluejays to be struck with food poisoning so they'll have to break, and as if in answer, they do. I'm out of Bowker's arms muttering, "Thanks," before he can stop his feet.

"Come on, Baby." I pull her arm. She comes up so lightly from the chair, I'm surprised. "Let's go to the john."

"Did you see Rose? Didn't Sonny bring his wife, even? What's the matter with him?" Baby fumes as we crowd into the bathroom.

"Lock the door," she orders. "I can't go when other people are around."

"What about me?"

She looks surprised. "Oh, you don't count."

"Screw you, too."

"Honey, relax. I just meant you're family. Wait for me. And open that window."

From the stall I hear an explosion of farts. "Ohh, this operation." There's another release. I breathe through my mouth. Then she belches.

"Baby."

"I know, I'm sorry. I can't help it. I've had this for a month now. Have to drink so much water I feel like the *Titanic*. I can only eat a teacup of food at a time. It all passes through. I have cramps all the time. Good deal, huh?"

I smile at my reflection in the mirror and mouth the name Tolson and I used to call her, "the Weeble Bag," because her huge stomach wobbled and weebled like Jell-O in a bag. We never said it to her face because we knew she'd crush us to death sitting on us.

She flushes and comes out adjusting something under her skirt. "*Des Moines Register* always runs those articles about curing fat. They should try this. I wouldn't do it again for the world. Imagine: diarrhea for a month! I'd rather die of heart failure or stroke. They almost had to hospitalize me for dehydration."

She lets out a big, round belch. " 'Scuse me. This gas, upset stomach. I don't even *want* to eat. It's so embarrassing. It's like swallowing a big rock that just sits there, pressing down and getting in the way of your body. Sometimes I want to take a butcher knife and rip out my whole stomach." She yanks her slip and skirt down.

"Baby . . ."

"Oh, what do you know? I'll tell you—there was this one guy I heard about while I was in the hospital. He was a lightweight—three hundred ninety-two. They stapled him three times, but each time he found some way to eat and pop the staples before he left the hospital. And you *do* want to. The craving's still there. Finally he died. They'd left him alone in the shower for twenty minutes, and he put his mouth to the spigot. Drank himself to death. Exploded his stomach." She rolls on some pale coral lipstick that is nice because it doesn't overpower her pale skin.

"Awful, isn't it?"

I nod. "I'm sorry, I had no idea."

"Yeah, people think the doctor gets out his Swingline stapler, zap,

zap, and everything's great. I love to hear those women who are ten pounds overweight talk about how great it'd be to have it done. I'd *love* to give it to them."

"How much longer do you have to—"

"At least another hundred pounds. But I don't know if I can make it. Especially with Daddy moving." She starts shaking.

"Baby, what's wrong?"

"I can't do this, Honey. I can't make it through this alone without him. You have to tell him, make him stay till I get the staples out, till I'm skinny. Please, Honey?"

She clutches my arm. She's not going to cry. She looks beyond that. There's real fear in her eyes, and it *does* move me.

"Okay, it's okay, Baby. Calm down. I'll talk to him."

"He'll listen to you, Honey. Thank you."

I have no belief in Daddy's listening, but I will try to help her, I decide. At least she didn't suggest that I move in with her.

"What about Sonny Boy, could he help?"

Baby looks at me in the mirror. "You've gotta be kidding. Golden boy? His only concern in life is pleasing himself. Look at him. A family wedding, the whole town's here, and he leaves his wife and kids at home.

Our only hope is that he *didn't* invite Twyla." She adjusts her hair, picking at it with her comb.

"I did."

She gives me a sharp look.

"I invited Twyla as my guest. Since I didn't bring a date."

She looks harder.

"It wasn't a good idea?"

Baby shakes her head slowly in disbelief. "Sometimes, Honey . . ."

"I know. But I wanted someone to talk to."

"It won't be her." Baby picks up the pink bottle of hand lotion the club provides for the ladies and squeezes some onto her palms. "She'll spend all her time entertaining Sonny."

I picture Twyla's pregnant stomach dancing with Sonny to a fast song.

"Gross, huh?" Baby grins as she rubs the lotion up her arms where the flesh is beginning to hang from the weight loss. "Glad *I* didn't invite her. Daddy and Louverna are going to have a cow." She turns to go.

"Baby . . ."

"Don't forget to talk to Daddy. Bye, love." She eases out the door, a three-hundred-plus-pound feather.

Back at the reception, the room is clotted with more groups of people. Louverna is just noticing the black face of the plastic bride when I arrive to introduce myself.

"Did you do this?" she demands.

"No." I sound like I'm lying. "I'm—"

"I know who you are. Did you *see* who did this?" Her tiny figure with a poodle hairdo and baby blue ruffly dress snaps at me.

When I shrug, she says, "I bet," and wipes off the icing with a white napkin. We both stare at the black greasy smear as if it's the name of the wrongdoer. Daddy is watching the room, pretending we've never met.

"Dad, uh, can I talk to you for a minute?"

He glances down like I'm a disappointingly cheap paper prize from a box of Cracker Jack.

"I wanted to congratulate—wish you well."

He puts his hands in the pockets of his baby blue tux. "Thanks." He shifts his gaze back to the dancers.

"Also, well, I told Baby I'd ask you—talk to you. See, she's really not in good shape. She's scared and sick, I didn't realize how sick she—"

Daddy waves a hand and nods.

"She shouldn't be alone."

"Move in with her, then."

"I can't."

"Won't."

"She's not my responsibility."

"She's not my problem. You kids are grown now—have to take care of yourselves."

It's a standoff. Poor Baby. I can't believe I'm saying this after my years of misery because she told everyone I was pregnant. Brewer's dead because of her. Now I'm standing up for her.

"Nice meeting you, sweetie. Julius is moving in with me after the honeymoon. Aren't you, Julie?" She presses her body against him. He puts his arm around her protectively. She's mine, keep away, his face says.

"You-all come by sometime," she drawls, pulling his face down and kissing him. She must be from southern Iowa. I move to the other side of the room, trying to avoid Baby and Sonny, who is dancing with a pretty high school girl. I stop beside Boyd Ziekert, the sheriff.

"All the best people in town here," he says, nodding his head toward Larue Carlson, who is now dancing slowly with Bowker, although the band is doing its version of "Rock Around the Clock" to a country and western beat. "Bowker looks like an old dog with poor teeth who's just found a fresh bone."

"Yeah, he does." I laugh.

"Glad to see your daddy settle down. That woman's buried two before him, though."

Good, I want to say.

"Your sister's losing some weight, isn't she?"

"It's making her sick, though."

Boyd nods. "I bet." We watch the crowd for a while. Sonny Boy is working his way systematically through the fifteen- to eighteen-year-old girls. As he whirls past us, gracefully, Boyd says, "I hate to see that."

"Yeah, I know."

"He's trouble, that brother of yours. Someday . . ."

"I know."

"You ever hear from the other one, what's-his-name? Tolson? Younger, wasn't he?"

I nod. "Nothing, never hear a thing."

"What bit his butt?"

I shrug.

"Probably just as well. Some need to get out of here or they end up in trouble, causing it, usually."

Boyd's in his fifties. His wife decided fifteen years ago she'd go back to college, be a potter or artist or something. Packed up for Iowa City. Never came back. Last we heard she was in Alaska, that's what the postcard said. He's never bothered with getting a divorce. He sees a few women, but nothing serious. Maybe he's still waiting for her to come back. He's not bad-looking for a man in his fifties. Better than Bowker. I might go out with him if he asks.

"Seen Jasper Johnson lately?" He asks it casually like it's not his sheriff voice, but it is.

"No, why?"

"Oh, you know how some of these hillbillies around here get."

"Well, I haven't seen him."

"Thought you two were—"

I shake my head.

"Probably just as well. I don't like to give those rednecks another opportunity. One black corpse on the books is enough. Hated to see that one, too. Nice-looking girl, good family, hardworking, and she gets killed taking a bus through here. The feds couldn't even figure it out. I'll know someday, though. I'll know who shot her. It's going to come out. Fifteen years or fifty. You can't keep a thing like that hidden forever. Someone just won't be able to keep it in. That's the way we're built around here. I'm gonna find out."

"What if it was an accident?" My hands are sweating, and the air of the room is suddenly so thick with smoke and voices, I can hardly breathe.

"Unlikely. Single shot to the head in the middle of the night? Sound like an accident to you?"

"I guess not."

"Those poor people, her parents, not knowing after all these years, who or why. I just feel sorry for them, that's all. The murderer, I hope he's rotting in hell." Boyd shakes his shoulders to loosen the tension.

"Anyway, I'll find him. Just you be careful. Johnson's okay. Minds his own business, works hard. Hate to see him get hurt. Or you, for that matter," he says as Sonny Boy appears in front of us again.

"I wondered if they'd show up," Boyd comments as Wolfgang and Faye, his wife, appear at the door. "God, she's a rough piece of goods. No wonder he spends so much time hanging around Twyla."

Faye's a dumpy blond whose black roots always look like acid eating her hair. Her face is rough and wrinkled from years of sunburn, and her body has that lumpy, distorted look of a cheap old cotton mattress. Her nearsighted eyes squint meanly around the room. Despite the money she spends on her wardrobe, she always makes what she has on look cheap. Today an emerald-and-diamond bracelet gleams like glass on her wrist. Twyla has the same one in sapphires and diamonds that looks like the crown jewels on her arm. I wish she were here wearing it. Everyone hates Faye, but we can't stay away from her. The stories she tells are so funny and vicious, they make us feel privileged, like we're somehow part of an inner circle to listen to the slander.

"Well, I wonder who she'll burn at the stake today," Boyd says.

"Twyla's coming."

"Uh-oh. I better stick around for that one. Don't want an infanticide."

"What?"

"Killing babies. Infants? She thinks it's Wolf's, I bet. Like everyone else in town. Or she will by five o'clock tonight when the other women get through telling her. Whose is it, really?"

"I don't know, Boyd. I'm not sure Twyla even knows."

"Let's see, correct me if I'm wrong: Wolfgang Reese: but he might be sterile since Faye doesn't have any. Sonny Boy Parrish: we know he's fertile as good river bottom. Of course, we can't leave out the husband, Tom Tooley: always the last to know. No evidence on his potency one way or another. And assorted others. Miss any major players?"

I want to hit Boyd, but what he says is true. I shake my head and lean against the cool painted concrete block wall, my hands clasped behind me. Boyd leans back with his arms folded and props one foot against the wall. Though he has a stocky, barrel-chested build, he looks fit, tough. He keeps his thick gray hair and mustache neatly trimmed, and his face is so unwrinkled that it creates an odd impression, like time had gotten mixed up.

"No offense, Honey."

"Twyla's just different, Boyd. She has her own rules in life."

"That's okay, Honey, as long as they don't cross mine." He pauses as Sonny passes in front of us again with another young girl. "I don't see them getting her very far, though."

"We'll see. She usually does what's best for herself."

"I hope so. I really do."

The band ends the song and picks up a flourish right away as Bowker stands in front of them with his plastic wineglass raised in a toast. "Let's wish the happy couple the best now, and watch them cut the cake."

Everyone claps as Bowker sips the cheap champagne and Daddy and Louverna plunge the plastic cake knife tied with a black ribbon into one of the black tiers of cake. They each pick up a piece of cake. All goes well when Daddy feeds Louverna hers. She even manages to lick the black rim from her lips. Louverna holds the cake in front of his open mouth like Eve with the apple, daring him to come for it. He takes one chew of the cake, smiling, before he spits it out in her hand, where it sits as a nasty black lump as he grabs his glass and gulps the wine. "God, Louverna! What in the hell did you use licorice for?" he yells.

Before she can answer, Twyla, in a blood-smeared yellow linen dress, rushes into the room. She scans the crowd until she spots Boyd and me. "Hurry," she says. Thinking she's going to have the baby, we sprint out with Sonny Boy and the entire reception behind us. We look like the posse chasing the robbers out of town.

"Twyla," I call after her, staring at Jass lying on the backseat of Twyla's Oldsmobile before I understand it's not the baby being born.

12

Revenge

The blood on the pearl gray velour upholstery and Jass's face and clothes matches the stains on Twyla's dress. A fly lands on his chin and climbs up the torn cheek, stepping carefully over the dark clots sheeting the face. The swollen, split lips quiver, and a moan whistles through a broken front tooth. The sound shivers through me. I'm standing next to Boyd Ziekert, staring numbly when the feeling hits. "Jass, Jesus Christ—"

"Get some towels," Boyd calls over his shoulder, and goes around to the other side to have a closer look at Jass's face. Since the eyes are swollen shut, I can't tell if he's unconscious or not. I'm afraid to touch him. His shirt hangs in tatters, and there's cuts and scrapes all over like he's been dragged on concrete or gravel. His knuckles look swollen and bloody, and one finger is crooked. His beautiful hands . . . Who did this?

Boyd is carefully examining him for broken bones. When he moves one shoulder, Jass groans, and Boyd says, "Broke his collarbone." Then someone brings the towels and hands them to me. At first I don't want to take them, don't want to get closer, but the towels keep pressing into my hands. I crawl in on the floor of the car. There's room enough if I don't mind getting my dress dirty.

"Just wipe enough blood off so we can see what we're dealing with," Boyd says.

The sides of his face are scraped raw, and bits of gravel are embedded in the flesh. It almost makes me sick, but I force myself to concentrate, saying, This is Jass, this is Jass, over and over inside my head.

"There's a big cut on his forehead—that's what's bleeding. Nose, too. Must be broken."

Boyd stands back and says, "Pull that arm across his chest so the collarbone sits still. This boy's taken a beating, that's for sure." He looks up and addresses the crowd: "Someone call an ambulance. He'll have to go to County in Good Earth."

"Why don't we just drive him, Boyd. Faster. Take my car," Twyla says.

"Okay. Someone call ahead that he's coming in. Honey, you okay back there? I'll drive." Boyd climbs in while people close the car doors.

"I'm coming, too." Twyla's in the front seat before Boyd can object.

As Boyd spins the car around and heads out of the parking lot, I watch the crowd break up, leaving the stranded newlyweds staring after us. Off to the left Baby stands smiling as if she couldn't have done better herself, and Sonny Boy, flanking the couple to the right, stands rigid with his fists at his sides.

"Jass, are you awake? Jasper?" I whisper. "It's all right, you're going to be all right. Just hang on now."

"Where'd you find him, Twyla?" Boyd asks. We're doing seventy-five, and the speedometer's rising.

"On our road. In front of Honey's place. First I thought it was just some old clothes blew off a motorcycle or something. Then I saw it was a man. Dumped there. I didn't know what to do, so I came to find you and Honey. Figured everyone'd be at the reception. That's where I was headed.

"You didn't see it, but his back's all torn up. They must've dragged him, like the side of his face. Made me sick. Lucky I didn't try to eat today. He woke up enough for me to get him in the car." She looks down at her dress, brushes at the dirt and blood. "My dress is ruined." She states it so abstractedly that I watch the side of her face closely. Is she in shock?

"Twyla, I'm—"

"It's because of you, Honey. They beat him up because of you. He woke up enough to say he went to pick up salt blocks and feed at Reiler's and some guys jumped him."

"Oh, God."

"I know. Those shits." Twyla glances at Boyd. "But I don't know who it was exactly. Maybe Jass will tell."

Boyd shakes his head. "Sons of bitches."

Jass groans, and I squeeze his hand, forgetting about the broken finger. He groans louder, and I drop it. What's wrong with me? I'm getting leg cramps squatting, so I try to sit, stretching my legs out in front of me. To hell with the dress. To hell with the wedding. I wish I could hold Jass, make the hurt go away, but now I'm afraid to touch him. I squeeze the bloody towel in my hands, trying to pull and tear it. "Fuck them, fuck them," I mutter.

"What?" Boyd glances in the rearview mirror.

"You know who they are, Boyd. You have to put their asses in jail."

"Have to get Jasper to file charges first, you know."

"Was my brother part of this?"

Twyla's back stiffens.

"Got me," Boyd says.

"I bet he was." I remember the exchange between Sonny Boy and Terry at the bar of the reception. They were all in on it. All the men. This was their way, their thing. Something ugly, violent.

I pinch a shred of blue shirt hanging from Jass's side. I'm not going to let go of him, not again, damn it.

I lost Clinton, but I'm not going to lose Jass. I'll take on the whole town if I have to. I've been so stupid since I met him. I don't know what I could've been thinking. Maybe I just got so used to being around people who didn't care much about me, I stopped caring, too. I've tried to be like Twyla, but I'm not put together that way. Jass is a good man. But his reaching out keeps pushing me away, like I've had to maintain a certain distance between us. It's a rule, something I'm going to break now.

Jass tosses his head as we hit a dip, and his body shifts. Drops of blood spot the front of my white dress. They are so red, so pure. New. I watch them soak in, spread, darken, diffuse like paint. The blood will never come out. But that's okay, I don't want it to.

Four hours later I'm sitting beside Jass's bed in the ward, which is empty except for a recovering heart patient five beds away. Jass is sleeping or unconscious. Mild concussion. Broken collarbone, nose, finger, two ribs. Sprained ankle. Ten stitches on the forehead. Back that looks like pounded round steak. Twyla and I picked gravel and dirt out of it for two hours. Got most of it.

He looks like a child now, breathing deeply, his eyelids fluttering with dreams. They've cleaned the blood and dirt out of his hair, which he's let grow since I last saw him. It fans blue black on the white pillow. I can't stop myself from stroking it, following the remarkable silkiness out to the coarse pillowcase. The light from the nearby lamp seems to catch each strand, like a prism. Clinton had hair like this. So sweet, like a child's, straight and fine. These men are children, and in a way they're mine. Somewhere inside of me I know, I've always known, I'll probably never have babies. I can feel it. But these men—they're mine, as sure as if I'd had them myself.

I look at the rich tan of Jass's skin, something burnished, polished, about it. As if he's the jewel of all those races, bloods, mixed, hardened, decanted, and fired to this one perfect moment. Now they're trying to hurt him, and I'm going to get even. Sonny and the men in this town have run things their way long enough.

When I lean over to kiss the side of his face that's not raw, Jass speaks. I'm so startled, I pull back.

"Where am I? Is that you, Honey?"

"It's okay, sweetie. It's me. You're up at County. You're going to be fine. You're a little banged up now, but you'll be fine." I press my hand along the good side of his face, careful to avoid the puffed shut eyes.

Jass tries to sit up and groans when he feels his collarbone and back. "What the hell—"

"Broken collarbone. Do you remember anything?"

"My back . . ."

"Looks like you got dragged. What happened?" I try to soothe him by stroking his chest gently.

He shakes his head. "Don't remember, tired . . ."

"Just sleep. I'll stay here, don't worry." His breathing slows and deepens. Watching Jass, I realize that I've missed him. I was just pretending, lying to myself about quitting men. Thinking of what I did with Terry makes me feel ugly now. I was ashamed. That's why I avoided Jass over the past month. Now I can't tell him about it even, after what they did.

"Honey? We gotta get back. Come on now, he just needs to sleep it off." The blood on Twyla's dress has darkened so now it looks like an abstract painting with brush strokes attacking the pale yellow cloth.

"Look at your dress." The evening light is cool, making all the edges in the ward distinct—beds, chairs, tables—as it glides along the yellow mint green walls.

"It's okay. Come on now. Can't leave you up here like this. Your dress looks pretty nasty, too, you know."

I look down and brush at the dried blood and dirt. It looks like *I've* been in a fight.

"White, you wore white to the wedding. Only the bride . . ."

I smile. "I know."

"You *are* a bitch sometimes." Twyla laughs.

"I know."

"Well, let's go. I'm so tired I could crawl in bed next to Jass there."

Twyla is leaning on the rail at the foot of the bed. There are dark hollows under her eyes, and her cheekbones poke out of her skin unnaturally. When she smiles, her teeth seem too big for her face. Jesus, she's a wreck. Why haven't I noticed?

"Twyla—"

"*Come on.* You can drive back in the morning. Tomorrow's Sunday, you don't even have to work. But if you don't get your ass in gear, you'll be carrying me out."

Nodding, I put an arm around her waist, scared that it fits in the bracket between her ribs and hipbones. She used to be so strong, muscular. She was never skinny, bony. The baby rides safely in front of her, looking stuck on, like a pretend pregnancy, a pillow or ball. "As long as we're here, why don't you—"

"They already checked. Boyd stuck his big nose in it. The baby's fine. I'm not. What's there to say? I figure it'll kill me or I'll kill it. Same difference, so forget it." She pulls free of my arm, straightens, and walks with more determination slightly apart and ahead of me. The Exit sign

glows danger red in the dim corridor.

"Did you notice that the paint on the walls is the same shit they used on our grade school? It's enough to drive you crazy, isn't it? Thank God I don't have to stay here," she says.

Watching her thin legs teeter on the spike heels, I feel my stomach lurch. She looks the way she did in those early days when we first put on her mother's ancient high heels and practiced walking on the linoleum in the bedroom. Twyla was always better at it. I had to concentrate so hard, I couldn't talk and walk at the same time. I still trip and wobble in them. Now she looks like she does, too. Stop it, eat, I want to yell at her. Don't do this. Can't you take care of yourself? I want to make her behave. Make her clean her plate and go to bed safely.

"Give up the baby."

"What?" Twyla stops with her hand on the Exit door.

"Look what it's doing to you. Give it up, stop it." I stare into her eyes. There's a hard center to them I don't understand.

"I can't—I won't—" She pushes the door open. "Besides, it's too late." She holds the railing and descends the flight of stairs carefully. At the bottom she turns and faces me. "You don't understand, I've always wanted a baby, a child. It's the only way I'm going to leave anything that says I was here. Who cares about the rest? Fucking and fixing hair. What's that? No, this is *mine.*" She rubs her belly with both hands, watching it as if it is speaking. She looks up, reaches for my hand, and places it on her stomach. A ripple of something passes over the surface, then back again.

"This is the only real thing there is anymore. For a while I hated it for making me so sick. Now, well, now I listen to it, feel it, and I know everything's going to work out the way it should."

I can't stand this. "What about that stuff a minute ago—'it killing you, you killing it'?"

"Oh, that was just a mood, Honey. Relax. I say stuff like that all the time. Doesn't mean anything. Come on. Boyd's waiting in the car for us." She pushes open the door to the lobby, and I follow.

We ride silently until the outskirts of Divinity, when Boyd says, "I think it'd be better if you two tried to stay out of this. Don't talk about it. Anyone asks, you don't know anything. Or better yet, tell 'em to talk to me." We both agree, and Boyd pulls into the Riverbank Supper Club parking lot, which is full with the usual Saturday night crowd. I wonder if the reception's over as I say good night to Twyla and Boyd.

Leaving the lot, I head for town instead of home. I don't feel much like being alone, and maybe Baby needs me to talk to since Daddy's gone off with Louverna. Even saying her name puts a bad taste in my mouth, like a spoiled pickle.

As I approach the house, I see all the lights on, as if a huge family lived there. Slowing down, I notice two figures sitting on the porch under the yellow bug light. One is broad, dense. Baby. The other is tall, thin, and flat as a table knife. He sits with an arm resting on each side of his wooden porch rocker, staring out at the world. Although I'm not quite close enough, I think there's surprise on Daddy's face. Surprise maybe at the empty house all lit up like a holiday behind him. Or maybe surprise at finding the big body of his oldest daughter beside him instead of his new wife's. I almost turn into the driveway behind Daddy's car, but another figure appears in the doorway behind Daddy and Baby, the dark glass of a beer bottle outlined in his hand. I haven't even seen Sonny's car. He must have come back with the rest of the family.

Although they're staring at the street, none of the porch occupants seem to recognize my car. It's just as well, I decide as I step on the gas and leave them waiting like shipwreck survivors. I guess having a family wedding didn't work out the way anyone planned. Maybe it's just too late for that kind of gesture.

13

The Fall

■

Just stand there in the middle, let Buddy do the work, Honey," Jass advises from the chair he sits on next to the door. "Now point the whip at his butt and say, 'Trot.' Cluck. That's it. Just keep his body between the whip at one end and the lunge line at the other. That's

it. You stay in place, let *him* circle. Teaches him balance."

The two-year-old chestnut colt wavers on the circle, distracted by a sparrow that lands and takes off next to him. I tug the line to get his attention as he trots past the far wall lined with plastic inserts at the top to let in daylight.

"Good, that's it. Talk to him, too. Remember, baby horses are like kids—short attention span. They want to play all the time. Curious, too."

I'm concentrating so hard that my hands are sweating, though it's one of those cool days that come in September as a warning. This is the third time I've lunged. The horse flicks his ears, arches his neck, and lifts his trot so he's floating when the figure of Azium Boardman enters the arena.

"God, relax, will you, Buddy?" I mutter. The colt pulls hard on the part of the circle away from Boardman but caves in and speeds up when he has to go close to him.

"Let him walk for a minute," Jass says just as Buddy breaks into a wild, sprawling canter, his lead shifting as he speeds to catch up with his own legs. He looks like he's going to fall down, and his momentum is jerking the circle into zigzags. I drop the whip and try to brace with both hands on the line so he can't pull me off balance as he tries to run off the circle.

"Hang on," Jass calls, laughing, as the horse yanks me forward, and I have to let go or get dragged.

"Just wait till he gets it out of his system," Jass says when I walk over to where he sits.

"You could've waited," I say to Azium, who stands grinning beside the chair.

"No big deal. Look at him. He just needed to get his bucks out. If he's a smart one, he won't get tangled in the lunge line. Tomorrow we'll turn him loose in here first. *Then* we'll put him on the line."

The colt is running flat out, pausing only to duck his head and kick his hind legs straight up and out. When he comes by us on his third lap, he twists, snorts, and kicks in our direction, sending bits of dirt over us.

"Watch it, Buddy," Jass calls to him. "You're a cocky little shit, aren't you? Real cocky." The colt slows at Jass's voice, and by the next round he's trotting, then walking. His shiny red coat is splotched dark with nervous sweat. The colt nuzzles the ground in the far corner, then follows his nose along the side like a dog. Careful not to step on the lunge line dragging from his halter, he ambles over to where we wait.

"Okay, good boy. Now, Honey, walk up to him slowly, holding out your hand, rubbing your fingers together like you have a treat there. Say something quiet and touch his shoulder. Then work your way to the line. That's it, good, yeah. Now put the line in loops again like I showed you. Pat him. Start all over again."

I'm scared but walk to where I've dropped the whip. The horse follows as if the past few minutes never happened. When I bend for the whip, he nuzzles my back, then I feel a tug on my shirt as he grabs the cloth between his teeth.

"Cut it out." I bat at his nose with my hand, but he won't let go. "Let go." I say it growly between my teeth, and he does. He raises his head and stares at me, surprised. I rub his nose. "I'm not another horse—keep your teeth to yourself."

The men are laughing as I start the colt on the circle again. "You two can take over anytime."

"No, no, you're doing great. Besides, I don't think Buddy'd like us half as much," Jass says.

I go back to lunging the colt. When Jass was released from the hospital a week after the beating, it ended up easier for me to stay at his place than to drive back and forth. Cindy Reiler comes out to help with feeding and heavy work. Azium Boardman just showed up. Said he'd cook, run errands till Jass could drive. It's weird, like in those days with Clinton again.

At first I was driving to work every day, until Marylou suggested I take some vacation. Since I haven't been off in three years, I've taken two weeks so far. Bowker complained at first but went along and hired Tom Tooley's mother to come answer phones and type. She's had years of doing farm budgets, so she can work on the numbers, too. I worry if I'll have a job when I go back. Maybe it'd be better if I didn't.

"Pay attention," Jass calls.

"I *am.* Let me do it if I'm supposed to do it." The colt has relaxed and dropped his head so far that he's in danger of stepping on the line. His coat is drying.

"Whoa, Buddy. That's enough for today, Jass. He's calm. Gave in." I gather the line and walk the colt to the big sliding doors that lead from the arena out to the stalls. Jass looks surprised.

"Open up, Azium." Best to keep these two in line. They could get sassy, like this colt. I turn Buddy into his stall to think about the lunge lesson.

"What's for dinner?" I ask Boardman, who's pacing in that jerky shuffle like an old rooster because his knees are bad.

"Spaghetti. Your friend Twyla called. Sounded upset."

"Why didn't you tell me? Jesus—" I run to the tack room to call her. Jass walks in, carefully sitting on the couch we made love on last spring. He grimaces and cradles the arm strapped to his chest. "Ribs or collar-bone?" I ask.

"Both. Back, too. Guess I'm a goner." He smiles at me.

I listen to the busy signal and slam the phone down. "Not till I'm through with you."

"The old man—" Jass gestures to the door.

"I know. I was just going to give you a kiss, if your mouth is better." I lean over him, bracing myself on the wall behind him, and press my lips against his. They've healed faster than the rest. They part, and his tongue touches my lips, asking. There's some magic in his mouth that shakes me and makes it hard not to fall into his lap. His tongue teases mine and slowly rounds the curves of my mouth. It's the kind of kissing that makes me feel like I'm already having sex. His good hand touches the neck of my pullover and moves lightly down the front. When the trailing fingers of his big hand touch my breasts, I run out of breath. He lets his hand continue past my waist until it rests between my legs. Heat flares through my jeans, then the hand is gone.

"Better call Twyla again," he murmurs. There's a sexy smile on his lips when I pull back. The swelling is almost gone from his eyes, leaving only dark bruises that give them sexy promise—bedroom eyes.

Straightening up, I glance down at his pants. The bulge is pushing at the seam. Jass catches my look. "We're doing it tonight if it kills me."

I nod. "It might. But I wish Azium would sleep more. It's creepy with him up at all hours." I don't tell Jass about Azium, Clinton, and me. How we'd catch the old man spying on us. Clinton would just laugh, but it made me nervous. Jass is the same way, like he's blind to the crazy way Azium stares at him.

While I'm waiting for Twyla to pick up her phone, Azium appears in the doorway. "Boyd Ziekert." He jerks his thumb toward the house.

Jass struggles to get up. "Shit."

"Why don't you just tell him?" I ask.

Azium and Jass look at me like I've just suggested we burn down the barn.

"I have to live here. Do business. Besides, I like to settle things my own way." Jass limps out the door behind Azium.

Jesus, what a pair. "Come *on,* Twyla, pick up the goddamn phone." I wait ten more rings, then slam down the receiver. "Fuck it." She's probably with one of the expectant daddies.

At the barn door I pause to watch the men, who are arguing by the house. Boyd has his hands on his hips and is still wearing his state patrol mirror sunglasses. Someday I'll tell him he doesn't need those. His eyes look like chips of beer bottle—they're scary enough. Jass has one foot on the porch steps, like he's going to abandon the whole thing any minute. Azium is above him on the porch, his hand fluttering wildly through his hair, his mouth open like he's having trouble breathing. Great, with our luck, he'll stroke out and we'll have a repeat performance to County. Azium reaches out and tugs at Jass's arm. Jass shakes him loose like he's an annoyance.

Now Boyd bangs on the side of the patrol car with his fists and takes a step forward. Azium jumps like he's being shot at. Jass pushes his hair off his face. He hasn't cut it in a while, and sometimes he lets me put it in a ponytail when no one else is around. I make him wash it every other day to keep it shiny, smelling good. Watching these three, I wonder if someone will get hit or hurt. You never ask that when women argue, but it's always there with men. With the horses, I notice, the females fight as often as males. If being human and civilized means anything, why is it that only the women stop pounding on each other?

I slip out of the barn and around to the back where we've parked my car so people on the road can't see it. I've got to find Twyla. She's due soon, but spending all this time with Jass, I've only been talking to her on the phone these days. She sounds more like she did at County. She's stopped whining. It's like she's high now, even though she's still losing weight. She'll be okay, though; Twyla's good at surviving. I keep telling myself that. The sticky heat of September isn't helping her, I bet. It makes your skin feel just like those burrs drying by the road are pressing into your skin. If you walk there, the ragweed sticks to your socks like yellow-green caterpillars that feel like they're crawling up your legs. You get these pinpricks now with everything drying. In summer things just push out of their skins practically, trying to grow, up and out, wet and green. Now it's the opposite, like the sun is making the skin shrink and dry. There's a little rattle as you pass the tall weeds. By October everything will have it. The corn goes from the green rustle and squeak of July to this rattle and crackle, like old newspapers. The fat ears of corn droop and harden against the stalks.

The sumac reddens first, and later the poison oak I have to be so careful about. Then the elms and maples and oaks, with the weeping willows almost the last. So you notice their branches turn gold like women's hair in fairy tales and sweep to the ground. Maybe the prince was only climbing a willow in "Rapunzel" after all. Hair like Twyla used to have. Will again, I correct. Across the hayfield, the alfalfa tints the stubble green. It won't stop until hard frost. Jass got three good cuttings this year. The fourth was lost because of his "accident," as we refer to it now. An accident of what? I want to ask him. Race? Color? Sex?

The brood mares are walking their fat bodies across their pasture. Their winter coats are starting to shag their legs and necks. Three pastures away, the weanlings startle and bounce as a group across their field. Their long legs get awkward sometimes, and they bump each other or stumble like a bunch of junior high kids, afraid to be on their own. They're as round and thick-furred as cockleburs today. Their thick short baby tails stick out like industrial broom heads. When they collide to a stop and turn back, they look puzzled; they've already forgotten what made them run. The first one drops his head to pull at the grass with baby teeth, and the others follow the experiment. Ten days ago we started the weaning. The mares seemed relieved to get rid of their babies. Most of them are carrying next year's crop. The babies set up such a ruckus, I didn't know whether I could stick it out. When they finally settled and began to eat without looking around for milk all the time, Cindy and I led them to their pasture. It's a lot easier having baby horses than baby humans, I decide. Wait till Twyla realizes that.

Jass has laid out the pastures and paddocks as spokes from the hub of the barn. It's easy to move animals in and out of places that way. He's replaced the barbed-wire fencing with board stained dark brown. He's got almost as much tied up in board fencing as he does in a couple of his best horses. Between the mares and weanlings, I notice that the yearlings, two- and three-year-olds, concentrate more on eating. In the mornings they buck and run, but by afternoon, when the sun is making them hot in their new winter coats, they sleep and graze, only coming to life again if it turns cool or at suppertime, when they jostle and crowd each other to get taken in first.

I should be going to Twyla's, but as I watch the fields, a flock of blackbirds swings across the sky in a huge graceful curve, as if they're one single bird instead of all those little ones. They flow up and down, scalloping the air in front of me, sometimes breaking apart as if a rock has been thrown into their midst, then rejoining and executing another design. Finally they settle in the windrow at the end of the pastures, and their calling reaches my ears. I'll miss it this winter when there's only the crows prancing and cawing at dawn and dusk, like a black clock.

"Honey?" I hear Boyd Ziekert's voice boom across the fields, almost echoing as it ricochets against the metal siding of the indoor arena. "Honey, come here." He hollers again, in his best sheriff tone.

I turn from my car and walk through the ragweed weeds and burrs back to the front of the barn facing the house. I wish Twyla were here to see this. All three of them are on the porch now. Boardman is handing out beers. With an apron on. At this distance he resembles one of those tall, strapping farm wives who start wearing their husband's overalls and flannel shirts. Underneath they wear T-shirts instead of bras, and their breasts hang flat and floppy like half-empty flour bags.

Boyd has taken off his sunglasses and hat and is loosening his tie as he accepts the beer. Jass is staring at me. Even from that distance I can feel his eyes. He says something, and Boyd looks at me, too. "Come here, Honey," he calls softly, the way he would to a shy dog he was trying to make friends with.

Nobody seems real happy. I take a look around me, as if it's the last time I'll be seeing this, sigh, and walk to the porch. Now each man has chosen a different place to put his attention. Jass is examining the knuckles on his right hand. Boyd is reading the beer bottle label as if he's never seen one before. And Boardman is busy polishing his librarian half-glasses with his apron.

When I reach the bottom step, he hands me a beer, already opened, and gestures for me to drink. I do. Everything's suddenly so quiet; the cricket chirp and bird twittering, the rustle of something in the bushes by the porch, and the occasional stamp of a hoof dislodging a fly are the only sounds we pick up. We're like radios, bringing in the raw static, then the true forms of voices and music. On the road a truck lumbers by, loaded with hay; we hear its muffled engine struggle over the washboard. Iowa, its big tires thump, Iowa.

"What do you want?" I ask finally, and take another slug of beer, liking the way the cold burns at my throat as I stand there.

"It's Twyla," Boyd says, bringing his eyes up to my face.

I don't want to ask. My head stops numb as the beer bottle chills my hand. "What? What about her? Boyd?"

The pause is an arctic year. "She's—she . . ." Boyd stands up, facing me. He leaves his bottle and the porch as he steps down to where I stand. "Wolf just called. She didn't make it, Honey. She was on her way, in the ambulance, and the baby was coming, and—"

I'm shaking my head. I can feel myself doing it, but it doesn't feel like me at all. "No—goddamn it, don't tell me that—damn it, no!" And Boyd has his arms around me, and I can't catch my breath against the hot wool smell of his jacket. I'm trying to cry, but the tears won't come out. This is so much worse than just tears.

"She just called here," I accuse, as if that means he's lying.

"She was on her way out the door. Wolf called the ambulance. She was almost unconscious when he found her."

"Found her?" These words seem so stupid, so meaningless—a jumble. I can't make them say no. That's all I want to hear—no, it's not true—but I can't find those words. I push away from Boyd. Jass is standing above me, staring. It's your fault, I tell him silently. Yours—and yours, I say silently to Boardman. You men, you make us put you first, take care of you before anyone else. You make mothers of us all, you bastards. It's your fault. You kept me away. I'd be with her, she'd be alive if I'd stayed with her, not you, Jass. I should have been with her.

Then it comes struggling out. "Twyla . . . oh, no—" And the tears come against my hate trying to hold them back, and my words disappear. For a while I'm in the cardboard box my crying pulls on top of me. I don't know I've closed my eyes until I open them and the light shines like a five-watt bulb. Cheap and flat. The way everything looks puts a taste in my mouth like I've been chewing the plastic off a cheap ballpoint. I can't make my fingers, my arms, move, so I just watch Boyd climb in his cruiser, dip his head at us, and start the engine I should hear but can't find the sound of. Finally, there is nothing to say as Jass holds me with his good arm and Boyd drives away. I hear each piece of gravel *ping* against his car. Each one, and I don't even know I'm listening, trying to hang on to something in this moment that I won't forget, that won't slide away in the hours and days to come. Each distinct note of metal chimed by stone.

14

Deficits

Twyla always said she'd donate her body to science. That was just another thing she lied about. I figure we all tell these lies, then we have to be careful we don't start believing them. Like Jass. He wanted to come, but I wouldn't let him. He didn't like Twyla alive,

why would he like her better now that she's dead? We fought until I had to move back to my place just to get some time to think about her.

I'm waiting for the service in the little room off the chapel. Reverend Prouty keeps ducking in and out, as if he expects me to have turned into a whole crowd of family while he's gone. But her parents are dead, and no one knows where to find her sister. Tom is probably somewhere being goofy. The other two men—I almost feel sorry for them.

I wait on the donated couch, covered with an avocado green throw. Two bright orange and green pillows sit together at one end like witnesses waiting to be called. The beige carpet with quiet stains is worn thin. Two armchairs, also in disguise with orange throws, guard the doorway. There's a little altar at one end of the room for anyone overrun by holiness. "Good luck," I mutter to it. The lavender mums next to the cross clash violently with the room, but that seems right. This could be Twyla's trailer, cleaned up. I was there again this morning. I keep wanting to go back to the scene of the crime. What was the crime? Letting her die. Making the choice for Jass over her. Listening to bullshit. Hers. Mine. Theirs. The pronouns seem like small pieces of failure when they line up that way. Small. I put my name, my failure, on the wall chart this morning back at my place.

I'm keeping track now, counting the cars that go by my trailer toward Twyla's. Wolf. Tom. Sonny. Sonny. Sonny. Wolf. Tom. Somehow, without Twyla, they seem like the steel balls that fall out of a plastic toy you smash. They lose their function without the levers and springs.

I look at my stupid navy pleated skirt and white blouse. I'm dressed like a Camp Fire girl. Stupid choices. Why does it come to this? I can ask the Rev, but he'll squeeze his hands and look distressed. He's learned that face. He never wears it at the municipal tennis courts in his white shorts and T-shirt. I've always wanted him to wear his collar when he's playing, but he never does.

First his head, then half of Reverend Prouty's body appears in the doorway. He's embarrassed, tentative about intruding. "It's filling up out there," he says in a stage whisper.

I nod, and he disappears again. A good "house," something we'll talk about for years to come in Divinity. I wonder where Tom and his mother are.

The organ, which has been squealing quietly for a while, picks up strength and bellers. They're getting ready. People will hush now, except for the whisper passed in the cup of a hand.

This time it's an arm, covered in black, that beckons me through the door crack. When I pull it open, there is another man beside the Reverend, his elbow stuck out like it's grown in that position. If I don't take it, what will he do? I feel Prouty's hand in the middle of my back, giving me a gentle push. I glance sideways and catch the expectant expression on his face as he looks down the short hallway to the chapel. We march out like bride and groom.

The usher deposits me in the front pew, next to Tom's mother. I try not to look at anything, but even the blond grain of the pew is saying something. If I keep my eyes away, I won't know what it is. But the body is a betrayer. My ears are listening despite me, and my eyes follow their lead. I'm turning to look before I can stop my shoulders. Behind me sit the other "girls" from the Curl-Y-Que Hair Shop, looking like aliens with their wild shellacked hairstyles. Behind them are scattered Simpy from the diner, Boyd Ziekert, Larue Carlson, Jonesy, and Twyla's customers. They seem to stare back at me like I might have killed her. No, I want to tell them, look at the brown roots of my red hair. She's the only one I trust to color it.

"Crazy," Clinton suddenly says. "Careful."

"Where have *you* been? How come you didn't warn me, you shit?

Just like always, huh, going gets rough, you disappear. Can't take the heat, Mr. Full of Advice?"

"It was 'heat' that made me take a break, Honey. Your little interlude with Terry sort of did me in. I figured you must want to be left alone if you're doing that stuff."

"Is that all it takes?" I accidentally say this out loud, and Mrs. Tooley leans over.

"What, dear?"

"When is Tom coming?" I whisper back.

Her eyes fill as she thinks about her son and her new granddaughter. "He had to change after he got back from the hospital."

I nod.

"They won't start without him, will they?" she asks anxiously, putting her hand on my arm.

"No." I pat her black-cloth-gloved fingers gently. We turn our heads simultaneously to stare at the wall opposite us. The sun outside the church makes the stained glass as bright as neon and almost as fake in happy blues and reds and yellows. The disciples march down the church walls like Rotarians: white men with good jobs, a Chamber of Commerce for God. Everything's so clean, as if they're always in their best clothes. Not a hair out of place. Even the passion of Christ has positive thinking stamped on it. There's not much blood, no dirt or sweat, and the agony looks about like Bowker's when a deal falls through. Why shouldn't it, though? He has an inside track—he knows this isn't going to last long. He'll climb down and go home when it gets dark. The angels of God look more like dashboard saints and Christmas tree ornaments than real angels. They probably couldn't fly any better than a chicken.

The organ hits an odd, wheezing note, and my head swivels to the front despite my intentions. The white enamel steel coffin looks like the commercial ice chest from Reese's A&P. I can see the baby pink satin lining peeking out in ruffles along the edges. Twyla'd shit.

"Lovely, isn't it? A friend of hers paid for it. Tom and I couldn't."

"I know." I pat her hand, which has remained weightless on my arm. I don't tell her that I know which "friend" that would be, too. I wonder if Wolfgang is here. Avoiding the coffin again, I swing my eyes upward, catching the heaven-turned eyes of Christ—He's so out of it, He doesn't recognize me—and look around the church for Wolf. He's not here. The place is only half-full, so it's not hard to see who's made it. There's more women than men. Strange, since Twyla knew more men than women. I guess they're too embarrassed, or their wives and girlfriends have come to see that she's really dead. Like villagers in a Dracula movie, they want to make sure the wooden stake is secure in that heart.

As I'm inspecting the crowd, the door opens and Tom is framed dark against the bright September day. When he steps forward and the usher tries to give him a program, I notice his arms holding something as he sits carefully.

The single choked cry of the baby makes Mrs. Tooley turn. "Oh . . ." She puts her hand to her mouth. We look at each other. Tom has taken the baby from the hospital and brought her to her mother's funeral. The image of careless Tom handling that tiny life makes both of us shift uncomfortably, as if we'll be called on to rescue her momentarily. A whisper and rustling passes through the people behind us. The organist pushes the squall of music louder, as if she suspects us of resisting her. "Calm down," I whisper to her.

When I look back again, Tom, dressed in black with his dark hair newly oiled, flipped, and slicked, is very competently holding the baby. Its wrinkled pink face nestles in an armful of white blankets he has carefully wrapped her in. He alternates between looking up at the coffin and down at the baby. Expressions of grief, confusion, and joy flick across his face. He is sitting up for the first time in his life.

"Oh, dear." Mrs. Tooley's hand grips my arm tighter.

I pat her hand again.

Reverend Prouty stalks to the podium now, sets the hymnal down with a thud, and grips the wooden edges with huge hands. He's almost too big to be a preacher. The equipment of his job looks too delicate when he touches it.

"Let us pray," he begins.

I try to, but it's only Twyla as she was recently that I see—starving, gray, determined, like in some phony Hollywood pioneer movie. I don't have anything to say to God. Jesus. I figure they bowed out a long time ago. So I talk to Clinton instead.

"How come you didn't tell me about her, Clinton? If you know so much, why didn't you warn me? I could've—"

"No, you couldn't have. Everyone makes their own way."

"I don't believe that. I could've stopped it, I *know* that."

"What, forced food in her mouth? Lived with her? Made her body *not* be sick?"

"Thank you, Lord," Prouty says in his too loud voice.

I squeeze my eyes extra tight. I won't give in, but the tears begin anyway, freely, naturally, as if I am going to cry forever now, so I might as well get used to it.

"You can't stop other people from living their lives the way they want."

"Just shut up, okay?"

"Today, we are gathered to say good-bye," Prouty begins. I grab my purse and yank it open, searching for Kleenex. A hand holding a small white cotton handkerchief appears in front of me. I take it and nod thanks to Mrs. Tooley.

I try not to listen to the service. Twyla wouldn't have, why should I? It's the usual stuff, talking, singing, talking. The idiots from the shop say their pieces—funny hair stories—but since I know Twyla hated them, I won't listen or smile. They were dumb shits to her.

It is the loud, familiar sigh from the back, which occurs in the lull as Prouty is flipping the tissuey pages of his Bible, that makes me turn around. The usher is trying to hand Baby a program and lead her forward to an empty pew, but she's standing her ground, blocking the light from outside. Then a taller, thinner shadow appears behind her wide one, and she moves to follow the usher.

Sonny Boy stands alone, stunned, like a shot steer just before it drops. He seems afraid of the coffin, of Twyla, as if it's sending a force field pushing against him. I expect to see him grab both sides of the doorway to keep from being blown backward out of the church.

"Come here," Baby says, not even trying to whisper. She is safely wedged in a pew, holding the maroon hymnal like a hall pass. Sonny Boy walks numbly. For once he looks as graceless and destroyed as the rest of us. His light blue shirt must be yesterday's. His navy sport jacket hangs oddly, as if it's been on a bent hanger for years. His gray trousers are too tight and too short. He looks like a kid who insisted on dressing himself for the first time.

"Sit," Baby orders. She's a table-size version of bright flowers splashed on white. Jesus, this is a *funeral,* not a church social, I want to tell her.

Sonny Boy sits tentatively on the edge of his seat, leaving one leg in the aisle, gripping the pew back in front of him. He stares at the coffin. I can tell he's torn between wanting to run up here and wanting to run back out.

"Good luck," I whisper to him, and Mrs. Tooley pats my arm again.

* * *

Sitting here, I remember the last time we went to the movies together, before I even knew she was pregnant. We had to go to Pottersville because Twyla said, "I'm sick of that fat greasy Mahoney at the Iowa. He even sweats grease. His head looks like a piece of that old popcorn he tries to palm off on us. And that 'free' candy he keeps giving me? It's so stale, I have to dump it on the floor when I sit down."

We saw *Reds* that night, and on the way home I felt so moony over Warren Beatty, I told her, "God, when he says, 'Honey, don't leave me,' to Diane Keaton, begging and crying . . ."

Twyla just looked at me. "What about it?"

I kept my eyes on the road since I was driving. "Well, I would've gone across Siberia for him, too."

"That was Finland, you dope."

"Yeah, well, I'd still go across Siberia. Those eyes, God, those *sweet* eyes. I'd love a man with eyes like that."

As we were passing Sorenson's dairy and the manure smell flooded the car, she said, "It stinks worse than the girl's john at the Blacksmith on Saturday night. But Warren Beatty, I wouldn't. I wouldn't go anywhere I didn't want to go just for a man. Especially one with those damn sweet eyes." And I could tell she wanted to add, You shouldn't, either.

She was probably right about Clinton and Jass. But Jake, where did he fit in? And what about her? How far did Twyla get following her own advice? Pregnant, didn't know who the daddy was, and now dead. I feel so bitter now. Pissed off to be sitting here at her funeral.

We drove a ways more that night before I said something about the smell of spring. "It always seems like I'm walking the bottom of a pond when the air's so thick and green. Feels like it catches in your nose, and you can't get your breath, doesn't it?"

When I got in one of those moods, Twyla usually let me ramble. She was a good friend that way. Once she said, "You have a way of making things interesting, even if you're mostly wrong about them."

I remember I said, "Nights like this I'd miss. If you could miss anything afterward. I mean, I worry about regretting things, like Clinton."

"What do you mean?" Whenever I brought him up, Twyla got uptight.

"Twyla, look at the way those little farm lights wink back at us out there. It's so good and predictable."

"Yeah, that's what's wrong with it. I've seen enough cows to last a lifetime. When I get to Chicago or New York . . ."

"I just wish I had a house instead of a trailer. That's all I want. Someplace solid, built *into* the ground, not just resting on top."

Twyla laughed. "We got time enough for that, Honey, after we're dead."

We rounded a curve, and the car wobbled, then straightened.

"Careful."

"God, you sound like Jake, Twyla."

Twyla shifted on her seat. "That's the first time you've mentioned him in weeks, Honey. I don't see how you can be divorced such a short time and never even think about Jake—like he's been vaporized or something. And then Clinton, who's been dead, what, fourteen or fifteen years, he's like *living* here still. It's weird. Don't you ever hear from Jake, even?"

I shake my head.

"You never *did* tell me exactly what happened, you know."

"What can I say? Things fell apart."

She smacked her gum. "Well, I never thought it'd last as long as it did, you know."

"Thanks, Twyla. Why didn't you tell me, save me the trouble?"

"You never listen to me about men. Heard from Jass lately?"

"No. I guess this is going to be his deal—check in just often enough to drive me crazy."

"Well, you don't have to be home the next time he calls, you know."

"I couldn't not answer the phone. I'm not made that way. Besides, he can always find me at work, like last time."

"Stand him up. That's what I'd do. He'd get the message."

"Yeah, I suppose." I had let the silence of the countryside fill in the rest of it. I could no more stand him up than I could ignore the phone ringing. I wasn't in so much demand that I could afford those luxuries. Not like Twyla, at least. Men loved being insulted, ignored, hurt, by her. At least it was *some* form of attention.

We were quiet then until I pulled in front of her trailer. During the drive there I had decided to try to tell her about Clinton, his visits.

"Twyla, listen, it's weird, okay? I know that, but I have to tell someone." I pulled on the hazard lights and waited for a minute while they click-clicked in the dark.

"What's going on, girl?"

"Okay." I took a deep breath and shut down the head and panel lights. "Well, it's like I can hear Clinton."

"What!"

"No, really, Twyla. Like his voice is here. I hear him."

"*Honey,* this is bullshit. Excuse me, but this is plain bullshit." She rolled up the window, almost jerking the handle off as she yanked it around. "Goddamn mosquitoes. Roll your windows up."

"Twyla, seriously. I think I hear him, and I don't know what to do."

Hearing the catch in my voice as she wound the window, she reached out to pat my shoulder. "Okay, I'm sorry. I just hear such crap all day from the customers, I wasn't ready to get it from you. Not that what you're saying is crap. Sorry. Didn't mean that, either."

I turned to face her. "You didn't ever know him the way I did, Twyla."

She nodded.

"You thought he was a goof, but he wasn't. He was . . . well, I don't know. He was different from that. God, I miss him. It drives me crazy sometimes to be without him. I mean, it's like my arm or a leg or something inside, a lung, that's been taken away." I covered my face with my hands, and for a few minutes the car was dark and silent except for the clicking hazards and the seesawing croak of the frogs in the ditch beside the road.

"Honey? Hey, Honey, talk to me." She rubbed my arm, and I dropped my hands. In the moonlight I knew what she saw—what Clinton always told me he saw. "Your face has this crazy purity," he said, "like an eight-year-old girl, completely trusting everything and everyone. But it keeps changing places with this hurt look, the kind you see in pictures of kids after they survive a war or real bad poverty. Their eyes look way too old for them. You got nothing to offer them. You both know that. 'Take 'em out and shoot 'em now, save yourself the trouble later,' I want to say every time I see that look." He scared me. Maybe it was true. Maybe I couldn't survive this town, my family, my life here. Maybe I wasn't meant to be here—like Billy Bond or Clinton.

"You want to tell me I'm crazy, don't you. Well, I'm not."

"If there *was* a way for Clinton to come back, he'd do it. I know that. So would I, Honey. It's just that . . . well, I gotta go now." She opened the car door.

I had nodded. She probably didn't think I saw Sonny Boy's car, the way it fit almost perfectly in the shadows behind the trailer.

Now I wonder if Twyla will try to talk to me, try to come back. Or if being dead is just a big relief for her.

As the people begin singing "Amazing Grace" a few notes out of step with the organ, they all get up and march past the coffin as if Twyla

Tooley is a dead president or movie star. I see a few fingers reach out to touch her, then jerk away. The beautiful woman we knew and feared or loved is gone. We're not sure exactly what this substitute is. She looks like one of those thirties' dust bowl pictures. An Oakie who fell into a *Glamour* magazine make-over contest. The girls at the Curl-Y-Que have had their revenge. Twyla's hair is teased and sprayed and curled into a huge Dolly Parton style. The color is gone, though, and the hair is dry and stiff as a cheap wig. Her starved face grew old over the past weeks. The thick orange makeup can't totally hide the dark splotches beneath her eyes, the caved-in look of her cheeks.

In her hands, crossed peacefully on her chest in a way Twyla would never do, is a white rose. Someone has glued blue-red Lee Press-On Nails over her chewed ones. The effect is so cheap, it looks like a joke. I feel myself smiling and have to cover my mouth with my hand. She's wearing a pink floor-length taffeta that must have been her prom dress in high school.

I stop beside the coffin, and people flow around me like water until at last it's just Baby and Sonny Boy, who stand opposite. She is holding his hand. To keep him from running, I suppose. I expect Baby to say, See, I told you she's dead, but she doesn't. They just stand there until Baby begins to snuffle and dig for a Kleenex. While she's drying her eyes, Sonny Boy reaches out with a trembling hand to Twyla's. Before I can say anything, he's snapped off one of the fake fingernails and, clutching it in his hand, is running down the aisle. Baby and I watch as he stumbles, catches himself, and, with his coat flapping behind him, leaps the stairs and disappears in the bright September light.

"He made me come," Baby explains. "Believe me, I wouldn't have. It reminds me too much of Mama."

I've grown so numb, I can't react. I don't even know whether I'm crying or not.

We notice Tom approaching the coffin at the same moment and step back automatically. The baby looks around, blinking its blue eyes. Tiny spasms of expression move her face, but there is something still unfocused about her eyes, like she doesn't know where she is yet.

Tom stands close to the coffin and tips the baby toward it. "There she is, Twyla. She's real pretty. Tamara. Tamara Julia, like you wanted."

Tom is holding Tamara facedown over Twyla's body, lowering her until the two faces touch. When the baby whimpers, he snatches her back, wrapping her protectively in the blankets as if *we* might try to do something to her. Tears begin to trickle down his face as the organ finishes the last notes of "Amazing Grace."

The ushers and men from Kramer's Mortuary are standing around us discreetly, waiting to close up the coffin. I have a sudden moment of panic now. Don't go, I want to say. She's still alive. I concentrate and will her to move—even a fingernail—so I can fight them off, hang on to Twyla forever. But we all step back and yield the body to the men. In a minute she's being rolled out like a Frigidaire on its side. Twyla would have liked that idea.

At the graveyard—I can't bring myself to use that town word, "cemetery"—there are fewer people standing around, so it's easy to spot Wolf's black Riviera hovering around the curve of the gravel drive. I guess he's the one I feel sorry for. He can't even get out of his car with his grief. The hole is banked with flowers, big good-luck horseshoes in white and red, as if she's won a trip somewhere. The fresh dirt is discreetly covered with Astroturf, the cheap, too bright green stuff we lay around our trailers to pretend we have real yards. A few clods of dark brown dirt have tumbled onto the real grass around the hole. Twyla looked like she was going trick-or-treating in that outfit they put on her. If she's really going to be all right, like Prouty says, then why disguise death so much?

I stand between Mrs. Tooley and Baby now. The men have put the coffin on a scaffolding over the hole. We're all supposed to pretend the hole isn't there. The coffin is draped with a huge blanket of white carnations with T'N'T'N'T spelled out in pink. Tom, still holding the baby, stands at the head of the grave. He's the man of the house now, he can sit at the head of the table. Have the biggest and best portion of everything.

As Prouty begins the prayers, I glimpse Sonny Boy a few yards behind us, halfway between his car and the grave, as if he can't make up his mind whether to come closer or run away. His hands are jammed in his pockets, and his head is bowed.

"He's back there, isn't he?" Baby whispers.

I nod, watching him take a few steps closer.

"He's scared," Baby says.

Too bad, I want to say. Too damn bad.

When Prouty gets to the part where we're supposed to mumble along, a gusty wind starts blowing. Mrs. Tooley anchors her black pillbox hat with one hand, and the Reverend disciplines the flimsy pages of his Bible.

Finally we're all picking up the crumbles of dirt and dropping them on the coffin, splotching the white with dark. And with Tom watching, Sonny Boy, having taken off his pants, breaks between Baby and me and, ripping the flowers away, tries to open the coffin latch. He fumbles with the catch, squatting, his bare ass sticking out at us. When the lid pops up with a hiss, Sonny pauses, then puts one leg in like he's testing the water, looks around hopelessly, and bends toward the body. Boyd Ziekert and one of the mortuary men who have been standing with their jaws gaping, step forward and grab an arm and a leg as he starts to lie down beside Twyla. Her dress twists in the struggle, rising up her thighs to the white cotton underpants that have been placed over her panty hose. The men pull, and Sonny tries to anchor himself with her arms. When she begins to rise, following him as he's dragged from the coffin, Sonny looks in horror at the cold solid flesh of her arms, screams, and drops them. He's frantically rubbing his hands on his suit jacket as he's led away.

Twyla's right, he is hung better than Jesus Christ. She must be laughing her head off if she can see this: Sonny Boy, pantless, being led to the sheriff's car, howling; Wolfgang, paying for everything but afraid to get out of his car because even all his money can't protect him from his wife, Faye; and Tom, with clean fingernails for the first time since he was ten, standing up straight with the baby in his arms like he's done it a hundred times before.

"He's such a natural father," Mrs. Tooley sighs as she turns to leave, ignoring Sonny Boy's antics as if that is the normal course of affairs in Divinity.

Baby is crying for real now. After Sonny Boy's display she doesn't know how she'll hold her head up. Get a strong neck, I could advise her. But she floats away.

I can't bring myself to leave yet. It's like Tom and I are having a contest to see who'll get the last word in before the hydraulic works and Twyla go crashing into the dark hole. I keep pressing and crumbling my handful of dirt. It seems wrong to make this the last thing I'll ever give her. I wish I had a six-pack or a pint of tequila—something she could take with her instead of just sending her away in that stupid dress and hairdo.

Tom and I are standing there, waiting each other out, when Jass limps up to the coffin and lays a big bunch of goldenrod and purple aster on the coffin. Pasture flowers. They're so simple, I want to cry, but I don't have anything left. Then he turns and puts his good arm around me. "Say good-bye now, Honey."

I kiss my fist and fling the dirt, trying to hang on to each *ping* as it bounces on the metal surface.

Jass tightens his arm around my shoulders and turns. I go with him, feeling the rush of hopelessness and failure pushing everything else out of the way. When I look back, Tom is still standing there with the baby, like one of those dogs faithful to its dead master. Like Sonny Boy was never even there.

15

Larue Carlson

The air coming in through the door we've propped open is a notch too warm, like the press of another person's hand on your skin, their breath fogging your forehead in July. It's one of those Indian summer days in October when everything prickles and irritates. Bowker and Marylou have been sniffling and sneezing all day. Allergies. Hay fever. Not me. I just feel like stabbing someone with my Bic ballpoint pen. The numbers in the accounts payable don't make sense.

I hallucinate their marriages and divorces. Bowker must be up to fancy footwork again. One call to the IRS and he'd spend the next fifteen years explaining. When I tell Marylou that, she just smiles like she has a secret.

A few minutes ago Bowker called her to the storage closet to help him stack centennial flyers. He's just lucky it was her; the mood I'm in he'd be wearing a stapler down there.

Last night Jass and I decided to stop seeing each other for a while.

"Give you a chance to recover," he said.

"Meaning what?" I asked, knowing exactly what he meant. Lately I've been in one of those frames of mind where you want to make other people do stuff, say things out loud that can hurt you—or them. He didn't fall for it, though. He just shook his head and climbed out of bed. I didn't offer to help as he clumsily pulled on his jeans. His collarbone is healing a little slowly.

Seeing his slim hips and muscled torso held briefly in the candlelight that way didn't move me. It was just another curiosity. More like the candle itself Jass had lit to make love by. I felt as numb as the wax dripping and freezing in a little puddle at the bottom.

"See you around," I called to his retreating back. He slammed the door on his way out.

I guess he didn't like the idea of making love to a corpse, but I don't want to be moved by him now. I can't fake it, either. Every time he tried to kiss me, I closed my mouth, refused the sour taste of his tongue. I've started picking on him, too, in my head. I make fun of him—his greasy, too long hair, his dirty-looking skin, the musky smell of horses. It's good he left, before I said or did something bad.

There's a burst of giggling, and the closet door swings open with Bowker's hand on the knob. He stretches his arm and leans as if he's letting Marylou out of his house. She brushes his body as she passes, adjusting her blouse and pulling her skirt straight. I feel a twinge between my legs as I watch. Stop it, I order, you're supposed to be dead. In the bathroom, Marylou is running water. Washing him off her hands, no doubt.

"Honey?" Bowker says, pulling his tie up to his collar. I'm so fascinated by the fat knot and the way it makes his collar points rise and stick out, I don't answer.

"Honey!" He says it louder. "Take the papers on my desk over to Larue Carlson, wait for a signature, then come back and close up. Marylou and I have to, um, business outside town. Understand?"

I nod and look extra hard at Marylou, who is busy gathering her purse and sweater. Her kids must need winter coats. Bonus time. His and hers. She avoids my eyes as they leave. Why not? Who the hell am I to judge?

Walking to Larue's, I'm so tired I stumble on the piles of leaves by the curbs. I want to lie down on the sidewalk—give in, give up. I take a detour that adds two blocks so I don't have to go past the Curl-Y-Que where Twyla worked. The "girls" played hearts for her customers, I heard. Dying can be beneficial.

"Honey," Clinton begins.

"Don't even start," I tell him. You'd think he'd be happy now with Jass gone and Twyla not around to bad-mouth him. But no. He's hassling me worse than ever. What does he want from me?

Before I can think about that, I'm at Larue's. The big two-story white frame house stands stiff as a Methodist lady, Miss Ethel, maybe. The top is crowned with a cupola, like an old school. Sometimes when I'm out prowling late at night, I see someone up there pacing from side to side or perched on the railing. Smoking. I imagine it's Larue.

I go around back and take the stairs. Larue will be up there this time of day unless there's a big game in the parlor below. Now that the seed company shut down, and the canning company's only seasonal, Larue Carlson's game might be the only place a man can make an extra buck. Outside of driving all over two counties, that is.

I don't even have a chance to knock before Larue's calling for me to come in, it's unlocked. She's left the big door open and has all the windows thrown up. Still, it's pretty stifling as I stand in the kitchen.

"It's me, Larue, Honey Parrish, with some papers from—"

"I know. Why don't you take a load off while I get my glasses and a pen." She points toward a pressed back oak chair set that surrounds a huge round oak table in one corner. Sitting there, I realize that this is a big old-fashioned country kitchen, the size of most people's living rooms. There's a tin ceiling painted off white and a brick fireplace on the back wall. The floor is covered with orange brick tiles. Although she has brand-new stainless-steel appliances, there's an old-fashioned icebox that looks like it was attacked by a bunch of viny plants. There's even an easy chair next to a small table stacked with books in one corner near the fireplace. And pictures on the walls.

"Different, huh?" Larue says as she goes to the fridge. "Want something cold? Sparkling water? Pop? Beer?"

I shrug.

"Come on, you have to have an opinion on that."

"Surprise me."

She stiffens but gets something out and clunks it on the table in front of me.

I stare at the green bottle. Cold Spring mineral water? That's what I get for being a smart ass, I guess. The bottle seems to stare back defiantly.

"Here." Larue reaches over me and twists off the cap. "Ice?"

When I shrug, she sits down, too. I watch as she uncaps her water and pours it over ice in a glass. It fizzes coolly. She takes a long drink and survives, so I try it.

"Not bad, huh?" Larue smiles.

I smile back despite myself. She's not wearing the doll makeup, and I can see the age sitting in little wrinkles around her eyes and mouth. She doesn't look too bad, really. A little lumpy at the jawline, maybe. She's wearing a pink velour sweatsuit, though it must be eighty-five degrees in the kitchen. She daintily pats a Kleenex at her throat and lips. "Hot."

I nod.

"I had the men take down the air conditioners for winter, now this . . ." She gestures around us like the whole room is sweating. "I never miss a chance to sweat, though. Good for you, keeps the skin young." She pushes the sleeves of her top past her elbows.

"You want to read these first?" I pick up the papers and place them in front of her. When she pulls them closer, I get a whiff of her Shalimar perfume lying heavily on the still air. She's almost as bad as Jass, crowding me now.

She glances at the papers, shaking her head. "I never do. Bowker'd be crazy to cheat me. He's cheap, but he's not crazy." She laughs, and I smile.

Signing the papers, she asks, "Heard from Jake?" without even looking up.

My stomach tightens for a moment at his name, so unexpected it feels like a slap stinging my face. I shake my head, take a sip of mineral water, and pretend to read the form lying on the table in front of me. It's the one we've sent out to everyone in town to apply for a centennial activity or sponsorship. What would *she* be doing that'd be public?

"Just as well. We may be cousins, but he's a different tribe as far as I'm concerned. What did you ever see in him, anyway? Aside from his looks, I mean." She signs the last page and looks up. Her half-glasses perched on her nose that way make her look her age. I have an urge to tell her so.

"Can't say I married anyone for any better reasons myself. Talk about a gallery of losers." She laughs. "How's that Jasper doing these days?" She leans back and takes another drink from her glass, watching me closely.

"He's okay, I guess. I don't know, really, I'm not—"

She waves her hand. "Sorry. Prying as usual. When I first moved here I got in the habit of trying to keep on top of things, keep track. In my business you kind of have to, you know?"

I nod, watching my fingers, short, stubby, knobby knuckles too big to slide rings over easily. Larue's are long and elegant, like those of ladies in TV commercials. Her red fingernail polish looks like delicate daggers at the tips of her fingers. If I wear polish, it looks like red balls I'm comically juggling on each finger.

"You'd be surprised at what I see, what I know." Larue watches me over the rim of her glass as she drinks.

"Okay." I'm not biting today.

"Your family, for instance. Julius is still living with Baby, and Louverna has half the county—she's related to everyone in the world—coming by to talk to him about it."

I smile and nod. "I believe it."

"Louverna's a tough old hen, though, she won't give up till he's living in married bliss in Pottersville. Even if she has to take a contract out on Baby to make it happen."

I'm watching the last of the summer flies crawling on the heat of the windowsill, buzzing helplessly against the wire screen, so I don't catch the beginning of the next sentence.

". . . and Leigh Hunt will probably ask her out in the next week or so."

"Who?"

"Baby, your sister? She's formed the Famous Fats Club? And Leigh is real taken with her, I hear."

"Maybe Louverna's paying him," I say.

"Hardly. He's rich as God, practically. More likely he'll pay Louverna to get her husband out of there so he has a clear track. When the Hunts want something, they generally get it. Baby's lucky."

I sip my water. "Maybe. If you think having a man is any sort of luck. I'm not sure I do."

"You're sort of grim today. What's biting your behind?"

I shrug.

"It wasn't men killed Twyla, you know. She *had* a choice in the matter, Honey. Wolf would have flown her to the Mayo if she'd wanted. She was too self-centered to believe anything could really go wrong in her life. She thought she had it all under control." Larue gets up and goes to the table by the easy chair. She comes back with a cigarette and lighter. "I let myself have one a day."

I'm trying to ignore her remarks about Twyla because they're the things I've said to myself. I hate it when other people have the same insights I do these days.

"You know it, too, don't you?" Larue blows out a thin stream of elegant smoke. If more people looked like that, everyone would be smoking. She's probably the only person in town who can get away with it, though.

"I had a brother who drank himself to death—same difference. Nobody could tell him anything. He knew it all, and now he does." She stubs out the cigarette in an ashtray on the table. "Yuk. That tasted terrible. I just do it to remind myself how bad it is. I used to smoke two packs a day. Almost died of the pneumonia one winter. Doc found spots on my lungs. I left Chicago as fast as I could. Came back home and opened up here." She spreads her arms.

"You've done okay," I agree. Better, really, but she knows that.

Larue stares at me for a minute, and I get nervous. "What?" I finally ask.

"I'm just wondering about you. You and that family of yours. You'd probably be better off living away from here, you know that, don't you?"

I'm getting tired of her attitude. Who is *she,* anyway?

"Well, I'm here. This is my home. And be careful about my family—they're all I've got." I'm getting up when Larue puts out a hand.

"Relax. No biggie, okay? You look like you need a friend, that's all. Want some more water? With ice this time or are you still going to be stubborn?"

I nod and smile. "Thanks, yeah."

"You wear your heart on your sleeve, you know. God, don't ever play cards." She puts the glass and bottle down in front of me. "What's wrong with Jasper and you? Tell your old aunt Larue. I'm great with men."

The last woman who claimed that is dead, I want to say. But she's trying to be nice, even if her attitude does get on my nerves. I let my eyes circle the room for a minute, trying to figure out what to say. "Those real paintings?" I ask finally.

"Yes. If you mean by 'real' are they original. Yes. In Chicago I invested in work by young artists. It was a cheap way of building a collection of things I like. Some abstracts, like those over there, some lithos and watercolors in the other room, and some more recent new representational."

"Oh." I'm impressed and confused.

"I'll explain it the next time." She says this like we're going to make this a regular feature. "Why don't you answer my question now?"

I can see why she's a successful businessperson. She has good timing and real authority. I find myself opening my mouth to answer before I can stop it. "He wants me to . . . he wants things to be . . . oh, you know—he wants me to be a certain person, the one I was only I'm not now because—"

"That explains a lot. You could get a job writing for the government."

"Christ, Larue, I hardly know you."

"We were cousins, for a while, at least. Through Jake?" She grins. "Just family, Honey."

There's something about Larue that charms me. I guess I miss being close to another woman because I feel myself leaning toward her side, her view of things. Let go, the voice in my head urges, tell her everything. What can she do to hurt you?

"I just got so mad at all of them when Twyla died. Don't give me a lecture, I know it's not their fault. It's the way I feel. I was out taking care of Jass, and I should've been with Twyla. That's all. Now I can't let him close again. I try. It's driving him crazy, as close as we were before. I just feel like everything's doomed anyway, so why try?" I lean back, fold my arms, and look at her pale blue eyes. They seem curious, disarming.

"You'll get over it. He wants to fuck you into his life. He's probably scared. You're trying to juggle all this other stuff. Don't worry. If it's meant to be, it'll happen."

"Jesus, Larue, what kind of comfort is that?" I laugh bitterly.

"You didn't say you wanted comfort."

"Yeah, but this Doris Day crap, 'What will be will be,' is pretty worthless, don't you think? My whole life people in Divinity have said that. It's like they think their lives are weather—acts of God and climate. A drought . . . well, it's meant to be. Murder? Mayhem? Meant to be. Jass gets beat nearly to death—just a freak storm, can't stop it, have to go with it. Come on, I thought you were a step above that shit."

Larue stares at me coolly. "You're an honest bitch, aren't you?"

"Only lately."

"You want to know who or what's behind those things around here? Ask your brother, ask Sonny Boy Parrish. But you want to know about love, you ask me. That's what I *do* know. I've had a few more tries at it than you have, let me tell you." She taps her long nails on the smooth oak tabletop.

"What about you, what are you going to do? Spend the rest of your life viewing the wreckage, or are you going to get back on the train and ride? You've had some bad luck lately." She raises her hand to stop me when I open my mouth to disagree. "I know. All your life. People have died around you. Close to you. It happens, Honey. Eventually, everyone ends up dead. It's so simple, it sounds stupid, right? The thing is, you can let it mark you, stop you from living. You end up tapping your toe, counting down the minutes, the hours and years, till you're dead, too. Then what—what was the point of being around to begin with? Some sort of death watch? If that's all life is, we should all put a gun to our head now." She pauses and rubs her hand back and forth on her forearm as if to reassure herself.

"Let me tell you something, you let yourself go on this way, let yourself stop feeling and start counting instead, things will happen that'll make all this business so far look like 'Sleeping Beauty.' You sit back and let that train with Jass and the rest of your life go on without you, and you'll end up as someone you don't even know or like. It can happen like that." She snaps her fingers in front of my face, making me jump.

"Larue . . ." She's scaring me. I'll have to get her off my life.

She laughs carelessly and tosses her white blond hair. Even though she's without makeup, her hair is a carefully styled cloud around her face. "I know. Just listen to this old crow, Honey. She knows a lot. How do you think I got all this?" She spreads her arms like she's at some mansion instead of a house on a side street in Divinity, patrolled by the fire sirens night and day.

"Doesn't look like much, but I started with nothing. And coming from nothing, this is a whole helluva lot, Honey. I may not be the favorite of some people here, but I run my own business, I pay my bills, and I please myself. That's what makes me happiest. You ought to try it."

Her smugness has excluded the town gossip that says she does more than run a poker game in some of the dark rooms up here. But that's her business, I figure, not mine. Actually, it's the men in town who cause Larue the most trouble. They can't stand the idea that a good-looking woman who isn't married is happy. Their stories about her always have sex in them. That's how we know the men have started it. It's hard to tell which makes them feel worse: Larue getting it or not getting it. The women only focus on her because the men take such an interest in her.

"Larue, can I just ask you one thing?"

"Sure, what is it—as long as it's not how much money I make—that's between me and my maker." She winks, flirting with me a bit, like she can't help herself.

"What happened that time Fred Seagrim's place caught on fire? A lot of people blame you."

"That was so funny. Wish you could've seen them—Daffy Duck and all the other Loony Tunes."

"Well, what?"

She tries to stop laughing. "Some of the volunteer fire guys were here playing, and Smitty was supposed to answer the phones in the station, you know. I guess he was in the john with his pants down reading girlie magazines. Took him twenty rings. By that time the fire'd spread from Seagrim's hay barn to the corn crib, and they were wetting the house down with a garden hose Mrs. had on the roof. Fred was pissed.

"Smitty put out the call, but he knew a lot of the guys were over here in a big game. At first I wouldn't let him in the door because of the pot. None of this coming and going when it gets over a couple hundred. Then he managed to sputter it out and comes bursting in just as Harold Spitzer is hauling in the line, bluffing his way straight down the middle. When Smitty said it was a call, Harold said, 'Wait a minute, 'til we finish this hand.' And Smitty said, 'What for, you only got a lousy pair of threes.' I grabbed Harold's arm before he could break Smitty's jaw and made 'em calm down. Had to promise another hand after the fire was out. Smitty doesn't play poker, you see. Let me take a drink, there's more."

She finishes the glass of mineral water, chasing the cubes with the pink tip of her tongue. "About then everyone woke up to the fact that they'd better haul ass out to Seagrim's before the whole farm burned down. As it was, most of them were so tired and drunk that they lost the barn and corn crib entirely. The new dairy barn was just starting to smolder, and they had to work like all hell to keep the silo from going up. It was some fire, sparks flying around and catching on little patches of dried-up grass. Seagrim was running like a crazy man, threatening everyone with a lawsuit because he paid his dues as a volunteer, he supported them, and by God they let his barn and corn crib burn up, and if even one single spark got on his house . . . The men did take that to heart and climbed up to help his wife wet it good until it started leaking into the attic. Seagrim's wife only remembered to shut the upstairs windows after they started spraying, so they had a fair amount of mop-up in the bedrooms, too, but the house never caught. It took over five hours to get everything out because it was so dry. They'd just get it all wetted down and the air would dry it and it'd start up again. The poker players worked extra hard because they were all thinking about that two-hundred-dollar pot I was holding. I make some of that back in food and liquor and a percentage for the house.

"Things would have worked out okay for everyone if Smitty hadn't decided to show up about the time the fire was put out. He came barreling down the road in that old Rambler of his, raising dust and shouting once he caught sight of the ruins. He drove into the farmyard, spinning up dust and gravel, and burst out of the car crying, tears actually running down his face, shaking his fist at Harold and the boys as they stood around exhausted and dirty. 'I told 'em, Mr. Seagrim, I told 'em to leave that gosh-darn poker game and come to put out your fire, I told 'em, I swear I told 'em! They didn't care, they just wouldn't come.'

"Seagrim had just gotten calmed down when Smitty arrived, but when he heard that, he started in again. It took everyone another forty-five minutes of hard talking to convince Seagrim to keep his mouth shut or he might not get the insurance money. And the boys had to promise to throw in free labor when he rebuilt. Smitty scooted out of there when no one was looking. He knew what was good for him. That was the last time he came to my place. He always phones the alarms now. I make them bail out faster than a drill sergeant. Once the story got around, though, I ended up with all the blame. The wives especially wanted to believe that their men would stay home and wait for fire calls like they should if it weren't for me. Funny, huh?"

I nod and laugh with her.

"Necessary illusion," Clinton used to call that kind of blaming. "Can't take everything away from people, then they get wobbly, like a car with one wheel gone, and they're likely to crash into something, most likely you. This way, you keep them on the road, and you just maneuver around them. Honey, just learn to drive defensively, didn't they tell you that in driver's ed?" He'd grin and take another toke on the joint he kept in the ashtray in his car. I always figured they'd bust him for that, but they never did.

"So that's my story, Honey. What's yours? How'd you end up staying here?"

The sun has dropped to an angle that splashes light in the window
onto the tile floor, setting it on fire. Seagrim's barn must have glowed like this. Why *did* I stay? I can't remember.

"I know you won't believe this, but I guess I forgot to leave or something. I mean, everyone else has left I was ever close to—Jimmy and Brewer, Clinton, Tolson, Mama, now Twyla. It almost seems like you have to die to get out of here. Besides, I feel like I should stay and take care of things. Sort of." Lame, lame. What a jerk. Just tell her—it doesn't matter anymore.

"Jake got out of town."

"Yeah, but he never really invited me to go with him, or meant it if he did. But I didn't care, it turns out. I probably wouldn't have gone anyway. Not then. Now I can't." I'm startled by my words.

"What I mean is, I can't now because of things. Twyla's baby, and stuff." Lame. I grimace at how stupid I sound. Why should I apologize for having stayed, for having no ambition? As she said earlier, what's the point if we all end up dead?

"How is the baby? What's her name? Tamara Julia? How's she doing?" Larue is letting me off the hook.

"She's fine. Living with Tom and his mother."

"He's the only one with legal rights, I suppose."

I nod, wanting to add that he's the only one with guts and feelings enough to claim her as his, too. "I guess the others wouldn't be much better, anyway."

Larue smiles. "She's lucky. The Tooleys are good people. Tom is going to grow up now. Saw the same thing happen to his brothers before they moved away. Some men need to be made responsible for another person's life before they grow up. With others, any responsibility at all keeps them acting like kids. Some have it in them, some don't."

I agree, thinking of Sonny Boy, whose children hardly know him. He should've married a Twyla, a playmate, instead of a Rose Bevington, a wife and mother.

"There's men like Jasper, too." Larue pauses, eyeing me. "They're good men alone, and even better when they find someone to be with. Loyal. Hardworking. Stubborn. I like those traits in a man. Not many have them, though. But not many women can really handle it, either, I guess. I know I couldn't when I met one. Thought I needed more craziness, excitement. I was scared, that's all. Scared shitless. I passed on him. He's the only man I'm still curious about now. None of the others matter anymore. Jass could help you, Honey. You shouldn't give in to being alone now."

We both watch the light finish crawling across the floor and start up the wall. I wonder how she knows so much about Jass. Aside from flirting with him at the Blacksmith that night, what else has she done? You're too old for him, I feel like telling her. Keep your hands off. But the jealousy keeps flip-flopping with something else that makes my muscles go weak. I keep telling myself that I can't let myself care anymore. It's a death certificate.

"Sonny Boy keeping his clothes on these days?" Larue asks suddenly.

The image of him at the funeral comes up, and this time I can laugh.

"He may be your brother, Honey, but you have to admit there's something wrong with him. He's not all there."

"I know, but there's nothing I can do about that." I don't really want to discuss my brother. He's disappeared, as far as I can tell, and that's perfect. He must be staying home with his family.

Larue picks up her glass and presses its cold, sweaty side to one cheek, then the other. "Who said you had to?"

"I always feel guilty when someone brings him up—like it's my fault that he does stuff or like I should stop him since he's family. But I don't even feel related to him. He's a stranger. He always has been a stranger who doesn't much like me." I brush at a fly that's left the window to circle my head slowly, buzzing laboriously like a record on the wrong speed.

Larue shrugs. "That's the breaks." She presses her glass against her velour-covered chest. I watch fascinated as a dark splotch appears around the glass between her breasts.

"He'll have to replace Twyla, you know. I wonder who it'll be?"

I get up from the table. "I don't want to think about it. Anyway, I gotta go. Thanks for the, uh, water."

Larue just turns and watches me as I go to the door. When I'm closing it behind me, she calls, "You-all come back now."

It's not until I reach Bowker's that I realize I've left the papers. "Oh, well," I mutter, "let *him* go get them next time." I'm up to my eyeballs in Larue Carlson. She's so full of information, she should open a library.

16

The Long Night

Driving down Main Street on my way home, I notice a new sign over Sally's Gifts and Cards, which closed a few months ago. It proclaims FAMOUS FATS CLUB in black and red on an electric blue background with a silhouette of a fat king on one side, a fat queen on the other. Someone has pasted posters of Mae West and Orson Welles in the window where Sally used to put her holiday theme displays. This must be what Larue was talking about. How did I miss it? Are they on the centennial mailing list?

I have to brake suddenly as I come up on the back of a baby blue Lincoln Continental swinging into the diagonal space right in front of the FF Club. Leigh Hunt's gigantic profile fills half the front seat. Leigh Hunt, Sr., ordered four Continentals the last year they made the yacht-size ones. He figured he'd wait out the trend toward small cars. Americans were used to size—they'd miss it. Looks like he was right. Anyway, all his cars are baby blue with HUNT 1, 2, 3, or 4 on the license plates. Hard to miss them. Or the specially built seats.

Since I'm not in the mood to see Baby, I step on the gas and hurry past. I've had enough inspection of my life for one afternoon after my little talk with Larue.

Outside of town, the trees in hot oranges, reds, and yellows wave in the wind like people in a game show audience. They're at that last full stage of color and fullness, just before the cold blows down from the Dakotas and strips them. It seems to happen in a single day or two, the leaves pouring like water off the trees sheeting the ground below.

Then it's suddenly November. I forget to watch that translation of form, of time. Even Halloween is an abstraction now that I'm older. That was the good thing about being a kid—time was the part you had to go through to get to the next holiday when something interesting would happen: Birthday—Fourth of July—Labor day—Valentine's Day. Now I don't know what makes things interesting. Death, maybe—Brewer's, Clinton's, Mama's, Twyla's—and what Tolson and Sonny know about.

Crossing the little bridge over the place where Savage Creek runs toward the Mercy, I notice the phosphorescent sparkle of water today. Usually murky, almost black, the water looks yellow and blue. The wind is pushing the algae and weeds with the current. On the other side, down a ways, stands the figure of Billy Bond in his worn overalls, hands grappling with the cottonwood saplings along the creek bank. "Billy, Billy Bond," I mutter, and honk the horn and wave. Then I realize that my gesture might startle him too much, but as I slow down and look back, Billy acts as if he hasn't heard. I step on the gas.

If I were Billy Bond, I'd know about September—October—April—May—the time it took Bluebell to be born, grow, become the prize-winning 4-H pig at the Iowa State Fair, and then that long, long day in early October when the town was celebrating Homecoming, and Reese from the A&P butchered Bluebell for the pig roast. The afternoon he climbed the bank roof and stopped the Homecoming parade by shooting his BB gun at people, Billy stepped out of this life and into another place. Hell, maybe a place where his beloved Bluebell became the smell of roasting pork that drew us to the park by the Mercy River. By the time Boyd Ziekert pulled him down from the roof the next morning, after a hard frost, Billy Bond was gone. His body grew clumsy overnight, lost its boy grace and became mechanical, awkward, like a project someone would build in junior high shop class.

Mostly Billy doesn't recognize any of us now—like we stopped being people he wanted to know the day we ate Bluebell. Or maybe in his new time we just don't exist. Sometimes I want to grab his arm, stop his drunken moon walk, and make him look at me. "Remember me?" I'll say. "Remember the county fair you took me to when we were fourteen? I wanted you to win me a stuffed bear and kiss me, but you spent the day with your pig. Remember?" But that's the problem, see, I can't get around the fact of Bluebell. In Divinity, we're as locked in time with her as Billy is. If he woke up one day and said, "Oh, I must have been dreaming—I'm okay now," it wouldn't matter. He'll always be Billy Bond who ruined his life for Bluebell, a prize-winning hog. And we'll always be the cannibals who ate her.

"So what's the deal?" I say out loud, trying to draw Clinton or someone in. "Is Billy just taking up space, oxygen, molecules?"

"What, does everything have to be practical, have a reason?" Clinton asks.

"I knew I could get you, Clinton."

"You don't care about Billy Bond."

"Of course I do. I don't want to marry him or anything, but I care, sure."

"Then why *did* you eat his pig? He tried to tell you how he felt."

Clinton is right. At the time it seemed minor, almost silly. Everyone just assumed he'd get over it. We'd put out of our minds the pictures of Billy romping with his pig like it was his dog or posing for a newspaper photograph with his arm around Bluebell's neck like a boy at the movies with his first girlfriend.

I turn onto my road, slowing down to avoid skidding on the gravel. It's rained enough lately so the dust is down. Twyla would've liked that. Somehow with her gone, the road seems too open, vulnerable, though. She's not guarding the other end. Anyone can get through now. Parking the car, I ignore the dry rattle of the corn in the fields around my trailer and go quickly inside. I kick off my shoes and drop my skirt on the floor, heading straight for the built-in linen cabinet. When Tom packed up Twyla's place, I helped him, though it was a pretty awful job. I thought we should just torch it but didn't have nerve to suggest that. It took us a week to pack and clean. We threw out most of the stuff, all of Wolfgang's food. Twyla would've gotten a kick out of Tom picking up a can of pâté and trying to puzzle out what it was from the label printed in French. But he made me take the liquor. There was a big load of it—Wolf again—good quality. Twyla never let anyone treat her cheaply. When Jake moved out, he emptied the linen cabinet, which he'd used for his stuff. We only had a couple of towels and two sets of sheets to begin with. Now it's my "liquor cabinet." I say it that way every night when I come home from work and select something to drink.

Tonight I'll try the Chambord. It smells like cherries or raspberries. Hard to say with these cough syrup–colored ones. The ornate round bottle makes the contents look more interesting, even though it probably won't taste like much. I've discovered this sweet stuff usually goes down better mixed with pop. I pour a quarter of a glass of Chambord and fill the rest with Diet Pepsi. Then I add ice.

It tastes like a cherry Coke. After drinking one glass, I mix another and pull a box of Shredded Wheat from the cupboard. I'm out of cheese and crackers. The sun is exploding behind the corn, flooding the sky with orange and red, tipping the stalks and trees with sharp points of light, when there's a pounding on my door. I jump up. "Jesus Christ."

I've forgotten I'm in my blouse and half-slip. Jass is standing on the steps with a bag of groceries. He grins. "Didn't interrupt anything, did I?"

I return to the kitchen, leaving the door open. He comes in.

"You ought to leave the doors and windows open. It's getting a little sour in here. I can take out that garbage, too. That'll help." He nods toward the big black plastic bag that's so full, it threatens to spill.

"Leave it. I like the smell." In fact, I haven't noticed it even. Now I do. Two weeks' worth.

Jass sets down the grocery bag and asks, "Can I have one of those? What is it?"

"Chambord and Diet Pepsi. Help yourself."

"Jesus, that's disgusting. Here, I brought some beer." He reaches into the bag and starts pulling things out. When he finds the six-pack at the bottom, he pops one and takes a long drink.

"Who's minding the horses?"

"Oh, Boardman's there. I put 'em to bed early so I could come see you." He glances at me. "That okay?"

I shrug. "Thought there was a moratorium."

Jass puts down the beer and starts looking around. "Yeah, well, maybe I changed my mind."

"Maybe I didn't, Jass." The second drink is making me cocky.

"Well, I got to thinking you might need someone to take care of you for a while. I've been a little selfish lately. Didn't want you to feel so bad, so I tried to hurry you. That was wrong." He reaches down and tries to kiss me, but I turn away. "What the hell do you want?" He picks up the beer and drains it, staring at me defiantly.

"Nothing. I mean it. Nothing." I do mean it. I don't want anything from anybody. I just want to be left alone to figure things out on my own. Besides, I don't want the responsibility of another person—not anymore.

Jass shakes his head and looks around the room, hands on his hips. "Look at this. What's going on, girl? Your place is a wreck. I bet everything you've worn in two weeks is on the floor of this trailer. You look terrible, too. Look at yourself. What are you eating tonight? Shredded Wheat? Shit." He picks up the box and slams it down again. "And what is that shit on the wall over there?" He's about to reach out and grab one of my lists from my survey. It's the BIG/GOOD one.

"Don't you dare touch that." I half rise in case I have to fight him for the chart.

"Relax, crazy woman." He steps back. "You are, you know, you *are* getting crazy. I can't stand it, either, and I'm not going to. You're going to quit drinking that shit now." Before I can stop him, he grabs my glass and throws it at the sink, where it shatters against the stainless steel, showering us with bits of glass.

"Smart," I say.

"And you're going to quit eating this shit." He grabs the Shredded Wheat and dumps it into the garbage bag. This is just enough to topple the bag. We watch as it spews rotting food and booze bottles.

"Christ Almighty." Jass makes his hands into fists at his sides.

"You said it, Bud. Now you can clean it up, too."

Jass looks unbelieving at my tone and attitude. "Clean it up yourself. Or better yet, leave it. Somehow that suits you better. And here"—he reaches into the food he's stacked on the table—"throw this in there, too." He tosses the steak onto the spilled garbage. "Hell, dump it all." He throws all the food there.

"Nice, very nice." It pisses me off to see that kind of waste. It pisses me off even more to hear how angry he is. He doesn't have the right.

"We're not married, you know," I explain to him.

"What?" He flops onto a chair.

"You don't have the right to act like this in my house."

Then he does a useless male thing. "Oh, no problem. So long." He gets up and leaves, slamming the door so hard that the glass insert rattles and cracks. I watch as it darts in slow motion across one corner.

"Interesting," I say, and get up for another glass.

I'm lying on the floor in the living room, half under the coffee table with the comforter from my bed over me. I must've slept for a while because it's dark outside and my head aches dully. My mouth is so dry I feel like I've eaten part of the comforter.

It takes almost too much effort to get up and go to the kitchen for water. I have to grab the doorway to keep from falling. When I step on something sharp, I remember the broken drinking glass. Sure enough, there's a sliver I pull out of the bottom of my foot. It releases a bead of blood, which I ignore, tiptoeing to the sink.

When the living room window blows in, I'm draining my second glass of water. The full can of beer explodes as it ricochets off the edge of the coffee table and rolls, spewing beer across the carpet.

I'm so afraid, I stand there in my slip and shirt outlined in the kitchen light. A target. It finally sinks in, and I squat by the sink, still holding the glass of water. There's no sound outside. Then I remember the unlocked front door. My heart is pounding so hard I can't get my breath. It's like the can of beer hit me in the stomach. The phone is on the wall by the kitchen table, and I duck-walk there, still crouched, ignoring the sting of glass on my bare feet. As I dial the sheriff and wait out ten rings, I watch the last of the beer dribble onto my gray rug. It's a piece of crap, but it's mine, damn it.

When Boyd answers, he tells me to keep down. He'll be right out. I forget to tell him about the unlocked door. There's nothing else I can do but duck-walk over there and lock it. I take one look at the hole in the living room picture window, half expecting to see a face. It's just a black space, though.

I edge along the perimeter of the kitchen to the door, reach up, and turn the lock. Then I slide down with my back against it; sitting on the floor, I look around me. Two broken windows and a kitchen full of glass and garbage. No wonder my life isn't working out.

"Clinton," I whisper. "Clinton, what am I going to do? This is making me crazy—my brother, Jass, Twyla." Outside, the wind has picked up, and gusts at the trailer hard enough to shake the curtains in the living room.

"It's so lonely here. I just don't see how this all happened." But he's not answering tonight. Since Jass got beat up and Twyla died he's been unreliable, more like when he was alive. I always forgave him, though.

I listen real hard, waiting for Boyd or something else, but all I hear is the muffled *twing* of the trees rubbing and scraping in the wind, and the distant *ping* and rattle that might be beer cans, rolling around out there. I think maybe I know why Clinton was naked in that car at the bottom of Spirit Lake. "Clinton?" I whisper again.

The quiet knock on the door behind me startles me so much that I almost fall face forward trying to get away. "Honey?" Boyd's voice calls. "You all right in there? Open up now, it's me, Sheriff Ziekert."

I suppose it is his official title that makes me stand up and look as I unlock the door. He must've been sleeping when I called. There's still sheet wrinkles pressed into his cheek. I forget I'm only wearing a slip and a blouse until his eyes take it in as he scans the trailer.

"Sorta made a mess here. This you or him?" He looks at me. "The person who threw the can of beer through your window—he do this, too?"

Shaking my head, I say, "No, this was me. I had a visitor earlier, but he . . . they . . ." I move toward the living room. "Screw it. I'm a pig. My house is a mess. Did you see anyone out there?"

Boyd inspects the window. "Hole in one. Naw. I parked down the road, trying to sneak up on him. Nothing out there 'cept a pile of empties blowing around. Probably parked across the road, watching the place and drinking a twelve-pack."

"That's a lot of beer, Boyd."

He turns to me, again letting his eyes sweep my half-clothed body. "Yeah, know anyone who's pissed enough to—"

I laugh. "You mean aside from my family, the guys at Reiler's, and half the town?" I shake my head. "No, aside from that, no problem."

"Why don't you go get some clothes on while I make some coffee. We should talk." Boyd looks away from me, carefully examining the pictures of Bob Dylan I've saved from magazines and recently taped to one wall.

Something perverse gets hold of me then because I close the space between us. When he looks surprised, I take his face in my hands, stand on tiptoe, and kiss him long and hard on the mouth. His lips part and the tips of our tongues meet, tentatively. It sends an electric shock through me, and he puts his arms around me and presses me so tight against his chest that I can hardly breathe.

We break away at the same moment, hands resting on each other's hips. "Okay, now go get dressed." He takes a deep breath and turns toward the kitchen. It doesn't feel like rejection, so I'm not mad. I decide to follow orders, keep it simple.

In the bedroom I find the answer to who was outside the trailer. There on the mirror in lipstick, Sonny Boy has printed, "BITCH." I know it's him because he used to do that when we were growing up. I was always the bitch. It hurt at first, but after a while it didn't matter. I just assumed he was right, whatever that word meant to him. What bothers me more is the way he's gone through all my stuff, turning drawers upside down, digging my closet out. I've been letting things go, but this is ridiculous.

It's odd, though, I actually have to debate calling out to Boyd. The impulse to hide what Sonny Boy does is so strong from years of doing it that I have trouble deciding. Maybe this is a private war. Family only. Maybe I'm breaking some rule even having the sheriff in the house.

I paw through the clothes heaped on the bed and floor until I find some jeans and a sweatshirt. The nights have gotten chilly, and the broken window makes it feel like air-conditioning in the trailer.

Back in the kitchen, Boyd is sweeping up the glass and dumping it into a second garbage bag collapsed next to the full one, which is again upright. "Where're the twist ties for the bags?" He doesn't stop sweeping.

"In here." I pull a couple from a drawer and hold them out to him. He waves me toward the bags. As I lean over to close the full one, my head gives a vicious knock from the drinking. "Oh . . ." I straighten, holding my head between my hands.

Boyd leans the broom in a corner and takes my head in his small meaty hands. Pressing near the ache, he says, "Here?" He continues pressing and shifting until it feels like my head is soft and pliable as bread dough, the ache gone.

"Better?" He drops his hands and steps back.

I nod. "Thanks. I got a little out of hand, earlier, with drinking."

"Oh, I hadn't noticed. Just thought you were a bad housekeeper. Can you make me some coffee now? Long night . . . never know what other damsels in distress need to be rescued." He grins at me.

"About before . . ." I begin as I put hot water in the kettle.

"I know, I was going to say something. It was just a friendly kiss. I got trouble enough with women, Honey, without taking you on." He stops when he sees my face. "I didn't mean that. You're a full-time job, that's all, and I've already got a couple of part-timers."

I reach down the instant coffee, left over from Jake. "It's okay. I'm off men now."

Boyd gives a final swipe at the floor and leans the broom in the corner. "Yeah, well, I was going to talk to you about that. Think that was a disappointed suitor out there tonight?"

He uses the old-fashioned word in such a casual manner, I'm reminded that Boyd only pretends to be a good old boy. Actually he grew up in Ames and went away to college in California. Majored in history but somehow ended up in Divinity as sheriff, talking like a redneck farmer.

When I don't answer, he presses. "Who was here tonight with you? Jasper?"

The kettle whistles. "It wasn't Jass, Boyd. You know that." I reach down a mug, measure the coffee, and pour in the water. "I'm outta milk." I hand the mug to him, and he sits down at the little maple table Jake's family loaned us when we got the trailer. It's old and rickety—that's what I like about it. They've never asked for it back, so I guess they've forgotten.

"No, I know Jasper wouldn't do something like that. He was here, though, wasn't he? That might explain the other thing. Sonny Boy could be on the prowl." Boyd takes a sip of coffee. "Couldn't he, Honey?"

I shrug. The family defense. Pulling out one of the wobbly chairs, I brush the seat with my hand to make sure there's no glass and sit down.

"Aren't you people ever going to wise up about that brother of yours?"

Staring at his face from the nose down, I notice the grizzle graying his cheeks. His mouth is wide and full without seeming soft. I let my eyes drop to his hands. The knuckles are scarred, and the skin on the fingers looks rough, grimy. Then I remember his gardening—hours and hours in dirt and water. They must feel like stiff old leather. Without realizing it, I reach out and pick up a hand.

"That's enough, Honey," Boyd says quietly. He doesn't pull it away.

I put it down, though, and get up for some Diet Pepsi. "Sorry, I just have a thing about men's hands. They're interesting, tell a lot. Like yours." I open the fridge and pull out a can, opening it over the sink in case it wants to spray.

"Maybe it *was* Sonny, Boyd," I say, sitting down again. "He's always on me about the men I see. Well, he's always on me. Except when I was married to Jake. He didn't mess with Jake. It started with Clinton, you

know, that was the beginning. I never could figure out why. They used to hang around together before Clinton went to Vietnam. Right away, though, after the Appreciation Day for Mort and Roger, things seemed to change. Clinton didn't like Sonny at all. I could never figure it out. Sonny kept trying to stop me from seeing Clinton, too."

Boyd holds the cup in both hands, staring at the bubbles on the surface like he's telling fortunes. He's a good listener. Probably how he knows so much about Divinity.

I slug down some pop, liking the burn in my throat and the hot flood in my stomach as it hits. Outside, the wind keeps thrusting this way and that, gusting through the broken window in fits like it can't make up its mind about something. It sounds lonely out there. Just me now on this gravel road, unanchored. I could go sailing off in a big wind, the whole road ripped loose like a piece of cheap ribbon, flung away.

"What did Clinton do in the army?" Boyd finally asks.

"Why?"

"It might explain some things."

My impulse is to keep it secret, like I've always done. Except when Boardman and I worship at the Church of Clinton. Clinton always told me to keep it quiet. Maybe it had to do with his discharge, not wanting his mom to know or something. I don't know what the big deal was. Everyone kills in a war. Maybe Boyd's right, though, and he could piece all this together like Clinton that summer when all he wanted to do was drink wine with hunks of fruit in it and put together puzzles.

We'd do them in Boardman's backyard, or on Clinton's mama's front screened porch, or beside the Mercy River on a blanket, out of everyone's sight. He'd go all over buying these puzzles, the bigger the better. Five hundred to a thousand pieces, at least. He liked them hard, too—the ones where most of the pieces are the same color—and I'd be so sick of it after a while that my eyes felt like they were minnows trying to get out of the way.

But not Clinton. He'd arrive armed with boxes, new or used from junk stores, the Salvation Army, old folks' porches, and off we'd go. Sometimes there'd be pieces missing; he'd like that even better. Sometimes I'd get so impatient, I'd hammer two pieces together with the palm of my hand, ignoring the gaps between them. He'd just take my hand gently and put a new pair in the palm, and they'd always fit. And sometimes while we worked on the puzzle, Clinton would talk, tell me a story, to keep my seventeen-year-old attention, I used to think. Later I guessed it must have been just part of the puzzle he knew I'd end up owning.

My stomach starts to growl, and I get up again. "Want something to eat?" I ask, but Boyd shakes his head.

The only thing left in the cupboard is a can of Green Giant Baby Peas. I remember liking the idea of "Giant Baby" so much that I bought them. There doesn't seem much point in heating them up, so I just open the can and grab a spoon. I hold the can out to Boyd, but he makes a face. He doesn't understand that this is a step up from dry Shredded Wheat.

"You know," I say between mouthfuls, "he was just a grunt. Then they put him in Intelligence." Boyd is listening carefully, pretending to be casual. "He told me this whole thing that blew him away. I've never told anyone else." Clinton taught me to eat like this. Whatever you have is a meal. A jar of spaghetti sauce you can drink. Pickles and jelly. "In American homes you're almost never out of food," he used to say. I'm savoring every pea now so I don't have to tell this story.

17

Clinton's War Story

I set the can of peas down on the table. "This is the deal, Boyd. Clinton didn't ever want anyone to know stuff about him. He said it wasn't what *he* did so much as what *they* did.

"Eight months in he was rotated to an intelligence unit as an orderly. The guys in his unit interrogated wounded and dying Viet Cong in the base hospital just outside Da Nang. He was supposed to help the senior interrogating officer, a guy named Timothy C. Goodman, who had been a Catholic priest until he quit to become a philosophy professor at a college in Nebraska. Seemed weird how Goodman ended up in Vietnam doing that kind of work. He believed in the war, though, and was good at his job.

"Every few days they'd get wounded VC or NVRs in, and he'd go buy a couple of six-packs of beer and some Marlboro hard boxes—'slope favorite,' he called it. Then he'd make sure the miniature tape recorder had a new cassette in it and was going good.

"The two of them would walk into the room where med staff'd wheeled the 'gook' bed. Place was like a house. Windows on two sides overlooking a ball field on one end and the barracks on the other. Homey and safe, wasn't like any prison you'd see here. First day, Goodman told him, 'The whole procedure is designed to make the prisoner feel at ease, feel the logic of the world he's in, to remove fear and defensiveness.'

"Goodman'd go first, with Clinton behind carrying the cold six-pack—he'd stash the other one outside the door—the cigarettes and matches, and the tape recorder, which he'd sneak onto the little table next to the bed. He'd put the beer on the floor next to a big old stuffed chair he'd pull up next to the bed for Goodman. Once he was sitting, he'd open the cigarettes and hand them to Goodman and the 'gook' and offer to light 'em. Then Goodman would cut Clinton loose with an offhanded wave, meaning he was to wait just outside the room.

"Goodman was real good at his job. Clinton used to listen to him through the door. Government saved a lot of bucks building cheap with paper-thin walls and doors.

"First Goodman would introduce himself, sounding like Pat O'Brien in the movies, counseling teenage boys, but he'd talk in Vietnamese, not an Irish brogue. Then Goodman would open a can of beer, like it was the most natural thing in the world. Clinton'd hear the little pop and fizz, as the beer had already started going warm in the heat. Clinton said that was the worst morale problem the army had—keeping the beer cold. The next thing Goodman'd do was offer a can to the prisoner, whether he could drink it or not. If he accepted, there'd be a second pop and hiss.

"Following these sounds, there'd be a couple of minutes of quiet as they sucked on beers and cigarettes. Goodman worked hard to establish that scene. Finally he'd draw a deep breath, sigh tiredly, and start in explaining to the prisoner, 'Essentially the war is over for you. You're wounded, captured, you'll spend the rest of the war in a camp after you've recovered.' Or, if he were terminal, Goodman would remind him that 'the war's over for you, and I just want to save lives, end the war, do the right and humane thing. I'm certain we share this goal.' He'd talk so good-natured and reasonable, Clinton'd be nodding his head in agreement, too.

"Usually took the whole first beer and most of the second before a little conversation got started. Goodman would keep reassuring the prisoner that they were both such 'intelligent and sensible men, talking was really the best thing we could do in the face of such vast unreason as this war.' If it started to stick a little, like with tougher, older soldiers, Goodman, using the same reasonable and tired-of-it-all voice, would remind the prisoner that the South Vietnamese soldiers were right outside in the hallway, dying to get their hands on him, and they weren't nearly as reasonable as he was. Then he'd shake his head, like he really didn't want to see that happen, and press another beer tab open with his thumb, being careful not to cut himself. Goodman had a very high success rate in interrogation.

"There really were South Vietnamese troops stationed at the base with their intelligence unit, and hardly anyone came back alive after a visit with them, so Goodman felt like he had a mission keeping the prisoners out of their hands. Occasionally a few were given to them anyway. Goodman pretended not to see it. Clinton couldn't stand how easy it was for these men to die. There was one grassy spot, beyond the ball field, beside a clump of trees, where they liked to work on the prisoners when it was too hot inside. The red sandy clay beneath the grass was stained darker there. Rains didn't even wash the blood out. It just made the grass grow better.

"When Goodman was getting ready to go home, everyone thought he'd been such a lucky bastard, not even a hangnail the whole two years. They'd wanted him to reup, but he wanted to get back into the classroom before he forgot everything. Clinton had gone to headquarters to say good-bye. Even though Clinton was an enlisted man and he was an officer, Goodman had treated him okay, and Clinton thought he deserved a send-off. It was nothing, really, middle of one of those hot afternoons. It hadn't rained in days, but the clouds had been waiting, clogged up on the nearby mountains, and the men expected something to give them a shove any hour and they'd be over in a few minutes, pouring water on your head till they thought they'd drown if it didn't stop.

"First, they thought it was just thunder, but that was the way the

place lulled them into mistakes. So the three planes were almost overhead coming in very fast before they went into reaction-time fear, running for cover. The strafing must have started a second after they spotted them running. Clinton was looking over his shoulder to make sure the other men were under cover, that no one was out in the open, when he saw it. Goodman standing there, frozen in the middle of the sidewalk, midstride to the jeep that was due to take him to the airstrip, and then suddenly he wasn't. He was a clump of brown clothing you wouldn't even notice from a distance. Clinton said you could have missed him. It would have been easy to miss him. Then the three planes flew off, or were driven off. He was never sure. Just that it stopped, and they crawled out from under and behind things and went to where Goodman was. Not a mark on him. It couldn't have been neater if he'd done it himself. And the way he lay there when they got to him, his arm bent up, as if he were trying to get the sun out of his eyes so he could get a real good look.

"A month later Clinton got drunk, real, real drunk. He drank everything he could find in the barracks. They'd been under heavy bombardment, planes pounding in on them nightly. Driven off almost as quickly as they swept in, but the big guns positioned several miles away kept pouring shells on them, never close enough to actually hit one of the buildings, but making them so nervous they dozed with their arms around their heads and their knees tucked up in their stomachs.

"Lots of guys were in the underground bunkers every night, but something happened to them when they went down there. They never got over it. Their hands shook a little too much, and the whites of their eyes got yellow, like an old dog's that'd been kicked once too often. Clinton stayed up on top. But it wore him down. He decided to be ready that night when the bombardment started and get so drunk he'd forget where he was.

"When he accidentally dropped an empty pint bottle of vodka and stepped on some broken glass trying to clean it up before the other men got back, it was a while before he felt anything, he said. In fact, he tracked the whole floor with bloody little blossoms before he noticed. Even then he had to squeeze the cut hard to connect it to himself. It kept feeling like someone else's foot. He was only watching it bleed. That scared him bad. He decided that he'd lost feeling, that he'd die if he couldn't feel when he got hurt, so he went back to where he'd dropped the bottle and started throwing and breaking other things, too. Like the glass he'd been drinking out of, a couple of other empties, and a small mirror that hung in his locker. Then he walked over it. Back and forth, back and forth, until he started to feel something from his feet.

"The sergeant got back a little after that and put a stop to it, calling the MP's to wrestle him down and take him to the hospital to get his feet bandaged. They had to keep him sedated for two weeks after that because every time he woke up he ripped off the bandages and clawed open the cuts so he could make sure he was still alive. Clinton knew if he hurt, if he could feel it, he was okay. He'd be all right.

"What scared Clinton was the hole in Goodman's hairline that looked just like someone had drawn it on. A blackish purple bruise, but no blood. No blood came out the way he'd expected. It scared him. Sometimes, after he was back here, he'd get drunk and talk about the way that bullet hole looked. *That's* what scared *me*.

"While he was under he kept seeing Goodman, dressed like a college professor, a smart-ass grin on his face as he pulled the front of some girl's dress down, asking her, 'Do you believe in God? Can you give me the ten proofs?' Looking at Clinton the whole time. Or dressed in his priest clothes, he'd take a gun and shoot the crotch out of an empty pair of pants. Then he'd laugh like crazy. Clinton didn't know what that was all about, but it scared him shitless when Goodman would hand them over and order him to put them on in his dream.

"He started doing things then—got into too many weird scenes. He didn't care when they kicked him out. He figured by then they all got what they deserved, even Goodman. That's what he told me."

"I can see why he'd want that kept quiet. He went nuts, didn't he?" Boyd says.

Getting up to pull another can of pop from the fridge while Boyd is shaking his head over the story, I think of the other part. The day Clinton told me his war story, we were in Bevington's pasture on Clinton's scratchy brown army blanket, doing a puzzle. Only I'd given up on it and was lying back watching the white-blue cloudless sky, like a movie screen, where the pictures of Clinton's story were being shown. Then I dozed off.

When I woke up, he was gone. I could feel it even before I looked around. I sat up. Beside me, the puzzle of a giant hamburger in a field of yellow sat completed on a stained piece of plywood Clinton brought along. Beside that his car keys on the roach clip sparkled against the brown blanket. Clinton's shoes sat beside the keys. I waited until dark for him, then drove slowly back to town, hoping to see him walking along the way. When I reached Boardman's—I didn't want to drop the car at his folks' place and have to answer to Broderick Crawford's *Highway Patrol* interrogation about Clinton—there he was. Who could figure that out? I didn't even try.

Now, I don't even have the giant hamburger soaring in a yellow sky like a shuttle to Mars puzzle. In fact, living in the trailer, all I have room for is one we'd never put together. A Middle Ages deal, a tapestry with hundreds of flowers like little jewels and lots of guys in dresses and horses, big heavy ones. Some skinny dogs yapping at them. "The Pilgrimage," it says on the box. I bought it a couple of years ago in a heat wave. The deep blue was so cooling. And with all the detail, I figured I'd have the patience. But all I ever do is take it off the shelf and pour the pieces in a pile on the kitchen table and wait.

As Boyd and I sit here in the kitchen, I wonder where that puzzle is. Under the bed? Did Sonny Boy find it and dump it on the floor?

Sometimes when I'm alone on hot summer evenings, I just turn each piece over and over, feeling how the lick of air makes the colors on the paper damp, sticky. And sometimes when I sit back and squint my eyes, all the colors run together and take shape. I don't have to work to make this happen. The answer is always going to be the same one in the pile of puzzle pieces, if I ever bother to put them together.

Boyd is looking around him as if he's just noticed he's living among aliens. I feel relaxed for some reason. Familiar territory, maybe. "More coffee?" I ask him.

He nods and clears his throat. "Can I ask you a couple of questions?"

"Sure, shoot. I'll do the best I can." I take his cup, add water to the kettle, and get the instant ready.

"What *is* this stuff on the walls here—all these pieces of paper with arrows and names? Oh, there's other words, too. Am I on here, Honey?"

I turn to follow his gaze. I've forgotten about my survey, which is turning into a study of evil or something. Some days I wish I'd never started it.

"Billy Bond and Bluebell, under Large, but Baby's got a circle around her name and an arrow leading her . . . wait—there, three pages over. What is this?" Boyd tilts on the shaky back chair legs and folds his hands behind his head. The gesture stretches his shirt tight across his barrel chest in a way that makes me want to cradle my head there. Jass be damned.

"That's just some research I'm doing. About people, things that go on. Circles of heaven and hell." The kettle whistles. I hate that goddamned thing.

"Gluttony, Avarice, Lechery . . . this sounds more like hell than heaven, Honey."

Pouring water into the cup, I let the steam bite my hand. "Yeah, well, it's turning out that way. I found those subheadings listed as the Seven Deadly Sins. I don't know why there are only seven. I can think of a lot more than that, but I figure maybe people weren't so inventive back when these were made up or something."

Boyd laughs. "Keep going. I think you'll find seven is plenty when you look hard enough."

He stirs the coffee I hand him. "Say, am I on there?"

"Not yet. Lechery maybe?"

"Yours or mine?" He grins.

"Both? Haven't found a place for me yet, either."

He nods. "Sonny Boy is up there a lot, isn't he? You ought to color-code this stuff. Use different color inks. . . . Clinton," he reads. "He's here at the start and the end—and the middle, too. Couldn't make up your mind?"

I sit down again. "You know how it is."

Boyd shakes his head, leans forward, then leans back again, forcing a groan out of the chair. "I never could see it with Clinton. What the attraction was. He just seemed like this crazy, bigmouth doper. A tease—

he was going to get popped, you know. He was going to go down for dealing. Just a matter of time, Honey. That's all it was. If he hadn't died—"

"Okay. Just shut up. I don't want to hear it. He was my—I loved him. Nobody can take that away. So just drop it."

He holds his hands up and pats the air. "Fine. No big deal." Taking a sip of coffee, he seems to be reading the charts again, which makes me feel truly embarrassed. I must seem like some damn high school kid to him. But he nods and says, "This is okay. Good idea. I wish more people would take the time to think about things, besides what's on TV or who they're going to screw next. I'd like to see this when you're done. Print it up as a guide through the moral geography of Divinity, Iowa, for the centennial. Should sell like hotcakes, as many righteous as we have here."

We laugh and watch the march of paper and words like a chair rail around the kitchen.

"Oh, and the other thing . . ." His casualness is deceptive. "Was Clinton a good shot? In the army, I mean. Did he win any of those little marksmanship medals?"

"I don't know," I lie. "No, I don't think so. Why?"

Boyd pushes his chair away from the table and stands up. "Just curious. A weird sort of thing. How about Sonny? He do a lot of hunting? Jake?"

Again, I shake my head. "I don't know."

"Jimmy Bevington? Brewer? Any of those boys good shots?"

My breathing gets tighter. "No, I don't know. Why?"

"No reason. Just something that I thought of tonight when you mentioned the Appreciation Day. That girl got shot that night, remember? Anyway, you okay now, Honey? I should get going. I think whoever it was, they're gone now."

"Sure, I'm fine." Except for those damn questions, I want to add. "Thanks for coming out, Boyd. I was truly scared shitless."

He puts a friendly hand on my shoulder. "No problem. Get that window fixed soon. We could get one of those freak early snows."

I'm standing in the open door getting ready to wave good-bye when he stops and turns back. Pushing his hands into his pants' pockets, he says, "You might want to stay somewhere else for a few days, if you can." He looks off down the dark road. "You're pretty isolated here, got anyplace else? Twy—" He catches himself. "Sorry. What about your sister or Jasper? Either one, unless it's Sonny Boy who's hassling you. May be safest at Jasper's. Call him up."

"I can't. We broke it off tonight, so I can't." Saying that makes me feel stupid and hopeless. Why *did* that happen?

"You two are dangerous. *I'll* call him and set it up."

"Boyd, don't."

"Just for a few days. Sleep in the barn if you have to, for God's sake. Pride—you can't afford much of that now, Honey. Go in and check your charts. P-r-i-d-e."

"His, too, Boyd. Don't forget that."

"Yeah, I've already had a dose of his. The Lone Ranger bullshit. 'Night, Honey." He walks into the darkness to his squad car. A moment later I hear the motor catch, and the car appears. He stops and opens the door, half stepping out so he can talk to me over the roof.

"One more thing. Any of those boys ever own guns? Hunting rifles? Deer-killing size? That you know of?"

"I told you, Boyd, I don't know anything about that stuff." I shiver, remembering not only Clinton's guns, but Sonny Boy's, Jake's, and Jimmy's. Brewer hated guns. Locking the door, I'm struck by Boyd's lumping those names together. I did hear that Clinton and Sonny Boy got into a fight at Tippy's in Centerville one night after the Appreciation Day. I wondered for a long time if Clinton was bragging about getting into my pants. But suddenly I *can* see them together that night. Drinking. Kidding around. Only five years separating oldest from youngest. Not long after that, they all drifted apart, and after his tour in Vietnam, Jake wouldn't go near Sonny. Jimmy had taken off. Clinton and Brewer were dead. You'd think Jake and Sonny would pick up being buddies again, like before. I guess I'd always assumed it was the war changed Jake's feelings about things. Sonny Boy didn't like Jake, either, though. And Jake married me. Me. Why? I've always asked myself that. Why marry *me*?

As if it carries an answer, the wind howls through the broken living room window, and outside, tatters of leaves scratch the metal siding of the trailer.

"Clinton?" I whisper, but he's silent.

18

Hiding Out

Bowker's out for the day appraising property for the bank. Farms are going bust all around us. He goes to auctions every week, coming back with more junk for the office. It's getting crowded. A few days ago he hauled in an oval mahogany dining room table with two center pedestals. "For office meetings, centennial planning," he said, as if the three of us had trouble getting together.

Marylou keeps watching me this morning, trying to catch my eye, but I'm disgusted with her for leaving with him yesterday. Besides that, I was so scared last night, I slept in my clothes sitting on a chair in case I had to make a run for it. Today, my hands shake whenever I try to write in the column of figures. Finally she taps off her machine with a sigh. "Honey?"

"Yeah?" I answer without looking up from my records.

She swings her chair away from her desk and backpedals to mine. Our desks guard the front door on the right and the left. There's a little mahogany gate Bowker got from a church closing sale that monitors the center aisle on the way to his desk behind us. In the corner next to where Bowker sits is the walnut podium the minister used to read Scripture from. Now it holds the huge old *Webster's International Dictionary* Bow-wow got at a school auction.

Marylou leans an elbow on my desk and waits for my attention. I glance down at her perfect size 5½ foot, encased in nylons. Her red toenail polish matches her fingernails and lipstick. The Mary Kay look. Her slim legs are crossed, showing enough knee below her pale blue wool skirt to cause trouble if Bow-wow were here. I let my eyes follow the blue up, past the matching sweater and single string of pearls to her face. Marylou was not born pretty. She made herself attractive, though. Men always go after her like she's safer than someone truly beautiful, like Twyla. Maybe they're right. Marylou always looks the same—nothing wild, unpredictable. The only out-of-character thing she's ever done is getting pregnant with Mike and having to marry him.

"Honey," she says when I meet her blue eyes, "we got a problem."

"What?" As far as I know, we both have plenty of problems, but not one in common.

She gestures toward Bowker's desk.

"Hey, don't get me involved with whatever you two are up to."

Marylou's eyes sharpen, and her mouth tightens. "Well, you *are* involved, whether you like it or not. He's doing it to *both* of us, and we have to stick together or—"

"*That's* what you're talking about?" Marylou and I both look at the storage closet as if we're in it right now. A wave of sourness passes through my stomach.

"What do you want to do?" I drop my voice as if he can hear us.

Marylou smiles brightly, leans back on her chair. Drawing her legs up under her, she says, "I'm checking on some things." She looks at the big charts hanging on the wall to the right of the front door. They catalog the growing list of centennial events and the money and sponsors raised. "Bowker's proud as a peacock about being elected chairman of the committee, isn't he?"

I nod. She's looking pretty proud, too. It worries me. I have enough problems at home without work getting out of hand, too.

"Thinks he's king of the world. The town worships him. We're just the peasants." She spits these words out between her teeth.

"Marylou—"

"Shut up. You're such a wimp. What do you ever do—"

"Right. Okay. But what about you? You went off with him yesterday."

She laughs. "That was research, dummy."

Oh, shit. She really *is* up to something.

"See, I've been doing some research. Saw it on *Donahue* one morning when I had to take off 'cause my baby-sitter was sick? Anyway, we can get him, Honey, for what he's done in the closet. We can *sue* him." Her face relaxes with the joy of her announcement.

I hate to bring in reality, but it's my job, too. "Just who'd take our side in Divinity, Marylou? Get real."

"You may think this is the universe, Honey, but I got news for you, there are lawyers and laws outside this town. This is a *federal* offense, and we could win. Would, in fact. I've checked with a lawyer." She moves her legs, stands up, and begins pacing.

"Okay. Who *is* this lawyer?"

"He's from Omaha, we're corresponding about the case, documenting it. That's where you come in." She stops and sits on my desk. "You have to sign an affidavit about your experience, first of all."

"And . . ."

"You have to help me tape-record our storage closet episodes."

"What! I can just see myself trying to fight him off knowing it's being taped. Come on. We'll lose our jobs."

She leans over the desk at me so close that I can see the greasy pores on her nose where the makeup has melted. "No, we won't. We *can* change it. Stand up for yourself, Honey. Didn't you see *Nine to Five?* They did it." Marylou gets off the desk and sits down on her chair again. "Dallas, the lawyer, says the *best* thing is if we *both* are in it."

"Let me think about it, okay? This is kind of sudden." Screw off, I want to tell her. Get a real problem—like someone trying to kill you.

Marylou scoots her chair back to her desk. "The centennial in May would be the best time to strike, you know. He'll do anything to keep his name clean then." There's a particular viciousness about her tone and face at this moment. "Small," Mama would have said.

At lunchtime I go to Bob and Shirley's and poke at some hot dish Simpy's made out of beets, turnips, carrots, potatoes, and pork. It's a weird color from the beets. The farmers are all looking defeated. Record harvest. Prices will be down so far, they won't make the interest on their loans. I know what this is like and try to avoid watching their faces, the way they go blank with failure and resignation. They keep adjusting their hats until they're pulled so far down over their faces, only a grim set of mouth is left.

The afternoon drags on. No Twyla to call and joke with. Larue Carlson calls for Bowker and asks me to stop by after work, but I'm not in the mood. The wind is shifting, bringing in heavy clouds and an icy edge to the air. I'd better get the window fixed, but I don't know who to call. Jake always did the repairs on the trailer.

As we're finally locking up, Marylou asks, "You make up your mind?"

"Give me a few days." I turn to walk to my car, but the sheriff pulls up. Marylou and I stand there gawking like a couple of sheep. He leans across the front seat and opens the door. "Honey, get in."

"Must be official," Marylou smirks, and walks away.

Great. I grab the handle, open it, and get in. "What now?" I hope I sound annoyed.

"Close the door." Boyd is already pulling away from the curb.

"Hey—" I struggle to get the door closed. He smiles a little meanly. "What the hell's going on, Boyd?"

He ignores my question and takes a right turn a little too fast and in another two blocks pulls up in front of Boardman's. Jass's truck is in the driveway. I'll refuse to leave the car, that's it.

"Get out," Boyd orders in his real sheriff's voice, and I do. His hand's like a cattle prod in my back, pushing me toward the house.

"Boyd, I—"

"Skip it."

I notice a new dent in the side of Jass's truck. Now it looks more like it belongs here. He probably got it drinking like the others. Boardman's scrawny arm snakes out to hold the door open as we go up the steps. His face has that funny glow it used to get around Clinton and that he now wears almost permanently because of Jass. Like a steer in love. Can't do anything about it. Just act moony and keep the others away.

We walk through the showroom into the kitchen. Jass is leaning against the fridge with his arms crossed, grinning like a dog with a woodchuck. Boardman oozes around us and begins to get down cups for coffee and tea. It's too crowded in here, but when I take a step toward the living room, Boyd grabs my arm and Jass steps away from the fridge.

"Get real! What is this, gestapo headquarters? Want to come to the bathroom with me? Fine. We'll see how many people we can squeeze in there."

The men fall back, trying to put their eyes someplace safe while I head for the bathroom. With the door closed, I turn on the sink tap and sit on the toilet lid. Women's business. We always run water. I know we'll get to the point of this meeting pretty soon. It's just the *idea* of it that irritates me. Like *they* know what's good for me, better than I do. A framed picture of Clinton brooding on an overstuffed chair hangs on the opposite wall. I've never noticed that before. When I look around, there's other changes: pink bath mat and towels. A basket of dried flowers on the back of the john and a cheap jar of scented bath oil on the corner of the tub. What the hell is this? I look back at Clinton, whose dark eyes stare out as if they see all of time, even this moment I've come to, in Boardman's bathroom, and he doesn't like any of it. Here's a good example of male competency, I want to tell the men in the kitchen. How come you couldn't keep Clinton alive?

"Clinton," I say normally, as if he can climb out of that picture, "you're an asshole like the others out there, aren't you?" He doesn't answer. It never works with pictures, anyway. I guess that moment is too far stopped for him to speak from. Like ice that never melts. Antarctica. That's where time goes.

"Fuck it." I get up and turn off the faucet, give myself a brief, hopeless inspection in the mirror, and unlock the door. I don't have to go along with their bullshit. It's still a free country, right?

"Wrong," Clinton says.

"Where have *you* been? If you're going to eavesdrop, at least answer when I call, goddamn it."

"I can finally do what I want."

I stop in the hallway. "That's a *big* achievement. You mean you only have to die to get that? Gee, I should rush right out, drop myself in the middle of Spirit Lake, or just stop ducking when Sonny Boy shoots something at me, huh? Then I could come back and bug the shit out of someone, too."

"Honey—" Clinton sounds hurt.

"Oh, no, I'm sure it was worth it. There must be *tons* to do now, huh? That's why you can't leave me alone, right? God, I envy you, Clinton."

"I know."

"No, you dumb-ass—"

"Come back in here, Honey," Boyd's voice interrupts us. He rounds the corner. "Who're you talking to?"

Damn. Did it again. Sometimes I get so involved, I forget to have the conversation silently. It doesn't seem to matter to Clinton either way. I shrug, "Singing, Boyd. I was just singing."

He looks skeptical.

I smile and walk around him into the kitchen. Jass has moved to the table and is sitting with his hands folded like a good citizen. All traces of the beating have disappeared, though there is a new bump in his nose and his broken finger has healed slightly crooked. Boardman is hovering near Jass's chair like his mother or something. I want to ask him why he redid his bathroom in trailer chic.

I sit opposite Jass, avoiding his smiling eyes. Boyd stands by the sink. "Okay, what's this summit conference about?"

"We're worried about you," Jass says.

I make a funnel of my hands and mouth, "Fuck off," so he can see it.

"You can't stay at your place until it's safer," Boyd says. "Or you get someone to stay with you. Boardman here has volunteered—"

I shake my head and look at Boyd. The old man would drive me crazy in that tiny space.

Boyd shrugs. "Okay, then you have to go elsewhere."

I push back the chair and get up. "Now, look, just because you're men doesn't mean you can order me around. I'll be all right. Last night was probably just an accident or something."

"Oh, like the can slipped out of his hand and hurled *itself* through the window? And what about the propane tank?" Jass says.

I turn and look at him. "What about it? What're you talking about? And what were you doing at my place, anyhow?"

Boyd steps closer. "He went to fix the window. Used a credit card to pop the lock. Real safe, Honey. The gas was leaking into your trailer. The shut-off valve was broken. It was only a matter of time before it blew up."

I sit down. "Are you sure? Are you *sure?* Why would anyone—"

"That's my job. Yours is to stay safe. Take your pick between Jass or Boardman. Or call your family. Up to you. I can't stand here all day, though." Boyd walks to the doorway. "Well?"

"She'll come home with me. She can stay upstairs, I'll stay down. Azium'll come out and stay, too. To chaperone." Jass gets up.

Boyd nods. "Just need a few days to take care of this."

"I'm glad you all have this under control. What if I don't agree?"

Boyd grins and hooks his thumbs on his gun belt. "Ever spent time in jail?"

"Okay. But I'm only *sleeping* out there, right? Nothing more."

Jass nods his head, with a twinkle in his eye.

"A couple of days, right? While you men play detective. It'll turn out to be some animal that's goofed up the gas line. I can guarantee it. But if I can get you three off my case, it'll be worth it. What about my car?"

"Leave it parked where it is. I'll take care of that," Boyd says over his shoulder as he's walking out.

It's just my luck that as I'm about to climb into Jass's truck, I see

Baby waddling down the street on the opposite side. "Now what's *she* doing?" I ask.

Jass and I pause, waiting for Baby. The gathering clouds hang low now, smothering the late afternoon light. Through its smoky filter, Baby seems smaller, more fragile, pinker, like a real baby. Though she's older than Tolson or me, she remains the baby of our family. I don't know what that makes us two.

I get ready to talk to her as she approaches. It always takes preparation with Baby. But as I open my mouth to call hello, she sweeps by, staring at the cement walk. She seems to be concentrating so hard, swinging her arms as she marches along like she's in boot camp, maybe she doesn't see us. I think about calling after her but decide against it.

"Let's go, Jass, if we're going."

He climbs in but doesn't start the truck. "Have to wait for Azium. He'll only be a minute."

We sit there in silence. Jass looks out across the little town lawns blotted with leaves from the trees that line the yards and street. I watch him. I don't know why I'm doing this to him. Beneath the anger or whatever it is, there's another feeling. I don't trust it. That's how it always starts. Then I get in trouble. And people, men, leave or die. I sometimes feel like the Typhoid Mary of love.

Boardman opens the door, and I have to slide over next to Jass. All the way out to his place, the heat of his body burns into my side. I try not to look at his elegant hands, try not to think how they've stroked my skin over the past months, taking me to a place I thought I'd lost forever with Clinton. More reason to stop it now, I remind myself. You want it to end up like with Twyla? Or Clinton?

It seems automatic to help with evening chores. We're settling the horses for the evening, getting their water, grain, and hay. Jass is checking each one to make sure it hasn't hurt itself in the pasture. Boardman's in the house cooking dinner. Finished with my part, I'm watching the crew of young barn cats with their tails straight up in the air crowd each other around the food dish.

"Come here," Jass calls from midway down the aisle.

I walk slowly to let him know how I feel.

"Remember her?" He leans over the top of a stall door. Inside is a weanling.

"Your namesake? From last spring, Marvel's baby? I was so out of it when you were here last time, I forgot to point her out. Pretty, isn't she?

Come here, sweetie." Jass coos to the filly and puts his arm over the door to rub her. She doesn't pull her head out of her feed bucket. Instead she swings the rest of her body around so she can be scratched.

I laugh in spite of myself. "She's quite the pet."

Jass scratches her back and flanks. "The orphans usually are. Lucky I found that wet nurse or she'd have bonded too much with me. They need to remember they're horses. Need a mama to teach them how to behave. Our version is too skewed. There was this lady used to come to the track—some trainers would use her for problems, like breaking or injury or if a horse quit running good . . . whatever they couldn't figure out."

"And . . ." I prod him after he stops talking for a minute.

"Oh, so she'd come and talk to the horses. It was pretty strange, but after a while word got around that she was hitting well over fifty percent of the time. That's damn good in the racing business. The grooms all talked about it. How she'd diagnosed a sore shoulder or back before the vet could find it. Or she'd said this certain horse didn't like its exercise boy. Another one wanted its old blanket back, something that'd been thrown away because it wore out. Lots of 'em were worried because they didn't know whether they could race and win. Some just plain hated it. A couple were sent home to grow up after she talked to them."

It sounds screwy.

"When the trainers changed what was bugging the horse or laid them off or doctored them, the horses would get better."

I watch the filly lift her head, sink her back, and stretch as Jass hits a spot that feels good. She has a thick baby winter coat now, half fuzz and half hair, like a cross between a baby bird and a horse. "What's the woman's name?"

"Beatrice Leidekker. I even went out and bought two books she wrote, gave me good ideas about raising and training horses. Imaging. They need to see the picture of what you want. Works. Really does. They do it back, too."

I shake my head and smile. "I don't know, Jass."

He slips his free arm around my shoulders before I have a chance to move away. Without missing a circle on the filly's back, he tightens his arm and hugs me. It happens so smoothly and quickly, I don't have time to resist. It feels good, too, until I remember I'm not supposed to like him anymore. Before I can push away, he drops his arm and turns his face back to the filly. It's like being dropped out of an airplane without a parachute. I tilt awkwardly and have to steady myself on the stall door. "Knock it off, Jass."

He ignores my reaction. "As long as you're here, I figure you should learn to ride. No reason you can't ride. You're built right, not overweight, in reasonably good shape. Be harder if you were topheavy, but—" He looks me up and down like he's buying me at auction. "You're just right there."

"Screw you, Jass." I turn to walk away.

"Okay, that was out of line. Stay here, though. I mean it about the riding. Let's go get the old mare who wet-nursed the filly. She'd be a good starter horse."

I follow him down the aisle to the mare's stall. She's done eating and is just standing with her head in the back corner, hipshot, back sunk, lower lip hanging.

"Sleeping. Hey, Mama, come here." Jass speaks softly. The mare lifts her head a little and eyes us sleepily. "Come on over here. Meet Honey. You gotta teach her sorry ass how to stay in the saddle." The mare sighs like she's spent the day plowing forty acres and lumbers across the stall to us. Laying her big head on Jass's shoulder, she sighs again and half closes her eyes. "She wants me to scratch her ears. Watch, this

relaxes 'em." He begins stroking her ears, pulling them gently through his hands. Her lower lip quivers and droops more.

"She'll fall over if she relaxes any more," I say.

"Yeah, she knows to take her pleasure when she can get it. Not like some people I know."

I punch him in the back. When he jerks, I remember the healing ribs. "Sorry."

He turns suddenly and grabs me in a fierce hug, startling the horse, who throws her head up. He keeps pushing me until I'm up against the stall. Then he catches my hands and forces them over my head and kisses me hard. I kiss back with my teeth, and he uses his. When they clank together so hard it feels like we've chipped them, Jass pulls back. Releasing my hands, he rubs his lips. "Your crooked tooth got me."

"Well, those two eyeteeth of yours could draw blood. You filing them to get those points, or are you Count Dracula's son?"

He grins. "Stick around and see."

"Maybe." I shove him so he loses his balance and comes close to hitting the floor.

"Careful. Zee riding master demands strict obedience or zee crop on zee buttocks."

"I figured it was just another ploy."

"No, really, we can start tonight or tomorrow. Your pick."

"Tomorrow. I have to think about this."

Jass combs his hair with his fingers. "No, do it. Horses are so much more fun to be around if you ride, too. Otherwise you're just cleaning up after 'em. 'Sides, I need someone your size and weight to ride a few."

I back up a couple of steps. "Not me—no way."

"Not now, dummy. I know that. Later."

"What happened to Cindy?"

He looks at me for a long moment. "I asked her not to come out anymore."

I'm surprised. What is he up to? "Why? You scared of the Reilers?"

"No. God, you are the densest person. You're as thick as an old pine. Don't you get it?" He stares at me, and an image comes into my head.

"Stop it. Don't do that. You're doing that thing, aren't you? Stay out of my head, Jass. Leave me alone. I mean it." I turn and walk quickly out of the barn without looking back.

Outside the sky is a heavy Prussian blue, growing darker as a cold mist begins to fall. Tonight will be one of those early bone-chilling times when I'll miss Jass's warm body in bed. What I'm doing is as much for him as me, though. He'll stay healthy longer. They only beat him up the first time. Another image appears as I'm walking to the house: Sonny Boy with a rifle, his deer-hunting rifle. "There's no deer around Divinity," I once remarked. "Out of state," he'd said, and smirked. If Tolson was right, maybe Sonny Boy could do it again if Jass pushed him far enough. This time it'd be someone I know and care about. A gust of cold wind shoves at my back. I shiver, but not from the cold. It's the feeling that passes through me every time I think of that dead girl and my brother—the feeling that I *should* do something, raise the question, drag my brother out . . .

Maybe it was only coincidence—his leaving the house with the rifle wrapped in an old bath towel and the way it got "lost" a few days later. But how could you turn in your own brother? Even Sonny Boy. It isn't like I was there, myself. Not like I saw him pull the trigger. I *know,* but *what* do I *know*? It's the same old argument I keep having. That's why I try not to think about her—it—him.

If Sonny Boy were *smart,* he'd stay out of my way so I'd forget he exists. But he doesn't know that I know, does he? Does he? I shiver again and pull open the porch storm door and go inside, trying to leave these worries in the cold yard.

That night we're all in our separate beds by ten. The house has that tension of motels where strangers sleep close, where you hear things you shouldn't because there's nothing else to listen to when the room goes so dark. A cough, a toilet flushing, a voice murmuring. Outside the mist turns to rain *ping*ing the window glass as if it is already winter. I'm so lonely now, my warm island surrounded by sheets so cold they feel like January snow when I forget and move a leg. I'm wearing Jass's old sweatsuit because he won't turn on the furnace until Halloween. Says he does it that way every year. I'm a little worried about Boardman sleeping in the other room. His lips were pale blue when he went to bed, and he sleeps with the window open. Probably be frozen stiff by morning. Serve Jass right being so cheap. He's cheap in funny ways—different from Jake. He has a whole shed full of scraps of wire, metal, wood, anything broken, motors, buckets, bottles. Might need these someday, he says every time he stores something else in there. Bent nails. Rusty. Cans of them. But he drives a new truck, dresses okay, eats good. I'm tempted to toss a match at the shed each time we walk past. It's the old grain store. Abandoned because horse grain has to be very clean, he explained. When it comes to the horses, he doesn't scrimp. They're treated as if they're kin. I wiggle my toes to get them warm, thinking of Jass's horse-faced relatives. If I got up and put on a pair of socks, my feet would be warm, but I'm too lazy and fall asleep telling myself I'll be warm in a few minutes.

19

Baby, Baby

Ten days later, on Halloween, I'm still staying at Jass's. Nothing's changed. I'm a POW. Trapped in some circle of hell even Clinton can't identify. Boyd's deputy stakes out my trailer every night but can't figure how more piles of empty beer cans appear and two more windows suffer bombardment. We're not bothering with glass anymore. Christmas in black plastic will look wonderful. In fact, we could wrap the whole trailer in black plastic, put a bow on it, and haul it to Sonny Boy's. He's the only person mean and smart enough to get those windows broken and not be seen. Besides, it's Budweiser, his brand.

I asked Boyd to dust for prints, but he just laughed himself half to death. "Believe me, it hardly ever shows anything." He went off muttering, "Cop shows."

This morning when I get up, I remember the costumes Bowker wants Marylou and me to wear. "Something traditional." Thanksgiving turkey? Madame DeFarge?

"Twyla?" Clinton suggests.

I run downstairs in Jass's sweatsuit, one hour from work time, yelling, "Help, I have to go as someone."

Jass and Boardman freeze at the sight of me in this outfit, pants sagging around my ankles, sweatshirt sleeves to my knees, and hair standing in strange clumps.

"That should do," Jass remarks.

"No, really, I have to have a costume for work. Help—" When the men laugh, I hear myself sounding just like I did in third grade. Somehow

Halloween always snuck up on our family, and we always acted like someone changed the date just to get us. We only had four costumes, which we had to rotate until Sonny and Baby and then I outgrew them and could be something else. There was a devil in red flannel, a tiger in striped flannel, a baby gown in long white flannel with a bonnet, rattle, and bottle, and a pink ballerina with tutu and slippers. The year Mama made Tolson wear the ballerina was the last time anyone saw that one. I never blamed him, though the velvet sequined top was my all-time favorite. That year Baby had to wear the baby, Sonny took the tiger, and I was too big for the ballerina, so I got the devil. Looking at the faces of Jass and Boardman, I realize they've never had to think of such things.

"Costume?" they each say as if I've announced pigs coming through the septic system.

"Come on, help, what can I be? Traditional."

Boardman sips at his coffee, scowling in concentration while Jass cradles the bowl of waffle batter and thoughtfully stirs with a wooden spoon.

"Cowboy?" Boardman asks.

I shake my head.

"Witch? You're good at— Just kidding," Jass says, holding the bowl in front of him to ward off my attack as I start for him.

"Bum? I got plenty of old clothes out here," Boardman says.

Jass pours some batter in the waiting waffle iron, closes the lid, and wipes his hands slowly on a dish towel as if he's thinking hard. "Azium, watch this; when the light goes off—"

"I know, I know." He waves Jass on.

"Come on, Honey," Jass says, "to the attic."

On the way up he explains, "Must be three generations of clothes, furniture, whatnot here. I spent a whole afternoon last summer pawing through this stuff. Hotter'n Hades then. It'll be cold now, though." He pushes up the overhead trapdoor at the top of the stairs. The cold, stale air pushes down to meet us.

"Pew, what's that smell?" I cover the lower part of my face with the neck of the sweatshirt.

"That's why I came up here before. Had a regular zoo living here. Squirrels, sparrows, pigeons, mice. Even a big old rat snake. He wasn't as efficient as the poison I laid out. I blocked all the holes. That helped, though some got stuck in, not out. After they died, the smell was awful. Now with the cold, it's getting better."

"I'm glad," is all I can think to offer.

Jass goes directly to a matched set of steamer trunks, the kind that stand on end and split open with drawers inside. He opens one and begins pulling out clothes, throwing them carelessly on the dusty floor.

"Hey, wait, stop, you'll wreck those." Uncovering my nose, I discover that the smell is tolerable once I get used to it.

"I'm looking for one particular thing. Oh, here it is." Jass carefully unfolds a long indigo velvet dress with silver star-shaped sequins scalloping the full skirt and scoop neck. "This was Marvel's. It's her trunk." He holds it up to me.

Of course I fall in love with the dress. The material is that old-fashioned velvet that's so expensive now, soft as new butter between your fingers. "Will it fit?"

"Bring it downstairs and try it on. I'll find the shoes. I know I saw them last summer. . . ."

By the time I'm dressed, I'm already half an hour late, but the effect is amazing. I barely recognize myself in the mirror. Jass quickly fashions a coat hanger into a wand he winds a silver Christmas garland around, the shoes are tight but endurable, and I've just colored my hair red with one of those home kits. It's a little bright but goes perfect with the costume. I even feel a little magical as I step into Jass's truck for the drive to work.

"The Good Fairy," Boardman calls as we drive off. "Tell 'em that."

Even Marylou is stunned as I sweep through the door. Bowker looks up at the clock, ready to say something, but ends with his mouth hanging as I glide to my desk, stash my purse in the bottom drawer, and sit down with my wand in my hand.

"You look wonderful," Marylou whispers. She's come as a ballerina. Somehow she's managed to look like an eight-year-old *wanting* to dress up as a ballerina, not an adult. The natural-colored Danskin top flattens her already flat chest, and the off-white tutu wilts tiredly around her narrow hips. Noticing her skinny, straight legs in the natural flesh tights, I realize that Marylou needs the illusion of sex clothes can give her.

Bowker clears his throat behind us. "Good costume, Honey. You're late, have to stay late and make it up."

Nodding reluctantly, I look sideways at Marylou. She gives an imperceptible nod. We have an agreement not to strand each other in the office alone after hours. With two of us around, he gives up quickly and goes home.

All day people come in and out of the office to see the costumes. Most of the businesses on Main Street are participating in the annual costume contest, and since it's a Friday, this Halloween is a bigger deal than usual. There's a dance at the high school gym starting at eight for teenagers and grown-ups after the little kids have gone trick-or-treating. Costumes required. I wonder about asking Jass.

At noon Bowker goes home for lunch and comes back in his costume: a bear. It's the same ratty, matted fur thing he wears every year. Divinity will probably bronze it for the park when he dies. We always act surprised when he shows up, though, because he expects it, like a kid showing some lame trick to his parents. Marylou and I heave sighs of relief when he leaves early for the day to help judge the Main Street costume contest. We figure the crew at the Curl-Y-Que will win. They usually get something. This year they've all come as mermaids. Bowker will love the long hair tactfully covering their breasts.

"Good, now I can get home early and get my kids ready for trick-or-treating." Marylou puts her pen down as Bowker lumbers down the street to Shirley and Bob's Cafe to meet the other judges.

"You going to the dance?" I ask.

"No, Dallas is coming into town to discuss the case." She smiles almost shyly and ducks to search for her sensible street shoes.

"Take him to the dance. Put him in a costume, nobody'll know who it is."

She steps out of her three-inch heels, which have looked ridiculous with the ballerina outfit. "I suppose he could wear some of Mike's clothes and come as a bum—that's what everyone expects of me, anyway."

The bitterness in her voice surprises me. I've always seen Marylou as one person who isn't pushed around by the gossip in Divinity. "I don't think anyone sees you like that."

Marylou pulls the cover over her typewriter and stands up. "They talk about everyone, Honey, and they certainly aren't nice about it. I'm going to fool them this time, though. Wait and see." She's putting on her coat when I realize it's only four o'clock.

"What if he comes back?"

"Call me at home. Just say, 'The dog has a bone,' and I'll hustle back. And don't worry—things *are going* to work out."

Watching the door close, I believe her. If anyone can make things work out for herself the way she plans it, Marylou can. The phone ringing makes me jump. I grab it anxiously. It's Jass.

"Let's meet at the dance tonight. I'll wear something so no one will recognize me. Okay?"

I've agreed and hung up before I remember I'm not dating him now.

I'm trying to keep a safe distance so things don't get confusing again. But I'm lonely. What I need is a girlfriend, someone to go places, do things with. Even though Twyla was getting caught up with her men and baby at the end, I could still call her and talk things over. Now I'm in the stupidest situation: living with two men, not sleeping with either one. Twyla would have taken them both on. The only satisfaction I'm getting is closing the door on my bedroom at night as Boardman lets the last of his whistly farts and Jass clears his throat for the hundredth time in an hour. Eating with the two of them has been a special form of abuse. Jass's jaw clicks as he chews. After a while it has the soul-searing effect of a dripping faucet. I'm tempted to punch it just to see if that helps. Boardman is another case. He litters the table and floor with food like an old parrot. I can't understand why he can't keep food on his plate. After every meal I have to get down on my hands and knees and wipe the linoleum. I want to shove the sponge in his mouth and make him suck the food off it. Then I hate myself for being so uncharitable. I can't win. I sure as hell can't keep living with these two.

The answer arrives bright and obvious as a new car: Go home. My old car is out front, parked where I can watch it. Nobody's touched it, and regardless of what Boyd Ziekert thinks, I know it's an animal at the trailer's gas line. Mice, squirrels, racoons, will chew on anything. It's happened before to my car, trailer insulation, wiring. What do you expect, putting a trailer in a field? And it has to be Sonny Boy pitching beers. His style. His aim. I'd just like to know why he's so mad. Or crazy. I'm beginning to understand how important Twyla was to his balance. And the town's and mine. Given the opportunity, Sonny Boy could cause more trouble than an overturned cattle truck. I'll just have to be careful. Keep the lights off, put boards over my windows, maybe even get a dog I can turn loose on him.

"Honey?" Baby's voice startles me as I'm locking the office at five-thirty. When I turn to look at her, I'm stunned. She is wearing a huge version of the baby costume from our childhood. Little blue and pink lambs cavort across the expanse of white that falls to the pink, floppy-eared rabbit slippers on her feet. Hanging from her wrist on a pink ribbon is a pink plastic baby bottle.

"Where's the bonnet?" I try to hold my giggles inside.

Baby grimaces and points to the satchel hanging from her shoulder. "This is stupid enough for now, don't you think?"

Nodding, I pick up the skirt of my velvet dress and step off the curb to get in my car.

"You look beautiful. That dress, where'd you get something like that?" Baby's voice carries wonder in it that softens my usual defenses.

"From a friend. How come you decided on the baby? No devils, tigers, or ballerinas around?" I smile to remind her of our old struggles for the choice costumes.

"It's so stupid, you wouldn't believe it. We just started this club, and I'm already sick of it. Mind?" She sits on the hood of my car before I can object. The metal sinks and creaks ominously until she hitches a hammy thigh over the front fender to relieve the stress. She halfheartedly brushes at the dirt from the hood smudging her nightgown. "I don't care if this thing turns black. I told Leigh I didn't want to come as a Famous Fat. I told everyone." She drops her shoulder so her big blue woven vinyl bag slides onto the hood next to her. It rattles and clanks.

"What's in there?" I frown, thinking of the splotchy but still unrusted finish on my car.

Baby shrugs. "The usual—measuring cups, spoons, food scale, vitamins, plus my makeup."

"Oh." I lean against the hooded parking meter. Boyd has designated this as my spot.

"Oh, yeah, you haven't heard. I got the staples out. My weight was leveling off, and I was so sick, they decided to try something else. Now I have to walk two miles a day and measure all my food. Believe me, I'm not hungry."

"You look good. How much have you lost?" With Baby you always have to be positive. Lie. In fact, she looks tired, her face gray and drawn like a sick person.

"I lost a hundred and thirty total, down to around two seventy-five now. I like the walking—feels good after all these years. I don't know, though. Things have gotten very . . ." She pauses. We both face west, measuring, comparing the sunset. Is it as good as the last one? The best yet?

"You got some time? Right now, I mean, to talk?" She lifts herself from the car. Somehow the weight loss has made her awkward, as if she can't gauge her reaction times, her own physical space, anymore. She was graceful as a huge fat woman, the way elephants are. Going in slow motion, lifting their trunks and heads rhythmically, without haste, as if their size gave them grace in time, as if more of everything were given with the gift of size.

"Where do you want to go?" I stand waiting while she thinks. "Bob and Shirley's?"

Baby shakes her head. "People always stare at me there—especially getting in and out of booths. How about the house?"

This time I shake my head. "The house" means our old family one and running into Daddy and Sonny, too.

"Okay. Your place. You drive."

Surprised, I stand there until Baby pulls on the door handle. "It's locked."

I unlock my side, reach over for hers, and wait while she stuffs her bulk onto the front seat. Actually, she fits for the first time in years.

"Are we just going to sit here or what?" she says when she's settled.

"Oh, yeah. . . ." I start the car and back out into the street. The Valiant is chugging asthmatically. "Needs a tune-up."

"I'll say. It's not going to die, is it?" Baby looks around her anxiously.

The notion of being stranded on Highway 11 in these outfits makes us look at each other and start laughing.

"Just be nice to him and he'll get us home. You don't want to hurt his feelings." I pat the dashboard, and Baby folds her hands in mock prayer.

"Please," she says.

When we turn onto my gravel road, I slow down. "Baby, the trailer's a bit of a . . . well, it's a little messy. There's been some, uh, trouble, and I haven't been able to clean up in a couple of weeks."

Baby blinks her big blue eyes and says innocently, "Is that why you're shacked up with that Jasper character?"

Rather than fight with her, I nod and wheel abruptly into my driveway. We both take a deep breath. I'd underestimated the mess. The place looks trashed. Empty beer cans everywhere. Food cartons and wrappers. Something must have torn up the garbage bags. And of course there are my three broken windows covered in black plastic.

Baby doesn't say anything as we pick our way to the door. I'm prepared for an even worse mess inside, but it's really not so bad. In fact, things look neater than I left them. Jass must have picked up for me. Why can't I trust a man like that?

"Want anything to drink, Baby? I've got all of Twyla's booze." I go to the linen closet/liquor cabinet.

"Got any Campari and soda?" She flops on the sofa. Apparently she's already forgetting those years of having to sit carefully to avoid breaking furniture.

"Campari?" I begin to shift bottles around. If it exists and Wolfgang could find it in the five-state area, Twyla would've owned it. "Yeah, here it is. And soda?"

"Soda." Baby is definite in her desire.

"Where'd you ever learn to drink this stuff?" I hand her the glass.

"Leigh Hunt drinks it. Says it looks like you're having strawberry pop while you're getting popped." She giggles until she realizes I'm not with her as I stand watching.

"Here, try it." She holds out the glass. I hesitate, then sip. It's oddly bitter. I try again, thinking that it looks so sweet, it must be good. I'm that way about a lot of food. Still bitter. I hand the glass back. "Think I'll have some Bombay on the rocks."

When I come back and sit down with my drink, Baby says, "Kind of spooky drinking dead people's booze, don't you think?"

"Morbid, maybe." I taste the gin, feeling it curl its perfume on my tongue.

"She was pretty spooky the way she screwed around, Honey. Lucky she didn't give that kid any diseases."

"Well, it would've been our brother gave 'em to her." I take an angry gulp of gin and feel it claw my throat.

"Okay, let's not get into it about her. She's dead and gone. And I wish she wasn't the only one, believe me." Baby looks around. "Cozy here, isn't it? I wouldn't mind living out here, away from Daddy and the rest of them. Sonny Boy and Leigh." She makes a sour face. "Can't believe all these men. All their stupid programs." She pulls her legs up on the sofa, stretches out, and rolls to her side facing me. "They don't have a clue, do they? I don't understand it—how they manage to stay alive, even. Half the time it's like watching beetles on their backs, legs waving in the air. You turn 'em over, do they scurry off? No, they tip right over again, legs wiggling." She raises herself against the armrest and takes a sip of Campari. The sofa squeaks like the joints are suddenly dry. She catches my concerned expression and grins. "Don't worry, I haven't broken a sofa since I lost the weight."

"I wasn't—"

"Yes, you were. Don't start lying now. You'll end up like Sonny or Daddy. Those two *are* driving me crazy, you know. Leigh wants to come over all the time, but those two hang around like a couple of bums. We don't get a moment alone. You'd think we were fourteen instead of thirty-eight. Leigh's even older. He's forty-one." She says this proudly as if he's accomplished something, like a cure for cold sores.

"Let me ask you a question, Baby. Why doesn't Daddy go live with his wife?"

"Damned if I know, Honey. I wanted him to stay for a few weeks 'til

I got to feeling better. This is ridiculous, and now that I'm more mobile, they want me to cook and clean!"

I shake my head sympathetically. I want to laugh. Serves her right after all those useless years on the couch while the rest of us had to work.

"Louverna is driving me nuts, too. She keeps calling and crying into the phone. I know it's her when I pick it up now by the hiccups she gets when she cries. Daddy gets on and they yell for a while, and he hangs up. When she's not calling, she comes over, for God's sake. The woman has *no* pride. Drunk! All hours of the night. I'm glad she's not *my* hairdresser these days. I wouldn't want a pair of scissors in *those* hands. She must be so hung over, she doesn't know what being sober feels like anymore. But the more she chases him, the stubborner he gets. He's like that big old boar we used to have on the farm, remember? You couldn't *make* him do anything, had to kind of just nudge and guide him with that wood panel. You sure couldn't push him, and you sure couldn't pull him. That's Daddy. If she'd ask me, I'd tell her. But she won't."

Baby rolls her lips in and smacks them. The trailer is getting dark as the last hint of blue fades outside. I turn on the lamp next to the overstuffed chair I'm sitting in. Another donation from Jake's family; its soiled green brocade is worn to the cream stuffing on the arms. It has a footstool, which makes it the most comfortable chair in the place. I've
even slept here. "Why is Sonny Boy there?"

Baby rolls her eyes, which seem larger, prettier, now that her puffy cheeks have shrunk a little. "He's crazy. Craz*ier,* I should say. He's always been a little, you know, *out* there."

I nod, but my recollections are a lot different from hers. I see him with a gun in his arm, striding from the house in the middle of the night.

"Since Twyla died, God, wasn't that *the worst,* most embarrassing thing on earth he did? Anyway, since that, it's like he forgets where he lives. When Louverna isn't on the phone, Rose Bevington is. She even sends the kids to the house to get him. You know Daddy doesn't have any use for kids, grandpa or no, and Sonny just looks at them like they're collecting for the Heart Fund. The worst part is *his* crying, though. A grown man! Well, in his case we can't really say that, can we? He's Leigh's age, but he acts about sixteen, not forty-one. Every time I see them in the same room, I have to pinch myself to remember they graduated high school in the same year."

"Sounds like you have your hands full." I get up for another drink. "Want another?"

Baby holds out her glass. "You know, he's like a new calf just been put on the bucket. I don't think he's put in a week at work or home since Twyla's. He's in and out of the house all hours of night and day. I don't see how Rose keeps going. If Leigh did that—"

I finish pouring the drinks and bring them back. "So you and Leigh are . . ."

When Baby blushes, the effect makes her head look like a giant rose. She drops her eyes. "We *like* each other." She pauses and looks up. "Who has a chance to get closer with those men around all the time? I don't see how you managed it. No one's living where they're supposed to now. Even you. Why can't people in our family act like everyone else? How am I supposed to get Leigh Hunt to marry me when we act like this crowd of hillbillies? Why aren't *you* living here now? Someone said you aren't even going with that man anymore, and you're out there. What's the matter with all of us?" Baby struggles to sit up and begins to cry. In her costume, the tears make her seem like some sad giant child in a fairy tale.

"Baby, don't cry, please." I get her a box of Kleenex from the kitchen. She takes it, and her shoulders relax, though the tears seem to stream freely down her face as if she doesn't have to put effort or much feeling even into crying.

"You've always gotten anyone you wanted, Honey," she accuses.

I shake my head. "No, that's not—"

She nods furiously. "Yes, it is. You got all the looks, and you've gotten all the men. Why don't you just admit it?"

"But I haven't . . . I—" There's a strangeness about what she's saying. A wrongness that conflicts with me, the *me* I know.

"Yes, you have: Clinton, Jimmy, Brewer, Jake, and now Jasper. How many does that make? And what did you have to do to get any of them? Bring them home? Feed them meals? Lie to them about their looks? About how interesting they are? No, you never do, do you?" Baby slugs a third of her drink without missing a beat. She's certainly learned something in the past few months. Now she's a real member of our family. She can drink and make herself miserable in love.

"Baby, you don't know anything about me, so don't try to feed me that stuff about my love life."

Baby watches me quietly for a moment. It's my turn to act macho, but when I slug a big gulp of straight gin, I get dizzy and have to fight for breath. This conversation has taken such a twist, I hardly know what I feel now. Usually she's attacking me for the men in my life; now she sounds like she almost envies me. You're welcome to them, I should tell her.

"You've always gotten all the love. Everything you wanted, you got. First Mama and Daddy, then your friends and those men. You've never had to work for it, Honey. Not like me." She speaks so quietly that it scares me, like a new, more dangerous Baby has entered the room, our conversation.

"But that's not true, Baby, it's just not true."

"They never hit you."

"No—"

"They never made you feel worthless, ugly, stupid, or did things to you—like they did to me."

"No—"

"They loved you."

"No—" I resist the logic. "No, I had to watch. They made me watch. I had to *witness* what they did to you. I learned to run away, to hide, not to get into those fights with them. I learned to go along with whatever crazy, mean thing they wanted to do or say because I didn't want to get hurt. I was always afraid, Baby. I was chicken." I rub the scar on my forehead—the one time he hit me was enough.

Baby ignores my words as if they're just so much wind in the trees. My chest and left arm ache from the tension of my discovery: my role as witness, feeling helpless and cowardly. Even the gin can't seem to cloud the memories of family fights at this moment. I didn't want to get hurt. It was that simple. I watched Mama and Daddy and Baby and Sonny fight, and I figured out how hopeless it was, like in a cartoon. It was a setup. The Roadrunner would always beat the Coyote. Daddy and Mama, older and bigger, could always beat their children.

"What about Leigh? Think about him. He loves you, doesn't he? Doesn't he want to marry you? And he doesn't even mind you the way you are. God, everybody wants to hear someone say that. You need to trust his love."

She gives me the once-over and goes back to staring into space. "Sure, it looks good, doesn't it? From the outside, I mean. Well, let me tell you something. Nothing's ever as good as it looks from outside. I remember as a kid walking by the Bungalow Bakery and wanting, just aching, to try all those creamy filled horns and bismarcks and cakes. Jesus, I'd almost faint, I wanted them so bad, and of course we could only afford to try one thing anyway. Not all of them. When I finally did get one home, when I finally begged hard enough, this one, precious tiny little pastry, this minuscule horn filled with creamy stuff, not only was it gone in two bites, but it *never, never* tasted as good as I thought it was going to.

It made me want to run right back there again, to that same bakery window, and try another one. And another, and another, and another. I always thought I would get to the one that tasted as good as it looked."

I can't think of anything to say, so I sink deeper in the chair, wrapping both hands around my glass.

Baby burps a short laugh. "Funny, isn't it? Most people would stop when it didn't taste like what they thought, when it wasn't as good as they wanted, but it always has the opposite effect on me. I can't believe it won't turn out different with the next one. So I keep on trying to find something good enough to eat." Her laughter comes rolling out of her like soft spilled dough looping onto the table and chairs and floor. More and more laughter. "God, this is funny." I try to join in but can't force out more than a big smile.

When she stops, she looks at me with a curious kind of expression. "You don't know what's so funny, do you?" She doesn't wait for my reaction. I'm interested, though. This is one of the only times she's ever laughed at her body.

"Well, the thing I was laughing at was how everything turns out the opposite. Like the bakery window. Like Leigh. Sure, I'm lucky. One of the richest farmers around wants me to be his wife. I can say it out loud.

Wants to take care of me, love me, give me what I've never had all my life. You and Sonny got all the love there was, whether you know it or not. You wouldn't see that, but there wasn't enough of anything in that house. Now I get what every girl hopes and saves herself for. And you know what? He likes me the old way. He wants me to go back to being huge. He wants me to give up just when I've started getting hold of my weight problem. Just when I'm finally able to do things I couldn't before—like climb stairs and come over and see you without having a stroke or something. Just when for the first time since I was a fat little girl, I can go to the Style Shop and find a blouse, granted the biggest they carry, a forty-eight, but still I can fit into it. Finally. And he wants me back the way I was. He turns around and '*accepts*' me. Now what am I going to do with *that*?"

"Ironic."

"What?"

"I said *it's ironic.*"

Baby shakes her head and dismisses me with a wave of her hand. "Don't bother explaining it. You always get so weird. I think it was Clinton did that to you. You were fine before he came along. I mean, not bad. You just gave up on yourself after Clinton. Everyone saw it. Broke

Mama's heart, you dropping in your tracks that way, like an animal that got shot. I thought for sure you were going to kill yourself for a whole year after that. Mooning around, not talking to anyone. Then Jimmy and Brewer. Daddy just washed his hands of you. Really, what did you think you were doing?"

There it is again. Family.

"Oh, fuck off. I mean, I'm sick of listening to stuff about how I screwed up. Don't you ever get tired of rehashing family history? Don't you ever just want to go off with Leigh Hunt and live happily ever after?"

Baby looks at me. Her face is like a surface of baking dough, smooth and full and pale, eyes sinking like raisins now. Then she sighs. "I guess I don't believe in Leigh Hunt, or I believe he'll turn out like everything else, just another trick. Another disappointment just like all those damn pastries. All my life I've felt disappointed in things. It's like I don't have any control to make them come out the way I want them to. Even in my own family. Mama dying and leaving me to cope with things when she knew damn well I couldn't. She knew it. She fed me, I know that now. Anything I wanted she bought or cooked, and stuffed me full as she could. Like I was an old bag of rags she'd put all the scraps, all the worn-out things, in. 'Give it to Baby. Baby'll eat it.' I remember her saying that from the first. When I was two and three, the only things I remember were Mama sitting in front of me, spooning food in, begging me to eat more, even after I was full, begging me, and then demanding and getting madder and madder and finally slapping me, until I cried, and when I opened my mouth she'd shove it in again. I learned, let me tell you, I learned. I ate and ate and ate. She never let up on me a moment, not a single moment, without offering me food, with that secret behind it. If I didn't take it, she'd make me."

She stops. There are tears in her eyes again, and her voice is roughened by memory when she speaks, lower and sadder. "I've never known why. She didn't do it to the rest of you. Only me. I watched, so I know, but I never got to ask her. She died, and I never got to find out why she did that to me."

Baby turns to me. "Do *you* know why?"

The hopefulness in her voice makes me want to say yes, tell her, but I don't know. I shake my head slowly. "No, I'm sorry. I just don't have any idea. I never knew. Really."

She shakes her head, too. "I tried to be *so good.* I tried to eat everything the way she wanted me to. I let her stuff me like a cushion. I never complained about it. I tried to make her love me that way. All my life I've been trying to make people love me, doing what they wanted. Daddy and Sonny and now Leigh. It's never worked before. They always end up turning on me, so why should I believe this is going to work out any better? You tell me that."

She's yelling practically, filling up the room with a huffing of hot air. I want to push her down on the sofa. Even though she hasn't moved an inch, it seems like she's rising up with her anger.

"Well," I start, but she interrupts me again.

"Don't give me any of your bullshit philosophy. You're sitting pretty now. A place of your own. It makes me sick. *You* make me sick. Miss Goody Two Shoes, Miss Little Snoop. How come she never made you clean up your plate? It didn't make them like you any more, believe me. You want to know something? Here's the secret, here's the best one of all." She pauses, and her eyes sparkle maliciously, hypnotically, like a snake weaving me to a standstill.

"They hated us all. Daddy told me once. They hated all of us. They didn't want any of us. He told me that. You were prettier, that was all, but Daddy wasn't the only one. Mama felt the same way. She died feeling like we were nothing, like we were all nothing. You weren't there toward the end, but I was, and Daddy was. A few days before she died she told me, 'My life's been nothing, worthless. I married and had a worthless bunch of kids. None of you'll amount to a thing. It's all been nothing.' She went on and on until the nurse came in and made me leave while they gave her a shot to put her to sleep. That was the end. It came down to nothing for her."

She pauses again, not looking at me this time, both of us looking at the garbage bags covering the windows slowly breathing in and out with the night air.

"It broke my heart. After all those years of trying to please her. When she said it, like she'd hit me again, and after I'd eaten everything up like she said. It wasn't fair. The next day I was so mad I wanted to go back in there, pull her up out of that bed, and make her tell me why. Slap her face until she said it. But she died instead."

I'm too numb to move. Baby smiles bitterly, awfully. "See? Nothing works out the way I plan it. So why should I believe in Leigh?"

"Maybe—"

"Don't be an ass, Honey."

The first thud against the trailer startles us. The second sound of a full beer can *thunk*ing through the plastic over the window, landing and rolling to rest at Baby's feet like an unexploded grenade, makes us jump up.

"Who did that?" Baby demands.

"Sonny, I think it's Sonny Boy."

Before I can stop her, she's grabbed the can of Bud and is out the front door hollering, "Sonny, you get your sorry ass out of here—and take this goddamn beer can with you!" I hear it explode on the road as it hits. "Don't you *ever, ever* come out here again or I'm telling Daddy. So fuck off." His car guns in reverse, squealing in protest on the gravel, then roars spinning and swerving away.

"Thanks, Baby. Really, thanks," I tell her when she comes back inside.

"Did he do all this?" She waves her arm at the blackened windows.

"I think so. I don't know why he's so mad at me."

She looks at me. "Maybe he thinks you drove Tolson off."

"Why would—"

But instead of answering she turns back to the door. "Can you run me back? FF is having their own dance to raise money for our centennial parade float, and I have to meet Leigh."

We're both silent on the way back to town, as if too much has been said and we have to go away now, to our dark holes, and think about things. Mostly I have to think about what Baby's said. Glancing over at her, I discover that what I *thought* I hated about her was her fat, but there's this real baby inside her, too. It's always crying out to me for sympathy: Love me, love me; for mercy: Hold me, take me; and for justice: You *owe* me, you owe me something for all that love you got. It's a muffled noise that comes out like static beneath her other, mean words. That's why she's always confused me. I've always heard both sounds and didn't even know it. Now I realize there's no answer, either. She'll never believe I've missed the same things she has.

As Baby gets out of my car in front of the Famous Fats Club, I ask, "Who're you supposed to be, which Famous Fat—in that costume, I mean?"

She tosses her hair. "Anybody's baby," she says, and closes the door.

20

Witches' Dance

After twenty minutes in the girls' john in the locker rooms of the gym fixing my hair and adjusting my little black mask over my eyes, I wander onto the gym floor. The committee has done their usual job with orange and black crepe paper streamers, balloons, and cardboard cutouts of skeletons and cats. Old sheet ghosts with pumpkin heads on stakes guard the corners and doors. Along the back wall, tables of punch and food are set up. We're supposed to donate money or food for the dance. The band is tuning their instruments on the makeshift stage at the opposite end. From their clothes, they look like aging rockers, which means the adults will be able to dance, too. In a community our size, you try to please the most people.

I station myself across from the entrance by the doors leading to the locker rooms and the rest of the high school. The gin buzzes at the back of my head, and the colors and figures in the room take on the bright intensity of new Crayolas.

Mike and Mona from the M&M Bowling arrive first, dressed as Batman and Batgirl. Their natural grace and good looks edge their figures like a comic book drawing. When the band notices a couple in front of them, they test the microphone and break into a decent version of "Sgt. Pepper." Mike's and Mona's shadows from their six-foot-tall figures rise like giant bats up the wall.

Then Velva McGee from the dry cleaners stumbles over the metal threshold. Thin as a broom handle, with a tongue like a sharp tack, dressed as a bride in a white floor-length gown with layers of net and satin. Velva's a joke version of a bride, eyes burning with the alcohol she's been sipping all afternoon. Her dry blond hair is matted on the side she's slept on in back of the dry cleaners while her mother, mute from the last stroke, waited on customers. It's that way every afternoon. Velva's dress drags on the floor, and the bodice hangs shapelessly from her shoulders to make her look like a child in her big sister's dress. It's probably something that got left at her shop. Velva has a habit of dressing from clothes people forget or abandon at the cleaners. She has no regard for size, though. I don't think I've ever seen a mirror in the whole place. She pulls down the waist of the dress as if it's creeping up. She must weigh one hundred pounds now. The drinking, we'll all say later, and click our tongues. Velva strides to the punch on the refreshment table, opens her purse, and pulls out a pint of vodka, which she empties into the bowl. Then she leans down and stares as if she's receiving messages from the orange chunks and cherries bobbing with the ice cubes. Finally she dips a paper cup full and drains it, smacking her lips together and sweeping the room with her eyes. My dark dress helps me blend into the shadows. I'm not in the mood for chitchat. I've got to think about Baby's visit and the one thing that bothers me the most now—she blames *me* for Tolson leaving. Where'd she ever get that? I'll have to do something about it without actually coming out and saying what Sonny Boy did.

Bowker, in his bear costume, arrives with his wife, Althea, who's dressed as a wild animal trainer in ski pants, high disco boots, and shiny black-patent vest, her whiplash dragging behind her. Her thin brown hair is slicked flat to her head, and she's wearing a fake mustache that somehow looks natural on her. After that, a regular stream of clowns, rabbits, princesses, cowboys, witches, ghosts, tramps, and characters from *Star Wars* arrive. There are two Elvises, three Clint Eastwoods in serapes with guns and Cigarillos, a Dolly Parton, a Marilyn Monroe, a devil, a chimney, a TV, a clock, two Grim Reapers, and others too difficult to guess.

It's as if I've come as the Invisible Woman, the way people keep passing by me without noticing. The musicians turn up the amplifiers and start a string of Doors songs. Their ten-minute version of "Light My Fire" wears out everyone over forty, who all collapse on the chairs at the tables lining the walls. Velva dances alone, her wedding dress flapping raggedly around her like a flag on a windy day.

Larue Carlson and Jonesy stop in the entrance to the gym as if they're royalty waiting to be announced. Larue is in fact dressed like a medieval queen—one of those on my favorite puzzle. Jones is dressed like

Robin Hood, gone to middle age and beer. The bow and arrows across his shoulder look like a child's.

How many dances like this have I been to? How many more will I go to? Larue and Jones link arms and walk like man and wife into the crowd. Behind me on the stairs sit a couple sharing a joint. Their hissing pull of smoke and words squeaking out between lips held against breathing remind me of my times with Clinton, smoking dope in cars, behind buildings, in movies, our parents' houses, school bathrooms, every place we could because the dare was part of the high.

When they notice me watching, the boy offers me a hit on the joint. I step into the hallway, take a few turns, and watch the world adjust like I'm rising on an escalator at Gold's in Des Moines. Everything looks brighter, more fake and hopeful, like a cartoon.

"What is this stuff?" I ask as the color volume goes up and figures go flat.

"Thai stick. Strong shit, huh?" the boy answers. The girl is gazing at the beige tile wall in front of her like it's a giant color TV screen. I watch the wall whirl and dance with hieroglyphs until it reminds me of tripping on acid with Clinton in Iowa City the time we sat staring at the brick facade of the telephone building for two hours while the meaning of life scrawled itself in designs across it.

"You don't need anything much stronger than this," I say. "Thanks." I'm just settling back in my place watching the room glow like a Las Vegas gambling strip when a voice pushes into my head.

"*¿Señora? ¿Qué pasa?*" The dark figure in black sombrero and black shirt and pants leans over me. His long black mustache almost hides his white teeth as he smiles. I look down. He's wearing tall black boots with silver-tipped toes and heavy engraved silver spurs. His silver conch belt glitters at his waist, and the full bandoleros crossed on his chest creak as he leans closer, his arm braced on the wall behind me. The smell of leather and oil almost hides his scent.

"Boyd! Where'd you get that outfit? Who are you?" I push at his chest, and he steps back.

"I'm Pancho Villa—George Washington of Mexico."

The costume makes him more a stranger, someone I feel awkward with. "What, how'd you get your hair like that?" I reach up and touch the long black hair. "Oh, it's fake."

Boyd looks impatient. "Of course it is, what do you think? Larue helped me fix it up. And I collected this other stuff over the years. When I was in California, and the wife and I used to go to Mexico. I got my badge on, even." He pulls the cuff of his glove off his sleeve to show me. There's boyish pride in his voice.

"Pretty authentic." I smile.

"You bet." The cowboy boots lift his body and make him more massive.

I wonder if Boyd would rather have been alive a hundred years ago. "You study that time or something?"

Boyd nods and leans back against the wall beside me. "History is my passion, you might say. Especially since the wife left." When he grins, I realize that he has actually made a joke about it.

"Good to have one, I guess." I cross my arms on my chest the way he has. I wish he were high so we could compare notes.

"Jasper here?"

"No. I haven't seen him, anyway." Annoyed that he assumes so much about my life, I add, "He's not my keeper anymore, either."

Boyd shrugs. His sombrero and mustache keep his face blank. Then he stiffens and straightens up, hands hanging loosely at his sides. "Uh-oh. . ." I follow his gaze to the door, where Terry and the men from Reiler's stand. None of them is wearing a costume; that would be expected. Their jeans and flannel shirts make them stand out as if they are the *only* ones in costume.

"Watch for Jasper," Boyd says as he walks casually toward them. His legs bow, and his hips swagger in the boots. Along the bass line of the music I pick up the jingle of his chunky silver spurs. The room is beginning to smell of heat, perfume, and sweat—and something else, as if the music itself tarnishes the air—metallic, rough, sweet. The way jewels would taste.

Terry surveys the room, passing over me, then coming back to stare as Boyd talks to the three others. Overhead a strobe and glitter dome have begun stabbing us with strokes and points of light. The stars on my dress are glittering. I'm suddenly a piece of neon advertising. "Don't, please don't come over here," I whisper, and try to push deeper into the tile wall as Terry leaves the others and starts across the floor. His ordinary looks seem menacing in the irregular pulse of light, and I am on the verge of running by the time he says, "Dance?"

I let him take my arm, though his fingers already feel like bruises. I let him pull me against his body so tightly that I feel the press of his belt buckle in my stomach, the outline of his pants zipper. I try not to touch his shirt with my face, but I can't help it. The plaid flannel rasps at my cheek. He's wearing some sour after-shave they advertise for macho men.

There's the scent of alcohol as he breathes out. We're slow-dancing to one of those songs you can fast-dance to also, and the kids keep bumping into us as they flail around. Terry's body tenses each time we're hit. I can feel the ridges of back and arm muscles from years of hefting feed bags, bales, and machines. I close my eyes and try to remember one good thing about that night in July we had sex, but nothing appears. He's a man who is so totally without distinction that I can't focus his face even now dancing against his body. He's like a model in the Monkey Ward's catalog—good-looking enough to be anonymous. I get ready to push away and thank him when he tightens his hold. "Dance with me."

"I—" But he's swinging me around and around, pumping our arms in a Texas two-step as the band leads into "The Yellow Rose of Texas." "Terry, wait—" I stumble to keep up in my long dress, which is tangling around my ankles. He half lifts me around the next rotation. The grass and alcohol make things spin faster. Closing my eyes, I feel a lurch in my stomach from the motion, his smell, and the light splattering and cracking the room.

Opening my eyes, I can't focus. We're whirling so fast now. Stomach acid burns up the back of my throat, and my legs get rubbery. "Stop—" I say it as loud as I can, but we're right in front of the amplifiers on the stage, and he just carries me, helpless, in tight circles until I'm so dizzy I know I'll fall down if he lets go. The music is a terrible clang in my head, and we're like a cartoon running too fast forward.

We hit the bird, or what I take for a bird. That's what stops us. The figure doesn't move, but we're shaken, and when Terry drops his arms, I almost fall into the curve of wing that is suddenly behind me. The surprise on Terry's face turns to anger as he realizes that the bird has taken his partner. He starts to step into the space, but the other man bows slightly to me so the brown and gold feathers on his hood and mask glitter and rustle. I move between them, taking the arm strapped with a wing offered me, and we begin the dance. Terry shakes his head and walks off the floor. A moment later I see him pouring a pint of something in the punch bowl, too.

My vision clears, and my stomach settles with the slow waltz my partner and I are performing.

"Honey?" The voice in the hood is too muffled to make out. Examining the arm and hand holding mine, I see only a cloth imprinted with feathers in bronze and gold. The hand wears a tight pale yellow glove tipped with long black talons. The wings are covered with a wonderful array of white, blue, green, bronze, and red feathers, layered carefully as if these are the real wings of some magical bird or angel. They flutter and follow the easy motion of his arms.

As we slowly turn, I lean back and look more closely at the headdress. The feathered hood resembles a hawk, the way it curves over the head. The elaborate mask conceals the face with feathers and beak. The overall effect is strangely threatening, yet powerful, like those *National Geographic* pictures of medicine men and shamans clothed as animals. There is a strange odor from the creature, too, earthy and hidden, stale and spicy both.

When the band shifts to a rock and roll song, we drift to the sidelines and stop. The bird stands looking down at me.

"Who are you?" I reach up to lift the hood, but he grabs my arm.

"Don't you know?"

There's something familiar about the way he grabs me. "Oh, Jass? Is that you?" I look him up and down. "What kind of an outfit is that?" His voice is so unfamiliar through the mask, I laugh nervously.

"How did you—" I touch the right wing carefully. The feathers are slippery, soft and hard both. I step back to get the full effect. "It's so different—intimidating, sort of, like you could make things happen, weird things, if you wanted."

He stiffens and raises his wings, lifting the air up into our faces. "I will." There's a rush of heat, not from the man, but from this creature with feathers so delicately shimmering in the broken light and cruel curve of nails and beak.

A feather drops, and I watch it rocking on air like a boat on water, following the rhythm down. The splinters of light capture it over and over, where it settles, but I'm afraid as I kneel to pick it up that when my hand reaches something else will be there.

When I straighten, the feather hot as a bird's body in my hand, he's gone. I look around, but there's no sign of him. Reiler's men are working the punch bowl pretty good. Another pint comes out and gets emptied into it. It's some ritual, I decide, the whole dance. It's like we're repeating some ancient moment. The hieroglyphs printed on the tile wall of the gym, the telephone building in Iowa City, the Pyramids in ancient Egypt, what difference does it make?

I start thinking again about my acid trip with Clinton and how later that night we watched a meteorite shower, unable to tell which were the meteorites and which were the stars we were making fall—like a sky full of silver buttons our eyes pulled off—there was an eternity more. Everyone was familiar that night to us, there were no strangers, each face stamped with a star, a hieroglyph, we'd seen before on someone else—the name, the place, just on the tip of our tongues.

"Lost something?" A Mexican bandit materializes in front of me.

"Oh." I peer at his face. "Boyd—oh . . ."

"Get a grip, woman. We just talked, remember? What're you drinking?" He leans close and stares into my eyes. "Or smoking. You're not on anything, are you?"

I reach out and touch his arm. "I'm fine, Boyd. It's just a little strange in here tonight, don't you think?"

Boyd looks out across the room. "Tense is more like it. Where's that damn Jasper, anyway, you seen him yet?"

"No, uh, I don't know. . . ." I scan the crowd for my bird.

"I don't like it—Reiler's men, the bar crowd. You know, some of these old boys don't want to have fun like regular folks. If you see Jasper, tell him to lie low." Boyd strolls away just as I catch sight of Sonny Boy. Twyla would've loved his costume. He's come as Spartacus or some Roman gladiator because he's naked except for a little Roman-style skirt, leather lace-up sandals, leather spiked cuffs, a sword, and a gold headband. His body glitters iridescent as a beetle. He's like a god come to walk with mortals. As he turns his head, a gold hoop flashes in his left earlobe.

Sonny has pierced his ear! Wait till Daddy—but then there he is, dressed in a tan military uniform. Beside him Louverna is the small figure of a harem or slave girl, barely clothed in gold chains, silk, and jewels. The couple from *I Dream of Jeanie.*

Stepping back among the other spectators, I watch the three of them sweep past as if they're extras on a movie lot. It's a relief that they don't notice me. The band turns up the amplifiers and begins playing "We All Need Someone We Can Bleed On," and the floor fills with costumed dancers, writhing and twisting as if a huge wind were boiling through or a house just burst by a tornado—an explosion of cloth and glass, wood and metal, whirled and tossed in front of me.

Even over the music, I hear the men laughing in that way of men at their meanest. I begin to push my way through to see what they're doing, but someone grabs my arm and hauls me to a stop.

"Wait," Larue says firmly in my ear with my arm in her grip. I tug to get loose. "No, let Boyd handle it. That's his job. You come talk to me." Larue pulls me after her across the floor before I can protest. She's surprisingly strong. She must fool a lot of people with that lady business. The hold she has on my wrist would have done Mama justice.

On our way downstairs to the girls', I see the same couple, still smoking. Only now their heads are collapsing against each other, and the joint is burning out on the floor where it's been dropped. I pick it up on the fly and take a toke. The smoke heats my chest, then pounds my head into wafer-thin silver.

I'm finishing it as we stop in front of the mirrors to do inspection. Larue looks at me, then grabs the joint from my fingers and throws it in the toilet in a single smooth motion. "Honest to Pete, Honey, what is the matter with you?"

I smile sweetly at her in the mirror.

She laughs. "And don't give me that flirting bullshit. Remember, I've been at it a lot longer than you have." She pulls out a purse-size can of hairspray and aims it at her platinum head. "Watch it—" She pushes the button. She repeats this with perfume, mouthwash, and something she sprays in her own face. She still looks perfect. "All natural, see? Beauty is best achieved with a pure body, unpolluted." She watches my curiosity in the mirror. "No drugs or booze."

I nod as if I agree. I will do that about almost anything, I realize. I'm the great agreer. I could get along with Adolph Hitler. Atilla the Hun. I'd just listen and agree. Christ, I get along with my boss, Bowker, with Boardman, Baby, Twyla, Boyd, Jass . . . Clinton, I got along with Clinton Busee! I try to sit down, but there's no chair, so I let myself ooze down the wall onto the white-and-black ceramic tile floor. Suddenly I'm outside myself, seeing me from someone else's perspective. It staggers me—this vision. I'm gutless. I don't have any values, anything I stand up for. I spread my legs and get fucked whether I'm having sex or not. "Oh," I moan.

"You okay? Not that you should be—you keep abusing your body, Honey, it's gonna catch up with you. Believe me, I know. It's cost me plenty to repair all the damage I did early on. Plenty. . . ."

She outlines her lips carefully with a lip pencil and fills them in with pink lipstick in a familiar pink case. "Mary Kay." I laugh. Are we being taken over by body snatchers? At least Larue knows how to put her makeup on. No pie-wedge cheeks or rainbow eyes.

"You know, Honey, Boyd is really putting himself out for you. I hope you appreciate it. I really do."

I nod obediently. Stupidly, keeping my eyes blank as typing paper.

"You could pay him back, you know. Help him out, so to speak." She pauses in the adjustment of her face.

I nod, turning back to watch the cold silence of the toilets squatting in their white-and-black stalls.

"He needs to know about your brother—what he was doing that night of the Appreciation Day picnic seventeen years ago, for Roger and Mort. You remember. And the others—Clinton, Jake, Jimmy, and Brewer."

I watch a big flat roach the size of a dead elm leaf stroll down the line of toilets like an officer inspecting the troops. If I ignore her, maybe she'll ignore me.

"Honey?" Something jabs me in the thigh. I strike at it with my hand but keep my eyes on the roach. It's not until the music upstairs stops midbar that I realize she's been watching me the whole time and nudging me with the pointy toe of her shoe.

"What?" I ask despite myself.

"What do you know about the murder of that poor black girl?"

"What? What do those guys have to do with her?"

I'm impressed with how quick my mind is until she says, "I saw someone in a car that night—heard, then saw. They were shooting guns out the car windows. Trying to have fun putting a few more holes in Stop signs and picking off those blue glass insulators on top of telephone poles. Boyd was on an accident, but I heard them. Got a glimpse before they sped off."

She's not making sense. "Who? My brother, out with Clinton and the other guys?"

"It was Sonny Boy's car I saw." Larue says it so quiet, her purse shutting sounds like the click of a hammer on a gun shell.

I nod. "Oh."

Shouts and whoops from upstairs stream into the bathroom. Larue and I exchange looks. "Maybe we'd better go upstairs." She grabs my arm and helps pull me up. "Nice dress. Where'd you find it?" She rubs her hand appreciatively on the velvet.

"Jasper's."

"Oh?" She smiles and walks out with me behind.

Reiler's men and a few others have formed a little group in one corner by the bowl, which must be almost pure alcohol by now. Someone has set up another bowl filled with lemonade in an attempt to offer an alternative.

I follow Larue to the group but stop by the punch as if I'm getting a glass. Pancho Villa is nowhere to be seen. Scanning the dance floor, I think I get a glimpse of my birdman, but it's too dark and confusing to be sure. I'm too fucked up to focus on anything much. The room is gradually dissolving into a cartoon for real now. Voices sound like insect squeaks. The music seems to be coming from a tin can fifty miles away. I pour myself a full glass of punch and turn to see what Larue's doing. The group has split apart for her. Sonny Boy is standing defiantly, his skirt flipped up so everyone can see the jock strap he's wearing underneath. It's outlined with sequins. Larue is staring at it. I turn away just in time to see Jonesy lumber up in his green jersey Robin Hood outfit. Tights and all. Larue is pushing him back while Sonny Boy is trying to pull out the sword he's cinched to his waist. Robin Hood steps forward, knocking the other men back with a sweep of his big arms.

I've seen the next moment so often on TV and in bars that I look down and take a big swallow of punch, closing my eyes as it hits my chest, taking my breath for a moment. When I open them, the birdman is standing over Sonny with a hammer or club in his hand. Two other men press toward the bird but are sent sprawling when he knocks their jaws, splitting skin and spraying blood with his weapon. Three other men step back. Only Jonesy remains, and Larue has him anchored firmly by the arm.

As if the bird can feel my eyes, he turns and looks at me fiercely. I step back against the table, but he uses his wing to sweep me in step and out the door. Pressed tight to his side, I have no choice when he growls,
"Run."

The familiar red truck is the only one running, I discover as we spin around the parking lot. There are enough slashed and flattened tires to let Fergie's Super 76 Station have an early Christmas.

"Jass?" I squint into the darkness as we drive without lights out Highway 11. Luckily the moon is bright enough for him to make my driveway and rumble past the trailer to park behind in some trees.

"Jass, you have to—" He puts a hand over my mouth and half carries me to the door, which he slips open with a small pocketknife he has ready.

Inside he neither turns on lights nor lets go of me. My face keeps brushing the sturdy wing feathers as he drags me down the little hallway to my bedroom. I am flung on the bed with him straddling me before I can protest. There is something both terrifying and sexual about the beaked face, the winged arms, as they pull the dress off my shoulders. I struggle, but only because it seems important to seem to—while I am moaning and twisting, trying to free enough of my body for him to have—take—use—all the words I hate. He forces my arms over my head and holds them while he lifts the dress to my waist and rips off my panties and hose. Then he brushes my breasts with his wing until my nipples are hard and aching. When his full weight finally crushes me, I spread my legs as far as I can, trying to take him all inside me, feathers, the horrible hard beak pecking my eyes, my face, and disappearing into the dark rush of his wings, I'm finally taken so far beyond myself, I can't stop.

21

The Silence of November

The next day is November, and I wake up alone, my room unfamiliar with its fake wood paneling and cheerless yellow nylon curtains. Nothing about this room is me. I kick at the covers. A cloud of feathers dances up and settles back like dark snowflakes. "Jass?" I call into the empty trailer, but I can feel I'm alone. The air is singular, unticked by other breathing. Outside my window the corn field is being harvested. The huge orange picker mows down the stalks, grabbing the cobs like hands. I don't even have to look to know that dust and noise, the tiredness of men at the end of the day. A pain shoots up the left side of my head and spreads like spilled acid along the top of my skull. Maybe, just maybe, I've overdone it this time, I decide as I carefully swing each leg to the floor and sit up. The action almost takes the back of my skull off. "Okay, relax, aspirin on the way."

By the time I've made tea and toast despite protests from my stomach and bowels, the corn picker has roared by my trailer twice, shaking the dishes and what's left of the windows. Why does there have to be a morning after? I lament each time the picker seems close enough to run through the trailer.

I'm just putting on my red-and-blue sweats when someone pulls up. Baby, with another car right behind her. Sonny's. Scary. Halloween's over, I want to protest. Sonny doesn't get out, and Baby only stands beside Daddy's car and honks.

"We're going to get your car," she explains when I poke my head out the door. "And Sonny's gonna fix those windows, so leave the door open."

I'm standing there with my jaw hanging when she says, "Hurry up. I don't have all day."

I pull on a blue Blacksmith Lounge jacket but hesitate at the door. I don't want Sonny Boy in my house. I know I don't, but I can't go through it all with Baby. I decide to hurry back.

"Was that Jasper in that bird thing? Leigh and I snuck out of the Fats' dance 'cause it was so boring and caught the tail end of the fight at the gym," Baby says when we get to the highway. She's a terrible driver, alternately punching and letting up the gas pedal with a rhythm that's making me carsick. We slip a little on the loose gravel as she enters 11. "Careful—" It's out of my mouth before I know it.

"Mind your own business. Was it Jasper? Sonny spent three hours getting his tires fixed." She chuckles. "I thought it was pretty damn funny. Louverna had a cow. Daddy had to get down on his hands and knees in the parking lot. Got his uniform dirty, so he's pissed. Didn't Louverna look stupid? She's too old for that outfit, don't you think?"

Baby doesn't need me to hold up my end of the conversation today. I glance at the car clock. One P.M.? I must've slept like the dead.

It feels good to be back in my car, heading for home ten minutes later. Then I remember Sonny's there fixing the windows. I wonder whose idea that was.

As my body stops fighting the bright sun, I notice the other aches and pains from the night, as if I've been having sex with wild animals. My leg and arm muscles strained, and my crotch bruised almost. Yet there's a sense of secret satisfaction, like I finally got something I wanted, with no thinking and talking, no problems. I feel stripped, naked, pure.

The ditches along Jass's road are chocked with dry grasses and weeds. The sumac has lost its leaves, and the red branches are like bent, accusing fingers. The browns of burrs, beggar's lice, and thistle are perfectly outlined against the softer tans and yellows. The wild aster is dried brown now with the faded yellow goldenrod going to seed and the milkweed seeping out of brown pods. I'll pick some on my way back for a jar of grasses and stalks before the snow crushes them.

Jass is in the barn when I track him down. He doesn't look surprised when he sees me or when I kiss him with more passion than we've had in over a month. The best thing is, he doesn't smile smugly. We practically have sex beside the manure cart in the aisle but manage to step into the stall he's cleaning and do it standing up against the wall. The aches and soreness seem soothed by his cock as he works it slowly in and out, probing for something. He's holding my legs around his waist, and

I'm watching the wood scarred and dented by hooves on the wall opposite, but letting the feeling take me. I've stopped fighting Jass—for now, at least.

"We're going to teach you to ride today," he says as we pull our clothes straight.

" 'We'?" My head lurches with a stab of pain.

"Me and the big yellow mare. She'll be a good teacher. Let me finish this stall, then we'll get you some chaps and shoes and get started."

This is one of those ideas that's better in the abstract, I realize as Jass is zipping a pair of Cindy's chaps on me. I'm wearing her low-heeled brown shoes that come up over my ankles, too. "Paddock boots."

"You sure this is okay?" I ask as he boosts me onto the mare's back and I have to scramble not to go flying off the other side. I'm too embarrassed to admit how hung over I am.

He laughs as I sit up stiffly. "Relax, let your legs mold around her sides. Feel her butt with yours and follow the motion. That's it, yes, good. No, don't tense your arms, relax them. Try to think of the reins as threads leading to her tender gums. Better, yes—"

Jass keeps up a steady stream of comments while I struggle to keep the list of instructions in mind and the mare from walking me into a corner and stopping. She's no dummy. We both know I'm clueless here.

A horn honking out front makes all three of us look up.

"Damn. I'll be right back." Jass starts across the arena.

"Wait, let Boardman—"

"He's gone home. Don't worry, just keep walking." He disappears through the door.

The horse's big body is surprisingly warm and comforting once Jass isn't there to make me pay attention to all those details. I loosen my legs, letting them swing with her walk. She walks faster, and I dig my heels in for safety. She starts a trot. With the first bump, I abandon the reins and grab the mane, clamping my legs tighter. She trots faster, traveling in erratic lines now that I'm not guiding her. I bounce higher and higher as she trots faster. I can't find that safe, stable balance place and feel myself landing all over her back. She weaves across the arena, and I begin to slide, bouncing as my leg is pulled farther and farther up her side. I grip the mane like a life preserver, afraid the hair will give and I'll be killed beneath her giant hooves. That's when she runs into the wall and I go sailing off into shadows and stars.

"Honey? Are you okay, sweetie? I shouldn't have left you, are you okay?" When I open my eyes, the world is sitting safe and still and Jass's worried face makes me smile.

"Doesn't even hurt, but I saw stars," I brag, rubbing the spot where my head hit the wooden stud. "Ow."

"Yeah. Let's put some ice on that. You sit here with Molly." He gets up, slapping the mare's flank and handing me the reins.

"No way. I've had enough of her. I'm fine." I stumble up and let him catch my arm.

"Okay, okay. Come on, then. I've got Aronson out there trying to unload his apples on me." He slips the bridle off the mare and turns her loose.

"From the orchard? Are you crazy? Those are great apples. Is he giving or selling them, Jass?"

Walking hurts a little, too, but I keep my mouth shut. A good soak will fix that up.

"Giving me apples. But why the hell would he do that? I'm not a charity case, you know."

"Nobody who'd ever met you would think that. Will you just relax that pride a little bit?" My ankle turns unexpectedly, and Jass puts an arm around my waist.

"You sure you're all right?" I nod and lean into him, it feels so good. I'd forgotten about this part. Aronson is letting down the tailgate of his black Dodge pickup as we cross the barnyard. In the back are six bushels of red apples. My mouth waters in memory of how crisp and juicy they are fresh off his trees.

"Now these are the windfalls, Miss Parrish," he says as he climbs slowly into the truck bed. "They'd make the pies and the sauce, but not so good the eatin'." He bends down to tug a bushel forward.

I look at Jass, who frowns and jumps lightly into the truck. "Here, I got it—" He lifts the bushel easily, climbs down, and sets it on the ground.

"Take 'em all." Aronson gestures toward the remaining baskets. "Got too many as it is. Brought 'em for the horses. Can't raise any myself, but I've always liked a good horse. Always have." He nods in agreement with himself and climbs down stiffly while Jass retrieves the apples. Old man Aronson has a lot more cross to bear than Marylou or most people in Divinity. His son, "Prince" Reinhardt, is sitting in Anamosa Prison for the rest of his life, and old man Bevington can't walk down the aisle of his cow barn without seeing that girl's body trussed up there like a new-slaughtered heifer after Reinhardt got through with her.

Aronson looks out across the paddocks and fields, where the horses are snorting and playing in the late fall sunlight. He pulls out a little tin of snuff, goes through his ritual, and blows on a big dirty gray handkerchief. "Yesss, the apples are for the horses. You give 'em one a day, it'll keep the coat nice and shiny. We always did that in our family. Keep 'em happy like today—glad to be alive. Good to see an animal so glad to be alive."

Jass walks over and sticks out his hand, "Well, thanks. . . ." He tries to sound grateful. "You come and visit the horses whenever you want. I'll make sure they each get their share."

The old man turns and smiles at me. "You steal an apron full and make him a nice pie, you hear?"

I smile and nod him into his pickup. He climbs in tiredly as if his joints don't bend very far.

As we wave Aronson down the driveway, Jass says,"Nice old fart."

"Jass—"

"You talking to me, woman? You get your apron and make that pie before I whup you." He takes a pretend swipe at my behind, and I grab his hand.

"Boardman's gone?"

He nods and smiles.

"We're alone?" I pause and let my face show what I'm thinking. "Come on, then."

Later, I think I hear the wasps humming lazily around the apples in the last of the late afternoon sun. I look out the window next to the bed and watch them walking the bruised surfaces, pausing where the juice has oozed and stuck. I think I can see the tiny hairs on their legs, the specks at the tip of their antennae touching, tasting the warm sweetness of apple. It's hard to believe that Reinhardt will refuse to see his father, who takes the best, the juiciest, mahogany blood red apples to Anamosa for his son each year. I can't imagine living anywhere else at this moment, being too far away to eat these apples each fall.

Jass is beside me, sprawled across the bed asleep as if he had a long night, too. There's no evidence of wings in the room here, and I'm tempted to go back to the attic. But I like watching him sleep in the special stillness of November when the sun can bring the noise of wasps or a fly caught in the window because, except for the crows who own the trees at dusk, sound has migrated with the birds.

I know Sonny Boy is in my trailer, reading the wall charts in the kitchen, running his finger down the lists for his name, Twyla's. I haven't told Jass he's there. Somehow, with Baby in charge, Sonny seems disarmed, harmless for the moment. I don't want to see him though. Larue said his car was out that night of the shooting. Is Tolson right? Was it Sonny Boy with Uncle Fred's deer rifle? I shiver, though the room is warm. Jass's skin is so smooth and uniform, it glows like good oak or leather. It's a skin for loving. But do I love him? As if the question pricks his sleep, he frowns, catches his breath, relaxes again. Or am I like one of those wasps, drawn to the surface because it's shiny and sweet? What's to keep Jass from becoming Clinton or Jake? I can't help remembering his bloody body in the back of Twyla's car. Then Twyla— It's just no good, it can't work. I keep getting suckered into it by the sex. "If it feels good, do it," Clinton said back then. Now I know what a lie that can be.

Carefully sliding out of bed, I reach for my underpants with the crotch still damp and cold against me when I pull them on. That's why I have to get out of here. When the heat is gone, you always end up having to do the laundry again.

I get dressed quickly and quietly. Down the stairs and through the door, I pause in front of the apples. Being careful not to irritate any wasps, I choose an apple, brush at it, and take a bite. The sweet, soft insides squish and juice in my mouth.

"Hey, what's going on?" Jass calls from the bedroom window above me. Without looking up, I bend down as if I'm selecting more apples.

"Just don't take a bite out of every one of 'em," he says.

"Don't worry." I straighten, looking up at his head and bare shoulders framed in the window.

"Tell him, Honey." Clinton's voice suddenly intrudes.

"Shut up," I mutter, taking another bite of the apple. The too sweet taste of a brown spot fills my mouth, and I spit it out.

"Nice. What's going on, Honey? Why'd you get up?" Jass's voice drops. When I look up again, he's resting his chin on his arms, folded on the windowsill. The screens are down for the season, but he hasn't managed to put the storms up yet.

Checking the apple before my next bite, I try to think of how to explain it.

"Just tell him about—" Clinton urges.

"Honey?" Jass calls softly, wonder and sadness in his voice now.

"Uh, I gotta go, Jass. That's all. I can't— I know you're a good man. You're good in bed—the best, in fact—but I can't rely on that. You'll find someone nice. . . ."

I shrug, waving the apple as a wasp tries to land on it. "I'm not the one. No matter what everyone else says, Jass. I'm, well, I'm already taken." I pretend to search for another good place on the apple.

"Oh. Sure, yeah, right, Honey. Who is it? Somebody I know? One of Reiler's men, maybe?"

"Don't be an ass. You know better than that. It's—"

"Tell him."

"It's no one around here—physically." I wind up and pitch the apple as hard as I can toward the paddocks. It falls so far short, Jass snorts.

"You'll never get a job with the Yankees. Wait there, Honey, I'll throw on some jeans and come down so we can really talk this over."

"Don't. Don't come down here, Jass. Just stay there."

"Say it, tell him."

I shake my head. "It's Clinton. I'm still in—"

"In love with him? He's a dead man, Honey," Jass says as if this is news to me.

"I know that. It, somehow, it doesn't matter. I can't do anything about it. My heart just feels, well, taken. At first I thought I could do it, have sex, have a good time, even love a little." I look up quickly to see how he's reacting. He's covering his face with his hands and scrubbing so hard, I wonder if it hurts. "Jass?"

"A little, Honey? A little? How would you know when you reached the right amount? Get on a scale? Check the gauge? And what was I supposed to do? Compete with a dead man? What, does he fuck better than me?" His eyes are so bright and hard, they fill me with shame.

"You can't compete, Jass. I know that, now. And the sex *has* been great. As good as—"

"Clinton!" Jass slams his fist on the windowsill, shaking the glass above him.

"I can't do this anymore, Jass. It doesn't work. Trying to love you while I love him. It's too big a job. I just can't face it. When we make love, it just reminds me—"

"Of what, him? So sleeping with me is like fucking a ghost?" He's shouting, leaning out the window now. It's lucky I made him stay up there, the way he's acting.

"Don't be stupid, Jass," I say in a low voice. "If anyone's a ghost around here, it's me. I'm a ghost—emotionally. I'm empty, a haunted house. When I said he took my heart, I meant it. I try, but—"

"This is shit, Honey. This sucks. What is it? What's he have that made you so—*dumb*?" Jass pulls back inside the window and settles on the floor so only his profile shows.

I sit down beside the bushels of apples humming with wasps. "He loved me."

"That's it?" Jass says in a tired voice. "*I* love you, don't you know that?"

My stomach gives a bump, but I squeeze it silent. "He was the first person who ever loved me, made me *feel* loved, worth something, *lovable.* He came into my life, took it over, and gave it a whole new shape. He taught me things, he helped me see that I could *live,* you know?" I push the toe of my tennis shoe at a pair of wasps tangling in slow motion on the side of a basket. "Then he died. And I never got a chance to thank him, to show him . . . I don't know, that I loved him, too, loved him so much that I would've done anything to keep him alive. But I never had the chance, he—"

"Committed suicide in Spirit Lake."

"No." I shake my head at how plain and wrong Jass's words sound.

"Some love, Honey. You're right, I can't compete with Clinton."

After a few minutes I look up again, but the window is dark now. Around me there is silence, as if the whole world is holding its breath. Even the wasps seem suspended, still. I get up and go to my car.

"I'm sorry," Clinton says.

"It doesn't matter—you can't help it." My words seem so sad, I have to pinch my eyes tight to keep the tears in.

The new windows at my trailer glitter in the late afternoon sun. Sonny has actually washed them, too. They make the other windows look clouded with dirt. Inside, he's cleaned up the black plastic and glass. The reformation confuses me. He's getting weirder than Clinton.

"I resent that—Sonny and Jake are cut from the same cloth, not me."

I grab a can of Diet Pepsi from the fridge and sit down in the living room to enjoy the sun setting in my new window.

"You're such an oracle today, Clinton. Why don't you solve some real problems like world hunger, war in Latin America, or who killed that black girl Boyd and Larue are bugging me about." My head is beginning to ache gently, like the low hum of a fluorescent light. Just below pain level.

"You can solve that thing for Boyd. I can see the other answers from here, but I can't change things." He sounds so sad, it makes me like him better again.

"What about Twyla? Don't you ever—"

"She isn't here, Honey. She's gone."

I catch myself nodding again. The sun explodes just under the lip of fields and licks the blue sky with red and orange that stretch out in long pink and salmon skids. I can't put it in words yet, but this is what makes me afraid. The red glow pouring into the room illuminates the fingerprint Sonny Boy missed in the right corner of window. Is that the finger on the trigger? Will Jasper leave me alone? If I am very quiet, very still, will my life grow as quiet as November?

A few weeks later the wind rises from the north and the west and blows across the fields, whistling through the tatters of remaining stalks at night, haunted by herds of cattle that move like slow machines through the rows, searching out the ears of corn that sit hidden among the yellow leaves. And beside the fence in farmyards, the dead hollyhocks wave their stiff fingers into the sky, and if you put your ear close, you hear the faint click of the tiny seeds jostled in their pods. In the moonlight, the dark fuzzy outline of farm horses, backed against the corner of the barn, butts thrust uniformly into the wind, stand silent now that the cold is all they have to look forward to, their backs glittering white with frost, a frost that seems to burn the air at night, nothing escapes it.

Inside the houses of Divinity, dotted silent by the coming cold, the moon escapes into rooms, spilling its milk into slippery pools along floors and beds. I remember as a kid staying up late in my attic room, slowly twisting the dial of the old RCA Victor radio, and sound pouring in from everywhere. Skipping out of beams and nets of cities, it landed occasional as insects, as casual as moonlight, along the little bands of numbers, Fort Worth, Springfield, Texarkana, Fresno, Wichita, Winnipeg, Halifax, and Binghamton. It was the smaller places that arrived with a peculiar clarity, as if there weren't as much to hold them in place. I dreamed of them as I listened to the talk, the list of streets and drive-ins and request-night all night, the late-night DJ's like good fishermen casting out as casually and indifferently as men throwing balls to each other in the park, the laziness of the flicking wrist. The effort disguised by its own effortlessness.

Along the ceiling of the attic bedroom, with Tolson's teeth grinding out the work of his dreams, I pictured the towns, starting up the Mississippi on one side and down the Missouri on the other, Moline and Davenport and Muscatine pitched like tents that never came down along the slow, flooding richness. Council Bluffs, Hamburg, crouched like dogs before water moving too fast to drink, and in between, the saucer scraped out by glacier, deposited with oceans of prehistoric animals, seas that sank into the earth, slowly sifting themselves. Leaving to us the rock, the soil, and finally the greenness that was pooled with water washing the rock down to itself, eating the animals and vegetation until anything could grow here, anything, and when the early settlers came across it, prairie and grass and soil dark like looking in a well, they built their houses, dotting the dark lushness so that at night the land looked like a sky turned upside down.

Years later the order of the land would appear as a giant quilt to people, carefully squared off, sown with a variety of colors. But to me, on those nights alone it sometimes seemed like the ticking of a metronome, keeping the rhythm of imaginary music, helping us learn the fingering of the parts, each square putting us in perfect timing with each other, with the land. As Clinton says, Iowa is a state of mind.

When I turn out the light over the trailer's little stainless-steel sink at night, my charts catch the moon, and the writing looks like veins and capillaries or the central nervous system of a body. Maybe human, maybe not. And although Jimmy and Brewer and Clinton and Twyla have tried to disappear, they are as visible as towns along the lines connecting them to me.

Wednesday before Thanksgiving, Marylou is wearing a special look, and it's not Mary Kay, either. Once as she passes, she slips a colored travel brochure on my desk. "Come to Beautiful Colorado," it announces. I slip it under the ledger I'm working. When Bowker goes for coffee with the Centennial Committee, I open it. "Mountains, Lakes, Romance of the Old West" accompanies pictures in that too enthusiastic color of brochures.

"My kids are dying to move there," Marylou says as she leans over my shoulder. She's a whole chorus of smells—foot powder to hand lotion to mouthwash. I'll bet she wears deodorant panty liners even when she doesn't need them.

"We might have to," she explains when I look up at her. "I don't know that he'll want us working here after the suit. He can't fire us. Don't get me wrong, but he can make us so miserable we want to leave."

"I'm just not sure, Marylou." Behind the innocent blue of her eyes, there's an edge like the blue that ice turns at a certain low temperature.

"Take your time." She goes back to her desk and sits. "I could really use your help, though. The case would be much stronger, and we could drive out there together. I don't think your car would make it, do you?"

I shrug. "I'll think about it. What're you doing for Thanksgiving?" I've been careful to wait as long as possible. Her children are loud, obnoxious, pushy kids who break half of everything they touch. Jake and I fed them one year. I didn't get the cranberries off the TV knobs until Christmas.

"We're fine," she says happily. "And you?"

"I don't know yet." I hate to admit it, but no one has asked me to dinner. I don't answer my phone at home, though, so who knows. Baby's with Leigh's family, she told me. Sonny with Rose and the Bevington clan. Louverna has Daddy convinced she won't spring any surprises on him if he comes to her place for dinner. In a way, this emptiness feels good. It's a relief. Twyla was the only one who'd ever have made me eat with people. Suddenly I'm on my own, I discover, except for Clinton's voice. I might have to give that up, too, if he keeps bothering me. I'm finding that I like people abstract, distant, like those radio stations from outside Iowa. If this is a ring of hell, I can handle it. It's empty, but it's painless. That seems like a good bargain. Who needs Colorado and the mountains, anyway?

I'm just reaching a perfect condition for solo holidaying when Tom Tooley opens the door, pushing a baby buggy awkwardly ahead of himself. Marylou jumps up to help him so the cold air doesn't freeze the pipes by the time he gets organized. He's not much better at steering a baby buggy than a car.

Tugging away the layers of blankets, he carefully lifts her out of the buggy. She's almost invisible in a puffy pink snowsuit except for two blue eyes and a sweet mouth.

"Say hi to Aunt Honey." Tom takes a pink stub of arm and waves it at me. Tamara Julia just stares. It reminds me of Twyla. Tom unzips the suit a little and pulls the hood off her face. When Marylou stands on tiptoe to see the baby, Tom shifts her a little closer to his body. Ignoring Marylou's inquisitive look, he says, "My mom and I want you to come to dinner tomorrow. For Thanksgiving, you know."

My first reaction is to say no, but he looks so earnest, so hopeful of doing the right thing. "Oh, I may have other plans, let me check, okay?" His disappointed look almost makes me say yes. Instead I ask, "How're you doing, Tom? Are you getting along all right, you and the baby?"

His expression brightens. "Sure, yeah, we're fine, great . . . well, you know how it is. I sure miss her—even though we didn't get to spend much time—you know. Still, just being in the same town was . . . well, you know, Twyla—" He says it as if *she* were a state of mind, and in a way

I guess he's right. "You should come over, visit the baby, Honey. Anytime, even if you can't do the thing tomorrow."

"Sure, yeah, I've just been so busy. . . ." It sounds lame even to me.

Tom stuffs the baby back in the suit and the buggy. When I peek in to say good-bye, only her eyes show like two dark holes in the pale blankets.

I help with the door this time as Tom leans over the buggy, saying, "We're going bye-bye, Tammy. Bye, bye, bye."

"You haven't seen her since the funeral, have you?" Marylou accuses me.

"I haven't felt like it, haven't had time." I sit down and stare at the ledgers, imagining my obligations and responsibilities in the debit columns. There's almost nothing for the credit lines. "And I'm not going to Tom's now, either," I mutter to the pages in front of me. "I have enough dead people to worship as it is. If I'm not careful, I'll spill the truth to Tom about who else Tamara Julia's father might be."

"You're talking to yourself," Marylou calls in a singsong voice like Julie Andrews in *The Sound of Music*.

"You going to the Tooleys, then?" She snaps the gum she constantly chews to annoy me when Bowker's out of the office. I know why I'm not going when she makes that sound. Too much noise with other people. I need the crackle of metal siding shrinking as the temperature drops, the wind tapping the limbs, the thump of whatever has moved in beneath my trailer for the winter, and maybe even the insistent hiss of my own breathing.

22

Safety

Something happens in Divinity between Thanksgiving and Christmas. Everyone goes crazy. I mean it. Now that I'm the unofficial UN observer to this war-torn country, I can be more accurate and honest in my reporting. Everyone is crazy. Some days I think the kids are fooling with the well water.

Houses and trailers burn down from overloaded wiring and exploding Christmas trees, people grow angrier by the day because they're borrowing and using credit cards for presents they'll be paying off till July (if they're lucky).

It's December 22, and I haven't heard from Sonny Boy's beer cans since Baby caught him, which is a relief now that really cold weather is here. Louverna is still trying to figure out how to get Daddy to move in with her—short of dynamiting our house on Bedford Street. The only problem with that is it'll leave Baby homeless, too. I could warn Louverna that she'd better relax before she strokes out or goes mental. Daddy will be along when Baby marries Leigh Hunt.

At work, Bowker disrupts us daily with new crises about the way the Christmas lights are strung over the streets or the way our windows look with their little holiday scenes and spray-on snow greetings or the way *we* look: "Not holiday enough." I've taken to wearing black. It's simple, and I only have two tops and one skirt to trade off. Easy.

The Famous Fats Club sent in a proposal yesterday for a centennial parade float and plans for an open house. Life-size cardboard stand-ups of famous town fats. They've decided to make "fat" a positive term, like "black" for Negroes.

We're getting proposals daily now for the centennial in May. Twice a day Marylou and I update the charts Bowker's hung. The twenty-four-hour bowling tournament, the pig race, the oldest returning native, the cooking contest, the raffles to win everything from cows to cars. And of course the parade, when as far as I can tell every motley character in the tricounty region will drag itself or something with sequins down the street. Personally, I'm thinking of leaving town for the weekend.

The fund-raising is over half-done. Bowker's even squeezing small children for their ice cream money at school. Forget starving people in Africa, earthquake victims, or refugees. Divinity *will* have its day of glory. "Dress a pig up, you still got a hog," Daddy always said. But I'm careful to keep my opinions to myself. Bowker's eyeing me suspiciously like I've got communist blood under my black clothes. I start wearing a garland of red tinsel in the office to please him. When he's out, I sometimes wrap it around my head. Marylou just cracks her gum, arches her eyebrows, and passes me another brochure on Colorado life. Durango? Fort Collins? Cripple Creek? Why not stay here, where you can at least *see* what's coming across the horizon at you? I want to tell her. When she came back from Thanksgiving, she was wearing a cheerfulness that surprised me even. Someone spotted a car from Nebraska parked in front of her apartment all weekend. The lawyer's doing house calls. If she keeps this up, she'll *have* to move. Mike, her husband, is at County Detox again, so he doesn't know yet. He'll have to get drunk when he finds out.

I've put off Christmas shopping. The only places I feel like going are local—no trip to Iowa City or Des Moines. It just doesn't seem worth it. I pause before buying the ten-pound box of candy in Steadman's window, but I hate to break tradition just because Baby's on a diet. This year I'm tempted not to get anyone anything. See if they notice the junk is missing. Hard to decide whether to get Daddy and Louverna a group present or not. I get the usual for Sonny's family: some candy for the kids and a poinsettia for Rose. A bottle for Sonny. Adding gasoline to the fire. Makes sense. Marylou and I exchange three packs of control top panty hose in special holiday wrapping. We get Bowker a new stapler, letter opener, and paper clip tray. In matching wood trim. I always wonder who buys this stuff, then every year at Christmastime, I discover it's me. I do.

Sometimes I see Jass's truck in town, but since I walked out that day, he's not bothering with me. The holidays are keeping people busy—less time for Jass and me to hassle each other. Every night I go back to the trailer and sit listening to the wind breathing at the seams and windows. Twyla's is abandoned. Kids discovered it and broke the windows on Halloween. Nobody's come out to fix them, so the weather and animals have moved in. I feel lopsided now, like the earth with one pole gone. I sleep with the lights on most nights, dropping off after a couple of pages of Dante, waking again later. It doesn't make much sense, except for a phrase here and there. I'm beginning to feel like Clinton. I could open the book anywhere and get about the same out of it. We've settled in for the winter, Clinton and I. The trouble is, it doesn't even worry me much.

Three days before Christmas, and I'm looking forward to spending another holiday alone. There's the little pitying part inside me that feels sorry for myself, but I grab it and give it a good shake every time it squeaks. On my way to work I notice the fields laid shiny and smooth with icy snow like a new linoleum floor. When I turn onto 11, the pile of mail I grabbed from the overflowing box this morning slides off the seat onto the floor. Reaching over to pick it up, my hand touches cold metal—the screwdriver from Reiler's. I drop the mail. Let it go to hell, too. Predictions about me are coming true. The unpaid bills swirling with circulars and cards from insurance men (Bowker, I addressed it myself) and banks tell the story. If there's a hitchhiker on 11 today, I'm going to pick him up just so he can put his wet, muddy feet right in the middle of that pile. Glancing down again, I notice Jake's familiar handwriting. It's some mealy-mouth greeting card, I discover when I open it out of habit.

When Jake came home last Christmas from his traveling job, he hadn't called in weeks. I tried to reach him sometimes at night, but he never answered. He was always "on the road," wasn't even sure of his schedule.

I was at the Blacksmith that night a year ago with Twyla, Jonesy, Harold Spitzer, and a few other assorted men. The usual Twyla gathering, having pitchers of beer waiting to see what the action would be.

Pretty soon there was this elbow in my side, digging in like it'd left something there, and I said, "Hey, watch it," to Twyla, but she nodded her head like a pointing dog, and I looked over. It was Jake, leaning against the bar, having a beer and watching us. Like he'd just landed with the first wave from Mars. I didn't like the look on his face, that bland nothing that scared me so much, so I hustled on over to him and tried to give him a big hug, which worked about like trying to cozy up to a pine tree. I told the bartender to give me a beer, too, and asked Jake what was up. He just looked at me, and I started to feel a little creepy. Someone dropped some money in the jukebox and played about a dozen of the country and western Christmas favorites that Jonesy puts on the box.

"How come you didn't let me know you were coming in?" I tried another approach. It didn't work. He just eyed me like I might have fleas or something. I remembered once when Jonesy was a little loaded, he told me about trying to be an encyclopedia salesman. How they'd train you to have all these things to come back with, to get the customer going in your direction. Jonesy said it was like herding animals. You just had to get them rounded up and working the way you wanted them. First you sold them the bookcases, and they were real nice, came in a variety of laminated finishes to go with any decor. Then, of course, you'd sell something to fill those fine-looking bookcases, and these turned out to be the encyclopedias themselves. The big thing was to always carry one with you, under your arm. The other arm hung on to those bookcases. But the one you carried was always K for Kennedy, and you always worked it so the book opened naturally to that first picture of JFK and Jackie, the family portrait. Once you got them softened up, you talked about the children of the house and their education. It made everyone believe they were going to have a little president on their hands, soon's they could get the kids to read those things.

As I tried to open Jake up, I kept wishing I had something to sell him first—like the bookcases. But I didn't have anything for him, only an above average piece of ass that he seemed to think I peddled all over the county, because he just took another deep drink of his beer and eyed me like we hadn't been introduced yet.

I noticed he'd bought himself some clothes, something that didn't look like Iowa. A nice tan dress shirt and soft-shouldered jacket of some natural fiber. He even wore a woven wool tie. Looked like a damn college kid with his short haircut. "Razor cut," we used to call it. Now it was blow-dried, and as I looked down I saw he had on loafers. Loafers, for chrissakes. That scared me. I didn't know what was happening suddenly, when the man I thought I knew showed up in loafers. It tipped the whole scale. He might as well have walked in there with an umbrella.

"You changed the way you look." That brought the first smile out of him.

"Yeah, you like it?" He even sounded different, worried about his appearance in a way I didn't trust. Then I noticed that he had lost weight, too.

"You been sick?" I asked.

"No, damn it, just losing weight. I was the fattest ever living with you. I just wanted to get back to feeling good about my body, get in shape." It was true, he did look better. "I took up jogging." Although it was the big thing to do in cities, no one around here jogged. No one except people on the football and track team. Or some college student. But by the time they moved back here they got that urge worked out of them. When we were up at Sleepy's one night watching the news and sports on his twenty-five-inch color TV and the Boston Marathon came up, everyone at the bar about busted a gut at those folks stampeding like a bunch of chickens.

"Does your family know?" The way I said it, so seriously, cracked him up.

"No, why should they? It's not like I took up dope smuggling or have terminal cancer, you know. I said I took up running. It feels good. Everyone in the city does it, so you meet lots of people and keep in shape at the same time." Then he gave me a once-over look. "You better watch that beer drinking, you're going to need something like running to keep in shape pretty soon, too." Then he took a quick drink, cleared his throat, and looked around him.

I kept wishing for bookcases and the letter *K*. John Boy, where were you when I needed you? "Why don't you come over and sit with us." I wanted to tuck him in there somehow, get him snugged up at the table, loosen the tie and step on the loafers once or twice for good luck.

"No, you go back. I just want to unwind from the trip a little by myself here. I got some things to think about, and you've got a good start with your friends there. When I get ready, I'll just go on back. I flew in to Cedar Rapids and rented a car. So I'll meet you at the trailer, okay?"

It was like the loafers, the rented car. No one rented cars around here. When I left him standing there, it was like walking away from a stranger you accidentally bumped into and had a little conversation with. The jukebox kept pumping out all these mournful tunes about making it home and not making it home and how wonderful Christmas was sure to be anyway, without him or her, but prison was as hard a place to be as any. And boy, I understood that. "I know I'm crazy, but it keeps me from going insane." That old Waylon Jennings line kept playing at me, round and round, so I had another beer, and when Twyla asked me how come Jake didn't come sit with us, I just told her he was busy planning his sales pitch.

"He's all strategy these days," I said, and drank half a mug of beer. Then I felt Twyla's boot under the table chunk into my foot.

Jonesy turned on his chair to look at Jake and gave him a nod hello. Turning back, he said, "Looks pretty spiffy. When'd he start wearing them shoes?" I heard rather than saw Twyla's elbow going into his puffed-up sides, because she almost shoved the wind straight out of him. "Look,

I was only kidding, right, Honey? You took it like a joke, right? Twyla here's about to massacre me. Tell her to lay off, Honey, or I'll have to spend Christmas up in the hospital with a collapsed heart, soon's she breaks all my ribs." We all had a little laugh, and people forgot about Jake standing there alone at the bar, watching me casually like he was thinking about coming and getting introduced, but maybe not.

What Jake was doing, acting like he was passing through town on his way from Iowa City to Chicago, spooked me. I felt stapled to the table, the chair, the people I was with, and he was the staple gun, throwing them with his eyes into my back. I couldn't leave. I couldn't help being what I was, drinking too much with my friends, my voice getting louder and telling coarser jokes and trying to outdo everyone with Twyla watching me like I was a poor misbehaving child and pretty soon she'd have to haul me out to the car for a slap across the face and a good shake. Later I'd debate about how to include my part in what happened: accident? fate? chance? Was that what Jake believed?

In a while Twyla did get up, and I watched as she went over to where Jake was standing at the bar and started talking to him. They smiled and agreed on something. Then there was a whole series of things she was telling him because he just bowed his head over his beer and studied the foam real intently and shook his head once in a while. He didn't say anything, and Twyla looked like she was delivering him his rights because she was being more and more emphatic. I saw him steal a glance my way once in a while, too, but there wasn't anything in his eyes that I could read. What do you know about a stranger, anyway?

After another beer and more Christmas on the box, I didn't care so much about Jake and Twyla talking there at the bar. What difference did it make, what the hell. It'd give Baby something to hiss about, and hell, my daddy, he couldn't care less. It was just going to be a little more lonely than usual. I could feel something breaking up inside me as I drank too much and looked at the faces around me. Like the ice in March on Spirit Lake, it grayed and cracked and then chunked off and melted in the most surprising way—happening almost overnight sometimes and always leaving me a little sad. Though the deep turquoise water should be a sight to see, I always miss the heavy white of the ice and snow, capping over, hiding, all that movement. For a little while, in winter, I feel like I have everything under control. Organized. Then spring comes, and the world springs up "boo" to scare me.

If Jake's brother, Harlan, and a couple of his biker buddies from Des Moines hadn't rolled in, it would've been better. The roads were clear from the last storm, and God knows it must've been fifty below on those cycles with the wind and cold, but Harlan liked to think he was tough enough to ride in the Arctic if he took a mind to it. So he came bursting in with a big cloud of frosty air and a red face, followed by two other guys, and there was a little reunion. A kind of uncomfortable one where the two brothers found themselves being friendlier than either of them felt, and caught themselves in a big hug. Harlan's two buddies just leaned, hipshot, against the bar in their black leather and looked cynical.

Pretty soon Harlan and Jake were having a beer together; Harlan had his arm draped over Jake's shoulder like they were old friends. When you looked closer you could see the white knuckles on Harlan's hand from the way he was digging into Jake, and Jake was tight as wood as he stood there, like he'd grown to the spot and Harlan wasn't going to get a chance to shove on him without having to uproot the whole thing. They'd always been like this, two brothers who needed to dislike each other. Jake running off and leaving the whole farm to Harlan hadn't helped, and then Jake getting married to me and going to Chicago. It just left Harlan no choice but to hate him. I was beginning to think Harlan had a point. Jake just walked out on things when they didn't interest him anymore. "Short attention span," they called it in school.

By this time Larue was back with us, wanting to waste no words with Harlan; they were on a nodding basis only since the time Harlan took a buddy over to Larue's for a poker game and they got in a fight with a couple of the volunteer firemen. It was hard to tell about Harlan. Some people thought he'd settle in once he got married and started eating Campbell's soup for lunch and worrying about light bills. I didn't know. He seemed like the kind of person that would die of disappointment in himself if he couldn't keep acting like the town's rowdy. Or if he didn't manage to kill himself somehow on that big Harley hog of his, he'd surely hate to live to old age, you could tell. But he wasn't quite tough enough to go out to the interstate and ram it down the wrong lane at a hundred miles an hour, taking some citizen station wagon with him when he got ready to go. Harlan just wasn't put together that way. Maybe there was a bit of Harlan in me. I knew about that disappointment in yourself—the town reminded me every day. But did you die of it—like it was a thing you didn't get for Christmas? Harlan and I would probably never take things as far as Clinton did, just to prove we didn't care. Which means we do, I guess.

I supposed things weren't moving as fast as I remember, but I was drunk and it looked like a fifty-second slide show to me—one of those "history of mankind" in under a minute deals. In the next frame Jake was standing in front of me, yanking me out of the chair to come home with him, then digging through my purse to throw the keys at Twyla, who all but took them in the face, but she was fast enough to duck. As we passed Harlan, he had this big grin on his face, the kind of happy meanness that made my stomach turn even later. Then he said something I didn't quite hear, like "for the night." I didn't get the front part, and Jake was shoving me against the jukebox and then standing over Harlan, who was suddenly on the floor spitting blood. Then old Willie Nelson popped into the noise with "On the Road Again," and Harlan was standing over Jake, who was rubbing the right side of his face like he wasn't sure it was still there. When Jake saw the blood on his fingers he was up again, and they were dancing around in another hug like two funny bears. Only when I looked again, they were pounding into each other's guts, and in another moment it was Jake on the floor again, this time with blood pouring out of his ear onto that nice sports jacket. Then Harlan was down under Jake and getting his face beat in a little, and by the time I was in the bathroom getting my forehead cleaned up by Twyla from where I cut it against the jukebox chrome, the other two were being held and talked to by Jonesy and Harold.

When I came out Willie was singing "Blue Eyes Crying in the Rain," and someone made a joke about black eyes closing in the snow. By then I was getting a little sober, that island of clarity that sits in the middle of being drunk, which I can get to if I don't try too hard to think anything. I saw Jake was busted up around the face, but it was nothing he was going to die from, and Harlan was back at the bar having a double shot of Wild Turkey, the bottle in front of him, laughing it up with his friends while you could see he'd have one hell of a time riding home that night with two eyes swollen shut.

Jones grabbed Jake's arm and led him out to the parking lot, and Twyla took me in my car. In the next moment we were home, and I was trying not to pass out in bed, with the room spinning like the tilt-a-whirl Jake and I liked to ride at the fair. Jake was sitting on a chair down the hall at the kitchen table. I could see him there, smoking a cigarette and taking little sips of the Jack Daniel's he must have found in the cupboard. At dawn when I woke up he was passed out on the couch in the living room, and I covered him with a blanket, noticing that the loafers dropped beside the couch were scuffed now, and one had a deep cut in the leather of the toe.

I hadn't been into putting a tree up. It didn't seem like it mattered.

But I did miss the way it made the place smell. I called in sick since Jake was home, and Marylou was going to cover for me. There was nothing to do all day but wait for Jake to wake up and see what he wanted to say to me. Whatever all that was about last night.

When the phone rang, I just sat there for a moment. I wanted to pretend that no one was home, but then I realized that it'd wake Jake if it kept on, so I grabbed it off the hook. Well, I could've saved my energy. It was Jake's sister, the one who worked at the bank, calling to check on Jake. It was news by the time the bank opened. Jake and Harlan got in a big fight. They were drunk, of course, and Honey was the one started it, but Jake beat her up, too. That was the story. By the end of the day I knew there'd be a lot more that got tacked on it as it went around. When I said that at least part of it was true, at ten A.M. in the morning, Jake's sister, Earnestine, had a fit but kept her voice low and controlled since she was at work. I got the general idea, though. "Well, I'll tell you," she summed it up, "it'll be wonderful when he decides to divorce you. You're nothing but trouble. You and that whole trashy family of yours."

It was so odd, hearing these things said in such a low, even voice, but they stung like a whip she'd sent curling around me. I could just manage to reply, "Well, don't let it worry you—and have a *nice Christmas,*" before I hung up.

A minute later I could hear the water running in the bathroom and the toilet flush. Then Jake came down the hall into the kitchen, rubbing his hand through his hair and looking like someone had been at him with Magic Markers, he was such an assortment of black and blue and red. "How do you feel?" I asked him, knowing anything I said would be the wrong thing.

"How do you think I feel, for chrissakes?" Then he pulled out the big pitcher of icy orange juice I'd made for him when he woke up. He always liked to cure his hangovers with that. At least, as I looked over his swollen and cut face, it was a relief to see that blank look wiped off. He sat down opposite me. "Where'd you get that cut on your forehead?" It was the first nice thing he'd said in twenty-four hours.

"You gave me a shove against the jukebox; it happened then." I was waiting for him to apologize. Waiting for the kind hand to come sneaking across the table to give me a pat and a squeeze. But all he said was, "Oh," and went to studying the orange juice in the glass. That was a habit he'd picked up in Chicago, studying the contents of glasses. Looking at nothing so hard, you'd think it'd turn into something just from all that concentration.

"How you feeling this morning?" I was getting uncomfortable, feeling I was back at the bar with the stranger in the loafers. The thought made me glance down. No, he was just in his socks.

"How do you think I feel? You sure got me pounded up good. How am I going to go back to work looking like I've been in a barroom brawl?" He drained the juice and looked around the kitchen again. "You got anything decent to eat here?" I was a little stunned as I got up and started making scrambled eggs, bacon, and toast. I couldn't think of anything to say at the moment that wouldn't start a big fight, so I figured I'd just lie low for a while till he got some food in him and was feeling more human. I knew he couldn't mean that I was responsible for the fight. He wasn't crazy.

He grimaced when I set the plate of food in front of him, and that pissed me off. Not the other stuff, but just the idea that I'd cook something and he'd make a face over it. "What's the matter? My cooking's not good enough for you now?" That got him a little because he shook his head quickly and pointed at his stomach in between bites to let me know he still had a hangover.

Then he choked out, "Stomach hurts a little from Harlan's punches. Food's good. Using butter now, huh?" I'd forgotten I should only use margarine with him. I shrugged it off. What the hell.

Because of Harlan and Jake's fight, we weren't going to his family's for Christmas. We spent the afternoon buying a roast beef and some treats to go with it for our meal alone together. I was feeling so good that I went out and blew every penny I had on a new watch for Jake. A Timex electric. It sure was a nice watch. But when he opened it, this wave of something came over his face, then passed quickly away, and I couldn't remember it well enough to hang on and figure it out. So I let it go. He strapped on the new watch and gave me a present. A Totes rain scarf in bright colors. It was nice enough, but it somehow didn't seem very personal. The look on my face didn't go away fast enough, because Jake was quick to explain that it was what all the women were wearing in Chicago. In fact, he'd gotten the idea from one of the secretaries at work. She always wore such beautiful things. She'd helped him pick it out. I tied it around my neck, but it felt big enough to make a whole dress out of. After that he gave me a set of aluminum bowls I knew he'd picked up at the hardware store in town and a bottle of Jack Daniel's.

I tried to get over feeling that we'd lost something in that exchange. When Twyla and Tom, together for the first time in a couple of months, showed up to welcome Jake and give us a little something, I wanted to break down and cry when she asked me to show her my presents. Jake didn't show his watch around until I reminded him.

Toward evening it started snowing, just that light powdery kind that looked like salt someone was shaking out overhead, but it was pretty in the yard light outside. Jake and I were sitting in bed, resting up from the day and feeling pretty good about each other, I thought, when Jake said to me, "Well, Honey, what're we going to do about this living apart? It doesn't seem to be working out so well."

I thought for a moment, shrugged, and said the first thing that came to mind, only half-serious about it. "Well, Jake, we could get a divorce."

It was like he'd been waiting to hear those words for days now. "Okay, let's do it!" He never even asked me if I meant it. It seemed to bring us closer, figuring out a divorce, and that was the part that fooled me. Because the next day when Jake left to go back to Chicago, it suddenly hit me, that empty space, he wasn't coming back.

"You got to be careful when things get easy," Clinton warned me that morning. "The hard things to do are usually the right things when it comes to your emotions." Clinton was full of advice, I thought, that day, watching Jake's car drive down the road out of sight, then later watching the snow start to fall in big furry flakes that covered up the last trace of tracks and even wiped out the pine trees across the road. I'd be snowed in by morning, but it didn't matter. When the phone rang at dark, I answered it, thinking it'd be Jake wanting to take it back, wanting to say he missed me already and he sure didn't want a divorce, the relief of getting things settled wasn't worth that. Instead, he just wanted to tell me that he was happy we'd finally gotten things straight, and if I needed anything to let him know, he would go ahead and file there so I wouldn't have everyone in town talking right away. That'd happen soon enough.

After finishing the bottle of Jack Daniel's Jake gave me, at midnight I called Twyla's, but I got Wolf Reese, pissed off about something, snarling at me, "She isn't here." He banged down the phone. I knew it was interesting, that he answered the phone and she wasn't there, but I couldn't deal with that right then. It was too far away. She always had something for herself she could put in the middle of all this like an island of safety. And Tom and Wolf and Sonny couldn't get through that part. They'd never even get close, if I knew Twyla. I was right and wrong, as it turned out. Nothing kept you that safe.

Driving to work this morning, I remember how long that night was, how waiting for the morning to come when I could talk to some human voice on the other side seemed to take a year. I know now that that's my problem—no island of safety. Nothing done well, done right, that I can feel my way back to when things get tough.

This year my lists glow in the snow-light-sprinkled kitchen. Dark grinning curves of relating lines that seem to prove I really don't belong here, to the town, to my family, to my friends. Even the dead have a story, a place. If I'd been able to say something concrete, for certain, then maybe it would be different, but I let Jake go. He was just part of an accident my life made, a piece that gets swept up later. Some of the pieces get buried—Clinton, Brewer, Mama, Twyla. Others just disappear from sight—Jimmy and Jake. At least X marks the spot for the dead. They gain something. A highway safety sign, "Accident Control Area." The others just spiral away, spun by the force of impact. Daddy, Tolson, Baby. Who am I to make a list? Does the survivor have the right? Even if my hands *aren't* on the controls, shouldn't they be? Aren't I implicated, the guilty party, all along. The one who survives has to be doing something wrong.

As I walk in the door at work, Marylou says, "Azium Boardman wants you to call him. It's important."

"What now?" I throw my coat on the rack by the door and stomp to my desk. Bowker has put plastic Santas and miniature candy canes on all the flat surfaces in the office. This morning he's added a plastic poinsettia plant whose spiky leaves menace my hand as I reach for the phone.

Boardman takes enough rings to answer that I consider sending the fire department to check on him. "What's going on?" I ask instead of the usual greeting.

"Honey. Oh, sure, yeah." He sounds breathless.

"Is everything all right over there?" I could leave now, I figure, and be there in five minutes.

He takes a deep breath and laughs. "Sure, I'm just trying to take care of some things before I— Anyway, I need to see you. Soon as you can make it. When's that?"

I'm at work, you crazy old fart. I have to work for a living, remember? That's what I want to say. "Uh, lunchtime? I was just going to wander around, anyway. Is that soon enough?" I keep my voice level, calm.

"Noon it is. Just bang hard and walk in. I may be out of hearing range, so holler. Oh, and tell them you'll be a little late getting back."

"Azium, this better not be"—he hangs up while I'm finishing my sentence—"about Jass."

Marylou watches me as I settle into my work. I don't feel like giving her the satisfaction, so I ignore her. Bowker comes and goes all morning, his face lit with a ridiculous smile. He's planning our Christmas "office party," which always ends up more celebration for him than us. No matter what Marylou's got planned, I'm not going in that damn closet again. I've decided. At least not without a weapon. Or leaving the door open.

Just before noon I look up in time to catch Jass turning away from the window. Before I realize it, I'm out of my chair. Marylou looks at me curiously. "I'm getting ready." I circle back to the bathroom. Staring at myself in the dim little mirror, I acknowledge that I've never looked good in black, and I still don't. It picks up the dark circles under my eyes. Sleep has become a game of chance lately. I keep dreaming of Nazi invasions and huge bills I can't pay. I wash my hands and flush the toilet, though I haven't used it. Lately I find myself wanting that assurance—that things are clean. "A lady never has dirty hands," Mama would remark after our visits with Miss Ethel at the Style Shop. Last night I found myself staring at my hands, holding them as close to my face as I could, to see into the pores and cracks for that telltale crease or bump of brown. When I caught myself at it, I got uneasy. What did it mean? I wondered, and went to look at the bar of soap in the bathroom as if it were spreading dirt, not taking it away.

On my way out the office door, I pull the sleeve of my coat over my hand so I don't have to touch the latch. It's a small gesture I notice I've taken on after I wash my hands. What's the point of clean hands if you smear them with other people's dirt, I reason.

Despite his promise, Boardman's door is locked, and I have to pound on it for a while before he comes.

"Oh, Honey, God, I'm sorry. People were bothering me, visiting the shop. Always happens this time of year with holiday vacations. Come in."

The shop looks oddly disturbed, as though things have been moved around or taken, but I can't tell what. A garbage bag and a cardboard box sit in the middle of the kitchen as we pass through. There's a bigger stack of boxes and a duffel bag in the middle of the living room. Boardman sits down at one end of his sofa and pats the place beside him. I hesitate, then sit at the other end. His face is struggling with a smile as he watches me. I look around the room. Some of the pictures and knickknacks are gone. There's an unsettled air in the room.

"Notice anything different?" he finally asks, recrossing his legs and grabbing his knee to rock himself.

"It's pretty obvious you're packing things up in here. What's going on, Azium?" I'm not really in the mood for this as I notice the dust dancing in the sun streaming in the window. Pretty soon it'll settle on me. I'll have to go home and wash my clothes.

"Take your coat off. This will take a while to explain." He's dragging it off my shoulder before I can stop him. I struggle out of the sleeves and shrug it off, and he puts it on the rocker in the corner. It's probably covered with dust.

"See these?" He pulls a packet of photos from his back pocket and brings them to me. "My new life."

They're pictures of brown and green hills, cactus, a brownish river winding between cliffs of a small canyon, and a village of adobe houses. The sun seems bitterly bright in each picture. Everyone is smiling from beneath wide-brimmed hats.

"Up in the hills, a few hours north of Mexico City. My brother found it. A few Americans go there to retire, but mostly it's still native. Unspoiled. Some interesting geology, too."

When I look up he's smiling like a kid who's just done something his parents told him not to do because he'd get hurt, but he didn't get hurt so he feels powerful and scared both. Is it all right? his expression asks.

It's so sudden, I hardly know what to say. My stomach has found a hole and drained. "So you're leaving?"

He nods.

"How long have you known?" This is the part that hurts, his secrecy. Even if I haven't talked to him much lately, we still have Clinton.

He folds his arms and looks over my head. "Not long. My brother's been writing me about the place for a few months. Then the snow started, and I just couldn't face shoveling that walk again. Just didn't want to end up facedown with the steps half-done. You get to be my age . . . So here I am, packing for Mexico. Leaving tomorrow, the twenty-third. First thing. Be there in time for Christmas. What do you think of that?"

I lean back into the soggy comfort of the old brown brocade sofa whose cushions are so loose with pounded stuffing, they look like they've been on a diet. "I don't know . . . it seems so . . . I don't know. What about all this?" I wave at the room.

His smile almost bursts the seams of his face. "It's yours. Merry Christmas!"

My ears bring the words in, and my body stands up, but my brain won't take the step of belief. "What? What do you mean?"

"Yours. This is yours. It belongs to you now. The whole thing except for a few personal things I'm taking and some specimens I've shipped to the two universities for archival purposes. The house, the shop, the garage, the yard. I'm taking my bike. Probably need that, don't you think?"

I nod dumbly, like that's a decision I really have a stake in making. "Why? Why are you giv—"

His face becomes serious, almost sad, and he looks at the floor, shaking his head. Then he walks back to the sofa and sits down. Staring at his clasped hands, he says, "Years ago, before he died, that is, Clinton came to me with an idea. A proposal, really. He wanted to do something to make up for, to provide, make amends, whatever, for things he'd done." Boardman looks at me.

"The war, right." I'm trembling. I can't stop my teeth chattering. I try to press my fingernails into my palms.

"Yeah, that, too. But there was more. And he was worried about you. About what was going to happen to you here. So he made me this deal."

I'm scared, and I don't know why. "What? What's going on, tell me." Boardman sighs and looks out the picture window facing the backyard. "He bought this house, for you." He pauses. "We agreed I would continue to live in it and so on until retirement or . . . then it would become yours. Free and paid for. I have the deed at Clement Collins's office. You just have to sign the papers. I've done my part. Clint and I drew it up years ago." His expression softens as he watches a cardinal couple land on the juniper bushes. The bright red male and the green-and-dusty-rose female pick hungrily at berries, taking turns listening and watching for danger. "It's all taken care of, Honey."

I'm stunned. What do you say when someone *gives* you a thing you know you could never earn, save for, win? "It's free? The house, the—"

Boardman smiles tiredly at me. "The shop, the whole thing. I'm throwing the business in the deal because I'm too old and cranky to be running it. This way, I get to start all over, too. It's out of my hands, like an act of God. I'm wiped out. Have to start a new life."

"Azium, you don't have to—" I feel guilty, turning him out of his home and business.

"Sure I do. I *want* to. It's a luxury. You'll see someday, what a freeing thing it is to lose your 'stuff,' to give it all away. Besides, I'm hanging on to a few things still. And I'll always know you're taking care of things here. It's not like I had a fire or something." He runs a hand through his thin white-and-yellow hair. "It's a relief. You don't know. To get away alive. Always thought I'd die here. Used to make me mad, that idea. Like it was a failure on my part. Like Clinton."

My arms are aching with tension now. My face feels stiff, like I have to work my mouth with strings. "Are you *sure* this is what you want, Mr. Boardman? Clinton didn't—"

He frowns. "No, this is good, like I said. I should've done it before. Ten years ago. I guess I just couldn't bear to leave the memories here. Just couldn't."

Although my legs are shaking, I get up and go to the picture window. My movement makes the cardinals circle up around the yard and land on the bare lilac bushes in back of the garage. "How can I take this, how can I accept it?" I don't look at him.

"What's to accept? Clinton is giving you a present. I got the cash, and some other stuff in exchange."

"Dope money."

"So what? I didn't ask. And the jade and a few other—"

"The jade you tried to give me?" I turn around.

Boardman nods. "It's very valuable, like I said. You should have taken it."

"God, you are making me crazy—all of you. This is *so* weird. Why are you all in my life doing this shit? Why can't you just let me alone, that's all I ask."

Flopping onto the maple rocker, I bang my elbows on the arms. The sting travels to my shoulders. "I suppose Jass and Boyd know, too. The whole frigging town. Now I'll be the 'charity case', or worse . . ."

Boardman starts laughing. He laughs hard in great heaving waves, as if he hasn't let go like this in years. Despite my mood, I start to smile, giggle.

"Well, I can't help it," I say gruffly. He gets up and pulls me to him for a hug. I keep a little bit of myself back, remembering who he is, but he's really as impersonal as a Methodist minister in our embrace.

When we separate he says, "Clinton said you'd put up a fuss. That's why I've waited. Didn't want to listen to it for too long. No time now, see. I'm out of here in the morning. You can argue with me all the way to the airport in Cedar Rapids if you want, but I'm going, and the house is yours or nobody's." He leans over to tuck in a box flap. "Anyway, this was as much for him as you, Honey. Don't forget that. You were only a *part* of things for him. Some other stuff went on here in town that, well, it's best left at that. Now, let's you and me tour the place. I have to show you the fuse box, furnace, septic, and a whole slew of other things."

Feeling dislocated, out of sync with the person I left at work, woke up as this morning, I follow his thin, bent figure to the basement. What else can I do?

In the basement he kicks at a corner piled with dusty boxes of rocks. "Sorry about the mess. Don't have time to clean. At my age, you let some things go. But you're young, you'll find the time to put this place shipshape. Help you learn the business, too."

Hopelessness sweeps over me. I can't learn what took him his whole life going to school and studying. I'm no good at this stuff. He must be crazy. Spiders have webbed the boxes to each other and the corner, with little gray notches of eggs like eyes suspended in the centers. When they hatch, will I be here? It's the first time I consider the possibility of what Boardman has told me.

"Anyway"—he continues weaving around boxes, stacks of magazines and furniture—"you won't have to buy much for the shop for a while. I've always accumulated more than I should. Give you some leeway until you get your feet on the ground. Here's the furnace. Sid delivers oil end of every month. Four-hundred-gallon tank he checks and fills. I keep it cool up there. Oil's gotten so darn expensive. You do as you want. Clinton left something I invested for the taxes and heat, in case you went through hard times." He points to a gauge. "Just check on this once in a while, make sure you've got the pressure. And take this—" He picks up a small oil can with a long, thin spout. "A couple a drops where I've marked twice a year. Fall and spring. Keeps the motor running good. Okay?"

Without waiting for my reply, he moves to a small room. "This is your fuse box. Here's extras. Just screw 'em in and out like this. Oh, and this is your washer and dryer. They're not new, but beats a trip to the Laundromat."

I think about that and eye the old avocado green Kenmores. No more gossip or sweaty laundry days.

"Here's the hot water heater. Got so sick of running out—I like a long soak in the tub for these old bones—I had 'em put in your commercial size. You got enough for four baths in a row now. Number to call's right on the heater there, see it? In case of trouble. Should be good for years, though. You getting all this?" He looks over his shoulder as he goes to a workbench along the far wall.

"I'm leaving most of my tools. My brother moved a lot of his down there already. Much as we'll need. I left you some for rock work. And the polisher. You'll see that stuff upstairs in the storeroom off the shop. Don't worry, you'll figure it all out. Just take your time. Let's head on up, then."

An hour later as I'm backing down the porch steps, he's still giving me instruction. "Gonna have to keep the furnace on or you'll freeze the pipes if you don't sleep over right away. Keep the taps on in the bathroom when it drops below zero—north wall plumbing some idiot put in, you know. And pick me up at seven sharp tomorrow morning. I can't miss that flight. My brother has a three-and-a-half-hour drive to meet me. And no phone. Call me later if you have any questions." He's waving good-bye as I let the storm door slap shut.

"Thanks, thank you. I mean, are you sure?"

He closes the porch door on my question.

Walking back to work, I'm confused by the sun sharpening the icicles on the eaves, by the sparkle of snow and ice on the rough gray-and-brown yards. Overhead, the sky is a uniform, but not quite indifferent, blue. The winter blue that is clear and pure like you imagine it as a kid. I grope for the dark feeling I had going to Boardman's at noon. Now, an hour and a half later, I have to stop myself from smiling. How could this happen? How can I have a house, take care of a house? Most of all, what will everyone in Divinity say? Especially my family, what will Baby say? I should be grateful, excited. I am, but I'm worried. What can I give Boardman in exchange? I'm taking his house, but it's not his. Clinton bought it. For me. That's what Boardman said. He *did* love me, then. That scares me a little. This is evidence, something's on trial here. What?

"Clinton," I call softly under my breath. "Thank you. I don't know what to say. . . ."

"Just love me, Honey. Don't let go—I need you. I really need you." His voice chills the sun and dims the blue as I cross the street to Bowker's block.

"I do. You know that. I'll never let you go." The words sound hollow to me, like I don't really mean them.

"Yes, you will. Merry Christmas, though. Stay safe. Stay in the house now. Get out of that trailer. You'll be all right now. Trust me. Listen to me."

The wind that always seems to blow straight down Main pushes his words away from me and tumbles the sound past Bowker's door and

Steadman's and the Style Shop, on toward Reiler's, which stands starkly outlined two blocks away. A picture passes into me: Boardman's house as a place I've been heading to all my life, even in my dreams. But when I get there, the doorknobs might only work one way, to let me in, never out. A little wave of panic makes the sound of the ocean in my ears—what I know of it from the conches at Boardman's. I can't help but believe what other people tell me, you see.

"Where've *you* been?" Marylou hisses when I open the office door. "He's going nuts! Wants you to go to Jasper Johnson's for a machinery insurance check. Then Tom Tooley came by and filed a claim on Twyla's trailer, so Bowker figured you could do the paper on that on your way home. You better get going, Honey."

"Merry Christmas to you, too," I mutter, closing the door again.

On the way out to Jass's, there's so many ideas and feelings floating in my head, I turn on the radio loud to some Christmas rock and roll and slap the dashboard in time. Bruce Springsteen's "Santa Claus Is Comin' to Town" takes me up to Jass's driveway. It's not until I see his familiar red truck that I catch myself. "Now listen," I say, "no matter how good you feel—or how crazy—you are not sleeping with this man."

"Bravo. About time," Clinton says.

"Oh—" Then I remember the house he's just given me and bite my lip.

When I find Jass in the barn, he's all business. "I told your boss I'd prefer someone else coming."

I guess I'm surprised. And hurt. "Where's the stuff I'm supposed to check on?"

"Outside. You can't go out there in those sneakers."

I can tell by his face that he remembers the last time he gave me boots, so I shrug and so does he. Walking behind him, I feel a little ache. He doesn't even care about me anymore. The snow slips over the rim of my shoe, and cold begins to wet my stocking. Fine. I step purposely in his big deep tracks that reach past the snow into the mud and water the horses have turned up today. Fine, I say to the water squishing between my toes and the mud flecking off his boots onto my legs and skirt. Perfect. I'll just do my job. He can be this way.

"I took delivery in early November, forgot to have it checked then." He comes to a huge forest green horse van, with red-and-tan trim and lettering. "Mercy River Farm" flows in soft script on the sides. Jass's name and address are on both doors, and across the back "HORSES" is painted in huge block letters.

"It's used, rebuilt engine, redone inside. Imperatore. Ten years old. Got a good deal. It was reported stolen, and the owner got a new one from the insurance, but someone saw his buddy digging it up where he'd buried it and the cops busted both of them. Sold at auction, cheap. I had the work done. Wish I'd gotten the shed built for it. Getting hurt and all, I ran out of time. Hope it doesn't have a hard winter." He pats the side and climbs up to open one of the big double doors. "Wanna see inside?" He's standing inside with his hands on his hips as I hitch my skirt and try to jam my foot in the step ledge. Grabbing the side of the door frame, I bounce and reach just as my wet sole slips off the foothold.

The front of my leg bone scrapes against the metal ledge as I fall. I try to land on my feet, but the ground is too slippery, and I slide halfway under the truck with my skirt to my waist. It only takes a few seconds to feel the snow in the back of my panty hose and a pain gradually sharpening in my leg. Jass jumps down as I roll onto all fours and crawl out. Standing up, I try to brush the snow from my butt without reaching under my skirt. It's stuck and melting, and I decide the only thing worse in life is the raw pain of my leg. When I hitch my skirt and look at it, tiny red beads are starting to seep out of the blue-white scrape. In another few seconds the blood starts to ooze more freely, wetting the rest of my torn stocking.

"We better go back." Jass turns to close the door.

"No, goddamn it. Let's just finish this. How many goddamn horses fit in this thing?"

"Six. Three and three, you can see it from here."

"Yeah, okay. Anything else I should know to fill out the form?"

"Some manners," Jass mutters as he closes the door.

My leg's hurting pretty good now, and I'm wet and muddy and cold. I push him just hard enough that he slips and almost falls like I did under the truck. I'm pissed enough that when he turns on me, I don't care. He must see that as he grabs my shoulders, shaking me so hard my head snaps back and forth, then pushes me away so hard that I sit down in the muddy snow. I won't give him the satisfaction of tears, so I get up and start back for my car, stumbling, sliding, and cursing.

It's because he lets me go that I come back, I tell myself as I back all the way down his drive and zoom right back up it. Clinton's calling me as I push out of the car, furious, and run to where Jass stands beside the barn.

"Get in here and get your leg fixed." He turns without seeing if I'm following.

A thousand mean things come into me, tiny northern pike teeth bite out of my pores. I want to turn them loose on him. I'm so mad, single sentences seem stupid.

"Sit." He goes to the medicine cabinet in the tack room. I notice he's added a pillow to the couch. Probably fucking Cindy here again. I punch it with my fist.

"Cut it out. Put your leg up here." He squats, pulls my foot onto his thigh, and tugs off my shoe and rips my stocking to the knee without getting his hands dirty. "What a mess."

"I agree," I manage through gritted teeth as he swabs at the foot-long cut with iodine-soaked gauze. "Jesus, *be* careful." I jerk my foot when he wipes too hard.

"Hold still. Don't be such a damned baby."

I want to kick his face in, but instead I bite my lip, and the raw pain brings tears that blur his fingers. They're still beautiful. I try to distract myself with that idea, forcing the pain and the chill from my wet clothes into the wool blanket covering the couch.

Standing up to get some salve, Jass notices me shivering. "Here—" He pulls another blanket off the back of the couch. "Take your coat off—it's too muddy and wet to help much. Looks like it's seen better days, too."

I glare at him as I undo my eight-year-old black car coat whose wool is worn so thin, you can see the weave where it hasn't become flat and shiny. He drapes the blanket over my shoulders and leaves it to me to pull it across my chest. It seems like a small, mean thing to do. Maybe he really has stopped caring. The idea hurts more than it should. Think about Clinton, I warn myself. Think about the house. No more trailer nights, listening to things knocking through it.

Jass applies the antibiotic salve gently, the way he would on a horse. The blood pushes through the thin yellow layer and makes a sickening color, like infection. He looks at it. "Better wrap it. Stop the oozing or it'll make a mess on everything." He carefully winds the gauze around and over the Telfa pads he's covered the cut with, keeping the pressure even and light. Taping the end at my ankle, he gently sets my foot on the floor and rocks back on his heels, his arms wrapped around his knees, and looks at me.

"You're a mess."

"Thanks a lot. You're no prize, either, you know."

He's staring at me, but I can't meet his eyes. "Okay," he says, "what if we do it your way?" He slips off my other shoe and dries my foot slowly, then places it on the floor next to the first one. I focus on the blue black of his hair. "We don't have to say a word; talk just gets us in trouble, doesn't it?" he says as his hands gently rub the backs of my calves, kneading the tensions loose.

Clinton, Clinton, I keep chanting while my eyes find the path at his neck into the V of his shirt and down the smooth skin of his chest. That's what I'm watching when I first feel his hands push my skirt up and the rush of cool hit my thighs. I close my eyes. Too much has happened today.

The next morning we drive Boardman together to the airport. We both sense the rip that's sucking our feelings away as we watch the plane take off, but two days later we decide to spend Christmas Day together anyway. I'm avoiding Twyla's trailer and my new house. And Clinton. Maybe I'm saying good-bye to Jass, to Boardman. I don't know. I don't know what Jass is avoiding, but I can feel it. Maybe it's something simple, like being in love with me. The day has a lifeless, mechanical feel to it as we open the one present each of us has under his tree. I give him a yellow-and-red-checked flannel shirt that clashes violently with his skin tones. It's the only thing I can find at the last minute. He gives me a pair of deerskin gloves that leave brown crumbles on my shirt cuffs and hands.

All day we try to avoid touching each other, as if the lovemaking three days before happened to two other people, a couple we saw in a movie. Jass's distance finally makes things equal between us. Now we're both empty, I want to say as we poke our forks hopelessly at the mushy pumpkin pie after dinner.

23

Stiller's Pond

One of the things I've always known is that Clinton should have been a Catholic. Not just to say what he'd done—you can do that with almost anyone. And a lot of people will forgive you, too—like they did with Clinton. What he needed was the priest telling him he was forgiven and giving him a bunch of chores to do—like on the *Sunday Night Catholic Hour* on radio when they hail Mary and chant the rosary. Finally what he needed was to step out of that dark, wood-lined closet, leaving his words behind. Safely stored, sealed in time and another person's vows.

Clinton said that what Americans need is "the Church of the Articulate Listener," but what we have is "the Church of Atomic Particles." I never knew what that meant, but like the Catholic business, I didn't discuss it with him.

I've always wanted to go to confession to smell the priest on the other side of the grate and the sweat of everyone who's been there. The way he's going to breathe interests me. If I stop mine, will I hear his? And the creak of his shoes as he crosses his legs? Will I be able to see his profile, the wrinkles in the sleeve of his robe, the shadowy slab of hand? Could I poke my fingers through the grate and touch his eyelids? Would I be that close to God?

In January we all stay indoors, nursing our holiday wounds and thinking. The temperature plunges and bucks like an unbroken horse, and there's nothing to do but wait. I start sleeping over at Boardman's. I still think of it as his house. I'm just a temporary, housesitting. I try not to disturb anything, leaving what he's left as it was when Jass and I took him to the airport. His heavy winter clothes hang properly in closets or remain folded in drawers. His slippers and snow boots wait alertly in the closet. I ignore the scratch and tick of the mouse building in there. It's not my problem. I have done the dishes, but I'm careful about the contents of the cupboards and fridge. I don't let my cereal and fresh milk nudge his. I don't want him to think I'm pushy.

Though the washer and dryer sit humped in the corner of the basement, I don't use them. He's left a load of laundry in each, and I can't bring myself to touch them. Something about the damp overstretched elastic of his graying underpants and the thinning heels of his stained white cotton socks.

Every afternoon after work I drive out to the trailer to get clothes for the next day and work on my charts, which circle the kitchen like a wagon train under attack. Only I don't feel like the white settlers in the middle. I'm always with the Indians trying to ride the wagons off their land in those movies.

Twice when I've gone out there, the propane gas has been screwed up. I know it's the animals chewing at the lines. Or just the cold.

It's a dark, alone time in Divinity, no matter who you're with. Somehow being alone this year feels more right. Bowker moves lethargic as a fat old bull snake after a big meal. He comes late and leaves early. No one's buying or selling right now, though there's pending foreclosure on several farms. The idea of money to be made doesn't seem to move him. With the holiday cheer gone, he's just another overweight businessman in a tight, cheap suit. An out-of-work Santa Claus.

Even Marylou has toned down her happiness. The car from Nebraska hasn't been seen since Christmas, and her husband, Mike, is out of County Detox with his drinking cut to a single beer he savors all afternoon long at Sleepy's.

The centennial five months away seems like some third-rate carnival no one's much interested in anymore. I'm not talking to anyone now because this is the time I hate the most. I feel like a tire that keeps running over the same damn nail, year after year. Clinton gets quiet now, too, as if he has to go ahead and drown again. I have to remember it, and he has to do it. So I'm bracing myself with hot tea and a package of Lady Finger vanilla cookies on the Saturday afternoon anniversary of Clinton's death, when someone knocks on Boardman's door. My hand's on the knob before I realize I don't have to answer it. I peek out the split in the curtain of the door glass. Boyd Ziekert in his uniform. Taking a deep breath, I open the door. Not wide enough to make him feel welcome. He presses himself forward while smoothly pushing the door open.

"Good to see you, Honey. Just came by to see how you're doing in the new place." He forces me back and aside by stepping into the showroom. "Still not open, huh? Well, you shouldn't let it worry you so much. Just open up and let the people have what they want. Can't fault making money, and I know Azium would want you to do it."

He says this like I owe something to someone and walks into the kitchen. "Can a man get himself something to drink around here?" He sits in my place at the table. Picking up my cup, he sniffs it. "Tea? Smells good. I'll have the same." Then he pulls a cookie out of the half-empty package. "Having a little lunch, I see." He bites it in half. "Not bad."

Although I haven't said a word yet, I feel like we've had a conversation.

"Tea?" He holds up my cup. When it's ready, I set down a fresh cup with a clunk that breaks the silence between us.

"Haven't seen you around much lately." He takes another cookie. "Have to get me some of these. Soon as I run out of those Christmas ones everyone gives me. It's a wonder I stay as thin and handsome as I do."

Trying to discourage this interview, I take a sip of my tea.

"Not talking, huh? Heard from Azium? I got a card the other day. He made it fine."

That Boardman hasn't written pisses me off. Don't I rate a card? Here I am keeping his stuff.

"Haven't heard from him, huh?" Boyd swings his eyes around the kitchen. "Haven't moved in yet, either, I notice. Planning on doing that soon?"

I avoid his gunmetal eyes and shrug.

"Sucking up the gas keeping two places, aren't you? Say, I know some folks, retired farmers, looking for a place. You interested in selling that trailer?"

"What's this all about, Boyd? You taking up real estate or social work?" I get up and dump the rest of my tea down the drain, then stand there watching the tan swirl and bubble in the stained, chipped white porcelain.

"It's three weeks since you got this place."

"I *have* a calendar, Boyd."

"Well, I just thought something might have come up. You might want to talk. And I got this retired couple—"

"Retired couple, my ass." I walk to the stairs going up, assuming he won't follow. I'm wrong. He's on my heels like a giant version of one of those nippy terrier dogs.

"There *is* a couple. A couple of couples. They're everywhere. All you have to do is post an ad." I turn at the top of the stairs in time to see him spilling some tea on the old rose floral runner.

There are three rooms and a bath upstairs. One holds the remainder of Boardman's library, what he didn't donate, and a big old scarred yellow oak library table he used for a desk. Another room, looking out the back, is his bedroom, which I've left as it was. The third is the junk room, where I'm sleeping on a cot.

I go to the study while Boyd goes up and down the hall, opening the other doors and inspecting. He's commenting as he goes, but I ignore him. Instead, I push aside two of the half-filled boxes and sit down at the desk. Boardman gave up packing and told me to keep what I wanted and give the rest to the public library. Over the years he'd read the library contents A to Z several times, so he had a good idea what was missing.

"What this place needs is a good cleaning, Honey. What're you doing on your behind?" Boyd steps over a stack of papers and walks to the window, snapping the shade up. Bright January light bouncing off the snowy porch roof fills the room, making it look even worse. The walls are covered floor to ceiling with raw, unpainted pine bookcases jammed with books and magazines. A veneer of dust covers everything, including the old-fashioned overhead etched-glass helmet for the light bulb. On the floor is a piece of old floral carpet, ragged along two edges where it was cut from a larger piece. It's a different pattern from the one on the stairs runner.

"Pretty grim in here," Boyd comments. "Bet you could use some help."

"Boyd, I don't know how to break it to you, but I'm not up to this today—whatever you think you're doing." Drawing my name in the dust on the table, I continue to avoid looking at him. Better tactic, anyway. I'm wrong again.

"Hello?" a woman's voice calls from below. "Anyone home? Hello?" A clanking and clanging follows.

"Boyd!" I'm on my way down, with him laughing behind me.

Larue Carlson is in the middle of my living room, standing in a puddle of buckets, sponges, and assorted cleaning liquids and sponges.

"Eleanor'll be in with the next load in a sec. She's got the vacuum cleaner, too," Larue says as if this explains everything.

"Larue." I'm going to put my foot down politely, but she stops me.

"Relax. My place is clean. Boyd's is beyond hope. I figured you're the only other person around who'd let me work off some tension this way. You don't mind, do you? It's my therapy." Larue blinks her beautiful blue eyes, and I can almost hear Boyd's heart tear through his shirt and clunk on the floor. I look at her hands, already encased in new rubber gloves, and her perfect makeup. She gives other women a bad name looking so good on cleaning day, dressed in a black-and-red velour jumpsuit and a pair of matching suede slip-ons.

A six-foot girl with dark downy arms, a shadow of mustache, and dark brown, shoulder-length hair hanging in greasy clumps drops another load of equipment beside Larue and stands, hands on hips, surveying the room like it's the milking parlor on her daddy's farm and she's responsible for hosing it down. Apparently this is Eleanor.

"Okay, then." Larue picks up a bucket and sponge. "Where shall we start?"

She asks me, but Eleanor answers. "Up. Work the dirt down." Eleanor has a low, melodic voice like a movie star. You could close your eyes and see Lauren Bacall, Debra Winger, miscast in this corn-fed Iowa body.

Larue pauses on the stairs as Eleanor loads up again. "You on duty?"
she asks Boyd. When he shakes his head, she says, "Come on, then. You, too, Honey. Unless you trust us to sort on our own."

I try one more time to save my day. "Larue . . ." She ignores me, pressing gracefully up the stairs with Eleanor banging and bumping behind her, like Marilyn Monroe on safari.

"Boyd . . ." I say between gritted teeth, but he grabs a load and heads upstairs, too.

"Now where shall we start?" Larue's voice is almost singing with Eleanor's low counterpoint.

"Doesn't anyone listen to me?" I mutter as I reluctantly trudge upstairs.

"Did they ever? Anyway, stop feeling sorry for yourself, Honey," Clinton says.

"Oh, and what do *you* have planned for today, Mr. Know-it-all?"

"Dying, I'm going to spend the day dying again."

His words make me grab the handrail and stop. There it is. The reason for everything, it seems, comes to this one day in January, and no amount of scrubbing is going to wipe this day off the year or out of my life.

The low hum of Eleanor's words drifts down to me: "My mama would tan me good for a mess like this. Think I should put his clothes in the garbage bags now?" I climb the rest of the stairs two at a time.

Many hours later they've gone home to bed and sleep, leaving my new house clean and neat, an entire box of thirty garbage bags now full lined up by the front walk. It's well after midnight when I'm driving past my trailer, looking marooned, like a boat in dry dock, and then to Twyla's place, which suffers almost nightly vandalism.

At Twyla's I stop, get out of the car, but leave it running for the heat. I'm wearing a sweatshirt, one of Boardman's holey old cardigans and a military-issue parka I found in one of his closets. It hangs to my knees, and the grease-stained sleeves are three inches below my hands, so I don't need gloves. It feels right.

The screen door flaps on one hinge, and the other door is lying on the living room floor, as if some rage had burst through. The living room and kitchen show signs of kids—beer cans and cardboard cartons and paper sacks everywhere. Someone has tried to start a fire on the living room floor, the sticks stand pyramided with charred ends. The sofa looks as if someone has grabbed fistfuls of stuffing out of it. I don't even go in the

kitchen. The scurry of mice and the dark jagged outlines of smashed dishes, beer cans, overturned furniture, and broken windows tell the story of travel back to some preformed time. Why are kids so savage? When alone, they attack. Why this hatred of houses, animals, buildings? Is it some ancient thing, an instinct that keeps their hearts wild until it gets killed and they grow up?

I don't go to the bedroom. Don't need to. The trailer's a loss. Twyla's lost. It's clear what I have to do next. I go to the car, find the matches in the glove compartment, come back, and, pulling more stuffing from little craters in the sofa, set as many fires as I can. There is a hesitancy about the fires, as if waiting to make sure I mean it, but when I turn my back to leave, the glow bursts open and fire begins to *whoosh* along the floors and up the fake wood paneling. The hot remains on my back as I hurry my car to a safe distance down the road and pause to look back. The trailer's yellow-and-red light bobs up and down like a boat in a storm. A sense of peace slides through me. There was nothing to claim there. This will make it easier for all of us. A total loss, I can write on the insurance forms for Tom, and he'll understand.

After Twyla's, the gravel road seems like a little world, a continent lost, left behind by events, time. If I really move into Boardman's, maybe the fields will reclaim the road. I like to think of having to fight my way through weeds and saplings over my head to get back to my trailer. Then the charts would be like lost scrolls, things to be studied, deciphered.

Heading west on Highway 11, I find my way by instinct, following the moon, to Stiller's woods and pond. On this night every year I park the car by the little path and walk through the trees to the field where the pond waits, frozen into these little waves, like they're starched on the top, from the wind. To one side are the dried cattails, where they found the Stiller girl so many years ago with her long blond hair tangled in the broken stalks. The man's body was found floating in a hole in the ice. I have to be careful walking out here, as if the fear and mystery could pull me under like those two, sealing me over with a skim of ice. Skirting the uneven, pocked edge of the pond, I look for a way onto the ice.

The thin moon lays a blue light across the snow, which turns purple and black in the trees behind me. Once when I look back, I think I can see the red of a fire smudging the sky. Twyla won't be coming back. I won't let her—she doesn't want to. We both know that. She's as gone as the Stiller girl, whose eyes were plucked out by the huge old turtles in the water below. Stepping onto the ice, I wonder if they hear me walking on the roof of their pond, the vibrations signaling them to drift up.

For years since the town's men dragged the two turtle-plundered bodies from the pond, parents have forbidden their children to come here. So they do. Boys like Sonny and Terry from Reiler's spent their summers trying to trap the turtles, then beat their huge shells with sticks and rocks. As if the turtles hold some secret—something forbidden and obscene—having eaten human flesh. And the boys must kill them in order to discover it. There is a mistake here, I want to tell them. But for the rest of their lives they attack the turtles as the cause of something, not just the evidence of it.

Why am I crossing Stiller's pond tonight, waiting for the first curious turtle claw to appear tentatively through the white pond surface? Spirit Lake is too far away. The Mercy River isn't deep enough. I have to make this pilgrimage—it's an annual event, walking the pond ice. Maybe like Clinton, I'll hit a hole, a dark place, and fall out of time. Maybe on the pond bottom Clinton's secret waits, like the turtles, living off the bodies winter and grief bring to them. All summer the young of Divinity try to beat the hungry turtles to death, and all winter the turtles eat their fill of what delivers itself through the ice. We're in some deadly embrace here, a cycle of pain we can't seem to escape from. And even Clinton driving off the edge of the world where the ice ended on Spirit Lake, hasn't escaped. He's merely changed one form of torment for another.

Above me the moon cuts into the sky like barbed wire, and the stars are caught and tangled on a mean stretch of darkness. A cold breath of wind stings my face numb. My toes pinch against the seeping ice underfoot. Pain. This is the place we keep it, store it. Not the cemetery—that's the dress-up place, the one we show to the public, like a front parlor. This is where pain goes. We pass the story down to the kids: how the father and mother refused the girl's body. How the man's face was eaten away, unidentifiable. How two men were missing: her brother and the hired man. How there was a burial and reburial of her body that refused to stay hidden. We know this story so well that even Clinton drove a hundred miles to Spirit Lake rather than come to Stiller's pond. It's not the falling through that would be so hard, it's what might be beneath you, sleepy and hungry as you sink.

"Honey, it's me, Boyd." His voice is eerie, like it's coming from the ice below me more than anything. I keep walking. "You don't want to do that now, just turn around and walk back, slowly, just the way you came. Remember, easy does it."

The recent snow has left the ice bumpy with little hills and valleys. Of course, nobody scrapes a skating place. Though there's just that sliver of moon tonight, it's reflection off the snow gives enough light for me to see the cattails to my left now and the dark rim of shore a ways ahead.

"Honey!" Because this time Boyd's voice is closer and the beam from his flashlight casts a thin yellow splotch at my feet, I stop and turn.

"What." It's a statement more than a question. Boyd is still close to the opposite shore.

"Good, now just walk slowly back here, Honey."

I think about it for a moment, listening to the stir of wind rustling the cattails and touching the trees. There's another sound, too, one I haven't noticed before. Maybe the noise in my head kept it out, or maybe it's been there like an undertow I chose to ignore. The creaking, spine-splitting tear of ice, rubbing, adjusting, and the tiny lap of waves against an edge.

"Boyd? I think the ice—"

"I know, Honey, just do what I told you. Walk slowly back. Just follow your track. You're okay. Just come slowly."

I concentrate on Boyd's dark figure standing motionless with the beam of light radiating from his center. But the ice seems to be breaking up beneath me. Before it seemed so solid, like walking on ground; now I think I feel the wet coming through my tennis shoes, dark holes appearing on either side of me. I can barely stand to put the next foot down. When it sinks through the snow before meeting the resistance of ice, I panic and stop. "Boyd, I can't do this. Help me!"

"Yes, you can. Just keep walking the way you have been. You're doing fine."

By now I'm standing in the middle of Stiller's pond. The dark spots around me might be the turtles, might be something worse. The low chorus of sound from the pond makes me shiver.

"Boyd, I think the ice is breaking up; help me." I keep my voice low in case the pitch vibrates the ice.

"No, you're fine. I'm freezing, though, so please get your ass over here." Boyd's yelling cuts my fear into obedience, and I begin to walk again.

"It's like 'Nam," Clinton remarks. "A mine, a tripwire, every time you put a foot down."

"Or Spirit Lake?"

"As it turned out, yes. Best stay off water unless you're Jesus Christ, Honey, that's what I learned."

"Great. You make it through mine fields and booby traps in Vietnam, and come home and fall through some ice in your car. That's either bad luck or bad brains, Clinton."

It's only a few more yards to the edge. Boyd has moved back to ground, and I can tell by his expression he's not happy. The flashlight is shaking in his hand, and there's a coiled rope hanging from his shoulder.

"This town has just as many booby traps as Vietnam. You don't know the whole story. Not by a long shot. Someday maybe I'll tell you, or maybe you'll figure it out. If you last that long."

Boyd grabs my arm and pulls me roughly to face him. "What the hell were you doing out there? Are you drunk? Here, let me smell your breath."

When all he smells is my bad stomach, he gets angrier. "Jee-sus, Chee-rist, you weren't paying one bit of attention out there, were you? If I hadn't come along . . ."

He tightens his fingers on my arm with every phrase. "Ow, let go, Boyd. It was a mistake. I have a lot on my mind, you know."

"You make any more mistakes like that, you won't have to worry about what's on your mind." He gives my arm another bruising squeeze like Daddy would have and lets go. "Don't you know this pond *never* freezes right? It's spring fed. Bottomless, some say. I don't think so. Just very deep in one spot. Come on, let's warm up in the squad car. At least I got a good heater."

I follow him following my track back to where both cars are parked. He starts the engine, and warmth begins to fill the car. "Not only that. We got so much snow, it's kept a lot of water around here too warm to freeze good and thick. Stiller's was never any good, though, like I said. Nobody should ever trust it."

I nod, scared to tell him how many times before I've walked out there. The car heater is putting out such hot air that it lifts the smell of sweaty wool and greasy musk from the car seats and our clothes.

"I got some hot tea here. You want a cup?" He reaches for the thermos on the seat next to him.

"Yeah, thanks."

"What were you doing out there, anyway?" He hands me the metal lid of the thermos half-full of hot liquid and pours some into a homemade pottery mug for himself.

"Just thinking. I come out here to think sometimes." I take a sip of the tea, and the smoky flavor surprises me. "What's this?"

"Lap-sang sou-chong." He draws out the syllables in a self-satisfied way. We sit there for a few minutes, staring through the trees at the pastures rolling to the flat of the pond. The night is very quiet, as if time stops when it gets this cold. As if cold reaches a hand into the chest of the planet and turns off the heart machine, or just holds it in a dark icy hand.

Then it occurs to me. "How come *you're* out here, Boyd?"

"Someone torched Twyla's trailer. I was patrolling, and saw the light from the fire. On a night like this, it looked like a damned supermarket opening. Know what I mean?" He pauses and watches me closely. "I don't suppose you had anything to do with that, did you?"

My silence brings a long sigh from him. "Never mind. It was an eyesore. A tin can. Even when Twyla was living there. You better hope your place doesn't have a similar accident, though. Know what I mean?"

"Yes, Boyd. You don't have to keep saying that. I *always* know what you mean."

Boyd taps his mug against the steering wheel in a Latin rhythm. "Okay then, tell me what you were really doing out there tonight. Nobody comes here 'to think.' You've been acting real odd lately, you know, real different. Sour. Here someone gives you a house and you go out for the Divinity depression team. Your sister cheers up and you cheer down. What's going on?"

Everyone is such a know-it-all here. That's what I should tell him. It's hard to live with this net of opinion dragging you toward them. Even now I'm irritated, though he's probably saved my life.

"Why in God's name does it matter, Boyd? Why is everyone so interested in my life? Can't you all just let me alone?"

Boyd laughs. "I suppose we could. Maybe we should even try to do that, but it wouldn't last long." He reaches for the thermos and pours more tea in the mug, then holds it over mine. I nod, and he pours some into my cup.

"*You* elected to live here, Honey. Your brother Tolson left. You could, too. If you stay, you can't expect the whole town to change, just because of you. What you want. Folks are folks. You know that. You're doing your little version of heaven and hell on your kitchen wall. At least I thought you were trying to understand how things stand around here. Maybe you're just another high-minded person who works things out so they stay above it and the rest of us are so much garbage beneath their feet. Is that it? If it is, Divinity is the last place on earth you want to live. Our faults, our sins and crimes, will drive you crazy, the way they hang right out in the open for everyone to see."

I don't want to admit it, but he's making a lot of sense. Before I can answer, the radio pops the tension.

"Sheriff?"

Boyd reaches for his microphone. "Yeah?"

"State troopers called. They're working an accident on Eleven. Twenty-five miles out. Don't need assistance."

"What'd they call for, then?" Boyd sounds impatient.

"I dunno, company? It's a cold night, they wondered if you'd bring 'em some coffee if you're coming over." The deputy laughs.

"Tell him to call . . . here—" Boyd flips open a small spiral notebook and reads a number. "Tell them to call that number. It's the sheriff in Pottersville at home. He hates those guys. This'll drive him nuts. Talk to you later."

"You two seem to have your fun." Boyd's handsome face has relaxed into a smile.

"Have to break it up any way you can. It's a better solution than Stiller's pond."

"Boyd, I was not trying to . . . you know. I really *was* just taking a walk." He's starting to worry me.

"On thin ice?" He rubs the back of his neck like that's where the pain I give him has settled.

"No, don't be silly. I've been walking out here for years. Nothing's ever happened." My pulse hurries a little at the image of what could've.

"Consider yourself lucky, then."

"Some luck." It's out before I can stop it, and we both stare at the words like an unwanted child in our laps. "I didn't—"

"That's what I'm referring to, Honey. You are not to be trusted these days. What is it? You want to end up like Clinton? You've spent half your life mooning over him. What a good example he set, what a nice way to show his love, how considerate."

I slap him hard enough to spill his tea. His reflex is automatic. He grabs my hand and twists it hard enough to make me drop my cup on the floor and put my face on the seat. When he releases me, we both try to clean up the tea mess.

"Sorry," he says gruffly as he pours what's left of the thermos into our cups.

"Me too." The steam curls thinly toward the windshield, as if the heater air were pulling at it. Outside, the wind is picking up, sending small shudders through the trees and the car.

"I still mean it. About Clinton and you. I never understood how you got mixed up with such a loser."

"Don't, Boyd." I try to gather my strength and patience. "He was nice to me. He helped me out when things at home . . . well, things were hard."

"Your father . . ."

I nod.

"What about the others? I never understood how you got hooked up with those fellas. Jimmy, Brewer, Jake."

I don't like the sound of that coming from Boyd. It's like a list of crimes of the condemned. "I really don't want to talk about my love life, okay?"

"Sure. Just wondering. Always wondering. Like what a Vietnam vet fuck-up like Clinton Busee would want with a sixteen-year-old girl. What'd you two find to *talk* about or *do,* aside from the obvious?"

I want to tell him the whole story. To defend Clinton somehow. Or myself. I don't know which. "You weren't sheriff yet when he . . . ?"

"No, I was still in Des Moines."

"Well, it *was* the sixties, right?"

Boyd smiles. "You mean you did drugs together? The 'innocent' kinds, I suppose."

"I don't do them now, if that's what you want to know." I figure a little lie won't hurt.

"Yeah, so?"

"Well, Clinton introduced me to smoking grass—pot. In fact, it was the Appreciation Day picnic."

"The night that girl got shot," Boyd says flatly.

"I guess. Well, after that—"

"Wait." Boyd looks at me carefully. "Don't you ever think about that? How this girl gets killed and we never find out who did it?"

I try to hold his eyes, but I blink when I lie. "No."

He lifts his hand and lets it fall back to his thigh. "Go on."

"We started smoking with him regularly after that, buying ounces, then pounds, together. Finally, we were all out looking along empty fields, roadsides, and railroad tracks for the stuff.

"Once, in September, we had a wiener roast. Only we built the fire with big drying plants, put a blanket over it when it was smoking good, and inhaled like crazy. Then we cooked the hot dogs. I didn't come down until Monday night, had to go to school that way, laughing through all the classes. It was a good time. Jimmy and Brewer were with us.

"Every weekend, Clinton would take us out somewhere and we'd do something we'd never done before. Like drive to Chicago to see a concert, or go down to Iowa City, only do it stoned or tripping, because by that time we were taking acid like everyone else in the state. At least it seemed so to us. We just assumed that everyone in the world was stoned, so it was okay, because we were all in on it together, like a big joke. 'A cosmic joke,' Clinton used to call it, and things like that he got off record covers and songs. Country Joe and the Fish. Jimmy Hendrix. The Doors. Jim Morrison wanted us to break on through, and we were.

"In late October the Methodist church took a bunch of us up to Spirit Lake to that lodge they have for things like spirituality. The kids in our group decided to trip while we spent the day alone in the woods. We weren't supposed to talk to each other. That was one of the rules. 'Wake up Saturday and spend the whole day until evening in communion with Christ,' they told us. It sounded fine. Get out of town and take a trip with God. So we all dropped acid with the orange juice at breakfast, then went our separate ways."

I glance over at Boyd to see if he's upset about the drugs, but he's just looking out the window.

"For about two hours I alternated between being stone lost in the woods and terrified that I'd never get home again, and being stone lost in the woods and feeling more happy than I'd ever been in my whole life. The whole time I kept thinking, Clinton should be here, he'd really enjoy the trees and lake. Once I took off all my clothes and sat in the pine needles and prayed to God to make us love each other better, and to give me a sign that he was there.

"I waited and waited, and all I could hear was the wind, tossing lightly above my head like someone breathing regular against the window, in and out, the little fog it made each time coming into my head, then pulling out again. I wasn't sure if that was a sign or not and finally got tired of waiting and went down to the water and took a swim."

Boyd looks at me curiously.

"It was too cold, but I managed to convince myself that the cold was warm and almost burned up in that lake. Then I started thinking about why they called the place Spirit Lake and remembered the Indians, and thought when I got back home I'd look up some stuff in the library about them. The more I thought about it, the more it seemed like I was an Indian and this was before white people and everything. That lasted for a while and was just fine. Finally, though, the acid started wearing off, and I went back to where I'd left my clothes and got dressed and wandered around until I found one of the other kids, and we talked until evening.

"It wasn't Clinton's fault that we all started taking drugs." I try to defend him against the cynical smile on Boyd's face. "It was just another way of leaving town for us. The older people were always complaining that we grow up and move away. Well, we stopped that for a while. We were plenty happy in our town spacing out and staying home. If they'd left us alone, we might all be here still.

"Those of us who were close to Clinton those months did know what was going to happen. We could sense it, no matter how stoned we were. The funny thing was that while the rest of us got happier as we smoked and took things, Clinton just got quieter and more detached. Sometimes, he'd cry and cry and cry. I spent a lot of time holding Clinton, like a child, cradling him and rocking him. He was my first baby, I used to think; I never told Jake that. There wasn't anything we could do, though. We knew that. The morning we woke up to the phone call about him, it wasn't news like snow in May, nothing the weather could be compared to. It was just the last thing. Like a stop sign he was coming to."

The wind bodies the cold against the car, and it shimmies. Boyd is silent.

"Driving across the Mercy River when it was frozen in winter was a game for us. We always did it late at night after a few beers and a joint. It was one of the last things we did before we went home. We'd follow the snowmobile trails and gun it, fast as we could, sometimes even following each other bumper to bumper to add to the risk of falling through. But we all knew that the Mercy wasn't too deep, six, maybe ten feet in the worst parts. We were sure we'd be able to crawl out. Besides, we figured if we drove fast enough, we could beat the ice cracking.

"So it wasn't queer, like they said, that Clinton was up at Spirit Lake that weekend he was supposed to be in Chicago seeing the Jefferson Airplane. And judging from the timing, it seemed accurate that he *did* see them, and decided to blast on home to tell us about it. Not waiting until Sunday like he'd planned. Probably it was just that he was tired, or bored, and wanted to do something none of us had done yet—drive across Spirit Lake. It was like Clinton to try something first, then help us follow. It was the uneven weather that winter that made the lake freeze that way. The snowmobilers that found him must have crossed that lake a hundred times a day. It was lucky they didn't fall in themselves, coming up on that big black hole of water in the middle of the night, but maybe they could see it. Because the way I figured it, he must have gone in more toward morning because he would have been coming back from Chicago. That's what I thought, although I argued with the others about it and they didn't agree with me. The only thing was that when they raised the car, which they had to do to get Clinton out, the way the body was jammed in or something, he was naked. Not a stitch of clothes on. 'Now you figure that one,' we said to each other. I tried to. I just couldn't."

The car heater ticks, and the tree limbs outside rub together like they're trying to start a fire. I know how they must feel. I wait a minute for Boyd to say something, but he doesn't.

"After that happened, I remembered about the Indians and being up there earlier in the fall, and I did go to the library, like I'd promised myself. When I asked where books on Indians were, the woman behind the desk just gave me this queer hard laugh, looked me over like I was spit, and said, 'You don't need a book on Indians.'

" 'How do you know, you old bitch,' I yelled, and walked out of there, stomping my feet on the old wooden floor."

Boyd chuckles.

"But the worst part of it was the funeral, because that's when everyone found out for sure about Clinton and the army. When his parents wanted the army to send over an American flag and put a little marker on his grave to show he'd been in the war, the army told them that his dishonorable discharge meant that he was disqualified for anything like that. The news got around quick, and the town seemed to feel satisfied finally. They were right after all. It's hard to forgive them for that. They didn't understand Clinton or me, as it turns out. What we shared—pain—was the one thing no one else seemed to bother with. He made me feel okay, sane, normal—he understood how crazy things were. Maybe I'm here today because he showed up to talk to me—some luck, huh?"

Boyd and I are quiet for a few minutes, letting my story soak through the car floor and leak out the slit he's keeping the window open to. Out the windshield I can almost see my words being walked to Stiller's pond by the wind.

"More cold coming from the north. Better get home now, before that old car of yours decides not to start." He pulls on his headlights.

"That's it? You don't have anything to say after I told you all that stuff?" I open the door and climb out.

"Start your car, let it warm up." He doesn't look at me.

I slam the door as hard as I can. After the battery whines a minute, Prince starts up, the engine putt-putting like a drunk with a hammer.

The steering wheel's so cold, I stick my hands in my pockets. Maybe

I can drive with my knees.

"I used to do that," Clinton says.

I ignore him, which is lucky since Boyd tapping on my window makes me jump. I roll it down enough for his big face to rest a few inches from mine.

"You have to learn to forgive these people in Divinity. First, though, you've got to forgive yourself."

I've heard that so often, it's another nursery rhyme spinning in my head. "Yeah. Okay. What about them?" My car's engine speeds up as it begins to warm.

"They forgave you a long time ago, Honey. You've just been too blind or stubborn to see it." He holds up his hands in defense as I start to reply. "Now I want you to go to Larue's for the night. No discussion. I'll be right behind you, so don't get cute. My patrol car is the fastest thing in the county. Ask your brother, he'll tell you."

"Boyd, why—"

"Because I don't trust you right now. Out here alone. Then that story about Clinton and you. It makes me worry. I hate that feeling. So tonight, Larue's in charge of you. She's still up. There's a game going. I'll meet you in her driveway. Now take it easy. Ready?"

There's no use arguing when he's in his sheriff mood, so I nod and turn on the heater. For an old car, the Valiant has a good strong heater, which I need after the cold from the open window.

On the way to town, I realize how embarrassing this is going to be—a slumber party with Larue Carlson. Hardly the social event Baby and Daddy will be glad about.

Passing my gravel road, I long to turn off, move back to the trailer, to the way it used to be, but time again. There's no hope in time. Everyone is lost, wasted, ruined. I feel so helpless in the face of the events since September, since I was sixteen, or fourteen or eight. I think very hard—concentrate—going back, hand over hand, like I'm lowering myself deep into a cave leading to the middle of the world. When was living a thing that belonged to *me,* that was my very own? When I was five? No, Mama whipped me for dirtying my dress, for letting Tolson out of my sight. Three? Infancy? The single baby moment watching Sonny and Baby play "ring a rosie" around my bed. There is no joy or sorrow in that scene. It just is. I am myself, complete without the complication of memory or feelings. Empty and whole. After that, every event in my life became tinged, tainted by others, by images, ideas in so much conflict, I have grown over the years less and less myself, instead of the opposite. Until I arrive here, driving into Divinity's deserted snowy streets, haunted by the voice of a dead man, missing that of another. Everyone else's is full of unwanted advice. How did I move so beside myself? How did I step so out of my skin that I feel like a battery-operated figure? I'd ask who has the remote control, but I feel the compact plastic cool my own fingers.

"That's enough of that." I turn onto Boardman's street when I can. Ignoring the flashing red lights behind me, I park in the driveway and get out.

Boyd springs to catch me at my front door. "I thought I told you—"

"Arrest me or go home, Boyd. It's my life. I get a chance to live it, too, so leave me alone. All of you—just leave me alone." I slam the door on his contorted, angry face.

"Goes for you, too, Clinton," I warn the dark as I climb the stairs. "Get your ass out there and die. I'm going to bed."

Falling asleep, I wrap my arms around myself, as if I can cradle and hold on to that baby that was the pure, unclouded me, holding her against the cold wind rocking the house.

24

Cupid

One of the problems with New Year's resolutions is that most people rush to make something up at the last minute. They're feeling like a pair of old underpants because they've gone through six weeks of holidays. The only thing they really resolve to do is open a Christmas Club account at the bank and quit drinking and eating so much. That's why I'm taking so long this year. I spend January sorting out the free calendars, deciding which to hang and which to keep in the drawer in case I need them, because you can't throw all those months away. I've tried, I know. And I get rid of the old calendars after cutting out any pretty or interesting pictures. Boardman didn't even get that far. I discover a waist-high box in a closet full of thirty years' worth of calendars, free pens and pencils, fans, key chains, address labels, brochures, and trial-size packets of soap and toothpaste.

I have more time now to sort and clean at Boardman's. I've brought enough clothes over so I only go to the trailer on weekends. Azium finally writes me a letter, scribbled by hand, barely readable with lots of messages for Jass I'm not going to deliver.

That's one of my resolutions.

When Larue and Eleanor cleaned my house, I made them leave the boxes and cupboards alone. The washed windows do let in the winter light better, but now the rooms seem shabbier, the wallpaper stained and yellowed, the paint chipped and smudged, the dark oak floors around the worn rugs looking as if someone has painstakingly rubbed gravel across them. Someday I'll do something about all this. That's another New Year's resolution.

After our encounter at Stiller's pond, I try to avoid Boyd Ziekert. Saving my life wasn't enough for him, I guess. He wants to save my soul, too, so I keep it short when he comes around every few days.

At work, Marylou is sighing significantly and taking mysterious phone calls in whispers.

The centennial is shaping up despite the fact I can't stand how self-important Bowker and his friends are getting. Every day we raise more money and more ideas on boasting the town. The Curl-Y-Que is going to give one-dollar haircuts on their front lawn. The only catch is you have to be willing to let them create the style they want. Twyla would've laughed her legs off. She was the only one knew which end of the scissors cut, she used to say.

Since she died, I'm scared to let anyone do my hair. I'm cutting it myself now. With my sewing shears, I'm a clumsy version of Twyla. Suspending a strand from the comb, I watch the scissors make a decision about length and cut. Some get cut short, some long. A poor imitation of the authority poised above my head when Twyla was alive. "Damn you," I address the absence of her in general. I haven't had any of those visits by her ghost, in dreams or such, so I guess she's satisfied by the way things turned out. She would've loved this. I pick up handfuls of hair and dump them in the toilet, then watch what's left curl and dry to a natural shape. Not bad, I decide each time. Twyla might not have liked it, but it will do fine. Near Valentine's Day, I dye it red again.

I'm not expecting any cards on V Day. No gifts. It's a holiday for lovers and rich people. I'm determined to make myself not care by celebrating alone. I wear a red sweater and skirt to work. The sweater is angora, and I spend the morning fighting the fur flecks out of my eyes and nose. It's a surprise I bought for the occasion, but it's like walking through spiderwebs to wear the thing. I go home at noon to change into a black top.

On my way back to work I spot the bear big figure of Baby lumbering ahead of me. Catching up with her, I'm surprised when she pants, "Oh, good, I was just coming to see you. Slow down, Honey, I can't walk so fast. These shoes Leigh gave me are hard to walk in. Like 'em?"

We stop and stare at her shoes. They're red suede with silver filigree over the toes and curling up the high heels. Despite Baby's size, she has very small feet, only a little pudgy.

"Leigh loves shoes. This is the ninth pair he's given me. He has stacks of catalogs. They aren't cheap, either." She eyes me suspiciously like I've suggested they are.

"No," I agree. "They look like they cost a lot." I try to shuffle my larger feet shod in scuffed black pumps out of the way, but where do you put your feet when you're standing on them?

"They don't even hurt my feet." She smiles shyly at the wonder of it, like a girl with her first corsage.

"Lucky the walks are dry. It'd be a shame to stain that suede. It's such a pretty color."

Baby nods happily and begins to walk carefully toward Main Street again. "So how're you getting along in your new place?"

A hundred questions come up, all sounding like Why haven't you come to see me? "I'm okay. It's a lot like your—our—old house. I thought you might be over by now. To see the place, I mean. I'm not so far away anymore." Making the turn onto Main, we walk slowly, Baby like a funhouse image of me locked in step at my side.

Baby glances at the store windows we're beginning to pass and trails her mittens along their glass, leaving a smear.

"Aren't you going to answer?" I ask finally, and stop.

Baby snorts. "I think it's pretty obvious. You've never invited me over. I decided you don't want to be disturbed. Maybe you're embarrassed or something." She lets her voice drop and linger on something as if I should be.

"Cut it out, Baby. You were too— Oh, never mind."

"Blame it on me. Go ahead. I know how you feel about me. I'm this big fat slob you like to make fun of." There's a catch in her voice, and she brushes at her cheek with her mitten, leaving a black smudge from the windows.

"I'm sorry. See, as always *I* end up apologizing."

"That's not true. You used me in October to stop Sonny Boy, then you ignored me. How do you think that feels? To be the one everybody comes to for help, then they forget?"

It's such a different angle on Baby's life, I pause. That isn't the way I've ever seen her. The helper? The rescuer? The fixer?

I'm just about to mention Jimmy and Brewer when she says, "And don't bring up the damn Jimmy and Brewer thing again. I feel sick to death about them. I didn't mean to *hurt* anyone."

"Well, that wasn't exactly helping things out, Baby. Telling everyone I was pregnant."

Baby nods her head. "I know. You can't imagine how many times I've wished I'd never said a word. I'll never forgive myself. I can't, and saying I'm sorry never feels good enough."

"You might try."

A bewildered look crosses her face. "But they're gone, Honey."

"No, dummy. *Me.* What about *me,* your sister? You ruined my life, practically got me killed. Doesn't *that* deserve an apology after all these years?" I'm almost shouting, and people passing are looking at us curiously.

A series of feelings confuses Baby's face. "But I *did,* didn't I? Haven't I, every time you bring it up?" There's a little quiver in her voice, and she covers the lower part of her face with her red wool mittens so only her eyes peek out.

I actually stamp my foot. "No. You've never said you're sorry. You've taunted me about it, that's all."

"You must be wrong. I'd *never* do that. I might not have said the *actual, actual* words to apologize, but I always tried to show you how I felt. And if I've been hard on you, it's just to help you get over it, don't you know." Her face looks like a cherub's: fat cheeks pink from the cold, round innocent eyes. She could be a doll with that expression—confident it is going to be loved.

A few doors down from us, Bowker pauses in front of the office, twists around, and brushes at the muddy slush dotting the back of his pants cuffs. Baby and Bowker have a lot in common. Their points of view are so absolute, nothing else is possible, so you just naturally have to try to see it their way. After a while it's scary, like now, how I begin to let her be right, regardless of the evidence. Maybe I did misinterpret the whole thing. There's probably a way to make all the pieces fit—hers and mine. I just haven't worked hard enough.

"Okay. Let's just drop it. Why were you coming to see me?"

"Oh, I forgot. No, wait. Oh, yeah. I'm so excited, and I need your help. Leigh is taking us on a cruise in March. A cruise. In the Caribbean. On a huge ship. And we're going first class. Can you *believe* it? It's so unreal."

A rush of envy makes me blush, until I push it back. "That *is* great, Baby. You deserve it. Really." I hope my words don't sound as stiff and flat to her as they do to me.

Baby shakes her shoulders, too happy to notice my tone. "It's just too amazing. Me, on a cruise. But that's the problem, too. I need you to talk to Daddy. He's going to be furious. He'll never let me go. You know how he can be. I mean, we aren't even engaged yet, but I think . . ." She laughs. "You know what I mean."

The week-old snow banked on the street seems dingier, and the wind rubs at my cold skin like sandpaper. "Baby, I'm not very good at talking to Daddy."

"How can you say that? He didn't move out when he got married. You talked him into that. This should be a lot easier. A lot."

"God, Baby, he did that because of *her,* not me, don't you know that?"

"No, that's just not true, Honey. Your talk helped a lot. And all I'm asking is that you do the same thing again. Just talk to him. Remember Sonny Boy."

"Oh, shit. When're you leaving?"

"Three weeks, and I have *so* much to do, you wouldn't believe it. Leigh's buying me a wardrobe, too. Lord knows, I need it. Did I mention it's a 'Big Is Beautiful' cruise? You have to weigh over two hundred fifty pounds to go. We might sink the ship, huh?"

"I gotta go to work, Baby. One last thing, how am I supposed to get together with Daddy for this talk?"

"Oh, no problem. Sleepy's at six tonight. I had to promise him Louverna *wasn't* the surprise. He'll be waiting, so don't be late, you know how that makes him."

"Okay. This isn't going to work, though. Just so you know. He doesn't exactly count me as the most moral person on earth."

Baby laughs. "I don't know where you get these ideas, Honey. He has plenty of respect for you. Don't forget, six at Sleepy's. Thanks."

"Happy Valentine's Day," I mutter at her retreating back.

My plans for tonight did not include talking to my father. He's the last person I would have chosen, in fact. By the time I park my car at Sleepy's, the lot is beginning to fill up. Sweethearts celebrating. By midnight half of them won't be speaking. They'll be so drunk, though, they'll find someone else to go home with for the traditional screw.

Daddy is in a booth by the front windows when I walk in. Worse luck, it's the one we sat in the night Jass came with us last fall. Now all we need is Sonny Boy. There's a glass of clear liquid on ice in front of Daddy when I sit down.

He looks at me surprised and wraps his fingers tighter around the glass.

"Hello. Baby sent me." I figure we should get it all out in the open. He hates surprises. Mystery dishes.

Daddy shrugs, takes a drink, and looks out the window at the parking lot.

"What do ya want?" The barmaid cocks her hip, staring at my father but asking me. He ignores her.

"Club soda or ginger ale. Whatever."

"Club it is." She eyes the level of Daddy's drink professionally and leaves. A moment later she sets the drink on the napkin in front of me. "Tab?" Daddy nods, and she's off again.

"This better not be about Louverna, Honey." He looks at me coldly. There is a new tiredness in his voice, dark chapped skin around his eyes, and a new sag to his cheeks. She's wearing him out. I don't know how to feel about it, either.

"It's about Baby. She needs—she wants to—"

"The usual stuff from your sister. I know. That fat rich boy wants to spoil her to death, then let me pick up the pieces. Right?" He takes a long gulp of his drink, emptying the glass, melting ice and all, then holds it up for service.

"He wants to take her on a Caribbean cruise." I say it carefully as the waitress replaces his empty glass with a full one.

"I know you think I shouldn't interfere with someone her size finding a man. I should be grateful. But damn it, your mother wouldn't have stood for the way you girls carry on, so I shouldn't, either. No."

Watching him drink like this, I'm reminded that he only does this when he's very upset. It's his way of not having to say the words out loud to anyone. Just sit in his corner and drink until the bottle's empty, the silence flooding from his chair in the living room. But he's drinking in public now, like his children. Not a good sign.

"He's probably going to ask her to marry him on the cruise. Besides, Leigh Hunt's not the type to break anyone's heart." He just looks at me and finishes half the glass. Must be gin. He hates vodka. Gin's a workingman's drink in England, he used to say, half-proud and half-ashamed.

"You can guarantee that? You know so much about men?" He leans back against the wooden booth and crosses his arms. "Maybe you do. Lord knows you've had enough chances to find out about 'em."

I don't know whether he's being a bastard or a whiner—the two types of men in our family. Then his face gets wrinkled and funny, and he stares so hard at the ice in the drink, I think I can see him melting it. We sit like that for five minutes until I say, "Daddy? What's the matter?"

It must be my voice sounding so like when I was a little girl coming to sit on his lap, the favorite for a while, enjoying that brief feel of love and the power it gave over my brothers and sister at his feet. Then, realizing how left out they were feeling and how that was the part Daddy liked, I couldn't bring myself to that comfort of his lap anymore. I had to join my brothers and sister gathered on the floor around his chair.

His eyes look hopeful for a moment before the old bitterness replaces it. Don't ignore me, please, Daddy, don't, I plead silently.

This time he takes just a taste of gin, clears his throat, and looks at the parking lot. "This marriage, it's getting me . . . down, I guess you'd say."

An enormous bubble rises in my stomach. Breathe, breathe, I remind my lungs as I wait for him to continue.

He shifts his gaze back to his hands, a larger replica of mine: thick, square fingers too short for the palm. Only his fingers are covered with pale orange prickly hairs.

"I don't trust her. That's the problem. After that cake and reception, who would? And she can't stand my kids. What kind of man would take that?"

I nod encouragingly, but I want to ask him since when his kids are important to him.

"I mean, can you imagine your sister unable to reach me if she needed help? Or Sonny Boy without a roof over his head, sleeping in his car some below zero night because those Bevingtons think they're better than God Almighty, let alone the Parrishes? Rose Bevington was *lucky* Sonny married her. *Lucky.*" He drinks to that idea.

"Now Louverna wants to keep all my kids away—you, too. 'They can come when they're invited,' she says. Well, I won't have it. She doesn't get to make the rules in my house, I do. Your mother always said that, she knew. She was a real woman, a good wife."

Beneath my father's brave words, I hear another tone. Fear. He's afraid. It comes home with all the force of his hand slapping my face. My father is a coward. He's afraid all the time. He even drinks the brooding coward's way: alone, in the dark, plotting.

"Is that why you haven't gone to live with her?"

He nods reluctantly, like he's admitting to shoplifting or something. "It's her house."

"Yeah."

"She earns more than I do." He admits this almost whispering, confessing it like a crime of shame.

"Oh."

"A-man—" He stops and toys with his drink. "Isn't-a-man-if . . ." He can't force the formula out. "Your mother . . ."

I nod again. She was all he needed her to be, and she died lonely and disappointed in life.

"I'm not some broken-down farmer Louverna can push around. I have to be the man of the house. You kids had to learn that the hard way, I know, but it was the right thing. If I'd gone around acting like a failure, you wouldn't have had any respect for me. I'm not a failure. Anyone could've lost that farm. Anyone."

Respect? This has all been about that? The word refuses to register in place of Daddy's usual anger. I'm confused tonight, light-headed with the way he's treating me. Not so much as a daughter, but as a person he talks to, someone he's not mad at because I'm related to him.

There's another lull, and we both concentrate on the parking lot as if Elvis Presley is going to make an appearance. Instead Sonny Boy pulls up, parks blocking three other cars, jumps out, and runs to the door. Our eyes follow his circle around the room, prodding and pushing through the dancers and standers. He pauses at the bar to grab a long-neck Bud and continues his pacing as if he's securing the perimeter. When he finally spots us sitting at the booth, he stops, slugs the beer, spins the empty down the counter, and pushes his way out the door. We follow his roaring, sliding departure from the parking lot.

"He's in a mood tonight." Daddy finishes his drink and holds up the glass as before. When the new one arrives, he tastes it, letting the gin roll in his mouth before swallowing. He looks at me somewhat surprised, as if I've just slipped in there or said something bizarre.

"You like your new house?"

"Yeah, sure, it's fine. Okay." I stick a finger in my glass, poking at the melting ice.

"Nice of him to give you the house." He says it too nonchalantly.

"He *did. Give* it to me. After Clinton bought it from him for me." I say this a little proudly. Of all the boys I went with, Daddy hated Clinton the most.

"You're lucky you didn't get that nut case with the house."

"Yeah, we already have one of our own in Sonny Boy."

Unexpectedly, Daddy laughs and drinks from his glass. "You do remind me of someone, Honey. You always have. You know who?"

"No."

"Your uncle Hubert. Remember him? No, you were too young.

Hubert: the faith-healing dentist. Best in the business. Always had his own way of seeing things."

"I look like him or something?"

Daddy grins. "Lord, no. The man looked just like Burt Lancaster. That's a fact. Even in his old age, when I knew him. Well over six feet with big, broad shoulders. A mouth that would turn you to stone if it went straight and hard, raise you to heaven when it smiled. And those eyes—like they were seeing right into you, like they could read your heart and see if Jesus Christ, your Savior, was written all over it, like it was supposed to, if you were going to be healed. Nobody came faking around Hubert. He was such a tough old bird, even at eighty-four he could make you confess your sins and holler to beat the band when he took hold of your jaw and asked the Lord to come down and have a look for cavities."

Daddy leans back smiling, reaches a cigarette out of his shirt pocket, and lights up. He looks at it apologetically in his fingers. "She started me again."

"Did he ever cure you?"

He smiles and says, "I never had a single cavity with Hubert and the Lord doing the dental work. Not a single one. Never lost a tooth, except the front one got knocked out by that baler; but Hubert even fixed that

for me."

He grins but keeps his lips shut tight over his teeth so I can't see the tooth that Hubert, who looked like Burt Lancaster, fixed. Then he opens his mouth, showing a gleaming white eyetooth that looks just like the others.

"You'd never know it's fake."

Daddy looks disgusted. "It isn't, can't you see that it grew back? Hubert and the Lord made it grow back, just like a natural tooth. Hubert said it would happen if I believed, and I prayed like the devil for a week, and pretty soon it got more solid in my head. Then I prayed again for another two weeks, and it started getting whiter, looking like the rest of them up there solid, you couldn't pull it out. And that's how come Hubert was so famous. He had the touch, I'll tell you."

He finishes his drink and holds up his glass for another. When she comes, he draws a circle over the table to include my glass this time, too. Then he takes a last puff off his cigarette and mashes it with his thumbnail in the ashtray. Farmers are always careful of their ashes and butts that way.

"The only time Hubert had trouble was right at the start. Family, of course. People were beginning to talk about him; he was getting more invitations to the camp meetings and revivals that every little town in Iowa had at least four or five times a year back in the twenties and thirties. It wasn't like today with these folksingers or rock groups coming in with their Jesus songs and fancy hairdos. This was an all-day, all-night, all-day, all-night kind of event. People would come from miles around, family packed in wagons and later cars and trucks, spreading out the blankets for picnics and people to sit on, and they'd go at it. If the healer or preacher had a big name, there'd be a big tent with wooden chairs. Since there wasn't any television then, this was what we did for fun. Went to the meeting, saw friends, got a chance to sing, jump around, cry, and beller like a mama cow for her calf. Mostly women did that, but sometimes men, especially when a good healer came along. Hubert was a good one. He worked with a Bible in one hand and a steel dental pick in the other, waving both of them around like he was conducting a band, and flashing those big white teeth he'd had since birth. Came out of the womb with a full head of teeth. My mama had hair like a grown woman, long and curly, and her brother Hubert had teeth. I guess her other brother, Walter, was fat, and nobody expected her sister, Amelia, to live."

The girl delivers the drinks, and we each take a sip.

"About the time he was starting, Amelia, his youngest sister, started
having real bad pains in her head, and when she went to the doctor he told her that she had wisdom teeth that had started to abscess, get infected, and she'd have to have them pulled right away. So she went home, and as soon as Hubert got back the next week, she told him she wanted him to heal her teeth. She wasn't going to any doctor in town for something the Lord and her brother could take care of.

"Hubert was flattered to get trust like that, especially from his own family since his father had been skeptical before he died, and his own mother had her teeth checked by the traveling dentist. This looked like a big vote of confidence, and he set in to do his job with everything he could muster, praying for a whole day to get the power for such a big undertaking."

The jukebox kicks in with Bruce Springsteen, and Daddy has to lean forward to be heard now.

"Amelia, sick as a dog, just lay in her bed, trying to keep her moans and groans quiet so she wouldn't disturb Hubert's praying in the next room. My mother was sitting with Amelia, helping her pray as best she could with the pain. Hubert had told them that she shouldn't have any of the painkiller the doctor had given her because it would cloud up the transmission of power between the three of them, Hubert, Amelia, and Jesus. When Hubert finally came in at three in the morning, he'd put on his best suit and gotten his best Bible and dental mirror out, and looked like some Old Testament judge, though he was clean shaven. His eyes were just flashing, and you could tell he'd had communication, he'd touched the divine spark, because when he came to Amelia's bedside, she relaxed, sort of let go, and she took on a glow herself, and later Hubert would say that was the Lord relieving her of her pain. After the examination, Hubert prayed some more, and the Lord told him not to pull the wisdom teeth or Amelia would be an idiot all her life, so he didn't.

"Instead, he spent the next two days and nights praying with her, his hands clamped around her jaw while be beseeched God to come and heal this woman's pain so she could grow to be a wise old woman. The whole time, Amelia seemed comfortable and happy, like the pain of the past few days had gone. On the third morning, when the rest of the family came up to see how it was going, Amelia was dead and Hubert was still kneeling beside the bed in prayer, this time with his hands folded in front of him, looking like a sampler with the figure of a child saying his bedtime prayers cross-stitched on it, my mama said. 'The Lord wanted her,' was all he told them. 'She was happy to go.'

"Your mother wanted to name you Amelia, after your aunt, but I told her it was bad luck. Even as a baby you were more like Hubert—independent, stubborn. You never caused me the kind of trouble the others did, not till high school. Then . . ." He picks up his drink and sips at it, watching my face. My scar burns under his gaze.

"Still, I never worried about you the way I had to the others. You always seem to go your own way, but you never ask for help. Your mama never understood that. I did, though. Hubert. I can see it right now in those eyes of yours. Poor Hubert."

I'm confused by his attention. Does this mean he likes me? After all these years of his anger, am I claimed as his daughter now through the connection of some crazy uncle? His voice interrupts my thoughts.

"Now Sonny, he's always in trouble. Always will be. He's tormented. I wish Hubert were alive today for him. Maybe Sonny could use Jesus. I don't know what to do with that boy. Louverna's just going to have to see I have kids. Grown-up, maybe, but they still need me." He eyes me. "Well, not Tolson or you."

In a funny way, it seems that Daddy, Sonny, and Baby *are* a family, and Tolson and I aren't. We stopped years ago. Or even earlier, if I count the times Daddy beat Tolson, threatened to kill him, pinning his thin, underweight body to the bed while Mama turned her back and I watched frantically silent. It's this memory that keeps me from Daddy now, won't let myself be on his side, trust him. I like it where I am, I realize, free to follow Springsteen. "Born to run."

"You never needed any of us," Daddy says matter-of-factly. "Tolson was always chicken, but not you. You just saw it different. Still do. Doesn't make the rest of us like you, but I'm not sure that's important to you—to folks like Hubert."

It's the closest to understanding I've ever gotten from him. Even though he's partly wrong, I'm grateful. I try to see myself as he does. Independent. Not part of the family. It hurts in a way. I want to tell him that I *have* missed him, missed being loved, liked, accepted, but I can see it doesn't matter. This is about as close as we'll ever get. Next time he'll probably be mad again.

"Are you going to move in with Louverna?"

He grins, more relaxed now that he has me pegged. "I might make her wait just a little more. She's starting to come around, but she still needs to understand how things stand. I'm not letting her bury me like she did the others. Besides, I'm not letting Leigh Hunt have my daughter just because she's too desperate to wait for a ring. The minute I move out, he'll move in. Nope, I'm doing the right thing. We've managed to avoid having little bastard babies so far, and I'm keeping it that way."

Although he's had a lot to drink, Daddy's hand is still steady as he bangs his glass down. It's so noisy and crowded in here now, no one notices. He won't show the booze until he's so drunk, he'll stiffen up and pass out like a dead man. Next day he's always fine, like drinking was just a seizure.

"If she doesn't go on this cruise, there's a good chance she'll spend the rest of her life on your hands, hating you."

Daddy considers this for a moment. "Yeah. Okay. But separate rooms. Separate. You tell her that, and make sure he hears it, too. I'll kick his fat butt down the courthouse stairs if there's any little Leighs without last names in nine months."

God, I hate playing Cupid. "Don't you think it'll mean more coming from you? If you tell her?"

He blushes and looks away at the crowd. "I couldn't say that stuff to Baby." He speaks so quietly I can barely hear him. "She's my daughter."

The way he says it, like there's some magic involved, makes me so sad that I have to shut my eyes. What am I? I want to ask. Why can't I ever be the daughter? Was it the day I climbed off your lap to make the others happy? Or the day I let you scar my face? When did I stop being one of yours? It seems like the kind of question someone's always been asking since families first started. I can feel the hopelessness of it, too, dragging all those tired years of disapproval to now. A minute ago I was safely independent, now I'm his child again—left out, left over. That's what family does.

"Okay. I have to go." I grab my purse, pull out a couple of dollars, dump them on the table, and stand up. Daddy looks puzzled. "I'll tell her what you said." I pull on my coat. "Thanks."

In the car, I pull the image he's given me of myself, my childhood, to my chest, wrapping my coat around it while the engine tries to warm up. There is a good pain here, like walking away from a car wreck with only a few scratches and a broken arm, knowing you could've been killed, you had every right to be dead. I was prepared for his anger, indifference, not this new view of myself he's accidentally given me, but I can't let myself trust him. Watching Daddy's hatchet face grow weak and afraid tonight makes me see the spin that fear and desire put on our lives.

Tomorrow I'll tell Baby to lie about having separate rooms on the cruise and to start taking the pill.

"Happy Valentine's Day," I tell myself in the mirror. I switch on the

lights, ready to pull away, when I see something stuck in the windshield wiper. I get out, pull it off, and sit down again. It's a red envelope. The cartoon pony on the card says, "Miss horsing around?" Inside it says, "Be my Valentine," signed, "The Lone Stranger." It has to be Jass. Who else? I smile despite myself as I head for home. I'm my own best valentine—that's my next New Year's resolution, I decide, and circle the block so I can head out 11 for my trailer. If you bother to make resolutions, you should write them down. Maybe I'll add Uncle Hubert to the charts, too. He had Jesus to help him, and I have Clinton. Relying on the dead—I guess we do have a lot in common.

25

Winter Dreams

Winter in Iowa is an alone time. Staying at the trailer the weekend after Valentine's, I look out my windows at the fields around me, notice the rhythm of work change, for a while, and try to place the pause everything takes. When the winter wheat is planted, the corn fields emptied and broken down, the cattle turned loose in them for forage, the black sunflower fields harvested, the oil sold and stored, the barley and rye, millet and flax, gathered by snowfall, the fields sit silent and exhausted under the thin noon sun, too soon obscured by the gathering clouds of snow. When the occasional bale of hay left wet and rotting in the field becomes a hump of snow smoothed and forgotten in the farmers' minds, they look out, strain their eyes into the whiteness of the fields, across to the black outlines of the trees, the windbreaks along the north and west. The corncribs are full and the silos are full, the pigs are penned for the winter with only their soft grunting and burrowing, and the steers munch hay in the shadows of the barn or bunch against the falling snow in the protective angle of the eaves outside, and the horses dark and whispery turn their rumps to the snow, deigning to mix with the cows, and the chickens cluck softly and flap in the hazy, straw-filled house where ammonia needles eyes and nose. The sheep in thick silence rest like huge stones in the pen before the storm, and the cows lie in their stanchions, heads curled to the side like huge birds asleep, with skin draped over hips like wooden chair backs. Inside the barn ticks the electric generator, metering fences outside, water pumps, milking machines, liquid manure machines, electric lights, and all the machinery that hums and clicks like another busy animal against the silence the farm becomes in winter when the snow reaches down in long curtains over the fields and houses.

Up at the house in the long afternoon, before evening chores and after them, in the evening, men and women go over the accounts, plan their breeding programs, read about bulls and boars and rams pictured in the artificial insemination service catalogs, stretched and posed like fancy show horses, with names attached to their virility: "Tom Jones," "Lover Boy," "Casanova." The cows and shoats and sheep as graceful as does or as lumbering as oxen line up in the farmers' dreams to receive their shot of it.

And in the basements and root cellars the vegetables rest in the dry, dark silence, their ripeness caught in the exact moment and held suspended there above decay. Potatoes and apples and squash and, around the corner on the shelves built fifty and a hundred years before, the jars of preserves, tomatoes, beans, corn, succotash, and pickles the family will eat through by spring.

This is the life our family lost. As surely as driving into a semi on the interstate, we were wiped out, wiped clean, pried from the land and chuffed off. Now the metal walls of my trailer *ping*ing with frozen bits of snow and dirt blown from the surrounding fields is all that remains of that life, and I hate to leave it. But, like Clinton, sometimes I don't see how I can stand witnessing what we're losing.

Mapping the resolutions on my kitchen walls, I remember when we sold the family farm and moved first to Omaha, then Des Moines, and finally came back here to Divinity when I was seven, so Daddy could drive by the old place once in a while just to make himself feel worse. I tried to walk there from our little house in town once, when I was eight, but I didn't make it. It was like it kept moving just beyond my reach, the kind of game you play when you're a kid and an older, bigger kid will hold something you want up and over your head, just to watch you jump up and down until you're exhausted and fall down crying. Keep away. When Mama finally drove down the shoulder and stopped just behind me, I was ready to get in. But when she drove me the rest of the way, it seemed to take just a minute.

"How far did I get?" I asked her.

"Only two miles. You must have been taking your time."

"No," I told her, "I was walking straight and fast."

"Then you're never gonna get very far in life Honey, 'cause you only made two miles in all that while. Here, now, here's the old place. Kind of pretty, wasn't it?" Mama was right, of course.

"Mama," I say it to the graying light of the kitchen, to the white squares of scrawled paper tiling the walls, iridescent almost. Mama and Daddy have their own pieces of paper now, and the rest of the world radiates from them like pieces of a house exploding or the just sun shining, depending on my mood. The king and queen of heaven and hell. There's nothing simple here. Talking to Daddy at Sleepy's a few days ago changed something. I've felt sad since then, like another thing has died. Today I start to feel better. Lighter. I'm not his baby. Never was. Never will be. I'm my own baby. I keep coming back to that image, like a photograph he's been hiding or holding hostage and just decided to release. A prisoner of war who could finally come home. Beside her, Clinton seems smaller, crowded. He complains about it. Keeps trying to tell me things I don't have time for right now. I'm on the track of something, like a good hunting dog, I smell it. Sometimes I press my face against the charts, breathe the light chemical smell of Magic Marker ink and squint my eyes to see if there's another pattern to be made, to be found in the evidence before me. Evidence of what? What crimes, what sins? What research, what history? Is there some object to be found, recovered, stolen? A valuable something—a something at all?

Lately I've been clipping stories in the newspapers Boardman kept for wrapping the rocks he sold: at the celebration for the Kentucky Fried Chicken Museum, they served roast beef. A farmer losing his farm shot his whole herd of dairy cows, smoked a cigarette, and shot himself. In the Amazon birds called honey-gatherers attract and lead people to honey trees with an elaborate series of songs and gestures. North Dakota is the geographic center of North America.

This all seems important somehow. Because my eyes found them, they must be messages, and on weekends I bring them out and paste them on the walls, too.

When I fall asleep at the kitchen table, my head on my folded arms, Clinton is leading me through a bunch of caves. They're more lit up than usual caves, though, like tunnels for mining or underground bomb shelters. We have a lot of trouble. Sometimes people are chasing us, sometimes it's natural things like snakes or mucky water. At the end of the dream, Clinton looks pretty goofy with long greasy brown hair straggling over his shoulders and a silly baggy outfit in purple, red, and yellow. Sort of a cross between a clown and a magician. With dirt on his face and his clothes, he's ragged, outdated, as he climbs the metal rungs set into the blond stone wall and pops the round cast-iron lid at the top. Outside, we're standing in the middle of a city street, and I realize Clinton and I have been walking through the sewer system the whole time. I'm both relieved and pissed off, unsure that I'm happy to be above ground.

I wake up because my arms ache from falling asleep under the weight of my head, and my neck is cramped from the position. In the time I've been asleep the sun has set, and outside, the fields carry the metallic gloss of Sorenson's bulk milk truck. That's the dream I haven't had yet. For ten years I knew it was February by that dream of having to drive in Twyla's truck, the one constructed by Tom out of barrels of jet fuel strapped together. The barrels were white and shiny with bright red warning letters on them. It was hard to get into the open cab on the passenger's side each year. I can tell the dream is gone. Maybe I left it in those caves that son of a bitch Clinton's kept me in.

"I led you out, dummy. Pay attention to details. Nice dream, by the way. I liked everything but my clothes. I looked so sixties, didn't I?"

"Clinton." I rub my neck to relieve some of the pain. "My head is not your private movie theater."

"The way you've been lately, I have to do something for entertain-

ment. You never want to talk anymore. I say something, and you ignore me. I could help more, you know. Look what I've done so far."

I get up to dig a Diet Pepsi out of the fridge. Since I started working out here weekends, I've stocked the kitchen with stuff that keeps for a while. I'll have to do dishes sometime, I notice. The stacks are starting to inch onto the stove and table. The smell isn't bad because I'm mostly eating Budget Gourmet, and I keep the garbage bag tied between visits.

Leaning back against the sink, I take a long gulp of pop and survey the walls. I've heard these complaints from Clinton a lot lately, and they're beginning to wear me out.

"You want me to move back here, is that it, Clinton?" I yell. "You gave me a house. Fine. I'm grateful, goddamn it. But you did not say I had to give you my whole life in return. Besides, I've tried that, remember? It doesn't work. I gave Jass up, what more do you want? Can't you just go do whatever dead people usually do? Why are you always bugging *me,* for chrissakes?"

The silence in the trailer scares me. It's dark in the rooms beyond the kitchen, and I'm talking to a ghost. I'm about to turn on the lights when Clinton says, "No, leave them off. This is what it's like here for me. So you'll know. It's all shadows and bits of light that seem to splinter off something I can never quite make out, beyond or above me. That's why I keep coming back to talk. It's so lonely, so unclear. I feel like one of those shadows is me. And I don't know it or something. There's no one else here. I'm all alone."

He sounds terrible, and I hate myself for being so mean. "What can I do, Clinton? I don't understand. Do we do this talking thing until I'm dead, too, or what?" Saying that makes me uneasy, like talking with him *will* kill me.

"You're right. I know I have to stop. And no, I want you to keep the house. Jasper, by the way, is *your* doing. I *am, was,* jealous. But don't blame your problems on me."

"I did it for you. . . ." I finish the can of pop, rinse it out, and put it in its special bag. The centennial committee has decided the town needs to try recycling for their celebration.

"No, Honey. You did it for you. Your problem. Not mine. If I were a woman, I'd fuck all day and all night. I'd have ten Jaspers. I wouldn't be caught dead playing your game."

"You were, remember?"

"A joke! She got it. Humor returns to Divinity on a rare visit."

"Funny, ha ha. Do you really have something to say, or are you BS-ing as usual?" I pick up the article about a pet python that tried to swallow his owner, who was saved only because the python's tooth got stuck in the man's forehead.

"Yes. I feel like I'm that snake. Or that snake swallowed me. I can't figure out which. Here it is, Honey. Here's a story for your wall. Remember when I came home from Vietnam and met you at Appreciation Day? We horsed around until about two in the morning when I dropped you off? What you don't know is that Sonny Boy picked me up in his car at the Mercy River at three. He was driving around with Jake, Jimmy, and Brewer. There was a gun. A hunting rifle wrapped in an old bath towel on the front seat between us. Does any of this ring a bell?"

My legs start to tremble, and I sit down at the table. "Is it true? *Did* he kill that black girl? Shoot her? Tell me, Clinton . . . Clinton? Don't you disappear on me now. Tell me."

"We all did it, Honey. We *all* killed her. You know that. It was all of us. One minute she was standing there under the neon bus sign, the next minute she wasn't."

"One shot, Clinton, to the head? All of you in one shot? Don't you *dare* walk out now, don't you dare do that again."

"I can't help it, Honey. Think about it, just think—"

"Clinton, damn you to hell, you come back." I know he's gone by the way the darkness grows impersonal, mechanical, and grayer, as if a special shadow is bleaching out of it. "Christ, what am I supposed to do now?"

The wind smooths the metal sheath around me, and I almost wish for the assault of Sonny Boy's beer cans. Were they all murderers? Or were they all along for the ride, except for one?

Tolson said Sonny Boy took a rifle that night. Later he claimed it was lost. Jake? What do I know about Jake? If he killed her, who is he, was he? Jimmy ran the night of the accident. One dead body too many? And Brewer, the sweet one. He hated guns, but that was after, wasn't it?

But who were the best shots? Boyd asked me that. Not Clinton; he was good, but he wouldn't have. Jake? What do I know about Jake, the war and Jake? But he did Vietnam *after* the killing.

Almost without realizing it, I'm at the table writing down their names like planets circling the center ball with "DEAD GIRL" printed in block letters. Boyd's right. One of them *did* do it. Tolson might be on target, but Clinton makes it sound like they all had a hand in it, but that doesn't make sense. The real question I have to ask Clinton is how I got mixed up with all of them.

Without meaning to, I remember that time with Jimmy and Brewer, our senior year, the fall after Clinton had died.

What happened wasn't anybody's fault. Not Brewer's. And not mine and not Jimmy's.

I remember that last time with Brewer, parked in O'Malley's driveway, the long one that winds over the stream through five acres of woods before it finds the house. It was almost three in the morning, and I knew Mama would be worried sick, if she was awake, but I couldn't bring myself to stop and go home. I just couldn't. We argued all night because I told him I didn't want to go out with him anymore. Then we did it, our first and last time. It was summer, and I jumped out of the car, naked, and stood on the little bridge looking down at the moon torn up in the jagged rocks the stream ran over. I kept wishing I could be like that moon, because in a moment Brewer was behind me, his strong body, slick with sweat, glistening like a pretty horse.

He pulled me around to him. "You're gonna get into trouble like this. This isn't right, you know that."

But I couldn't tell him then about sneaking around with Jimmy, couldn't stay with him, either. He was so good to me, I couldn't. Then he'd know that I'd been lying to him steady about loving him only, all along, and he wouldn't love me anymore. Somehow that was important, that he not hate me. So I wanted to be that moon all ragged in the rocks below us, not the person that was making Brewer's voice crack and the tears start rolling down his face. It's not easy to watch a man cry. I knew that as I hugged him and tried to say that I'd be all right. We both knew I was lying.

It was a month later when I realized how Brewer must have sensed something all along. Jimmy was acting strange, and I started feeling bad in the mornings. Oh, I knew what it was. Although I hadn't let Jimmy touch me in weeks, it had to be, but then I couldn't tell for sure. That was the problem. I wasn't feeling like I wanted anybody to touch me then, being sick as a dog all day long in school and getting hall passes to go to the bathroom to throw up breakfast or lunch or some yellow bile. That made me feel better, just the act of it. I kept thinking, Maybe I'll throw it up, maybe something will happen and it'll pop out this way. I knew it was silly to hope, but I had to believe that something could happen like that because I didn't know what to do. Brewer was calling me once or twice a week to see if I'd changed my mind yet, and Jimmy was acting strange, giving me excuses and showing up late when I snuck out to meet him. I was sick and tired all the time. I wanted to crawl in a hole and die. Mama noticed the way I was dragging along and wanted me to take vitamins, which I held in my hand and stuffed in my jacket pocket when she wasn't looking because if anything would make me sick right then and there, it was that sweet medicine taste of those vitamin pills. To this day, I can't stand that taste.

Finally, one night when Jimmy broke a date with me, I called Brewer, and we went out, driving along the country roads, and pretty soon I was pouring it all out. Only I didn't let on that Jimmy was in it, too, because I was afraid Brewer would know that the whole time I was seeing him that summer, I was sneaking out with Jimmy on the side. I just couldn't bear to have him think that about me. Brewer was loving and nice. After he got over being shocked, he wanted to marry me right then and there, but I said no. I wasn't going to start being a married woman with no high school diploma and a baby right away. He begged me, of course, but I couldn't, not with Jimmy and all, but I couldn't tell Brewer that. We went home after a while, both of us depressed.

A week later Jimmy and I had a big fight about the way he was acting. When he told me he was seeing Merry Alice Winters, I told him I was going to have his baby. You should have seen his jaw drop. Well, I thought, that fixes that. For a few minutes I was feeling pretty good, till

I realized he wasn't saying anything, just staring straight ahead down the gravel road we were parked along, looking off into the darkness, his hands gripping the wheel too hard. I thought it would break soon if he didn't let go, so I reached for his hand, and it came flying back at me, hit me so hard in the face that I was thrown back against the door, and my head went crack into the window. Things blurred out for a minute, and I could feel something coming up inside me, not the baby, but something else. I grabbed the door handle, yanked myself out of the truck, and hit the road running as hard as I could. Down the shoulder, then across the drainage ditch, full of dried-up stickers catching at my stockings and skirt, over the fence, and off across the field.

I was running so hard, I didn't hear him at first. It was train noise running inside me. I was stumbling over the molehills and piles of weeds and crying and yelling and heading for the dark woods that were just ahead. When I felt his arms tackle me, down we went, me struggling and kicking and scratching. I meant to hurt him. I fought as hard as I could until he was on top of me, holding my arms down and sitting with his weight on my stomach.

"Go head, squash it. You don't care, you don't give a damn about me." I spit at him then, and he lay down on me, crushing my breath out for a minute, and everything stopped. All the noise and all the anger. It all went clear like that fall night. Pretty soon I could tell that he was crying, the tears sliding down cool along the inside of my blouse and his body quivering like he was chilly. So I wrapped my arms around him and cooed to him, holding and rocking him. I didn't care if the baby squashed between us. I didn't care about anything.

Things looked like they were going to clear up then, like it would work out. Jimmy and I talked it over, were trying to decide what would be best to do. We met after school each day and went for long walks or drove out in the country. He held my hand when the truck ride made me sick and I couldn't help it. He was going to make a good father, I could tell, but I still couldn't bring myself to get married. It just didn't seem right. I knew I should just get it over with, tell my family, let the town know. They'd all know soon enough. Sometimes I wished there was another way, though, because I felt dark and trapped, knowing there was something inside me I couldn't stop from growing. Like an extra leg I didn't want on any account. Didn't need.

Then there was Brewer, too. He kept after me, accusing me sometimes of lying to him, other times getting so depressed that I was afraid he'd do something. He half suggested it a couple of times—that we finish it together, then and there, driving his father's car into the river, into a wall, off the edge of the world. But I just couldn't tell him about Jimmy, and I just couldn't tell Jimmy about him. It wasn't fair, no matter how you looked at it. I don't know even now, if things hadn't turned out the way they did, what I would have done. I really can't say.

It was the end of October when it all changed. Baby had been watching me pretty closely, and one day while I was in the bathroom throwing up, she came in. She had guessed but promised she'd never say a word if I told her who. I knew I shouldn't believe her, but we were sisters, and I knew she'd tell for sure if I didn't do something, so I told her: Brewer. A minute after I looked at myself in the dull little mirror over the sink and said, "Now, why did you do that?" It looked as surprised as I was.

That Saturday night there was a big dance for the school after the homecoming game. I was planning on going with Baby and her friends and meeting Jimmy there. The only trouble was that Brewer had been at me all day to talk to him, meet him someplace, he had something to say. I knew I'd have to see him somehow but didn't want him hanging around the house where Baby or Sonny Boy might overhear us, and I didn't want to be seen going around in his car where Jimmy might see us. Jimmy had been getting real tight lately, possessive. Anyway, I arranged to meet Brewer in his car at ten-thirty in the parking lot that night.

This is the part I hate, what came next. Of course, all the girls spent the evening circulating and telling each other the latest news, so it was just a matter of time before Baby topped them with my story, and it was just a little after that that the boys were all shuffling around on the dance floor shoving elbows in Jimmy and grinning meanly. At about eleven, while Brewer and I were sitting in his car, out came Jimmy running and walking, shaking his clenched fists in our direction. The next thing I knew we were streaking out of town in Brewer's car, Jimmy's pickup right on us, shoving us with its bumper every time Brewer took his foot off the gas. I was begging Brewer to stop and Brewer was telling me to shut up, and Jimmy was honking and bumping his truck into our car, so when we hit the dirt road to the quarry, we started sliding around each time he made contact. It was Brewer's brother's car, so he was furious and wanted to kill Jimmy, but we both knew that Jimmy was stronger and meaner, so we kept driving as fast as we could, swerving from side to side to keep Jimmy from coming up alongside and shoving us off into the ditch.

There are a hundred little farm roads crisscrossing outside of Divinity, and none of them have stop signs and nobody would stop if they did. I was screaming that we had to slow down, we had to watch it, and I was trying to grab the wheel, but it wasn't that that made it all stop. A cow in the road stuck in the headlights and we went plowing through it like it was a house, and that was the last thing I knew. The lights bouncing up and down on the animal and its eyes big as china doorknobs coming closer and closer and closer. And while I was swinging in the darkness that caught and held me, those huge eyes kept accusing, and I cried over and over, "It's not my fault, it's not my fault." But it didn't do any good, because when I woke up everything was quiet and dark, and Brewer was dead. Jimmy was out there someplace, running off for good, I could hear him. I was lying in the dirt, my stomach dropping out wet between my legs but nothing hurt, and when the moon came riding out of the clouds, ripe and whole, it seemed like it could drop right on our heads and we couldn't stop a thing from happening to us.

Afterward I could tell that folks were a little sorry that it was me and not Brewer and Jimmy that was still around. Baby and Sonny kept watching me like they were waiting for something else to happen. Only Mama stood by me in this town, telling all the liars to shut up and leave me be. I suffered enough. After Clinton, then Jimmy and Brewer, I was so alone, if Jake hadn't come back and started taking me out, I don't know what would've happened. I was getting real low about it all, couldn't even walk into Sorenson's Dairy Store without the two old bags working behind the counter whispering to each other while they mixed up my malt. No one ever stopped to talk at the booth where I waited for my malt. It was that cold. So when Jake came back from 'Nam and started taking me out, I was relieved. Just to have someone to talk about ordinary things with—like the way the moon could hang in the sky some nights, a big saucer of milk, and the sky like black velvet he could touch me with, his hands rubbing up and down my arms, my legs like softness itself, and oh, I'd be happy enough to give it to him, after all that had happened.

Now I can't make the connection between those boys, dumb and fucked up as they might have been, and the murder of a girl simply because she was there and black. Brewer kill someone? No, he was the good one. As a boy he had that sweet kind of look, with long eyelashes that made all the ladies hug him. People say around here that you can tell when a baby's going to have a short life, they're too pretty, too fresh and dewy, to stay long. It made the other kids dislike him because he got all that attention growing up.

With Jimmy it was the opposite. Kids loved to hang around Jimmy

Bevington, while the mere sight of him made the other mothers frown. What was he going to amount to? As it turned out, all he did to become famous in Divinity was knock up a girl and kill her boyfriend. Even then he had to share the fame with Brewer and me.

Maybe Jimmy did it.

Then there's Jake again. He was always secretive. Unemotional. Matter-of-fact. Not just about our marriage and divorce. While the war fucked up Clinton, it seemed more like on-the-job training for Jake. He didn't get a chance at college, so he did the best with what he got. The one thing he ever said about the war was a good example: "The war was boring. We had to think up things to do."

"What kind of a war story is that?" I asked him.

He shrugged. "Probably the only true one. Clinton was mainly full of shit, Honey. And crazy. He could be one crazy motherfucker when he wanted to be. So don't think his war was anyone else's. Most people did their time and came home and got it together, like me. The few like Clinton were always crazy anyway. Believe me."

When I read about a lot of other Vietnam vets who're in hell like Clinton, I know Jake was wrong. He was lying or blind. Could he kill an innocent girl waiting for a bus in a dark town in the middle of the night? Did her dark skin make her more of a target? Did he get hungry for it after the first time, is that why he went to 'Nam? Did he have the heart of a killer?

It wasn't Clinton. He was already tormented about the killing in Vietnam. I don't believe he would pick up a gun and do it again. He couldn't, could he?

I should leave and call Boyd Ziekert. I should do it right now. Give him the list, tell him what I know. But what difference would it make? The living ones can blame it on the dead or missing ones. There's no gun. Tolson didn't actually *see* Sonny Boy do it. Sonny attacked him when he brought it up, but maybe Sonny was only driving the car. It was *his* car. Clinton said they *all* did it—but whose finger was on the trigger?

The dark feels cold and moist, thick with my questions and fear. I quickly pull on my coat, grab my papers and purse, and leave the trailer. This will be the first time I've worked at Boardman's, but I can't puzzle this out sitting alone in that tin coffin in the dark.

As I drive off, I think I catch the glint of a car bumper in the trees across the road. I try to floor the gas pedal, but the engine sputters and dies. I glance at the blackness in my mirror as I restart the engine.

"Hurry," I urge its sputtering into a constant throb. I'm just elbowing the door lock down when a face, white and flat as a china platter, appears at my side window. Sonny Boy! I shift into drive, step on the gas, and chug forward. He takes a few running steps beside the car, leaning down to stare at me in the side window. As the Valiant gains momentum, he drops back. When I look in my rearview mirror, there's nothing but blackness.

I'm so scared he'll catch me in his car, I turn on 11 toward Jass's road because it's the closest. Running with my lights out, I turn quickly and stop around a bend so I'm invisible from the highway. I turn off the motor and lean my head on the top of the steering wheel. I'm so scared that I want to cry. I want to scream at him, Leave me alone, for God's sake! What did I ever do to you? I thought you were done with this? I want to take a knife and plunge it into him. Not to kill him, just to make him understand how much I hate this. His face like a white mask with dark eyeholes against my window—I'll be seeing that the rest of my life—and that mindless stare, frightening because there wasn't any feeling. Not even anger against me. "Somebody should lock him up, before he turns into another Prince Reinhardt. That's what I'll tell Boyd tomorrow."

I wait in the car shivering for an hour before I dare go back to town. Driving carefully, I imagine Sonny on my road again. Stung by the sour ashes of Twyla's trailer, maybe he has no where to go now. He's become a ghost. Most of all, that's what he looked like—some empty form with no intentions left. If Clinton is a voice without a body, maybe Sonny has become a body without a voice. How many ghosts are there in Divinity? Maybe we're all in danger of ending up like that.

26

The Heart of the Heart

For the next few days I think about calling Boyd, getting more details about the girl's death. I try to remember everything he's told me, Larue, too, at the Halloween dance. I've just been so full of myself over the past few months, I've ignored it. Maybe because Clinton said they were *all* guilty, I don't call Boyd. Which one pulled the trigger? That's the real question. There wouldn't be room for five actual fingers on it. Who do I accuse? Is my brother a murderer, like Tolson believed? Do I have to be the one to turn him in? As screwed up and hateful as they are, how can I do that to my family? Trade our lives for hers? And what if it's Jake—I can't even think of that. But *someone has* to be responsible. Isn't that the way it works? Isn't that justice?

There's another thing that nags at me: I'm at the center of this constellation, too. On the new chart I've pasted to the cabinet over the sink at my trailer, the black girl and I sit at the center like a bull's-eye. Around us are the names of all the boys and men I have been with from the Appreciation Day until my divorce: Clinton, Jimmy, Brewer, and Jake. Plus my brothers, Sonny Boy and Tolson. I've drawn lines trying to connect known facts with things that *might* be true, until the chart begins to resemble the night sky, full of related bodies, stories someone has to point out before you can recognize them.

March is the time of year when everyone is officially tired of winter and things get weird. I don't know why Clinton didn't wait to kill himself in March. There's usually so much craziness in Divinity during this month, I'm not surprised when Marylou gets a call at work on St. Pat's Day from a hospital in Iowa City.

"As far as I'm concerned, you can let the anatomy class carve him up. He's no husband of mine anymore." When she gets off the phone, she flashes me a big smile. "Valentine's present from Dallas, my lawyer, a divorce. Did it in Des Moines to keep the nosy Nellies from butting in."

Marylou answers the phone again. "Well, he *does* deserve the best—ship him to the welfare ward at the treatment center." She hangs up the phone, shaking her head. "Those bar wars—they've almost killed Mike this time. He quits his janitor job at the elementary school and starts living at the bars because the booze gets so cheap. He passes out at Sleepy's yesterday, bleeding from the mouth. If they hadn't needed the table for the lunch crowd, he'd have died. Now the hospital wants me to pay. Next time they call I'm giving them the numbers of every bar in twenty miles. They put him there, let them pay the bill." She looks at me hard and says, "What's your problem? If it were July, you'd be catching flies with your mouth hanging open that way."

I close it and open it again. "What bar wars? What're you talking about?"

"You still living here or what?" she asks crossly. "The bars got bored and started trying to knock each other out of business. It's been such a long, god-awful winter, people stopped drinking, just holed up in front of the TV. Jones at the Blacksmith and Sleepy are running neck 'n' neck. I'd like to burn them both out." She looks me over carefully. "You sure you're all right? How come you missed the news like that?"

I look away, smiling. "Just been busy, doing stuff."

She sniffs. "Oh, your 'new' house. Well, I've got more fish to fry than Mike and the drunks in this town. Grab the phone for me, if anyone else calls. I'm corresponding with the regional Affirmative Action office, you know." She's going to land on Bowker with those three-inch spike heels one of these days, waving a lot of official papers in her hand. I almost feel sorry for the dumb ass.

The next time the phone rings it's Larue for me.

"Meet me for a drink tonight, the Blacksmith at eight? Might as well take advantage of their largesse. They've taken all my business anyway. Hope Jonesy goes broke before I do. Okay?"

"Sure, why not. I haven't been out in ages."

"I know. Did Baby get off?"

"She sure did. Leigh bought her four suitcases of new clothes and a fur coat. Kind of surprised everyone. A fur on a cruise?"

Larue laughs. "You take it to show you can afford not to need it. Don't worry, she'll use it around here. This must be the longest winter in history. I'll be wearing my fur tonight, with jeans and boots. See you at eight."

The rest of the day moves as always. We get a confirmation from a congressman that he'll ride in a new car in the centennial parade as long as we keep the farmers off his back. Even Bowker's a little put out by that. "The farmers elect those jokers, then they spend all their time trying to avoid them. If the farm states banded together, we'd see a lot fewer families losing farms."

Even though he's making money on real estate these days, he doesn't like to see the town losing people. Much as I dislike his slogans, when he says, "We're all in this together," I have to agree. Marylou, whose heart is already in the mountains of Colorado, just nods her head dreamily. I know I should hate Bowker for what he's done to us, but I can't help thinking he's just a jerk. Nobody ever taught him to be different. He's probably been a jerk all his life. Even in grade school. The minute he got any power, like hall monitor, he was going to be a jerk. I can't explain this to Marylou. She's right, too. He needs to be taught a lesson, punished. But he's going to be a jerk about that, too. Marylou will find out.

I'm on time at the Blacksmith, but Larue isn't. At nine she calls to say she'll be late. By that time Jonesy is sitting next to me at a little table in the corner opposite the front door so we can watch for Larue. I'd like to think he's drunk as he runs his hand up my thigh. I'd like to think I am, too, as I let him. I haven't felt a man's hand on me in two and a half months, and it makes me shiver now with the beer inside loosening the warmth in my stomach and his fingernails outside scraping in a pleasant, tingly sort of way, riding my nylon like it's a fast rail up between my legs. The first couple of times I just reach down and pull his hand off, but he keeps coming back, hugging me in between, letting his fingers squeeze into the side of my breast while we laugh and tell jokes.

Once he whispers in my ear, "We're practically kin, Honey," like that's some kind of excuse. But I guess I don't need one because it's easy after a while to let it feel good, the beer, and me wanting to drop off to sleep with that hand nestling up between my legs. I'm glad I have on my panty hose. I can tell that if I didn't, he'd be in me in a second. His fingers keep scratching away at the nylon like a dog trying to dig itself under a fence. I think for sure someone else will hear it, but the music is playing real strong. It's "Willie Nelson and the Outlaws Night." That's another thing the wars are doing—putting good music on the jukeboxes, almost like a disco the way they have someone doing the selections for you. Even the red carpet in here seems loud, blaring back noise and sweat and beer at us.

When I feel myself soaking through the little panties of my hose, I get up and go to the bathroom. I stick a bunch of toilet paper down there, wash my hands, and try to comb my hair in the mirror but have trouble because my eyes won't focus up good and my hand shakes. I know I shouldn't drink so much. I know Larue is going with Jonesy. I know it's Jass I miss.

As I walk back to the table, the sight of his big heavy back makes me shudder. Jake and Jass aren't small, but Jonesy is what you'd call a big man. A side of beef man. He looks like he could arm wrestle a bull and win. So when I get back in my chair and he grabs my hand and shoves it in his crotch, I let myself take a big feel before I pull away. I don't know where any of this would've gone if Larue hadn't walked in.

Jonesy just gets up, adjusting his pants in front to make more room for the obvious, and gives her a big hug and kiss. She takes her time, moving real slow like a snake unwinding, then winding back up around

him, pressing her whole front to him. I haven't seen so much contact since I wallpapered the trailer bathroom. When Larue gets a moment, she gives me the once-over in a way that lets me know I'd better move my ass over for her to sit next to Jonesy. After another beer it's late enough that I make my excuses, put on my coat, and leave. Larue doesn't seem to be in the mood for socializing, and she seems to have forgotten why she called me anyway. We probably wouldn't end up being friends after all. Women like us don't make friends.

Out the front window at work the next day, I watch the street graying up in the late afternoon. Snow promised by morning. The farmers will be busy tightening things up for the storm, retying the tarps over machinery and storage bins, getting things into sheds, making sure the animals are penned. Around the houses you can see the bales of straw and old hay stacked against the foundation as insulation. The farmers will sit out this time like all the winters before, feet propped up on the edge of the white Norge stove to warm the toes that are a little cold and sip their coffee, watching the gray afternoon pull down upon them like a flannel blanket the late winter storm they always know is coming.

As usual, the phone interrupts my thinking. "Honey, is Bowker there? I got a problem." It's Jass. Maybe he only calls on days like this with snow moving in, when I have to shut down the twinge of longing in my chest.

"Jasper, neither he nor Marylou is here. But I'll go see if I can find Bowker. What's the matter?" I try not to sound happy to hear his voice.

"Oh, damn, I got a problem with colic out here. Three horses down, and the vet says we may lose one of them. I don't know what's causing it, and I guess Bowker'd better come out and check on the mare that's the worst. Tell him that we may lose her in the next hour, so he'd better come on ahead." Jass sounds tired and scared. Colic causes eighty percent of all horse deaths. A shiver passes across my shoulders thinking about the dying horse last spring.

"I'm sorry, Jass, is there anything I can do?" I can hear him taking a deep breath, struggling. "Not unless you can figure out what the problem is here. It's got to be in the hay, grain, or water. I don't know, I just don't know. . . ."

We hang up, and I run down the street to Shirley's, where Bowker is in the middle of a group of potbellied businessmen having coffee. When he sees me, he motions me over to the table. "This here is the best damn little worker in the whole town. Honey. Isn't she a honey?" The men inspect me like I'm live on the hoof and nod. I can just imagine having to put my hand against their putty-soft pant fronts in back rooms, too, but
I manage a smile.

"Uh, Mr. Bowker, we've got a problem that needs your attention. Can I speak to you for a moment?"

I try to look businesslike, but Bowker is bent on entertaining his friends. "Look at her, isn't she sweet when she gets serious? Makes you want to give her a big hug, doesn't it? Wouldn't you like to give her a hug, Casey? Go on, give her a hug." Casey, who has daughters my age, isn't happy. He just shakes his head, blushes, and looks at his coffee real hard like there might be a fly in it.

Everyone has a good laugh then, Bowker leading the way. They sound like a bunch of old honkers at the state fair. The ones with flabby pouches of skin hanging below their chins and lots of padding. I turn and start back for the door, figuring it will bring Bowker along, if anything can. Sure enough, I'm only to the pay phone against the wall when Bowker's hand on my shoulder catches me. "Say, what's wrong, Honey? We were only having a little fun."

I study the numbers and names on the wall around the phone: Clarissa, 268-0987. Is that the one I knew? "Oh, Jasper Johnson called. He's up to his ears in sick horses, colic, and he thinks one's going to die.

He figured you might want to come out and check for insurance. I told him I'd come and find you. What do you want me to tell him?"

Bowker is still for a moment as he looks outside, watching the way the afternoon is gathering gray and getting ready to snow. When his face sags for that moment, he looks like what he is: a tired, fifty-five-year-old small-town businessman. For a minute I see him as he must see himself in the morning, alone, staring into that bathroom mirror, the too bright light telling him the truth he doesn't want to hear about himself. Whatever it is he's been promising himself in life, whatever it is keeps him plugging away, has long since turned tail and headed for the hills. And left him, his face sagging into wrinkles and fat lines like an empty old pocketbook.

He looks back at the far booth where the other men are stirring their coffee and inhaling the warmth as they drink. Their faces have gone flat and soggy with worry and effort, just like his. "I think I'll stay here. We're talking about the centennial. We're having a committee meeting." He lands on the phrase like he's safe at first, a thumping satisfaction you can hear. His face brightens, and he takes on that look he gets when he thinks he's doing you a big favor. "You know more about Jasper and his horses than I do, and you did such a good job the last couple of times, why don't you go on out there? Take care of it for me, okay, Honey?"

I sigh. "Okay, but Marylou stepped out, too. You want me to close up or wait for one of you to come back?"

Bowker frowns, tapping his upper lip with a forefinger, taking another look out the front window. "No, go on and go. I can see the office from here. If anyone comes, I'll just whip on over. Damn that Marylou, leaving when we need her."

As he turns to go back to the booth, I say, "It was business."

He turns back. "What?"

"It was business why Marylou went out." I try to sound convincing. He just looks at me with a distracted, unfocused gaze. He isn't even thinking about us. That irritates me, that he could curse at her, then walk away and forget.

"I won't be back, probably, and I don't know if Marylou will. You'll have to remember to unplug the coffee and tidy up." I'll leave a note for Marylou, or better yet call her. Let him worry about the office housework for a change.

"Oh, all right. Hadn't you better get a move on it?" He shifts back to his old self, and I leave, pulling Shirley's storm door shut a little too hard behind me. Wrapping my arms around myself because the wind is rising and I've gone out without a coat, I start across the street. As I look back, businessmen at tables against the window are concentrating on their coffee and doughnuts, looking like the pigs at the county fair, with deep grooves of worried fat lining their faces as they root in the sawdust for something to eat.

I slow the car down on the gravel road to Jass's, but it spins and spits back against the underside, like we're under siege. I don't want to go fast here, don't want to get to this part, like last spring. I begin to see more flakes, and it's getting dark, though it's only the middle of the afternoon. In town, the streetlights will be popping on any minute. Something about coming here, about the misery of those too big, too dumb animals, holds me back, holds me back from Jass, even. Every time I get around those damn horses, I end up in Jass's bed. I have to be tougher, I remind myself.

In a moment I'm wheeling into Jass's driveway, out of the car, and up to the porch knocking. Naturally they're down at the barn, but I notice a little pile of the clothes I've worn other times and a note when I peer through the glass storm door. When I'm dressed in the old clothes and mud boots, I go down to the barn, too.

There's a strange scene in the indoor arena. One horse is lying on her side in the middle, not moving at all. Around her the ground is kicked and thrashed in sweeping arcs, like she's tried to make snow angels and failed. At the far end, Jass is leading a horse that keeps trying to pull back, her knees trying to buckle as if she wants to lie down, and behind her is Cindy Reiler hitting her with a whip, yelling at her, and I can see as they turn the curve the tear streaks glistening down Cindy's face. Jass isn't even looking. He's just pulling with sharp yanks on the lead rope. You'd think it'd snap the horse's neck, but she doesn't seem to mind. Her eyes are remote and hollow, like she doesn't know where she is. The jealousy that rises up when I see Cindy is replaced by fear. I don't want to be here, to see this again. There's just too much death.

At the end closest to me, I spot Roger and Mort, the vets, working on another horse. Roger has his arm, elbow deep, up the horse's ass, pulling out manure and shaking his head, while Mort holds the head, trying to make sure the horse doesn't kick or lie down. The horse, the big, bright chestnut I lunged last summer, is standing stiff-legged, knees locked, and grunting once in a while, like something hurts.

When they spot me Roger says, "Honey, pick up a whip over there and follow Mort while he tries to get this one moving, and don't let him go down, whatever you have to do—hit him, kick him, whatever, but don't let him go down. I got to check the others."

The first time the colt tries to lie down, he almost makes it because I can't bring myself to hit him with the whip. I want the colt to hear my voice, to listen to my concern and not do that. But Roger rushes over, grabs the whip, and gives the colt a smart crack across the hocks that sends him along, not jumping, just trudging sluggishly after Mort. "Like that, damn it, or we'll lose him, too." He thrusts the whip handle back at me.

Then I make the connection. The mare in the center is dead, and these could be, too. When I look over at Cindy and Jass, I notice they're having more and more trouble with their horse, even though Cindy has taken the lead line and Jass is behind now, cracking the whip across the back end of the horse, almost sobbing as he curses her into movement. When he calls out to Roger, Mort winces like he's been hit and says, "Shit, there goes another one." I want to go to Jass as he stands there holding the lead line in one hand, the other covering his eyes.

In a moment Roger comes running with a hypodermic needle full of yellow stuff. Checking for air as he runs, he calls over his shoulder to Mort, "I talked to Basko at Ames, and he said to try this. It has the opposite effect, it'll put her guts back to work. If that doesn't do it, we'll have to start operating somehow. But I don't see how we can get all these horses over to the clinic and take care of them at the same time."

After the injection, they all stand around the mare. "Let her down now, Jass, let's see if she'll stick." I watch, in between snapping the whip at the heels of the horse in front of me, as the mare stands, wobbly and wooden at first, then slowly crumples. She rolls on her back once, twice, then stops, letting out an explosion of gas. Mort turns his head and explains, "It's a gas colic. Severe. Can't tell from what, but it hit a whole section of the brood mares and two-year-olds. Six of them. One dead now, didn't get to her in time. She'd already had some good rolls, probably twisted her gut. Then these two."

Now Roger is running back to check on the others, shaking his head. "We need help," he tells Mort in a low voice as he comes past on his way to the stalls. Mort nods, looks at the colt we're leading, whose head is sinking lower with each step, even though he jerks hard at the rope to get his attention. It's like he's just disappearing from under us.

"Hit him along the sides, and yell, damn it, we got to wake him up again. Make him more afraid of us than he hurts. Do it!" Mort orders as the colt stops and wavers, like a person about to drop into the water. His knees and hind legs are folding, and oh, I want to let him go down, he seems so tired, so far away. But I hit him and feel the sting of it like it's on my own back, and hit him again and again and again, and start to cry as I see the welts it makes in his sweaty hide, but he's moving forward again, barely. Mort nods at me, but I can see his eyes are all shiny, too. I feel like hating Jass at this moment, for bringing me here, for making me have to fight all these feelings.

I think what almost breaks us is when Roger leads the fourth mare out into the arena and holds the rope out to Jass, who is still standing uselessly over the panting mare on the ground. She has quit rolling but let loose some gas, too. "I'll keep an eye on her, Jasper, you start with this one. It was probably in the feed, and it probably got all of them. We'll send everything to Ames as soon as we see how this is going to turn out." Jass takes the rope like he's asleep, gives a pull, and the horse follows behind reluctantly. Cindy follows with the whip trailing behind her, making a sad line in the arena dirt. I wonder if Jass is still buying feed from Reiler's and if those men would dare hurt the animals. I can't believe they'd take a risk like that—beating a man up is one thing, killing his livestock is another thing, especially in farm country.

Roger leads out the fifth mare and hands her to me as we all hear the sixth start to kick out the boards of her stall. "Christ," he mutters, running back to get her, "we can't handle any more." When he reappears, though, he has a big tired smile on his face, and right behind him are Harold Spitzer, Leonard Sorenson, Ken Morton, one of the Johnson brothers still greasy from the gas station, Silky Blue, who works at Reiler's Elevator and Feller's Ford Garage both, and Jonesy. I almost break down crying when Leonard Sorenson takes the whip and rope out of my hands and Jonesy relieves Mort at his lead line. The men give me pats on the shoulder and tell me to go on up to the house, where some women are getting food ready. But I stay where I am.

"Basko's on his way down from Ames with a crew, too," Harold tells Roger and Jass as he takes the sick horse from Jass. "You'd better keep track of that one that's down. We'll keep these babies going." I can see Jass clench his jaw tight to keep from breaking down as he nods and hands over the lead line, then goes back to stay with the mare that's down. Cindy kneels by its head, and Jass keeps stroking the flanks and neck, trying to reassure the horse as spasms shake it and the gas comes out in short harsh bursts.

"It's working, Roger, it's working on her. She's gonna make it if her gut keeps working," Jass calls out, his voice happy for the first time. It's a start. One out of six dead, but one out of six getting better, too. It should be me with Jass now. I know that, but I fight to keep down the sick churning in my stomach, the one that says, "You blew it, now he's with Cindy."

By midnight all the horses have been through the worst of it, and two have gone through surgery in the washroom that Jass keeps clean enough that they can sterilize and use it without great danger. The rubber matting helps save the horses when they wake up. After the first one's awake and up again, the team from Ames cleans up and goes to work on the second horse, cutting open the stomach to relieve the gas, checking for damage inside, emptying the stomach, and sewing her back up. Both horses make it out of the anesthesia and up again without breaking their legs, which Roger explains is the real danger of surgery. Now they just have to wait out the problems of infection, rupture of the stitches, and founder before they'll be able to tell for sure if the mares will make it.

By two in the morning Jass's little kitchen is crowded with people drinking beer, eating, and joking to let loose the tension that has built all afternoon and evening trying to keep the horses alive. A second crew of three shows up from town to relieve everyone once the crisis is over, and they're staying at the barn while the vets and everyone else take a break. Sleepy has sent over a couple of cases of beer and two jugs of wine, and old man Reese has the A&P make up a bunch of sandwiches, which added to what the women have fixed earlier makes quite a feast. It's a little like a Memorial Day or Fourth of July picnic, the way people stand around all friendly, drinking and eating. Cindy gets teased because her face is a mess. She's been able to cry. I've been afraid to.

"You cry over me that way, Honey?" Jonesy asks, putting his arm around me.

"Only if it looked like that gut of yours was going to explode." I give the round belly a little pat. Everyone has a good ha-ha about that, teasing Jonesy about watching what he's eating and suggesting he's never had a problem losing his gas.

After a while Jass slumps onto one of the kitchen chairs, and pretty soon his head is down on the table and he's nodding out. It's then that folks start picking up their jackets and getting themselves ready to go, being quiet so they won't bother him. By four it's just Jones and Cindy and me in the kitchen and Silky Blue in the living room passed out on the floor. We half carry Jass to the couch and bed him down there for the night. I'm wishing it was last April and I was there with him, alone. He's avoided me the whole time, except to hand me the mare's papers for the insurance claim. Roger and Mort have gone down to the barn to sleep in the tack room on cots, after starting the little stove there.

Jonesy pops the lid on another Pabst, the stuff Sleepy sent over, and Cindy sits down with a weary sigh at the kitchen table. Jonesy and I give each other a long once-over look. It's too late at night, and we've been through too much not to put a little truth in it. I keep trying to remember about Larue, but that hand on my leg the night before keeps pushing me somewhere else. Jass's face blinks on and off inside me. Maybe Twyla was right: concentrating on keeping something there between your legs keeps you tired enough to sleep at night and busy enough not to worry during the day. In another minute Cindy's head is slumped onto her folded arms and she's dropping off to sleep.

Jonesy comes over and leans his mouth next to my ear, shielding it with his hand so he won't wake her. "Maybe we ought to move her. We could carry both of them up to his bed, wouldn't that be something?" Then he laughs. I want to take back all my thoughts of the moment before. I hate him and Cindy both.

"They're just friends," I protest. But he gives me one of those looks. "Well, anyway," I add, "it's none of our business. Certainly none of *yours*. He can't even come into the Blacksmith!"

Jonesy gives me a look of disbelief and shrugs his shoulders.

"You go in any day or night and there's a couple of long-haired, half-drunk-on-their-asses know-it-alls talking about how 'it isn't the communists we got to worry about—it's them niggers and welfare people—they're gonna take over the country.' Then they haul out all their stories about going to Chicago or Des Moines or Omaha, to the *ghetto,* and what they said to the big coons that stopped them walking down the street about midnight, blah blah blah. Then the talk turns to guns. What works best, what you should always carry, especially in the city, especially in the glove compartment. And it's always getting worse. The niggers are always climbing in bed with some other group—recruiting. This year it's the poor people. They must be watching Reagan on TV or something. And they're as ragitty as anyone else."

Jonesy takes a swig of beer and snorts, "Now wait a minute, if he can't hack it, that's his problem. Nobody ever said he couldn't come in, for chrissakes!" He drains the beer and crushes the can with his big paw. It used to be more impressive before aluminum. Then he gets another beer out of the fridge and pops it open.

"You making money off the deposit on those cans over at your place?"

He grins and nods. "The last thing a drunk thinks about is retrieving his nickels out of a bunch of empties. Real steady boost to the business."

"At least Sleepy's has a gentler crowd. Sleepy doesn't join in with any of that hate talk. So Jass drinks there."

"Well, besides that, Jasper took the Appaloosa off Sleepy's hands last month, gave him a good price, too. That don't hurt none. Has to sell it back quick, though. If Annie comes back, she set a lot of store by that Appaloosa, you know."

I remember the story of Anne and Jack Masters riding double, naked, screwing. That *is* a special horse. Too bad Jass and I'll never get the chance, but he can try it with Cindy. I look at her sleeping at the table and don't hate her for being so damn angelic, good, why can't she do something I can hate her for, like a normal person?

Jonesy interrupts, "Jasper's getting a real good rep around now. Honest. Honest Negro."

"He's not a Negro, a black. Besides, what does that mean?"

"Hard worker. People are amazed at what he's done out here, cleaning up the old Kingman place. That earns a lot of points, you know. A credit to his race, that's what they're saying now."

"Races. He's not just black, Jonesy. He's a lot of things. I can't believe you're saying shit like this."

"Get off my back, Honey. I'm just repeating what the old-timers around town are saying. It's *their* words—not mine. Once Jass gets their approval, any form it takes, the younger guys will back down some. Like now with Cindy. He's been out with her a couple times since the bar wars started. People don't seem to mind so much especially now that he's tied up with that Olympic deal." Jonesy is watching Cindy sleep and sipping his beer.

The news of their dates is like touching a cactus, those hair-thin needles burrowing into my skin invisibly. "What Olympic deal is that?"

"Oh, you didn't hear? A horse he bred and sold was invited to work out with the coaches for an Olympic screening trial in jumping. In Des Moines. Word's getting around. People are calling. Folks around here like that. They respect the Olympics. Like saluting the American flag or singing the 'Star-Spangled Banner.' "

"That's nice." I'm happy and jealous again. Now everyone likes him, and I'm on the outside again.

I drain the beer I'm holding. It has that warm, grainy flavor I've always hated at the bottom of the can, like stomach acid coming back up on you. It always makes me want another right away to wash the taste out. Maybe that's the key to beer manufacturing. I turn to the fridge but think better of it. I'd best be getting back home; who knows what the roads are like. I've forgotten to ask or look since three in the afternoon. Besides, with that leer in his eyes, dripping down over his face like a mask, I have to watch it with Jonesy. I guess men like him just go ahead and take whatever they feel they want. They don't stop to ask does it belong to anyone else, is it related to me, or sometimes is it even human or alive.

I want to wipe that silly grin off his face. "So if you haven't made it clear, how come Jass doesn't come into the Blacksmith? Everyone in town thinks it's a 'white only' bar. Last fall we were there together and had to duck out."

His expression clouds up, and he takes a huge gulp of beer, which chokes him for a second, but when he regains his breath he replies, so loud that Cindy stirs at the table, "Well, it's not 'white only,' goddammit. It's just that some of the boys don't like coloreds, and since they're the ones come in and sit at the bar first most of the time, they tend to keep others out. Don't you see? Shit, there were blacks and Chicanos in my company in 'Nam. I lived with them. Hell, I ate and crapped with them, too. It's no big deal to me personally."

I shrug my shoulders, hoping it'll keep him on the defensive and off my tail.

"It's his fault he can't come in there. He got into it with a couple of bikers, few years ago. He used to come in once a month or so and sit down, have a beer or two, and leave. He and I shot the shit some. He was an all right guy. I didn't have nothing against him. Sort of makes me sorry, you know, because I don't have anything against him, or his people, it's just that I gotta do business with folks that spend the most time and money with me."

"Is that why you came out here? How'd you all find out about the sick horses to begin with?"

It's nice to see that earlier stuff gone from Jonesy's face. I actually like him when he isn't coming on to me, I decide, as he crushes another can and reaches automatically for the next. "Sleepy would send over Pabst. Everyone knows Grain Belt is a better beer, whyn't he send something a person could stomach?"

"So how come you showed up here?" I remind him.

"I heard you were out here. Thought it'd be my big chance." We both laugh. "Oh, you know how it is in Divinity: Roger's secretary told a couple of people. The operator who was putting the calls to Ames told a couple of others, and Bowker couldn't keep his mouth shut if it was sewed to his nose. Pretty soon Larue gets on the phone, lines up the fire department guys, who were having a game at her place, and then the rest of us decided to be neighborly. After all, nobody else around here ever does anything that gets us public attention, except to kill someone or die. I mean Archie Carlson, Larue's little brother, he pretends like he's from India, he won't even say he's from Divinity, Iowa."

"You weren't feeling a little guilty?"

Jonesy frowns, takes a smaller sip of beer, rubs his stomach, belches lightly, looks at me, and says, "Well, I don't know. I like him all right. Besides, I don't like my place being called a 'honky bar.' I may look like a redneck, but I ain't one. I don't want any labels on me." Then, as if reading my mind, he adds, "From you, either, little girl."

"Look, I wasn't thinking a thing. I was just going to say that it was real nice you coming out here. Saved his best brood mares and nicest colt, made him feel like he belonged for a change."

"Okay, okay. Let's change the subject. Are you going upstairs with me or not?" He isn't smiling this time, and he seems stone sober. Great, now what. I figure I might as well be honest, nothing else seems to work.

"No. Probably not. I like us this way. I don't want to ruin it by going to bed and having to sneak around Larue and everybody else from now on. Understand?"

I'm hoping he does. It takes him a couple of minutes of inspecting his belt buckle and the lint on the front of his plaid flannel shirt before he can look at me again. "Okay, all right." He begrudges me, I can tell. "Just don't ever say I didn't try." I shake my head. I'd never say that about him. "It's not something about me, is it? I mean, you know, the way I look or—"

I can tell this is costing him a lot. "No, really, it's just that I don't sleep around, especially with friends. You understand? It's not you personally. Hell, you'd be the first," I lie a little. I don't want him to feel bad now that he's down.

It takes a little more clothes inspection before he lifts the can in his hand, drains and crushes it, then throws it into the pile on the counter, but he doesn't get another one. "Okay, time to roll. You come in those clothes? Get your stuff and I'll follow you back to town. No use giving anybody anything else to think about. Their minds are already straining themselves with yesterday." I gather my things, and he helps me with my coat.

We decide to leave Cindy and walk out to the back. I try not to think about the two of them waking up and finding each other. I broke it off with Jass, I own the sweet sadness inside me now. Then on the porch, Jonesy stops me with a hand on my arm. When I look up, he puts his arms around me and gently kisses me in such a way that I feel the sweetness seep all the way down to my feet. It burns my soles and leaves me limp against his strong chest. With my head resting there, I can feel the engine of his body, deep within him, pumping tirelessly, and for a moment it feels like our two bodies are held and sustained by that same single engine, pumping in and out, the sound in my ear is both of us, and all around us the house wrapped in woolen silence, the wind swirling and the breathy swish of falling snow outside, the barn where the horses now sleep exhausted and safe, the men in the tack room dreaming, talking, playing cards, and the horse in the middle of the arena whose stiff legs thrown out in frozen galloping attests to what becomes of us, and I know it is that single, powerful heart pushing its rhythm through our body, through the single body of us all, that keeps us alive for a while, that holds us in its music, in its embrace. All at once, completely, I miss Jass.

When Jonesy speaks, I jump like someone waking up suddenly, but he holds me still in the comfort of his strong arms. "Don't worry, I won't bother you. If you want me, though, you can ask any time." Then he releases me and opens the storm door, and we step out into the snow. As he puts me into my car, he adds, "I heard you were straight. You're a good woman, Honey, don't let Sonny or anyone else tell you different. You deserve to be happy. Clinton was right. You're special. Remember that. Now drive carefully. I'll be just ahead in the pickup, keeping an eye on you. If you slide, don't jam on the brakes, go with it." He slams the door on my reply.

27

Old Scores

Honey, let me out. Goddamn it, Honey, let me out." Bowker's fists pounding on the closet door behind me sound like bowling balls being dropped. There's a wild clatter from the supply shelves he's bumping into. "The light's gone out, Honey, cord broke, let me out, I can't—" He begins banging on the door again, each fist producing a loud crack like a gun being fired.

I'm typing my little heart out. The harder he bangs, the faster I type. The letter of resignation is the third I've tried. Each one ruined by mistakes. You can't turn in a letter of resignation with typing errors—it condemns you. My hands are shaking too much to use the white-out.

"Honey, I'm getting sick in here. My heart—I'm gonna have a heart attack. I can't—"

Bowker's voice turns plaintive as a mama cow calling after her new calf is put on the bucket. I make two more mistakes and stop.

"I never hurt you, I never meant no harm. . . ." He begins to weep, slipping into his rural grammar as if what's happening takes him back to a time when he was a boy off the farm, arriving in Divinity to make himself a man. Maybe it's the weakness in me, but I *know* he's right—he never meant no harm.

I'm half out of my chair to unlocking the door before Marylou gets back, when the phone rings. "Jesus Christ," I mutter, picking it up. Bowker's noise stops as he listens.

"It's me, Baby," she says.

"You're back."

"Well, yes, I'm not calling from New Orleans."

Bowker lets out a howl.

"Honey, what is that?"

I try to cup the mouthpiece with my hand and press the ear part harder against my head. "Oh, well, Bowker hit his head. It's nothing. How was the cruise?"

"Aside from the food poisoning and the fire, just fine, just what you'd expect. Then we went to New Orleans, where Leigh's fancy relatives acted like the royal family receiving the Ayatollah. Your typical vacation. No wonder I never took one before."

"Help, help, let me out!" Fortunately Bowker's voice cracks to a wheezing in the middle.

"Uh, Baby, this isn't a good time to talk. Can I call you back?"

"What's going on there?"

I close my eyes and try to imagine a lie. "Uh, Bowker's got himself stuck in the closet; we're working on it."

"Why doesn't he shut up and act like a man? I don't see how you can stand to work for him. Anyway, I just called to invite you to dinner tonight."

"I don't know, Baby. It's awfully short notice." Bowker is sobbing quietly in the background. It has a soothing, rinsing quality.

"You *have* to come. It's a *family* dinner. Six P.M. See you then. Oh, and tell Bowker I said to grow up, men shouldn't cry."

I can almost hear the smack of Mama's Methodist lips pronouncing Baby's last words as she hangs up before I can tell her that if it's a family dinner, I definitely *won't* be there. Another of my late New Year's resolutions: Don't give my family a chance at me. I'm not a metal duck in a sideshow. Now I'll have to call her back.

"Honey, didn't I give you a nice Easter ham this year? Let me out." Bowker is trying a new line of attack—logic and guilt. "You'll be better off letting me out before Marylou gets back. I know she's behind this. You'd never—"

His argument is interrupted by Marylou and a tall blond man in a three-piece navy blue suit coming through the front door like there's a medical emergency and they're the operating team.

"It was a canned ham, and you won it at the VFW raffle," I call back to him. Glancing at the poorly typed resignation letter in front of me, I sigh and begin emptying my desk into a plastic bag I keep in my bottom drawer.

"You ready?" Marylou asks. She's still wearing the special glow of power she had an hour ago just after lunch when she got up from her typewriter and walked slowly to the closet, swaying her hips to some invisible music. Careful to brush the railing around Bowker's desk with the hiss of the satiny polyester dress swirled with purples and reds that accented her hips and breasts, she'd glanced over at me and smiled smugly. Bow-wow sat up on his haunches at the rustle of the dress. The next part was like a dog food commercial. Marylou opened the closet door and paused just inside, then called softly, "Honey, can you please help me here?"

Bowker was up bounding to the closet like Rover to the sound of a can opener. "I'll get it," he flung over his shoulder as he pulled the door to.

It was quiet for a minute, then a mild scrambling and crashing as if shelves were being overturned. As I stood up, Marylou burst from the closet and slammed the door. Flipping the lock, she turned to me. "See how easy that was?" she asked, and smoothed her dress, which had climbed up around her thighs.

"Did he—" I asked.

"Yeah, he got a hand on me. Tore my panty hose, but that was when I shoved him and the shelf gave. I'm okay. Great, in fact."

Bowker began banging on the door, hoping for rescue. Looking annoyed, Marylou turned and kicked the door, then banged it with her fists so loudly that I thought people on the street would need hearing aids. It must have been a sonic boom in the closet. Bowker howled.

"Bowker, hey, Bowker?" Marylou called. "You listen up, boy, now you hush, or I'm going to have you arrested."

There was immediate silence from the closet. Marylou turned back to me. "Easy, see? Now I have to run some errands, Honey. You stay and keep the old fart from getting out, you hear?"

In her new role, she was more like Joan Crawford or Bette Davis than anything else. I nodded dumbly and watched her swing out the office. It didn't occur to me to let him out. I just typed my resignation. I figured I had enough trouble in town without this, too. She must have seen *9 to 5* too many times. That stuff worked in movies. In real life you never got a good deal with your boss, but I guessed if anyone could, it was Marylou.

"This is my lawyer, Dallas." Marylou stresses *my* and smiles at him. He puts his protective navy blue arm around her as if I'm probably in cahoots with Bowker. I nod at him. He can figure it out. He looks smart enough for that and dumb enough to think Marylou is helpless.

"Marylou, you let me out of here now, and I *won't* call the sheriff. You're fired, though. You're both fired." Bowker is trying to sound like the Boss now. It fails because we can hear the tremble in his voice.

We all look at each other, and the yellow April sun outside seems to coat the office with a sheen of encouragement—not as bright and brassy as May or June, but a legitimate note of optimism polishes things here. One of the neon ceiling lights buzzes like a trapped bee.

"Where's the books, Honey?" Marylou takes a step closer to me. Dallas the lawyer lets his arm drop.

"In his desk."

"Cash?"

"In his desk, like always." I look down at the plastic bag lumpy with my junk. What is this worth, anyway, I decide, and drop the whole thing in the wastebasket.

"What're you doing, Marylou?" I watch her pull out the account books and cash box, then rifle the rest of his desk.

"He's skimming. I want the rest of the cash." She squats down to feel under the desk for taped envelopes, secret drawers.

"Honey?" Bowker calls in a loud whisper.

I'm a few steps from the door when Marylou cuts me off.

"I'm going to let you outta there in a minute, Bow-wow, but you need to think about something: I've got my lawyer here, and we've got the papers ready to file a sexual harassment suit. You have a wife and a town counting on you, so think hard about how you'll settle this. Out of court or in court. Either way you owe me, and it's payday. You hear?"

"Yes," Bowker says hoarsely. Before Marylou unlocks the door, I decide to get out of here. She's won, she's broken him. It's just such a dumb victory, like beating up someone half your size. On my way past them, I notice Dallas standing there like Margaret Thatcher's husband.

"Good luck," I say as I pass him, and I mean it.

"Honey, don't you want—" Marylou calls after me, but I shake my head and keep walking.

Moving as quickly as possible down the street away from the office, I figure out what's bothering me about Marylou's project. We should have told him no, first. Slapped his hands and then his face. Like a kid who won't keep his fingers out of the icing. Any mama can show you how it's done. But we never even warned him. Never said no. I don't like myself much at this moment. It seems like Bowker's getting what he deserves and more. If justice is so inexact, and vengeful, how just is it? "Small," I can see Mama's face saying.

Almost bumping into Tom Tooley and Silky Blue, I realize I've walked two blocks staring at the sidewalk. Tom's and Silky's hands are tacking up posters on telephone poles.

When Tom sees me, he stops and says, "Honey, lookit this—" He holds up a cream poster declaring the Divinity Centennial and Homecoming in big, red, old-fashioned letters. "Just ten days now. And look, I've entered Tamara in the Cutest Baby Contest. Mom's been sewing up a storm, cutest little outfits, Twyla would've loved 'em." He's got a new confidence about him, like a boy fresh back from college. His slicked-back hair has a big sassy wave in front that says, Look at me. He's almost James Dean today in his T-shirt, Levi's, and sneakers, except for the oil and dirt covering them. It's warm enough today to fool people into taking off their jackets, though there's still a spring chill under the sunlight.

I smile at the poster. "Where're you working these days?"

"Oh, me and Silky are over at the Mobile station. God, I love it. Get to work on cars all day. All night, too, when Mom brings the baby down and lets her sleep in the backseat of my car. I got a special bed set up for her."

Silky inspects the sidewalk and grins.

"Silky and me are a team. That's why we're out doing this Chamber of Commerce work." Tom seems to puff his chest a little in civic pride. I don't think Bowker would count these two as part of the club, but then they wouldn't care much either if they knew where he was right this minute.

"I quit Reiler's," Silky announces.

Tom and I stare at him.

"Jasper Johnson's okay. He ain't no nigger." Silky turns his face to squint at the sun, shoves his hands in his back pockets, and shuffles his feet like he's just announced he's running for president.

"We know *that.*" Tom punches him lightly on the arm and looks at me quizzically. I shrug.

"Tell him I said hello next time you see him, okay? Tell him I wanna buy him a beer, okay?" Silky ducks his head and picks up the box of staples and staple gun.

"We gotta move it, Hon. Stop over and see the baby. She's sure growing—looks like Twyla. Spitting image. Little blonde." Tom backs across the street, clutching the stack of posters under one arm while Silky's pulling the other.

I wave good-bye. What was Silky getting at? Were the men at the feed mill responsible for Jass's horses' colic? I wonder if I should say something to Boyd. Not Jass. There'd be a war if I did that. Was Sonny Boy up to his tricks again? Somehow I doubt it. Since Twyla died, he's been different. Weirder. Less tricky and more unpredictable. Scarier, maybe, like that night in February outside my trailer. If he hurt Jass now, it'd probably be an accident—because Jass got in the way, not a plan.

The rest of the afternoon I hole up in my house, napping and avoiding the phone. All afternoon the fresh dirt smell flows through the open window and tints the room with green. The robins, fat little Bowkers, pace the yard and argue in trees outside my window. The breeze fingers the limp brown curtains left over from Boardman and dusts my cheek with just enough cool to make me snuggle deep within my covers and dreams.

Unfortunately, this means that at five forty-five I suddenly wake up realizing I've forgotten to cancel with Baby. Now it's too late. I look at myself in the mirror. Hair rumpled, makeup worn off, shirt and jeans like they've been slept in. Exactly. If I have to go, they'll have to take me on my own terms, I decide, and pull the door shut as I leave.

I'm the last to arrive because halfway down the block I realize I should bring something, so I go back and pull some daffodils from the big bed behind Boardman's house. They're so yellow and perfect, I find myself touching them just to make sure they're not plastic.

"You'd better wake up before you get to your family's house," Clinton warns.

"I know. Don't worry so much, Clinton. I'm figuring things out."

"I know, Honey, that's what *does* worry me."

I knock on the front door, then pull it open. I'm always in that middle place with their house—half stranger, half family. Baby's look says I'm late. Daddy and Sonny Boy are pulling out their chairs as soon as they see me. In the middle of the table is a huge spread of spring flowers—tulips, iris, and daffodils. The ones clutched in my hand look home-grown, pathetic, next to these. A couple have brown spots on them as if they're aging right before my eyes. I go to the kitchen and quietly stick them in an empty Skippy's jar and fill it with water. They lean precariously over the counter.

"Nice flowers," I say to the back of Baby's head as she leads the way carrying a platter of roast beef into the dining room.

"Leigh had them sent from Cedar Rapids. He wanted me to have those baby Japanese iris. Hard to find close by. Well, let's eat."

Before I'm even seated, Sonny Boy has built a reservoir of mashed potatoes, taking up half his plate, and filled it with lumpy brown gravy. I've forgotten about Baby's cooking. I hope Leigh can afford to hire it done.

"Overcooked the roast again." Daddy hacks at the blackened mound, then slams down the knife. "Damn it, Baby, this knife's so dull you couldn't cut butter with it." Even Sonny pauses, breath held, a forkful halfway to his mouth, all of us waiting for Mama to lift herself tiredly from the table to get a sharper knife.

"Never mind." Daddy gets up himself and stalks into the kitchen and begins opening and slamming drawers. Sonny puts the fork in his mouth in slow motion. Baby begins tearing apart pieces of Wonder bread and wadding them into balls that she lines up on her plate like musket shot. We're all in suspended animation until Daddy returns. This time he slices the roast standing up.

"It'll be rare in the center," Baby says in a tiny voice.

"What?" Daddy stops and frowns at her.

"I read how if you start it frozen, it'll stay rare in the center, well done outside." Baby is on the verge of tears; her face grows splotchy red like an A&P tomato in the middle of winter.

"Damn dumb idea. Your mother never—" It's like an accident at the

blood bank, the way it pours out when the knife bites in. I turn away. Sonny watches fascinated, but not hungrily. Baby stares at her plate, missing the moment. A small tear slips down her face. Daddy sits down and passes the platter to me. I take a piece of outside meat bobbing above the red juice and hope it hasn't absorbed much.

Daddy's plate looks like a ritual sacrifice. Handing the platter on to Sonny, I try not to let our fingers touch. He takes a raw piece from the center and tips the platter so some of the bloody juice floods his plate. The potatoes turn pink. Baby takes a small chunk of meat, charred on the outside but pink inside, and motions for Sonny to put the platter down.

We pass the soggy green beans cooked gray and greasy with bacon. And the canned corn. Baby coats the entire plate with gravy until only the bread balls clumped like marbles are distinguishable.

Daddy looks at our plates with disgust. "Gravy's lumpy and potatoes are cold." He condemns the meal to silence. Baby struggles with her fork while bigger tears slide down her face. I hate to see them land in the food. The only sounds are from Sonny, hunched protectively over his plate, chewing with his mouth open and scraping the plate with his fork as he gobbles the bland food.

"Sit up, Sonny. You look like a damn dog. Stop chewing with your mouth open." We all freeze. Sonny is forty-one years old, but he does sit up and carefully lays his fork down.

When I dare, I steal a look at Daddy out of the corner of my eye. His meat is carefully squared, as if a surgeon were preparing the edges. The potatoes are squatting in a perfect round, and the green beans and corn have aligned themselves neatly on opposite sides like bleachers at a football game. I watch his fork lift a single limp bean from its friends and make it disappear smoothly, efficiently, as if it had never been there. You never hear Daddy eating. Even crunchy things go quiet in his mouth. The meat gets sliced in small slivers that disappear quickly also.

"Eat your dinner," he orders me without bothering to look.

Automatically I pick up the fork, then let it drop. The three of them look up, startled by the clang. I lean both elbows on the table and smile at them. This is the ultimate crime—I'm not on the edge of my chair, back straight and stiff, one hand in lap. I'm the nightmare of comfortable eating. Daddy automatically lays his fork down and picks up his table knife for the rap on the knuckles I'll get.

"Don't bother," I warn him. He slowly replaces the knife and continues eating. Sonny just stares at me, and Baby wipes her eyes with her paper napkin, a small grin beginning.

Pushing the plate away from me, I say, "What is this?"

"Roast beef and—" Baby begins.

"No, I mean, what's going on here? Why're we doing this? We're adults, why is he still telling us how to eat?" I nod toward Daddy.

He calmly lays his fork down, chews his bite, and says, "You can eat someplace else. This is *my* house." He doesn't even sound pissed off.

"No, no. You're missing the point. Besides, Baby invited me. What's the deal, Baby?"

Sonny and Baby have stopped eating, too, and are pushing their plates away. Before she can answer, though, Daddy gives his plate a shove that clangs it into his water glass and the gravy bowl. "Okay. Happy? Dinner's over."

I can't help it, I giggle. Sonny picks up the giggle, until he glances at Daddy. Baby looks worried. She sits up, folds her pudgy fingers in front of her neatly, and bows her head. "I'd like to make an announcement."

There is a collective intake of breath.

"I'm going to marry Leigh Hunt in June. He gave me this. . . ." She opens her hands to reveal a huge round-cut diamond ring. "Three carats."

"If that rich fat boy thinks he can buy my daughter . . ." Daddy says between gritted teeth.

"What? He can't have her? What's your problem? She has to stay here all her life while you make up your mind about Louverna? Honest to God, get a life." It's out of my mouth before I can clap a hand over it. Baby's jaw drops, then she stiffens her back.

"I'm marrying Leigh Hunt." She slides the ring on her finger. It's so big, it flops to the side. "He says I'll grow into it," she explains to me. There's a certain kind of misery in her eyes.

"He never even asked me," Daddy says, staring at Baby's hand like it needs surgery.

"She's an adult." I cover my face with my hands and rub my eyes. "You should be happy."

"They look down on us," he says.

"So what? Maybe this is our chance. Now they won't. Unless we screw it up. Right, Baby?" She just stares at me like I've been possessed by the devil. I glance at Sonny Boy. He's busy balancing his knife and fork on the top of his glass of milk with the salt shaker riding between them.

"I don't like him," Sonny says.

Baby's face gets red again.

"Who gives a shit?" I actually bite my tongue. Swearing at the dinner table, in front of Daddy, I must be going crazy.

"Keep your foulness out of this." Daddy slaps the table with his palm, making everything jump and clatter.

"No, *you* keep *your* foulness out." I throw my napkin at the center of the table. "Why don't you just admit it? You failed—we're all failures. Go ahead—we fucked up. That's right, *we're never going to amount to anything*—just like you always told us. Admit it and let go of our lives—leave us alone, for chrissakes."

"Honey, don't, I don't want him—" Baby struggles to push her chair back.

"Let her talk, Baby, she's always hated me, from day one, she's like your mother's family—this town—Leigh Hunt—they all look down on you, think they're better because they're different, think they're smarter." Daddy's thin lips stretch meanly.

Sonny is staring at me now with a mixture of awe and terror, like he's seeing the face of God or something.

I take a deep breath. "Look, enough is enough. Daddy, you have got to let Baby get married. Let her grow up, try living on her own. You've had your chances—you even have a new wife. So you go live with Louverna. Or you divorce her. What you're doing now is chickenshit."

Since I'm on a roll, I turn to Sonny Boy. "And you, you go home to *your* wife, Rose, and your kids. Twyla is dead. Stop hassling everyone else. Grow up. Start supporting yourself. Stop bugging me or else . . ." I let the threat hang in the air and watch with satisfaction as fear registers on his face.

"Baby, get married. Forget the family bullshit. Have a life—fucked up or otherwise." She rubs the diamond with her forefinger as if it's Aladdin's lamp and Leigh Hunt the fat genie who lives in it.

"And who made you head of the house, Miss Hotpants?" Daddy leans back, probing his teeth with a toothpick.

"I did. Me. Someone has to say something. You're like a bunch of crazies living in this place together, letting it fall down around your ears. Why don't you *really* want Baby to marry Leigh, Daddy? Is it because she might turn out better than you did? Sonny marries Rose Bevington—that's pretty good. But do you ever tell him to get his butt home and act like a man? No, you let him stay here. And you. You won't live with your wife because you're scared. We're all scared. You helped make us that way. I'm scared to love a man now, scared he'll die or leave me or something. Christ, we're the biggest bunch of cowards in the whole town. Different? You think I'm different, Daddy? I'm just like the rest of you. You just never realized it, that's all."

I get up, struggling to get my feet unhooked from the chair. I want to tell them how I left work today, too afraid to take a stand on either side. How I left Jass, too afraid to let him love me. How I talk to Clinton still, too afraid to let him go for good.

The banging on the back door makes me look at the staring faces at the table. No one has a word left to say, I realize with satisfaction. When I open the back door, Louverna is standing there, purse clutched nervously in both hands, face a little older, less confident, than the last time I saw her.

"Come in, we're just getting ready for dessert." I lead her into the dining room and pull out the chair opposite Daddy's. Her rightful place. She sits, hesitantly, wearing a confused look on her face.

Maybe it's because of my outburst and the fact that she's an ally now against me. Daddy leans forward, smiles, takes the toothpick from his mouth, and says, "Hello, sweetie, how've you been?"

She stumbles and stutters but smiles and blushes enough to play the woman to his man.

Baby sighs and gets up to clear the plates. Sonny starts rebuilding with the silverware and glass.

"Let me know how this turns out," I whisper to Baby in the kitchen.

"You really should've stayed out of it. I was working on it." She opens the fridge and leans in. I have an urge to give her big behind a push.

"You'd have died of old age first."

"Yeah, well, now I *have* to marry him." Her voice resonates off the hard surfaces of cold food.

"You don't know how lucky you are, Baby."

She pulls her head out long enough to give me an evil stare. "No one in this family has any luck, Honey. Don't ever believe that." I'm not sure I agree, but it seems like good advice for the moment, so I slip out the back door while the getting's good.

28

May Day

The phone ringing wakes me up late the morning of the centennial. Outside about five kinds of birds are raising such a racket, I picture a treeless, bushless backyard. Then the heavy perfume of lilac rubs the room purple and heady. I take a deep breath and lie back. As if it holds me at bay, I'm waiting for the ringing to stop before I get out of bed. I'm more careful about answering the phone since Bowker fired me from the closet and I told my family where to go and what to do with it. Who else would call?

When it finally stops, I leap up and hurry to the bathroom. I suppose taking the phone off the hook would be a kind of solution, but then I'd feel *really* out of touch, not knowing if someone was even *trying* to reach me. If it's urgent, they can stop by, try to catch me outside in the yard before I see them. I spend all night prowling the house and reading, fall asleep at daybreak. Spills of wax dot the sink and outside the tub from the candles I use. Electric lights just attract attention.

Today I search the mirror for what I was planning. My face looks tired, hollow. I can't eat here, and I don't want to go out and answer the questions about work. Today I was going to empty the freezer and cupboards of Boardman's old food. Maybe I can bring myself to eat something then. Besides the apples I bought a month ago.

The banging on the door must be another person trying to visit the rock shop. With spring, they're stopping by constantly on the weekends. Driving me crazy. They see the rocks on display over my shoulder when I come to the door to discourage them, and that only makes them push harder to get in. I keep promising to open in a few more days. When they go back to their cars, shaking their heads and muttering, I look around at the shelves I haven't bothered dusting in months. I feel satisfied by the dulled gleam and sparkle. "It's my party and I'll—" Well, it's my store, and if I want that petrified wood to go back to being more petrified than pretty, that's what'll happen.

A little bit of Mama's in me these days. I've avoided visiting the trailer and my charts lately, so I have to carry the voices and ideas in my head as I move from room to room. My head's so full today, I'm distracted as I walk downstairs, through the store, to the porch door to send away the customer. I guess it's my distraction that keeps me from noticing Boyd's cruiser in the driveway.

"I'm closed." I open the door a few inches.

Boyd's fingers come around and hold it steady as he pushes it open against me. "Hello, Honey. How're you today? Hm, a little behind in the old dusting. I'll tell Larue to send Eleanor over just as soon as this centennial is done with." He's on the porch and in the showroom before I get a chance to say another word. No wonder he's the sheriff—his smooth power is hard to resist.

I'm wearing an old red T-shirt of Jass's and a pair of faded print boxer shorts I found in Boardman's stuff. Boyd looks me up and down. "Nice outfit. Been on a diet?"

Shrugging, I go behind the counter to avoid his eyes. I can feel how my breasts stick out through the worn T-shirt material. I'd like to pull a coat on over them. Instead I cross my arms and lean across the glass top.

"Can't you read?" Boyd asks, resting an elbow on the glass.

"What?"

"Says, 'Do not lean on counter,' right here." He points at the sign, and I grimace. He's in his summer-weight uniform: khaki-colored, short-sleeved cotton shirt and cotton pants. It looks new with creases so sharp they could be drawn on. He's sporting a new haircut, too. Even his eyes look brighter, fresher.

"You're looking spiffy for the centennial."

He smiles crookedly. "It's all these people coming back for the weekend. I don't want them to think I've gone to seed like the rest of you." He looks around again. "Speaking of which, what's going on here?"

"What makes you think anything's going on, Boyd?" I stare at the pink scalp showing in his part as he ducks his head to study something in the case.

"Nice quartz and pyrite there. How much?"

"Come on, Boyd, you're not here rock shopping."

"Okay." He stares me in the eyes. "You don't look good, Honey. In fact, you look like hell. This place's a mess. Besides, nobody's been able to raise you on the phone for two weeks. So I just thought—"

"You thought you'd come over and interfere some more. Well, I'm fine. I don't have to keep house to please anyone but myself now. And how I look is my business." I open the back of the case, turn the rock over and read the price. "And this rock costs twelve dollars. Do you want me to wrap it?"

Boyd laughs. "No, I'll take it as it is. Here, let me see . . . yeah, here's the exact amount, too. I've always liked a pretty piece of stone, yes." He turns it into the light streaming through the dirty windows. "Now, let me use your phone." He dials and hands it to me.

The voice says, "Hello," a couple of times before I realize who it is.

"Hello, Mr. Bowker." I feel like hanging up, but Boyd is wearing his sheriff's look, so I don't.

"You left me in that closet—"

"Yes." I try to sound neutral.

"I didn't think you minded. You never said anything. Why didn't you say something if it was making you . . . you know, what Marylou said?"

Boyd has moved over to the fossil display, opening the thin drawers below the counter, one by one, stopping to examine their contents. There are several loud honks into the handkerchief from Bowker's end of the phone. I can't think of anything to say, so I pull a rag from the box on the floor and begin to rub at the fingerprints on the glass.

By the time Bowker's calm enough to talk again, I've pulled out a bottle of Windex and sprayed and rubbed the glass again. "Do you hate me, Honey?" I can tell that this is probably the most important thing Bowker has ever thought about himself in his whole life. It's tempting to answer him with more silence.

"No, well, not exactly." I can tell from the way he lets his breath out that he'd been prepared for the worst. This is giving him courage, a way to hedge. He'll be on his feet in no time.

"So, I'm *not* a bad man?" He pauses. I think of the lists taped on the kitchen wall in my trailer, search for his name. It isn't under Evil.

"No, don't answer that," he says.

But I want to. "You're not a *bad* man. You're like a lot of men. You don't think about the way *we* might feel in the closet." I'm trying to make him understand, but I can tell that by not squashing him, I've let him escape. Marylou was right about not trusting me. I would have let him out of the closet too early if it'd been up to me.

"Well, I always gave you your chance. You didn't have to go along with it. All you had to say was 'Stop.' I'm not some kind of rapist, you know." His voice gets a little hoarse and crackly again.

"Oh, I know that. It's just that you're the boss. We were afraid for our jobs, don't you see that?"

"Well, I never would have really fired you. That's, that's blackmail, and both of you were married women. Didn't I give you time off for family problems, didn't I give you bonuses, did I ever try to sleep with either one of you? Did I? Was I dragging you by the hair off to the motel or over to Des Moines for the weekend, like some men I know? I always treated you square—I did—and now that Marylou . . . she just took me for ten thousand dollars. I don't even know where she is, with that lawyer boyfriend of hers. He ought to get disbarred. I should go after him. I could do it, you know; I got lots of friends around this state. One word from me, and he'd be in court before he knew it, defending *himself* for a change. I should do that—show them what it means. I could've died, you know that? I can't stand dark places. It made me so nervous, I almost passed out. My heart was pounding so hard, I thought I was having a heart attack—I did, I could feel it come jumping up like a big carp against my chest. I could feel it pushing out, and I was going to die there."

The memory of how helpless he'd been starts a new round of nose blowing that allows me to stretch the phone cord around, spray the front of the glass case, and start rubbing it, too. With the phone cradled between my chin and shoulder, I can hear him struggling back.

"Honey, are you there? Did you want them to kill me?"

"No, Mr. Bowker, I would have felt awful if that'd happened. I'm sorry you had such a hard time."

"Well, I should think so. You know a man my age can't stand that kind of treatment. It's too much for our systems, and I'm not in as good a shape as I used to be. Doc told me to cut down on salt, fatty foods, coffee, drinking. He didn't give me anything to enjoy in life. High blood pressure, he said, but I think he's wrong, don't you? I think they make a lot of mistakes, but I could stand to lose a few pounds, get back in fighting shape. I'm taking it easy, anyway." He's pumping himself back up, old inflatable Bowker.

"I couldn't let you out. You know how she is, Mr. Bowker. I was afraid not to do what she told me to do." I'm not lying, exactly. I had been afraid, even though I'd enjoyed it, too. The appeal for his understanding works, though. Finally we're on the same side.

"Yes, I know, Honey. She was a sick woman. It's better she's gone. You and I can get along just fine without her. I wasn't firing you, just her. I figured you misunderstood when you didn't show up for the last two weeks. I tried to call, but you never answered. I figured you'd earned a vacation. A *paid* vacation. Now it's time to come back. You can take over Marylou's job, too. I'll raise your salary by three dollars an hour, and then it'll be just you and me there. Both of us will come out on top once this thing is cleared up." He gives his nose one final *whank* and takes a deep breath that doesn't catch in his throat. He is okay.

"I'll think about it, Mr. Bowker. Actually I'm looking for another job. After all of that, you know, I don't think I could go back to things *just* the way they were before." I want to keep some hold on him for a minute more.

He clears his throat again, testing for the right pitch. "Well, of course, Honey. Like I said, all you had to do in the first place was tell me you didn't like it. I was only playing, a little fun to break up the day. But you're too good a girl to let go, so think about staying. I'll raise you four dollars an hour, and you can hire a part-time typist if you want when things get rushed."

It seems important for him to keep something in place. I can understand that. A part of me wants to help him, it really does, but another part of me thinks that now's my chance to bail out, leave Divinity, see the world, look up Marylou and her lawyer, or start a new line of work.

"I'll think about it. I really will. I'll let you know on Monday. This is too big a weekend to be worrying about all of this. You have to meet the congressman and get your cars ready, and I have to find some people from out of town. We'll settle it on Monday, okay?"

"You're right, of course. You always were the more sensible one. I have to get dressed and meet the congressman's aide. He couldn't come, but he sent his wife and his closest aide instead. You want to ride out with us, Honey? You're the prettiest girl around, you know."

I can't believe it, he's starting in again. "No thanks." I underline it sourly, setting down the Windex hard enough to rattle the case. Boyd looks over and frowns.

"Sure, okay, no problem. Like I said, all you have to do is open your mouth. But why don't you come in now, talk, we'll get it straight. I'll feel, we'll *both* feel so much better. Okay? An hour? See you then." He hangs up without waiting for me to agree. I figure he needs that.

"You going to meet him, talk it out or what?" Boyd asks.

"Listening, too?" I put the Windex and rag back in the box.

"You should answer your phone more often, get the whole place clean in a few hours that way."

I laugh despite myself.

"Nice trilobites here. So, what's the word? You gainfully employed or bumming? I might need a deputy." He faces me, hands on his hips.

"Is there anything in my life that isn't your business?"

He smiles with his lips, but not his eyes. "Damn little."

"Okay." I hold my hands up. "Okay. I suppose I might go over there just to see what the old fart wants, though God knows I'm not going to get involved with that same mess again. No way."

Boyd nods. "Good. And read your mail, too. You might have won the Publisher's Clearing House sweepstakes. Pay your bills. Be a citizen, Honey. We got enough of the other kind around here." He picks up the armful of magazines, fliers, letters, and bills resting on a display by the door and walks them to the counter, where he spills them out in front of me.

"Great. Maybe I won't stay here, then you don't have to worry about my citizenship."

"That's true enough, Honey. But somebody else will, so just take some advice from your old uncle Boyd and get on with it. This pissing it away stinks. You got a lot of future ahead of yourself. You got a house, a business, a job, and a place to live that isn't half-bad."

"And a crazy family, dead people, and no friends." I hear the self-pity and pinch myself.

"Okay. That's partly true, too—*and* you're in the middle of an unsolved murder that's going to taint this town and your life until someone steps forward. If you want to be honest about it, that is." Boyd puts his hand over my arm lying on the mail-cluttered counter. "And you *know* it, don't you? That's part of the trouble, isn't it?"

I shake my head, and he tightens his fingers around my arm until I almost feel them meet through the skin and muscle at the bone.

"You'll tell me. This weekend. I can feel it, can't you?" His hand squeezes harder, and my arm goes numb.

"Boyd—"

Releasing my arm, he turns and walks out the door, letting the screen bang. As I rub the red welts he's raised, I notice he's left his pyrite.

"Clinton? What's going on?" Picking through the mail, I pull out an envelope postmarked Omaha, a week after Bowker in the closet. When I open it a letter falls out, wrapped in a thick white sheet so it can't be read through the envelope by Delbert at the post office. Marylou.

Dear Honey:

By now you know that I did it—like I do everything I start out to do. Dallas says that's one of my good qualities. He's now a good friend. He's letting us live in a big house he owns, with him, and is being real sweet to the kids. So far they like it because he's bought them bicycles and promises a pony if they're good and don't bother us too much. You should see how that makes them sit up and behave! Dallas has everything set up for me here. I can take a job in his office, working for him. Is he handsome! And dependable. He never drinks and is real reliable, on time and dressed fit to kill. He says we make a handsome couple and has bought me a couple of new dresses you wouldn't believe. I can't believe it myself—what good luck I've been having lately. Though Dallas says people make their own luck, and I think he's right about this, too. Because if I hadn't figured out how to nail Bowker and file for divorce from Mike without his knowing it, I'd still be sitting in Bow-wow's realty and insurance come Monday morning. Like you will be, probably. But listen, that's why I'm writing this letter—mostly to thank you for not letting Bowker out of the closet. I know how you must have wanted to because you are not a very strong person. That's what Dallas says about you, though of course he only met you that once, but lawyers can tell these things at a distance I think. Also I hope you'll remember never to tell anyone, *ANYONE,* where I am. Mike, when he sobers up every once in a while, might wonder, especially when the rent runs out and he doesn't have any place to sleep it off. Maybe they'll take him to the county hospital for detox again.

I'm sick of taking care of men. Let me tell you, Honey, I'll never do that again. My kids get all my attention, let someone take care of me for a change, like Dallas. He says he wants to, and after this I believe him. Don't you? Oh, the other thing is that I fixed it for you with Bowker. I made him think you didn't know anything about all this, and that you were real upset about what he did to us in the closet, that you were going to quit. He promised to reform before I let him out on Friday. You should have seen him. It was a big laugh, let me tell you, I could hardly keep a straight face. Dallas kept having to pinch my arm till it hurt so I'd not break out into hysterics. Bowker came out of there with his face all dirty and tears running down it. What a mess. I don't know how he made such a mess of himself, and his clothes looked like he'd been crawling around on his hands and knees. He even tore a hole in the knee of his suit pants. And he was bawling the whole time we talked to him. Shaking like a leaf. What a big baby. You might have known, wouldn't you, that he'd be that kind of man.

Anyway, we got the money, more than I'd hoped for. When Dallas saw the way Bowker looked, he said we should hit him for ten, not five or eight. Bowker just handed it all over. You know where he keeps his cash? I know you don't know this because I'm the one been studying it for a year now. He doesn't even report half his business. He's skimming like crazy. Got it stuffed in manila envelopes back of the supply shelves in the closet. He must take out ten or fifteen a year that way. Maybe even twenty. Doing the books the way you did, I'm surprised you didn't know. But then you miss a lot, Dallas says. I have to agree. Though I want you to know that I appreciated your friendship in everything. Besides, you were always the only person who was ever nice to me in that whole town. Anyway, now I have a new life and am happy as can be. Take care.

Yours truly,
Marylou Jackson

Good old Marylou. I bet Dallas has his hands full and doesn't even know it yet. Or maybe she's just met her match. It's hard to get mad, though by all rights I should. She's pretty insulting, but what the hell. She's gone.

It's only Saturday morning, and things are already getting crazy for

the centennial. It's like all these people have held their breath watching me live for the past year, and now they feel like they can let it out at the same time. I'm going to get blown from one side of town to the other. Trouble like a big knot of mayflies bouncing in front of the car. You drive through it and they're all over you, and suddenly you're past and the road's clear. Just some black smears on the car, your arms. Trouble. Ahead you see this knot of mayflies—the only way to avoid it would be to stop the car. If I were at the trailer, I'd write TROUBLE in an empty space on the wall.

"Clinton, why does Boyd Ziekert think I know who killed that black girl?"

"He's guessing, Honey. He thinks you might have some clues you're not sharing. That's all. Ignore him. You're doing fine now."

I walk upstairs to the bedroom, where I've thrown all my clothes in a big pile on the floor. Since I haven't done laundry in three weeks, I dig out a pair of rumpled jeans and pull them over the boxer shorts. Turning around in the mirror, I see the lines of the shorts on my legs. I could go without underwear. Or wear the dirty ones. But I've already turned them wrong side out and worn each side once. I rummage in the pile for a big enough shirt to hang over the jeans, but everything is too dirty. I look in the mirror again and decide to wear the faded one I've been sleeping in. What the hell. Clinton says I'm doing fine.

Outside, the sun is shining so hard, I have to blink my eyes and go back for sunglasses. They're on the kitchen table with the rest of the stuff I've dragged from the trailer and never put away. I'm a bag lady with two houses.

The streets on the way to Bowker's are lined with big cardboard bins for trash and booths for food, crafts, and souvenirs. A few people have already set up their chairs for watching the parade. On Main, the banners of welcome flap overhead like brightly colored bedsheets on a clothesline. American flags hang in front of every business as if Divinity's existing for one hundred years is somehow a patriotic thing to do. I suppose God's on our side, too. We'll hear plenty of that today—like we always do when they've dragged out the flags.

The first time Jake and I made love was the day after the Fourth of July. He had a job taking down all the flags on Main Street and folding and putting them back in storage. Instead, they were in a big pile on his living room couch. We made supper together, hardly talking, we wanted each other so bad. We got along together immediately like a good oiled machine, no tappet or clang. We watched each other, and it happened like we were walking under water, heavy and slow with what we were
going to do.

After supper we took our bowls of tapioca pudding and sat on that couch among those flags. The first kiss was so long and sweet, I didn't want to come up for air, it felt natural to be breathing him. It'd been such a long time. I don't know which of us first used the pudding to sweeten our skins or how the flags twisted and slid us onto the floor, licking and loving so slow and good. The best it ever was between us. Blessed by all those stars and stripes. Afterward we took the flags to the dry cleaners, and Velva McGee just looked at the dried-on tapioca and smiled.

The memory is so strong that I almost run into Bowker with his arm around Larue. In broad daylight. On Main Street. Larue smiles primly at me, pats Bowker's cheek, and walks away, her hips swaying above her three-inch heels.

Still thinking of that time with Jake, I follow Bowker into the office, through the gate, back to a chair in front of his desk. He's been talking the whole time, but I've missed most of it.

"And I know you'll keep it quiet. It wouldn't do any good to let people know about this. It'd hurt the community, don't you see, more than just me and my business. So I thought I'd give you this token of my appreciation, regardless of whether you come back to work for me, and I hope you will. I mean that. People who come in like to do business with you. They say you're nice and efficient. They trust you. Jasper Johnson won't have anyone else come out to check on the horses. You know that. Why, you could start working to get an agent's license on your own." He laughs. Me as insurance agent. Or is it me the real estate agent—I can't tell for sure.

I look down at what he's sliding over the desk in front of me. An envelope with some fifty-dollar bills sticking out of it. When I don't pick it right up, he gets uncomfortable, then opens his right desk drawer and pulls something out. Another fifty comes slipping across the desk at me, sliding easily on the mahogany's polished surface. I look at that, too. I just don't seem able to make myself pick it up. Then another appears, and another. It's interesting in its own way, sitting here. I don't know how long it would have gone on if one of the bills hadn't slipped off the desk onto the floor and I hadn't bent down to pick it up. Somehow touching the money seals the bargain. Let's see, Marylou got ten thousand dollars, and there are ten fifties in my pile.

"That's all I've got, Honey. Marylou cleaned me out, don't you know." It's tempting. I don't know what to do. I wish someone were here to give me some advice, but I can't just run out, flag down somebody, and say, "Can you come in here and tell me how much I should charge for keeping my mouth shut? I mean, how much is it worth? How much am *I* worth?"

The other problem is that to take the money means he's paid for something. Knowing Bowker, once he's on his feet again, it might make him worse than ever, thinking he's bought me somehow. Then it will probably get a little cloudy, and he'll think that he's bought more than my silence, that he's paid for other services, too. He doesn't like to see his money spent foolishly. He's always preaching about value for the dollar, and he'll see he gets it. I have to get out of here and think.

"I don't want this money," I say to him. When I look at him for the first time really, I see him sag. If I don't want the money, what do I want? He picks up his pen. "Do you want a check for the rest? How much?"

"No, you don't understand. I don't want this. I don't want money from you. I don't even know whether I want to keep working for you. It just wouldn't be right. . . ." It's the years of doing fast deals in real estate, of pulling the wool over everybody's eyes, that saves him, because when he hears those words, something comes alive inside of him. He pops up on the chair he's slumped onto, swipes the sweat off his face, and breaks into the big grin he uses to reassure people that they are in the hands of someone they can trust. He puts away his checkbook in one smooth motion. Then the fifties disappear just as smoothly. Like a magician. First they're there, then they're gone, and we both stare at the high polish of wood between us that reflects us back as distorted patches of color.

"Certainly, I understand. You need time. This has all been, well, unpleasant, I can see that. I'll tell you what, I'll draw up a new contract for you. With a salary, not an hourly, and benefits. We can think about a company car, why not? You've been a good employee. Everyone in town likes you, we wouldn't want to lose you. So Monday when you come in, we'll sit down and have a little chat. Sure, you can teach an old dog new tricks. I always said that about you, Honey. You're a smart girl—uh, *person,* and we're going to get along fine."

He gives me his Chamber of Commerce smile and sticks out his hand. When I go to shake it, automatically, there is a folded-over envelope he passes to me. "Now don't you argue, this isn't anything but a little bonus for being a good worker. I want you to go out and buy yourself a new dress and a good dinner. You deserve it. Just my way of saying 'thanks' and apologizing. For not being more generous at Christmas—you always got less and probably deserved more. Sure, and why not? Now just let me make up for it a little. And I'll see you Monday, right? You'll come in?"

I have to hand it to him. I really can't resist his sales talk. It's big and persuasive. It makes me feel a little helpless. Besides, I can feel that it isn't much money. Not like before. Maybe it's better to take a little bit, just to make him comfortable. He couldn't trust a person he hasn't bought. He has to own a little bit. The money changing hands makes him feel like we're back at ground zero. The Employee and the Boss. He can afford to be generous, and I can't afford not to accept it. I let it stand. I'll decide later about coming in first thing Monday morning.

When we both get to the front door, which is still open, Bowker automatically starts putting his arm around me, then catches himself and gives an embarrassed giggle. I just smile and stick out my hand again. We shake. I start walking down the street—hurrying, but not too fast. I don't want him to think I'm running away. When I'm far enough away, I stop on a corner and look in the envelope in my hand. Three fifty-dollar bills. Good. Just enough so he won't ever know for sure whether he's really paid his debt.

Because I turned down the larger amount, he'll never be certain of the value of his money. For a man like Bowker, that will be enough to keep some power away from him. Or at least keep him from having power over me. I wish Clinton were here now so he could see how smart I'm getting.

"And if you're really smart," his voice says, "you'll put that money in the bank and save up to get out of here."

I think about it as I cross the street. "On the other hand," I argue with him, "you always told me to 'take advantage of the freebies in life. Just take the gifts and use 'em. Don't store up, there's always more.' That's what you always said, Clinton, 'There's more where that came from. More of everything.' 'Course you couldn't wait to find that out, could you?"

Passing a booth where a man is stringing "Divinity Centennial" T-shirts on hangers over a rod just above my head, I decide on my first purchase. I choose a turquoise T-shirt with pink lettering and a picture of Sorenson's old pig house, which was the first schoolhouse ninety years ago. They've left the pigs out. This will look better than the red one. I've forgotten to put on a bra, so I have to ignore the seller's fix on my chest as I hand him a fifty. He takes a long time to make change, even for such a large bill.

29

Historical Accuracy

Back at my house, I get in the bathtub for a long soak after I wash my hair and soap myself under the shower head. I've just closed my eyes when the front door bangs shut. This time the person hasn't even bothered to knock. Tourists. I debate not going down but don't really want them to steal me blind. I'm just wrapping a towel around myself when Baby's voice floats up the stairs.

"Honey? You up there? The door was unlocked, so I came on in. You're not 'busy,' are you?" Her giggling says she hopes I am, in that special way.

"Down in a sec, Baby," I call as I drop the towel and reach for the comb. "Not a moment's peace. Once you let the first one in, that's it," I mutter to myself in the mirror. Quickly combing my hair and applying makeup, I rub lotion on my arms, chest, face, and legs, and head for the bedroom. Faced with the same underwear dilemma, I smell the boxers and pull them back on. They're not as rank as the jeans. I dot some Obsession on the crotch before I pull those on. Twyla gave me the bottle Wolf brought her from a trip to the Bahamas with his wife. "She gets the trip, I get a lousy bottle of perfume. Duty free, even."

I'd had to catch it before it broke. "Eight ounces, Twyla, it must've cost a fortune. It's perfume."

"So what—take it." And she smiled that naughty-girl smile.

I smear some more around my breasts and behind my ears and along my wrists before I pull on the new T-shirt. It hangs way past my crotch, which is good, because I always feel like other people can see smells, especially bad ones, like they stain you or something.

In the mirror my hair is already starting to wave and curl wildly. The shirt is huge, disguising the fact that I have no bra on. I'm down to one bra that hasn't fallen apart, and it's disappeared. I could wear another T-shirt under this one, but it feels hot already.

Downstairs, Baby has squeezed onto a chair at the kitchen table, which looks remarkably like the one at Jass's. The two houses and furniture are the same vintage.

"Tea?" I ask as I go to the sink to fill the kettle.

"No thanks. Water, if you've got a clean glass." She looks at the dishes stacked all over the counters. I peek in the cupboard, knowing there isn't one.

"It's okay. I just stopped by to thank you for making those two behave."

Filling the tea infuser, I try not to spill any. I'm down to powder at the bottom of the tin. "Things are all right, then?"

Baby laughs. "If you'd answer your phone once in a while, you'd find out."

I shrug.

"I heard you've been on vacation, and Marylou ran off with some lawyer from Omaha. Seems like a strange time for you to take time off." She lifts a paper bag off the table and pulls my missing bra out of the pile of junk. "Lose something?"

"Wondered where that got to. Here, let me—" I reach for it, but she hugs it against her chest.

"Let's see, wait a minute . . . thirty-six B. Not bad, a little on the Twiggy side, but not bad. Here—" She throws it at me, but I miss, and it lands on the stove. One strap touching the red coil of the burner smolders and ignites.

Grabbing it, I throw the flaming bra in the sink, where it sizzles and hisses in a bowl of dirty water. "Thanks a lot, Baby. That was my only bra. Thanks." The kettle whistles, and I roughly spill some water into a semiclean cup and drop in the infuser spoon.

When I take it to the table, Baby is laughing so hard her stomach jumps up and down, shaking the table. "God, I'm sorry," she gasps. "You looked *so* funny."

"Yeah, well, anyway, I've got stuff to do here today, okay?" Reaching into the bottom drawer beside the sink, I pull out a box of big plastic garbage bags, tear one off, and clamp a side in the top drawer to make it stand up. I open the overhead cabinet beside the stove and start pulling down boxes. I give each a shake and examine the expiration date before I toss it. When I pull out the Quaker Oats, it doesn't sound right, and it's too light. I open it. Inside there's dollars, fives and tens and twenties. I pull out the wads and set them on the counter. Baby's eyes are huge. She has stopped laughing. The kitchen smells like burning cloth and garbage.

"How much is there?" she asks finally.

"Here, count it. I'm going to check the rest."

Every box has money in it, except for the Trix, which he must've been eating. He could've lived with Twyla. In the flour, which I pour slowly into the trash bag, while the dust rises, coating everything white, I find a Ziploc bag. Opening it carefully, I find five black opals. Dark and fiery, they blink up at me like small animals I've pulled into the light.

"Oh, Honey, those are beautiful," Baby croons. "And *so* valuable. Black is *so* valuable."

Leigh Hunt is teaching her something, it seems. I put them back in the bag and hand them to Baby. "Keep an eye on these."

I don't have time to react while I'm doing this. My skin feels nervous, tingly, and I can smell the Obsession coming off my body in big waves as I begin to sweat a little.

"Is that your *perfume*?" Baby asks.

The freezer I've left to last. It always seems disrespectful to clean out another person's freezer. Like going through their underwear or sock drawer and deciding what to keep. A freezer seems so full of time, of promise and failure. Foods we're always going to get to, those we never do. There's always something stranded there. Even if it's just one of those blue plastic packs of fake ice.

Sure enough. Wrapped in Saran Wrap, next to some fish fillets, coated with frost I have to scrape off, is a dead squirrel. Fur and all. I would've dropped it, but for Baby sitting there. I'm tempted to put it back, leave the freezer for later. Who needs a freezer, anyway? A bit of green catches my eye as I toss it in the garbage, so I have to dig it out again. Sure enough, money. Fifties and hundreds. My lucky day. Baby won't count it because of where it's been. We put it in a separate pile away from the "clean" money.

"What are you going to do with all this money?" Baby asks when I've emptied everything from the fridge, too.

"Keep it, I guess. Want some?"

She gets a funny look on her face, almost sweet. "No, you keep it, Honey. Leigh has enough for me. Thanks, though. That's so . . . well, it's a nice thing to say. And I *do* mean thanks about what you did at dinner. Daddy's moving his stuff this weekend. Sonny Boy's been sleeping at home most nights. Or at least not at the house. I think I can get married without anyone going crazy, maybe. A Parrish family first. Who knows, though, Tolson's still out there someplace."

I sit down to sip at my lukewarm tea. "He's not going to bother anyone."

"How do you know?" Baby's voice sharpens.

"Ask Sonny. He's the reason Tolson left. Him and Daddy. He won't be back unless they die or something."

She looks puzzled. "Sonny Boy? He said—"

"I know, but *he's* the reason. Ask him. Or better yet, don't. Just stay out of it. It's a long time ago, now. It's done. Go marry Leigh."

"One thing. Daddy and I don't know what to do with the house. *You* don't need it, I don't, Sonny shouldn't, and Louverna gave hers to Daddy so he'd move in with her."

"Leave it. Rent it. But keep it. Tolson might come home someday, or Sonny's kids or yours might need it. We already lost a farm, we should hang on to the house, at least, as long as we can. Keep it." I drain my tea and get up. "I've gotta clean up here."

Baby stands. "I know. The parade's in forty-five minutes, and I've got to meet Leigh. Coming?"

I shrug.

"Only happens once in a hundred years, Honey. You'd better. Besides, you can laugh at our dumb Famous Fats float. You ever notice how things that seem like such a good idea starting out turn into such a pile of crap later?"

"Oh, not me—no—"

We're still laughing as she floats down the walk. I almost hug her before she leaves, but I don't. Some people can't come to that moment together. I'm not sure Baby and I ever will, but that's all right.

The day's so warm, I step out to the yard, following the flagstone steps back. The yard's so big and deep, you lose the sense of town here. No wonder Boardman stayed. Big old apple and plum trees separate his property from the others. Tucked under the trees and lilac bushes, there's an edge of red roof and peeling white paint wall. An old shed. For a moment I can't remember what's in it. Then I do. Bowker's been trying for years to buy it off the old man. The '35 Packard, in good condition. Covered with a tarp. Sitting there since Boardman got it when his daddy died.

Bowker found out about it somehow and pestered Azium about three times a year. But the old man just laughed it off. He had no intention of selling it but liked the attention Bowker gave him, stringing him along with, "I guess not this year, but maybe later." It was something Bowker couldn't get his hands on.

The apple trees have just finished blossoming, and the plum blossoms are beginning to drop, too. It's lovely, the ground a mat of pink and white, the air almost drugging me with its heavy, sweet scent. And the canopy of leaves starting to thicken up so I have to duck into semidarkness to get back to the shed. Azium used to sit at his bay window and watch the birds with binoculars. Somewhere he has a bird book. If he didn't take it with him, I'll do that, too. Every spring he made me sit with him to watch for the lady cardinal who was building her nest. The pale pinkish green of her head and shoulders giving off a waxy glow in the dark flash of leaves and green.

When I look up, though, I can't see the nest. Suddenly my foot catches in something, and I almost fall against the trees. I look down and see the tangle of vines, then look up. Sure, the grapes Boardman let go. Clinton always told him to keep them pruned and shaped so they'd produce, but the old man got too busy. I wonder if it's too late. Probably not. Grapes grow wild in the woods, and any bit of light and relief from undergrowth makes them produce like crazy. All I have to do is chop out some of the excess along the ground and thin the ones that are too heavy along the back fence there, then trim the overhead trees a little for light. They probably need it, anyhow. The fruit trees could all be topped and do a lot better. Azium neglected that the past few years, said he was too old to be climbing trees and he'd be damned if he'd spend money on some yahoo coming in to saw a tree limb. Now I'll have to take care of it. For a moment, a surge of helplessness comes over me. I can't do that. This is already way too much for me. I can't manage anything, the shop, the house. That's a Known Fact: KF, known fact. Hell, I'll have to sell the place, move away, forget it. I just can't do it alone.

But then that feeling is gone. The next moment, as I pull open the old double doors of the shed, the rusty, paint-clogged hinges squealing in protest, one of the doors drops down with a *chunk* in the middle of its swing.

The gleam of a chrome bumper catches my eye just as a flurry of startled swallows and sparrows comes charging out. For a moment it scares me. I'm thinking of mice and rats and bats, but I remember that the neighbor's cats have always taken special care of the shed. There it is again, the chrome bumper winking and flashing in the sun that's coming in through the trees in patches and streaks. Most of the car is carefully covered with a green tarp that's blotched with dust and bird droppings. The right side, in fact, looks like a stalagmite growing in a gray dune. Above the car seems to be a favorite nesting place on the rafters.

I think about leaving it the way it is, but something makes me pull the tarp at one corner. The dusty glow of dark blue paint underneath seems more inviting than ever, so I carefully pull the back half up and over toward the right, then go around to the front and repeat it. As if the car is sighing with relief at finally being released from the obscurity of the dark canvas, it shines out brightly. The white convertible top is still there, only yellowing and spotting in a few places.

I open the driver's door and climb in, forgetting to dust off the seat and ignoring the little tufted nest of a mouse that has apparently survived the cats' reign of terror. I can drive this car, I think as I place my hands on the wheel and reach for the pedals. I'll have to figure out how to pull the seat closer. But I can drive it. "Hell, yes, I can drive it," I say out loud.

"Why don't you?" a voice from behind me asks, startling me so badly that I accidentally hit the horn. It works, and that surprises me even more. "What the—"

"It must still have a charge on it. Maybe you can use it in the parade today."

I swing around now, to see who's there. "Jass!"

"Sure, who'd you expect, the ghost of Christmas past?" He's struggling with his face, trying to decide between a cynical, cross look and a smile. It makes him look like a kid, trying to act serious and knowing it isn't working. Then something changes, and he goes flat.

"You got the car, too?" he asks, but in a different tone now, like he remembers something he's mad at me about.

I climb out and shut the door carefully, the way Boardman would do it, carefully so not to disturb the old metal. "I guess so. I mean, Boardman never said anything about it when he left. Just that it was all mine, the house and stuff—" I wave my arm around the shed, the old tools and garden implements hanging on the walls, things stuffed onto the rafters I'll have to look at later. "So I suppose the car's mine, too. Nice, isn't it?" I stroke the car door gently, like it's a horse.

"You probably deserve it," he says. Something about the way he says it means a lot more, like I've done stuff for it.

I walk to the front of the car, struggle to pull the canvas up partway over the hood. It's hard to do this without help. I look back at Jass, who is still standing at the rear of the car, blocking some of the light coming into the shed. I squint for a moment. "Will you grab that?" He stands there like a goddamn statue.

It's a few seconds before it strikes me that his body is also struggling with something he wants to keep down. "Do it yourself." He spins on his heel and disappears under the trees, walking very fast, his hands in fists at his side, unnaturally stiff, as if he holds them down there to keep from having them do something else.

"Wait—" I call out, and run after him. "Wait a goddamn minute!" He's almost to the side of the house when I catch up with him. "Jasper, you wait or—" I grab at his arm. It's hard as iron, and when he swings it back at me like a club, it knocks me down and I lose my breath.

"Get up!" he orders, and looks down at me.

I want to cry real bad then, watching his shoes and being unable to breathe right, but I know he'll just run away again. As soon as I can speak, I say in a stern voice like Mama would have used, "Jass, stop acting like a fool." It works. I look up at him standing there, the sun hitting the dark blue highlights in his black hair, his face older and sadder than I've ever seen it before. Then his hand comes out to help me up, automatically, I guess, because when I take it, he jerks like he's grabbed an electric fence, and I have to climb up on my own.

"Let's go inside," I order, again using Mama's voice. Not looking back to see if he follows, but praying he will, I walk to the house.

We sit in the living room. Me on the sofa, him on the occasional chair across from it, his back to the bay window. Behind him, outside, I can see the hint of the shed and try to remember to get back there to close it up again. "You want some—" I ask.

He interrupts me, "No," sighing so deeply that it almost makes the chair tremble. It makes me mad suddenly, him acting this way.

"What the hell's the matter with you, anyway, Jasper?" He shakes his head, looking at the floor. I get madder. "Look, I've had it. Whatever I've done is done. You'd better tell me or forget it." I start to get up, acting like I'm washing my hands of the whole thing.

"You know," he says, getting cold again.

I sit up stiffly. "No." I speak clearly and slowly, the way Mama would when she was extra angry. "No, I do not have any idea what is the matter with you. You may tell me, or you may go fuck yourself. I don't need this anymore."

"That's easy for you to say." He gestures around the house. Then he shakes his head. "Yeah, you always know how to get what you want." Then suddenly he's angry, his hands clenching and unclenching like he wants to hit me but his voice rational, icy. "Is that it, Honey, don't I appeal to you? Clinton, Brewer, Jimmy, Jake, Terry, but not me? You've handed it out all over the county, all over Iowa, and I'm not worthy?"

He scares me. I back into the corner of the sofa, trying to make myself a smaller target. "Wait a minute," I protest. "Wait, you don't understand." But my protests seemed to drive his mood because he laughs.

"*Understand?* Oh, I *understand.* I've spent a year trying to get close to you, finding out about your family, your life, and telling you that I understand." He laughs again, so bitterly that it scares me.

"What the hell are you talking about? You spent a year to figure out some big lie, some goddamn fantasy you made up? You're the one, man, you're the one with the problem." This seems to drive him farther away because he smiles distantly and bridges his fingers like a TV psychiatrist.

"I came here to confront you. I came to tell you that I know, I know the whole thing that's been going on. Boyd told me." He is sitting perfectly still, his eyes fixed, body stiff. He reminds me of Tolson, as a kid, when we'd be so angry that almost nothing stood in the way of our beating each other up. I expect him to start breaking things any minute.

"*What* did Boyd tell you?" I want to make him say it. I want to hear it out loud.

"That Clinton and his buddies killed that black girl, and that you probably know it, too. And you'd do anything to protect him. And the others. You slept with Terry at Reiler's out of revenge, that I can understand, but you won't stop your brother—you let him beat me up. You knew. I've finally decided you aren't worth it. I want to leave you like a piece of trash on the road, not worth picking up, not worth disposing of." He's in control now, relaxing his hands on the arms of the chair. I'm stunned. Hearing it out loud feels like he's knocked me down, it takes my breath away.

"But it's not true," I finally manage to say, softly, so he'll know I mean it. But he just stares at me.

"I trusted you," was all he says. Outside, behind him, I catch the flicker of red from the male cardinal, helping with the nest.

"Do you want something to drink?" I ask.

"You were the only one who seemed to have anything going for herself. The only one who seemed to have a glimmer of feeling." He shakes his head slightly.

"What about Cindy Reiler?"

"I can't stand it, thinking about it, thinking about sleeping with you, and all the time you've protected murderers. They could've killed me, too."

I shake my head no.

"I was torn between wanting to follow you around and verify it—and not wanting to know too much for certain."

"Why don't you let me fix you something to drink?" I'm pleading with him now. I need it more than him, but he isn't listening.

"I didn't give up. I just didn't want to know. God, I've loved you. Why didn't you tell me the truth?"

I look at him for a moment. He seems to have drifted away someplace. "I didn't know. Boyd says the same thing. But I didn't—I didn't—"

"Sure. The house is a payoff. Boyd didn't say that, but it is, isn't it? I can see that. But why didn't you stop them from getting me, Honey?"

"I don't feel sorry for you." The tears are streaming down my face, but I don't care. "You believe some dumb lie, and turn on me—I've been through hell, too, you know."

"Yeah, well, I don't know it's a lie, do I? You haven't proved it isn't true. You've barely even denied it."

"Would it make any difference? How the hell do you expect me to *prove* I didn't know something? Especially when most of them are dead. You just believed the first dirty-minded thing you could about me. All that crap about trusting me. How come you didn't come and ask me then? How come? Or were you just pissed off that you weren't getting it, too?" It's an off shot, but I get a horrible feeling about it when I see his face. "That's it, isn't it? Here you are, being so goddamn self-righteous about it, and you just wanted to get yours, too. Great. Just great!" I'm up pacing the room now, feeling how small the house is with my excited strides. Then the flicker of green and another of red through the window again, registering the dark oblong of the shed door I've left open. Now I want to hit him.

"Screw you, Honey, I almost died in some stupid fight because of you. And all you can say is that I'm angry about not getting laid?" He's on his feet, too, and I can see that we are heading toward one of our fights. It's too bad we can't hit each other, it might help.

"Don't you come near me," I warn him. "I warned you about my brother *and* Reiler's men. You were too goddamned cocky to listen."

He holds his hands up, palms out, to show his intention. "Don't worry. I wouldn't touch you if you were the last person on earth."

It reminds me of things kids say to each other. I start giggling. Not meaning to, but doing it anyway. Pretty soon I'm almost collapsing with laughter.

He looks puzzled and annoyed. "Can you find me something to drink? Pop? Or water?"

I stop laughing and look at him. He has dark circles under his eyes and sunken cheeks that match the thinness of his body. Like me. There's a thick black stubble on his face, and his nose shines with oil. "Why *did* you come here, Jass?"

"Look, can I get a glass of something? I can't talk, my throat is getting so dry. Just some water, then. It won't put you out any. *Please?*"

He shakes his head in disgust and heads for the kitchen, but I jump in front of him. "Okay, okay. Just wait here. The place is a mess. I was clearing some of the old food out, and the garbage bag is flooding, so wait here. I'll find something." I find a bottle of Pepsi and put some ice in a glass for him.

After a couple of long swallows, Jass sits down again, his back to the bay window, and I take up my place on the couch again. He looks at me carefully like he's playing Matt Dillon the marshal or something. "Were you really going to sell out and leave without saying a word to me?"

I stare at him. "*Leave?* I'm not going anywhere. I've been off, on vacation, trying to get some things straight in my head. God, you didn't even talk to me that day your horses colicked, so what's your problem now?"

He leans back, relaxing his handsome face finally. "Jeez, Honey, do you have any idea how crazy I've felt? I haven't understood one thing that's happened between us since we met. Maybe once—Halloween . . . that night . . ."

My body turns hot at the image of the wings beating over my body, and I nod.

"The rest, hell, it's anybody's guess. I get the shit kicked out of me—your family tries to ruin me, kill me, kill my horses—"

"Now wait, that wasn't my family. That was Reiler's men."

"Sonny Boy and Terry are buddies. What, are you stupid?"

I'm caught. I know it. He's right. I've missed all the obvious things. "But I didn't realize—"

"For a smart woman, you are so dumb sometimes, you know that? I suppose giving you a list would help—for your walls—but most of us don't need a goddamn map to figure out simple human justice, Honey. *What* is going *on* in this town? If you didn't know Clinton killed that girl and all the rest of this shit, what did you *think?*" He leans forward, holding himself on his chair by gripping the arms.

"No, you're wrong. I didn't know. I'm sorry. I tried to understand, I just didn't know. But Clinton didn't kill her. That I can say. Sonny or Jake, maybe. That fits, doesn't it?" I have a hard time making my voice loud enough for Jass to hear.

He crouches in front of me, taking my hand. "You were just so in love with him, you couldn't believe he'd do that. You still are. That's what's screwing us around, Honey, just like you said. Clinton. All those dead people. But Clinton, most of all. You have to let go of him, and Sonny and Jake, the rest of them will go, too. You understand?" He rubs my hands between his like it's cold out, and in a way it is. A big hollow-sounding wind takes over my head, and I sit there frozen.

I finally get up and go to the kitchen for the bottle of tequila I've brought from the trailer. I pour two fingers in a glass and drink it straight, holding back the scald and explosion in my empty stomach when it hits. Then I pour another three fingers and start sipping it slow but steady. I have to reach ground again.

In a little while he comes in. "Come on, parade's starting. Let's go." Walking to Main Street beside Jass in the crowds of people, I feel like I'm in a car tumbling down a mountainside, rolling over and over and over. Banging myself this way and that, knowing I'll never be the same, even if I manage to survive this wreck. I just hope the pint of tequila in my purse doesn't break before I can finish it. I need it just to stay normal, today.

Now that he's had his say, Jass seems happy enough. One good thing, he doesn't try to comfort me, and I don't ask him to.

30

On Parade

The alcohol makes it easy to slip out of my house, my mind, and join the happy outlook of the parade. Everyone around me is really here, in the present, I realize, with the bright new May sun beating a tap dance on their heads. Everyone except me. I'm in this weird other place, wiped clean by memory. Time again. I'm the hostage. Antarctica. Iran. I try to retrieve that whole baby I once glimpsed, the one without memory or other people's voices, but she isn't to be found in this present so present it makes me almost disappear. I have to hang on to Jass's hand hard and sip from my pint to stay with the pulse of sound and color around me. Like trying to do the dead man's float in shallow water.

The 4-H group is trying to ride in precise lines. The excitement makes the horses stiffen their front legs, and the riders trying to sit the up-and-down jog don't know whether they disapprove or enjoy the excitement with their animals.

Of course, there are the teams of work horses whose muscles roll and gleam through the coats shined with silicone polish until they remind you of chrome, smooth and full and round, the haunches a precision of machine pace and evenness. Perfectly matched. The Belgians, the Percherons, the Clydesdales—no longer used for plowing, now the sign of true luxury on the farm. The symbol that says to neighbors: This man can afford to keep animals whose sole purpose is to *not* work, but to be treated like royalty, shipped around in special, heavy-duty trailers, each one with a groom trained not to let dust and flies settle on their horse.

The manes and tails smooth and silky from cream rinse, braided with rosettes of ribbons and flowers. Each man competing with others for the envy of his neighbors adorns his work horses with gifts the way a man does his mistress.

And there is the patience of the great horses as people hover around each giant foot, shining it with special polish, combing and powdering the white socks. Standing while the patent-leather harness is dropped on them. The blinkers on the bridle cutting off the side view don't alarm them, nor the great collars, nor the clink and tinkle of brass or silver chains and rings, nor the great long shafts that pull the wagon, nor being lined up with the others, one before, one after, on each side until there are four, six, eight, nor the wagon itself, the replica beer wagon, milk wagon, laquered with twelve coats of glossy enamel, gold letters that cost hours to hand-paint, and white wheels.

And finally the whip, which comes slithering snake light along the back. The call from behind, "Geee-up, Betty" and the lead horse in front puts her great chest to the collar, and they all follow, the wagon coming after. They're off, lifting legs that little bit extra of wasted motion they'd been taught since now they don't have to make it last all day around the field.

Down the street they come. You can hear the great hooves stomping
the pavement blocks before, the heavy rumble and rattle of the wagons after them. And the men on top, handling the leather lines with an awkward grace of something learned lately. No smiles. Only the grim mouths, demanding something the event isn't going to give them. The wives perch temporarily like sparrows on the benches beside them, small, frightened smiles floating on their faces as they look out over the backs and haunches of horses with the force of deep water breaking over rocks. Their knuckles gleam white as they grip the edges of their seats.

In the parade, studded with horses, there are fire trucks, the antique ones that chug along, their engines tuned for the hour. All the years of fires marked by the happy occasion of men bringing out one more engine. Each cared for as tenderly as a horse, bright and shiny. Fire trucks from neighboring towns, neighboring counties, it seems like miles of fire trucks. LaFrance, Mercedes, Ford. Hoses folded like fine linen on shelves. Brass glittering. Even the tires scrubbed and sprayed black. The men in the trucks always happy, as if being a fireman is by its very nature of choice an occasion for celebration.

Then comes Helen Jansen Binger and her Texas husband, Wade Binger, Jr. First they flew in a private jet to Cedar Rapids. None of us were there to see it, but someone picking up the senator's wife says it was a real honey. Then they drove down in a rented limo, making a stop at Dirkson's for the use of his newest, flashiest car. But that wasn't enough for Binger. So he called around, located a breeder of Arabian horses a hundred miles away, bought two over the phone, had them driven in with a beautiful show buggy, the harness mounted in sterling silver (it cost him ten thousand alone). Just so he'd have something special "to show off his Helen," he tells folks who stand around to gawk as the man who brought the horses in tacks them up.

The horses are something to see: a matched pair of chestnuts with flaxen manes and tails and four white stockings. Not even stallions, they cost thirty thousand apiece. They look like they belong in a movie. All the kids press around because they hear that the horses are the Black Stallion's brothers.

Helen looks more beautiful than ever, big and full, like an overripe peony. Wade, her husband, can't keep his hands off of her, even after all these years. He keeps nuzzling and biting on her like a kitten going after milk. It's nice after watching so many married people who act like touching gives them acne. When Helen and Wade climb up into the buggy (Wade insists on driving), the springs groan, sink, bounce back, then settle in. These two make you feel like theirs is a good harvest, and that just being near it means you get some of it, too.

Some folks say he's showboating and taking over all the publicity. Just trying to get himself in the papers. It's pretty amazing, him holding the reins in one hand, keeping the horses at their showiest walk, which looks like a trot in place, their knees come up so high, the sparkle on their hooves glittering like stars against the shiny bodies, and with the other hand tossing out silver dollars, flipping them lightly through the air so they land like flowers instead of money.

It about drives the crowd mad. They ignore the politicians who are up ahead as word passes down the line and everyone makes ready to grab the free money. Until Boyd asks him to stop whenever the parade lags so they won't have any accidents with people trying to get at the silver dollars that spin up through the air like fish leaping into the sun and slipping back into the water again, hands waving frantic as reeds in the wind, me me me.

"It's a shame," you can hear the older people say, "teaching those children to beg like that." Pretty soon, though, when a dollar slips their way, they have that hand up grabbing at it before they even know it. Like people at a baseball game, wanting to touch the magic of the foul ball, scrambling among the seats for a fingerhold of whatever it is to own something that had passed through the hands of the great.

So people won't forget the time Helen Jansen Binger came home. Big old Helen, Helen the Bomb, who was pitied by all.

And the sun shines hotly. You can see the sweat on the animals and on Alvin Acker, who marches with his trained pig, having it take little bows every few steps, showing folks how it can dance on its hind legs until it gets too tired, and it jumps in the little wagon Alvin pulls so it can take a rest. The pig is a big hit with everyone. "Better'n *Green Acres,*" people say.

But the saddest thing is looking up at the bank building roof and catching sight of the hollowed-out face of Billy Bond, peering down at us like a department store mannequin. When the pig comes along, dancing and doing its tricks, Billy lets out such a yowl that you can hear it above the bands coming half a block away and the ones half a block beyond.

I haven't seen Billy this excited since the county fair all those years ago, when he first showed me the pig barn and his beloved Bluebell. Then someone whispers, "Oh, no, he's going to jump," because Billy is climbing up on the ledge that surrounds the roof. He is so unsteady anyway, we think he'll fall if he doesn't jump. We are afraid to say a word. It holds us there, that spectacle of Billy swaying and yowling on the lip of the building.

Then someone mutters, "Why, look at that pig." Sure enough, the pig is going through a little routine of tricks, with Alvin Acker standing back staring at Billy. As we watch the pig instead of Billy, with the red bow around his neck bouncing along in time, he does some little dance steps, then whirls around real fast three times, acting like a dog trying to catch its tail, and stands up, on its hind feet, walking back and forth to some invisible music like he's doing the rumba, his fat butt swaying rhythmically. Then he sits on his haunches, pauses for an instant, and does a backward somersault.

No one makes a sound for a few seconds, then we hear the clapping from above us, and we burst out roaring with laughter and clapping. As the parade continues forward with a jerk, everyone turns their attention back to the street, excited and relieved, ready for what is coming next.

When the marching band from Tipton comes along, strutting in a goose step like some camped-up old war film, Nazi soldiers in blue-and-red band suits trimmed with gold braid and high comic hats, the crowd sucks in its collective breath, not quite aware of what they are seeing, then lets out a long "Oohohhhahhhh" and claps for the precision and the energy with which they play the old Cole Porter tune "I'm in the Mood" to a disco beat.

And after that flash of sound, we get another old fire truck, and I realize we'd better not have any fires a hundred miles around, because the trucks all seem to be here in the parade, trying to preen like birds before the camera that has appeared down the street, mounted on top of a van, with a Des Moines TV station printed on the side.

As I watch the next marching band, the two head cheerleaders' thighs like shiny horse flanks working in piston motion as they trot in place down the street, I catch a glimpse of Sonny Boy just on the other side. A moment later he's gone, but the sad, angry line drawn across the mouth makes me uncomfortable. He's seen me with Jass. A second later Terry is in between the flashing silver tassels of the band's hats—and then he's gone, too. It's like running channels on the TV, the faces fleeing so quickly, I don't have time for more than a single impression.

A moment later the music of the band is disrupted and then silenced by a steady growing roar from behind, and as our attention sweeps uniformly to the right, the roar grows and the first cycles come into view. The biggest, darkest Harley hogs you could ever want to see. Strangely festooned with real flowers garlanded across the handlebars and trailing from the backrests that rise like spears welded behind the seats. Between the two leaders, who keep perfect time with each other, there stretches the name of a club from Des Moines. This time people don't move. As if they must hold their ground against this dark invasion, they stand solid. Only the children in the front seem torn between the urge to run out to the strange machines and the innate fear of the grizzle-faced men, too old for the machines they straddle like war-horses. The cycles, impatient to be off to the battle, cough and sputter and lunge forward, only to be held back by the thick, muscular bodies of the men who ride them. Behind them sit the women dressed in black leather and denim like the men, booted and scarred as if they've followed into battle like loyal grooms.

It is the women who astound the crowd. The one riding in the sidecar with the baby, a patch of skull and crossbones signifying the club already sewn onto its flannel blanket. The father, a proud warrior sitting high above it, his red hair and beard a stain against the black T-shirt belling down to cover his belly. His woman, a worn-out blonde, looks as if she were young once. She too is wearing a black T-shirt, which falls limply from her rib-thin shoulders. I feel an involuntary pull in my stomach when I see the tattoo on her upper arm. Branded like a cow, she looks around at us with eyes that can cut like barbed wire if we get too close.

Then the parade lurches forward, and I catch sight of the ballooning walk Baby has adopted for herself. Like someone who has trouble keeping her feet on the ground, she lands light and slow on her toes, rounding up and almost away as she rises to the next step. Behind her, gripped tightly by the hand, is Leigh Hunt. I can't figure out why they're hurrying down the side of the street, but in a few minutes I see the Famous Fats float. Built with Leigh's money, it features some of the museum pieces they're donating to the Historical Society, the fat furniture, and several of the larger members of the group. Across the top of the platform, strung between two pillars, the banner reads, "FAT IS FREEDOM, FAT IS AMERICAN, FAT IS THE FUTURE" in bright red block letters. Along the sides of the float there are large placards featuring photos and names of historical townspeople who were fat.

When something lands clunking me above the ear, I realize they're throwing things from the float, too. The people around me are scrambling to grab what look like gold pieces, but which the kids immediately recognize as coin chocolates. Giant versions of food rest on the table: a huge ice-cream sundae, a roast beef four times its normal size, plates of giant three-tiered cakes, and boxes of chocolates so big you can almost taste the creamy fillings. As the float lurches past, Baby and Leigh are being shimmied aboard like huge bales of straw. A happy smile is on Baby's face as she takes her rightful place among the family she has created for herself.

Then I see Sonny Boy again across the way. This time he is unmistakable. Rigid as a pole, he is staring across at me and Jass, but without even realizing what he is looking at. I can't tell what is wrong. At first I think it's because of Baby and Leigh. Then I realize he hasn't even seen them, and I wave my hand before I can stop myself. The motion makes his eyes waver, then his face changes, and he shakes his fist at me, furious. If he had a beer in his hand, I suppose he would have thrown that, too. Confused, I watch him for a minute, then try to melt back into the people behind me, pulling on Jass, trying to lose our place in the front; but they hold the line and stand firm. I am stuck in plain sight. I take another pull of tequila. The next band comes marching between us, and the deputy's voice carries from the front, where he is getting himself worked up about something. When I look through the rows of baton twirlers and drummers, I can't see Sonny Boy anymore.

Then the hollow clink of the posse horse the deputy is riding comes down the street, and the band is pushed over. Staying neatly in rhythm, they sway like a snake away from the horse, and the crowd pushes back impossibly the other way. Deputy Mel is shouting for a doctor, and from behind me a voice comes up, and a young blond woman squeezes her way through to Mel, who has stopped his hot, glistening horse in front of me. The heat radiates in my mouth and nose.

"Climb up," he orders. Fortunately the woman is wearing pants, so she puts her foot in the stirrup he offers and swings aboard, giving the crowd a little wave and smile as she settles onto the uncomfortable seat behind the big carved western saddle. The crowd claps spontaneously, and Mel wheels the horse around and clatters back down the street, pushing his way through the corridor that opens in front and closes behind him.

"That mother in the motorcycle gang—the one with the baby . . ." I hear people passing the information along.

"Fainted."

"Her husband got hysterical. Almost drove the bike right up on the sidewalk, he got so crazy."

"Probably on drugs."

"Yeah, they're all on drugs. That's what I heard."

"More likely booze, they drink a lot. That's how Harlan got his last night."

"Harlan who?"

"Harlan, you know, Jake's brother. They farm out State Road. Old man wants to retire, busted his behind for sixty years but can't get those boys to settle down and take over."

"Happens. Better to get the girls married and get the son-in-laws helping you. They got to work harder, or their wives'll kick 'em out."

"Sometimes. I look at Sonny Boy Parrish, though—Rose can't make him settle down. The old man can't, either. He's running like a stray dog half the night."

"Shhhhh. That's his sister up there—"

When the Twoanda Full Brass Band comes into view, I lose the rest of the conversations around me, but hell, I know they talk, we all do.

The sun is beating down on us pretty good by this time, and I've forgotten to wear a hat, so I can feel it drive through my scalp, lifting and drying the strands of my hair. I try shading my face with my hands, but I can feel it getting tighter and tighter as it burns. The parade has been going for an hour, and I'm almost out of interest when someone yells, "Who the hell is that?" We all strain our necks to catch sight of where he's pointing.

There are two rows of barefoot people with long flowing hair and long flowing white robes, not the kind you wear in your house, but the other kind, like a fancy nightgown. Some of the women have hair that runs down to their waists, and I wish Twyla were here to see it. She'd sure get a kick out of that. She always complained that everyone she worked on wanted the same old haircut, medium short with some poof to it. She'd love hair she could really get her heart into. Some of the people carry baskets and are throwing petals of flowers out of them. They all look happy. They look more than happy. They look, well, out of this world.

After that, this long, white Continental convertible comes into view, with someone perched on the backseat ledge and another person beside him. You can't tell much except that one of them has long hair, too. Then as he gets closer you can see it's a man because the pale yellow part on his chest turns out to be a beard. He is waving like a visiting Miss America. It's something. Beside Archie sits his sister, Larue Carlson, smiling coolly like she's saying "I told you so" to all the prognosticators in town. At least she had faith in Archie. Now it's paid off. Behind him come four more rows of folks, playing light, sweet-sounding instruments and dancing. The men around me seem to enjoy the way the breasts of the women jounce up and down while they dance. On the whole, Archie does fine.

In a minute someone repeats the question, "Who's that?" and someone else answers, "Why, that's Archie Carlson, 'member him?"

"Yeah, he got kicked out of school for vandalism. Never did nothing right. . . ."

"Well, I don't notice you driving around in a brand-new Continental, or maybe you keep it parked in that falling-down chicken house of yours." Everyone around me laughs, and Archie just sails by, large and mysterious.

With the sun dusting our heads and faces and bare arms like a fine powder we can't wash off later, the parade continues, including the float of Miss Dairy of Ramsay County, who rides with a big block of butter a man has sculpted of her likeness in a glass dairy case specially built at the center of the platform. It's big enough for everyone to see. The ladies all say, "My, isn't that nice," with a kind of longing, like they've missed something in life.

The men all eye the princess up and down and wish the artist had done a full-length, but they don't say much out loud except, "She's a looker all right."

Someone says, "My horse has a smaller set of teeth."

And someone else answers, "You been out measuring again?"

Toward the end, when folks are starting to shuffle around and get bored, the VFW comes along. It's always something to see the oldest soldiers come down the street, one white legging shorter than the other, their uniforms hanging on them like they belong to their big brothers. Their old toothless grins. The flag men hanging on for dear life to the pole, setting the flag to fluttering with their shaking.

Then each war gets younger men, until finally the Vietnam War veterans come along, and they're guys my age. They're pretty beat-up-looking, and they aren't walking so proud, you can see that a mile away. Some of them have their families with them, like it's a group effort to get out there and march along in front of the whole town.

The parade keeps going by, another Girl Scout troop, another 4-H group, more horses, more cars, a whole half mile of brand-new, shiny farm equipment none of the folks will be able to afford this year. Or any year soon. No scratches or weeds caught in the parts, it makes you want to taste the metal, it shines so good. You can feel the tension rise in the crowd like a muscle tightening in the arm as the parade of machines is pulled by. Everyone imagining themselves up high, high above the field in one of those tractors, air-conditioned with stereo and a little built-in refrigerator/cooler for a beer or lemonade as you spend the day in the fields. The big chair padded to the hilt. A person could almost take a nap working the corn in one of those. Put the tractor on cruise control, lock the wheels for the mile-long rows, lean back, close your eyes, though the special-tinted glass never lets too much sun in anyway. It's better than a person's own living room, you can tell. Nobody'd mind farming in one of those. With digital operation of the various implements behind: just push a button, the computer works the right mixture of seeds, fertilizer, and weed killer; push another button when the soil changes slightly, and you get an adjustment. It's almost like doing the work sitting at the kitchen table.

Around me, I can feel the collective heartbeat at the sight, imagining something that would make the backbreaking work easier, tools and machines that didn't break down on you, fields growing in perfect unity, perfect harmony, imagining even the weather a push button away.

Then suddenly almost in front of where I am standing, Sonny Boy comes pushing along the edge of the crowd, with Rose and the two little ones in tow, the baby in her arms. He ignores me, and I only get a glimpse of Rose's wild, exhausted eyes, walled in white like a horse gone scared, as she puffs along behind him. The hurry makes her blouse wet, and it's sticking like a big hand had struck her in the middle of her back, pushed her forward, and knocked the breath out of her. The kids are stumbling and whining with tear-streaked red faces behind her.

As they pass me, I hear Sonny mutter back to Rose through clenched teeth, "I told you to keep up with them, damn it. Now hurry up." He reaches back and gives her arm such a pull that it almost unseats the baby she's carrying. Rose stumbles, catching the baby as it lurches forward. The hands of people in the front row reach out to help, setting her back up, giving Sonny's receding back a dark look. Rose, looking more panicked, breaks into a trot, and the kids behind her start to run.

"She ought to dump him. He's a real bastard."

"Yeah, but she's one of those women likes 'em that way. The more he does to her, the better she loves him. You figure it out."

"Maybe it's for the kids."

"Yeah, maybe. But you can't tell. The women in that family been acting that way since I've known of them. The whole lot. They like their men mean, and the meaner they are, the better they like 'em. They stick around for stuff my old lady'd have a butcher knife on me for, I swear to God."

"Yeah, your old lady'd have a knife on you for stepping out the door to pee if she could catch you."

Everyone laughs at that, and I decide to struggle out of the niche I'm
watching from. Jass can stay if he wants. He hasn't said a word the whole time, anyway. Watching the parade reminds me of a dream—the kind where everyone you've ever known came by, and they all have tag ends of things to do with you, talk to you about. They all want something done, something settled, and in a way that's what living in this town is like. You keep running into yourself over and over, all your past mistakes, all the little slights and insults, all the old and new arguments you're having, over and over. But folks just keep going, forgiving and fighting, making up and starting over again.

I turn once when I'm through the crowd and standing on the steps to the bowling alley. I'm surprised to see Jake riding on top of a new baler waving at the crowd, and before I can stop myself I wave back. He looks like a boy I once knew. Smiling big and young. A kid getting a special treat. His company has sent the equipment, and the signs draped along one side say, "Win This Today—Buy a Ticket." I'm tempted by it, but I know I'd never live it down. Everyone would think Jake had fixed the drawing to make up for things. Does he have a new girlfriend here today? She'd never climb up on that baler, I bet. She'd never know what a sight

Jake used to be with his shirt off, sweat glistening all over him, the chaff from the hay sticking to his skin, his face streaked with dirt, but happy burned brown, his muscles standing out in long, smooth ropes, his stomach a series of those little ridges that made me lose my breath for a moment.

I remember the way he looked that summer he worked on the farm with his dad and Harlan, the way he'd come in to me while I was supposed to be helping the women with the food. They'd give me the worst jobs—skinning the tomatoes or plucking and gutting the fresh-killed chickens—but I wouldn't mind because he'd sneak off and come inside and grab me, pressing his heat against me, so when he left there was his damp outline down the front of me, and his mother and sisters would give me disgusted looks like I was trash on the floor.

I'd just shake my hair to get the hay flakes out and leave the smear of dirt on my cheek where they could see it. And without fail, one of them would snap at me, "Wash your hands," as I went back to my work at the sink. I let them do it. I waited purposely. I knew it made them feel superior for a moment, and then worse because they didn't, none of them, even the married ones, didn't have a man like that. But I was lucky to have had it even that one summer. I wouldn't have done without it, let me tell you. Maybe I can just remember *that* Jake—the boy who went away and in his place left this man, who isn't my type, anyway. He's more like someone in his family would marry.

31

Lost Causes

Talk to Sonny Boy," Clinton urges. "Ask him about that stuff Jasper told you."

"Shut up." I mean to say it under my breath like always but say it out loud instead.

Someone turns. "What?"

"Nothing, I wasn't talking to you, sorry." I push my way past the crowds watching the end of the parade. I've lost Jass, but after our last scene it doesn't matter. It *is* Sonny I have to find. Or Jake. They know. They can tell me. Clinton always warned me I'd end up tracking Sonny down instead of the reverse. He's always right, damn it. Damn him.

Looking through the crowd, I feel like I'm looking through old trampled snow, there are so many been this way before. How can I follow anything? It looks gray and used up, this life I'm looking at, and nothing big looming out there beyond us on the other side, where the highway leaves town, nothing but more farms and more towns and more people, with the litter that winter accumulates like an old ragpicker, lingering and collecting along the way. It's odd that I keep thinking of winter when it's a nice, hot spring day. I can't help it for some reason. Like I left something behind there, and I need to go back and get it before I can turn the calendar pages.

"You did." I hear Clinton's mocking voice.

"What do you want to be, Clinton, a weatherman or something?" I'm careful not to say this out loud.

"At least I did something about it," he reminds me.

"Yeah, great solution, Clinton. You leave me here alone, go off in that dim-witted way. For chrissakes, why'd you take your clothes off?" I've always wanted to ask him that, but we haven't had the kind of good clear channels we have today. I can tell it surprises him.

"It was hot, I guess."

It's such a stupid answer that I get mad and say out loud, *"What?"* The people milling around turn to look at me. I just keep walking, pretending that there was someone beside me a minute ago.

Clinton answers, "Yeah, I'd dropped some acid and got hot. You know how that stuff works. So I took off my clothes. It was a gas, driving along stone naked in the middle of January. I kept wishing you were with me. I remember that."

It pisses me off so much, I almost start to say something out loud again but catch it in the nick of time. "That's the damn dumbest thing I ever heard. I suppose you're going to tell me it was all a big accident now, a big mistake, right?" But when I say it, I can feel him fading like the reception is getting bad. "I can't hear you, Clinton—"

The transmission goes out completely. His voice is gone. I know he'll be back. We've been doing this for a long time. And he's just as frustrating now as he ever was alive. The time I tried to tell Twyla about him, about his voice in my head, she thought I was joking and put me off, saying, "Well, if you see him, ask him how he's hanging." When they tried to go to bed together, he'd always had too much to drink, he told me, couldn't get it up. We never had that problem, no matter how much we drank, but I think Twyla was so, well, beautiful that she affected men that way.

He told me, "Some women make you feel like you're in the army. You know, get it up, ready, aim, fire. On command. I have the same trouble with them I had in the army. I just hate doing anything on demand. That's what's nice about you, Honey, you never make me feel that way. We sort of slide into it."

I know what he meant, because later with Jake, and then a couple of others, it felt like I'd been inducted, the way their hand pushed against the back of my head, insistent, holding it down there, between their legs, making sure they could reach way down the back of my throat with their cocks, liking it when I gagged a little, pushing my head harder then, like they could reach into my lungs, into my heart, with their cocks, and they meant to. They didn't care what little marks they left, either. Afterward they'd always say, "Oh, that was great, Honey, just great." I always hated my name then. It was so easy for it to come out generic.

I'm feeling lower and lower as I push my way along with the crowd. I can't tell where we're going. My face and arms burn from the sun, and my throat is getting dusty and stiff from the booze. I don't see Sonny ahead. It doesn't matter. I'm getting tired of following him, anyway. Jass, too.

Every few yards there's a booth with folks milling like cattle in front of it. Beef on the hoof, that's all we are. And this town just a barn that hasn't been cleaned out in too many years, and there's all this muck you stand knee deep in, sloughing your way through just to stay alive. I'm fed up with the whole thing. I want to shove it and leave, like Jass is worried about. But what's going to make it different someplace else, right? Who knows, maybe Clinton's been right all along. It nags at me. That idea of driving your car out of town—to Spirit Lake or points unknown. What difference would it make?

Like the story Clinton told me of the girl who sat in her library and built a circle of books around her so she could escape. She stole barium chloride from the high school chem lab and swallowed it. Took her a while, but she made it through. I've always wondered, you know, what it took to do that. I've always been too scared to take anything, though I've thought about it once in a while. Don't we all? The same as having too many drinks and trying to drive your car home when the bridge abut-
ments are winking and joking with you. A part of me wants to, it really does, but I'm always too chicken. I hate pain. I wouldn't mind dying, but I don't want to be hurt. I imagine Clinton swimming like a pale fish in the car, making the decision that moment the air is running out that he won't unroll the window and swim up. His eyes get big and happy as he lets go of the breath he's been holding and starts breathing water. It might not be that hard. If it just didn't hurt.

"Hey, Honey, did you see they put your old place on a mug? Over there—they're selling them." A voice and a hand on my arm, then it's gone. I press through a little, trying to get to the booth where the mugs might be. At the little wooden counter, there is a whole display of them, hanging by their handles along the sides and top. Sure enough, the old farm Julius lost. Then I notice the others, printed in Kelly green on a creamy ceramic surface, with the dates and names like an obituary on the reverse side. The oldest places around here.

"You want to buy something?" the man behind the counter asks me. He means that if I don't, I should get the hell out of the way so someone else can.

"Sure, I'll take a mug of the old Parrish place. No, make it two.

Wait, no, make it . . . oh, make it four. I might break one or two." I'm tempted to buy some for the rest of my family as I fumble in my pocket for some dollars. But maybe it doesn't mean the same thing to them. Maybe they never set out walking there. Besides, they all have money of their own these days.

"Here, I'm all out of bags. You'll have to take them the way they are." He hands me all four mugs and the change at the same time.

While I'm juggling and silently cursing the man behind the counter, a hand touches my elbow and steers me like a car out of the way of other people crowding to buy mugs. I turn to look when my shoulders are clear. It's Jasper.

"Want to put something in those?" he asks me. For some reason his voice sounds low and musical. Like some cowboy movie star. It almost makes me want to ride off into the sunset with him.

"Sure. What've you got in mind?" As I answer, he reaches out those big, delicate hands. I could fall in love again just for those hands. I put the mugs in Jass's hands, noticing how easily they nestle there. "Now what?"

"C'mon." The crowd's so thick that we can't walk side by side. Although I'm relieved Jass has come along, I keep getting the feeling that I'm forgetting something.

As I follow him, I notice the weave of muscle under his shirt, the way his back tapers into his narrow waist and hips. Cheap thrills. That's what Clinton calls it when I watch men.

Jass is different. Of course, I can always find something good to say about a man. Twyla claimed that was my problem—I took Will Rogers to heart. But there is kindness in him, the way he touches an animal, the way he stuck to his work, his dream, but not at other people's expense.

"Besides," I whisper to Clinton, who reappears with that knowing snicker he gives just before I make another man-mistake, "besides, I have a right to some of it, anyway, cheap thrills or not." And to prove my point, I reach out and tuck my fingers in Jass's back pocket. The jeans are snug, and I can feel the hard buttock muscle as he moves. He reaches back with an empty hand to squeeze mine. "See, Clinton, it doesn't have to be only one thing." I notice Jass's walking with a limp.

"Ah, the pity factor," Clinton says.

At Larue's we go around to the back to sit on the white wooden steps. Downstairs, there's a big bingo game going. The Catholic church is mad, of course, because they see themselves as having the corner on that market. But Larue says there's room enough for more than one game in this town. Just like an old western movie. Only in those there always turned out to be room for only one game. She went ahead, though, and started her marathon bingo game, winner take the grand prize of a weekend in Las Vegas, with little hourly prizes thrown in of meat, appliances, gift certificates. I'm surprised the merchants haven't complained about being hit twice for bingo prizes, but I guess they know better than to turn down either Larue and her influence or the church and its.

She's moved the poker game upstairs for the weekend.

"Here, sit down. I'll be right back." Jass puts me and two of the mugs down at the bottom of the stairs and climbs up the back. I don't know what he's up to, but it feels good to sit after the heat and throb in my head from the tequila and our fight. Larue's backyard is full of fresh green grass and spring flowers. The trees and bushes separate it from the neighboring buildings, and like Boardman's it gives you the feeling that you're out of town with the lilacs nodding along, sending their heavy scent up and about the yard, like walking through lavender water, not air, and the pear and cherry trees blossoming. A little farther back, tucked under the trees, there's a table and chairs, like out of one of those old paintings. That's where I imagine sitting with a bottle of wine and two glasses, a man and a woman, in summer clothes. He'll be earnest and attentive, leaning toward her, but she'll be a little cool and distant, leaning back, making him work for it.

That's what Twyla called it, "making him work for it. Don't let a man ever get it easy, then they don't want it." Maybe that was what went wrong with Jake and me. I tried too damn hard to do it his way. He never had to scrabble along on hard stuff and get his knees or hands scraped up. It was Jake this and Jake that, and when it got too easy, he left. I should have seen that coming. I mean, nobody wanted something they could have.

"We all got to desire something," Clinton says. "Man is filled with desire."

For a moment, I realize, there is almost nothing as good, as satisfying, as an Iowa backyard. Desire or not. You just hang there, like smoke, and nothing comes along for a while to push you on. The good smells coming up out of the ground, off the trees, and the light just so, doesn't hurt you any, and you can almost go to sleep to the lazy rhythm of the bumblebees making their slow, heavy way from flower to flower, the *whooo whoo* of the mourning dove on the peak of the roof, or the quiet chittering of the sparrows. At that moment, I don't have any desire.

"Sorry it took so long. The game's really heating up, Archie's raising the stakes. He's a thousand down right now. You should see those guys, worse than the guys on the track. At least that's usually for fun." Jass lines up the two mugs and pours champagne out of the bottle in his hand. It's good stuff. Not the junk they serve at bars and weddings around here.

"Where'd you get this?" I ask as he hands me a mugful, the little bubbles winking like stars along the lip.

Jass just smiles, holds up his mug, and when I tap it lightly, he says, "To us, to spring, and to this godforsaken town. I don't know how it managed to last this long, but I hope it can do it again. At least long enough so our grandchildren can sit around and toast us a hundred years from now." We drink. It tastes so cold and good, the bubbles tingling my teeth and tongue, washing out my mouth, then sliding down and dancing into my blood and right back up to my head, spreading through me like a warm hand over the oily layer of burn from the tequila.

"Nice." I nod to him.

"Archie brought in a whole case of it for Larue, and she's busy handing it out as she sees fit. At least that's what she told me. She always liked me . . . I mean, you know. Larue takes to some people. And I guess she took to me. I don't pay her or anything." He's blushing like crazy, and I laugh and take another sip. Then another.

"Anything? She's getting generous in her old age, then."

Jass gets redder still, takes another gulp of champagne. "Oh that. Well, that was a long time ago. You know, just helling around. Besides, Larue doesn't hardly ever take money from a man. It's different."

"Like what?"

He looks down at his boot toe. It's been stepped on in the crowd, and he sticks a finger in the wine and brushes the liquid across a scuff. We both watch it darken for a moment.

"Oh, you know. Favors. A man feels grateful and does her favors. 'It's better than money,' she says. I think she makes a couple of 'em pay. Especially someone like, say, your boss, Bowker."

"Bowker?" I take a big gulp of champagne, choke, and feel good when he puts his hand on the back of my neck and holds my head steady for a second.

"You okay?" His voice is so kind, not like earlier at the house, I feel like crying.

I nod, and he goes on sipping his champagne and looking out across the yard, drawn in the way I am. His breathing gets lazy, and I think both of us wish for a blanket to put on the grass that will still have winter dampness in it.

"Oh, Larue gets value for her labor. If she sleeps with someone like Bowker, she's making it pay. She's got a pretty expensive life here. Not getting busted. Besides, I think she gets a kick out of being with old men like him. They aren't much trouble, you know. Zip it down, shoot, zip it up."

He's grinning meanly at me while he says this, like with my past, I must know all about it. I almost throw the rest of the champagne in his face. Instead I drink it down and hold out my glass for more. "Don't waste good wine on jerks," Clinton advises.

Still, I can't let him get away with it. "Don't be an ass, that's disgusting. And anyway," I say, "how the hell would you know? Does Larue discuss her sex life with you? *Or* her business life?"

He's still smiling as he pours more wine for me, then for himself. When he sets down the bottle, I can see the French label and know the bottle must have cost more than I used to spend on groceries in a week for Jake and me, and we're drinking it out of cheap ceramic mugs with a blurry green picture of some old Iowa farm on it.

"Tastes the same out of mugs as glass, you know. Don't let the labels phony it up for you. Good stuff is good stuff." Jass is sounding suspiciously like Clinton at the moment.

"You're just avoiding the subject of Larue. How the hell do you know so much about what she thinks?"

He watches me over the rim of the mug as he sips. "Men's intuition," he says after he swallows. "Let's just call it that." Then he laughs this silly champagne laugh and winks.

"Bullshit!" I giggle.

We tap our mugs in mock salute, drink, laugh, and he says, "Yeah, I know."

At least he's honest. Like the way he came and confronted me at the house. Awful, but at least he tried. We look out across the yard that has taken on that late afternoon heat and smell of things coming out of the ground, drawn out by the first few hot days.

"You got a sunburn today," he remarks finally, almost when I've forgotten he's sitting here, a step higher than me. Upstairs, the sounds of gambling whoops and downstairs the sounds of winning cries mingle with the lazy feel the champagne has given us, until it seems almost like we must be listening to birds and animals in the woods, not something coming out of Larue's house.

"Couldn't you stay here like this? I mean, it's so soft, so nice." I turn to look up at him again.

He watches me for a moment, his pulse fluttering in the vein like a small animal trapped at the base of his throat where his shirt opens, making me want to put my mouth there for just a moment, to touch it. I look up into his eyes, and it confuses me. They're so, well, *there*. It makes me feel naked and young again. When I look away, embarrassed, he puts his hand on my shoulder, and I can feel the warmth seeping through my T-shirt like another sun. I know I'll carry the print of that hand home tonight. Then he leans down, and with those lips that seem too soft for a man, too understanding for someone like me, he kisses me, gently, the way we would have done it as kids. Somehow it makes me sad that we didn't know each other then, and now I'm too old. Spoiled by Clinton, like he tried to say earlier. I've been married and taken by so many things that I'm not young. I can't bring anything like myself to him. I push away from the kiss, shaking my head, feeling the tears coming up the back of my nose and throat. "No, I can't."

He looks startled, leans back, takes a speculative sip of the wine, his eyes cooling off. It's like watching the sun setting.

"Why the hell not? Got someone else?"

Sometimes when you want to talk the most, explain yourself, it seems to overwhelm you. Like trying to drag a barge up a canal with a

thread tied to your tongue. You just know how impossible it is even though you give it a couple of tugs just to show you're trying, at least. So I do. I stumble around, then say, "Oh, Christ, I just feel so old, Jass. I'm older. Even though you're older in age, I've been married, divorced. I just feel so old. You're right, too—about Clinton. I don't believe he killed her, but he knows who did. And he . . . loves me . . . and I—I still love him . . . I guess."

He shakes his head and takes a quick drink that drains the mug in an efficient way. Then he pours out the rest of the bottle into our cups. He's drinking in that male way now, getting it down fast and hard so it hurts and those feelings come twisting up so mean you just got to punch someone, you just got to make something happen real fast and hard. I hate watching men drink that way. All my life I've lived with broken doors and smashed windows, dented cars and trucks, women with bruised arms, black eyes, from that kind of drinking. I'm tired of that part of it, and it makes me so blue, thinking about what I decided earlier—getting out, following Clinton or not.

"I don't know how you ever got the idea you knew everything. Who ever told you that? You don't make decisions about me. You don't know a thing about me. It's not like I asked you to get married. Relax, can't you lay back and enjoy it like before?"

Before I can answer, he takes a big male swig of the wine and grabs me, pulling me hard into his arms, and I can feel a wet spot where the champagne swings out of the cup onto the back of my shirt with his gesture, and then he leans down and kisses me again, hard and experienced. He presses so hard, his teeth bite into my lips, but not hurtfully, then soft while his tongue outlines mine. Then hard again and soft. I hardly realize he's stopped until I feel his hand on my back again, pulling at the wet cloth sticking to my skin. When I open my eyes and remember to breathe again, it comes awkwardly. Sometimes you just want to stop when things reach a point where they don't look like they can get any better. When I look at his face, he's smiling. He's right, and we both know it. Damn.

"Okay, okay. I guess you're not a virgin after all," I concede, "But—"

"No," he interrupts. "I don't wanna hear any excuses."

There's a silence then, and I'm feeling scared that this might get in the way of my resolve. I'm sick of the whole thing, too, and it seems like the only thing to do is to leave. I can't give up Clinton. Isn't it just like life to keep offering you desserts, when you're starving, just starving, for something solid? Icing, that's what Clinton calls it. Sometimes all you get
is sugar to eat. God knows that can make you sick as a dog.

"I know what you're thinking," he says. "But you're wrong. Sure, I've slept with some other women since we broke up, but I always meant to come back for you. I was waiting. Thought you'd come and tell me about it. Trust me. Boyd did. I went through hell for you, Honey." He taps his chest with his fingers. "So I don't want to hear any BS about you being divorced. I knew you weren't cookie clean, right?" He grins and reaches for my crotch.

I pull away and stand up, furious at his hand touching me there. "You think it's so easy? You dump this on me about Clinton, someone I've spent most of my life with, and then I'm just supposed to lie back and spread my legs? You *forgive* me for knowing stuff I don't have a clue about. You make me an accomplice to assault and murder, saying that's okay? Are you crazy, do you really think anything in Divinity is okay, right? The only place that happens is when you're *dead*, you hear me? Dead. Clinton's got it right. Working for that old fart Bowker who can't keep his hands off me, feeling like the town toilet because of this man and that. Christ, I'm so fucking sick of it. I'm *waiting* for *you*—or any other man—to *forgive* me? You're crazy—just like the rest of 'em—another arrogant bastard!"

I can't hear anything but the roar of that water coming over my head, and I get up, throw the mug, and turn as it arcs across the green into the sun, throwing a rainbow of liquid in front of it, the old family farm disappearing. I know I'll never get back there now. Just the way I've known since I was a kid that I'd keep losing everything that meant something, and that life isn't going to offer me much more than that. Family. Love.

I don't turn to look back at Jasper but take off running, ignoring the way he calls after me. Though my heart wants to believe he wants me to stay, I just can't. Not now. In a minute I'm out in the crowd again, heading like the rest of them over to the park on the Mercy River. I keep wishing I'd feel that big hand on my shoulder again. I keep wishing he'd come along and pick me up like Rhett Butler in *Gone With the Wind,* but I know instead he'll be long past that moment, and like Rhett, he's fed up. "Frankly, my dear . . ." I can never finish the line because it seems too true. And I've always known it to be.

32

At the Mercy River

At the park, I dig bills out of my pocket and buy food and beer tickets. I can still feel the hard print of Jass's mouth against mine and the tingle of his fingers between my legs. I want to wipe them off, drink them away. I can't afford to let them stay there. I'm careful to keep my distance from everyone I know and let the wine and tequila carry me over to where the cans of beer float like apples in the big iced stock tanks. We're trusting. We believe people will pay when they're asked to. So we do. I reach in, shocked by the icy water on my wrist, and pull out a Blatz, feeling the cuff of cold that reminds me of something else.

"It was like that. It burned me, it was so cold. I couldn't get over it. I wanted to feel what it was like, you know, to feel what it was like to feel something finally," Clinton says. I know I should listen, but the alcohol, the high pointed place I've been able to climb up to, won't let me come to where he is. So he just floats out there, bobbing up and down in his car like an apple, like beer in the tank, like another chunk of something that will sink along with the rest of us after a while.

"You should be here, Honey. You should try this. I kept wishing that night that you were here with me, that we could be kissing and making love in the car while it went down. Wouldn't it be funny, I was laughing to myself, to die coming inside of her. I wanted them to find me that way, with a hard-on."

I want to start yelling at him, but I know I shouldn't. Then I want to get rid of him, drown him out. I drain the beer, and without looking around me, I grab another, snap it open, and take a big gulp.

I don't hear him come up behind me. "Getting into life around here, I see."

"What?" I whirl too fast and lose my balance a little, tilting too close to him, so he has to reach out and catch my arm. I don't like the feel of his hand and shake it loose.

"Holding a grudge? I should be the one to do that. You haven't called since I've been in town. I saw you at the parade with that colored fellow. Now you're drunk. Getting to be just like everyone else around here, aren't you?" I hate the way his handsome face looks at me like we used to look at the others.

"What do you want, Jake?"

"What do I *want?*" He walks over and fishes out a beer, pops the top, takes a swig, and watches me. "What do I want. Well, Honey, I just want to see how you are. I just want to tell you that I still want to be friends. I just thought you might care enough about me to want to know how I'm getting along, but . . . well, I can see that you've become part of the scene here. You don't give a shit about anything. My family tried to tell me. But no. I kept saying to myself, Oh, she'll settle down. She's not a bad girl when all is said and done. Then I see you like this, falling-down drunk, stinking like a goddamn brewery, sleeping with half the old men in town. Just like before we got married. Christ, my family—"

"You'd better just shut up now, goddamn it. I'm sick of you and your fucking family, and you and your fucking ambition, okay? You didn't mind living off me when you felt like it. You didn't mind hanging out at the bars, shooting shit with every drunk in town. No, you didn't even mind going to Vietnam, did you? You shithead, you *liked* it there! And Clinton told me how you were in the car, shooting the gun the night that black girl got killed. And I wouldn't listen. I thought you were upset because you got blamed for some stupid mission that went down the tubes and you ended up getting busted and shipped out. But no, it was because *you* killed that girl, didn't you?"

It's a wild guess, and I'm watching him and draining the rest of my beer, trying to keep my hand from shaking when the can hits me in the face, jamming against my lips and teeth, smashing my cheek so hard that I fall down for a minute to my knees, not knowing whether it's beer or blood that's dripping down my cheeks. Then there's all these hands on me, helping me to my feet, putting icy towels to my face and dabbing at my shirt front, which is filling up with red. When I look around, dulled by the pain that's starting, I see some men holding Jake off me, yelling at him while he jumps around, trying to get back at me.

Let him go, I want to say, let him go. We'll just finish it now. I don't give a shit. But I can't talk, not until I can locate how my cut tongue is going to work. Then a wave of nausea hits me, and I try to jerk away from the hands. When they look at me, they figure it out because finally I'm able to go back to the bathroom and puke into the toilet. The smell of the outdoor john, freshly limed, makes me sicker.

When I come out, I'm still dazed. I know I should go home, but I don't want to. I have to settle things. I insist I'll be all right and go to lie down on a blanket spread out away from things, with an ice pack on my face.

At one point Roger the vet comes over and lifts the cloth with the ice mostly melted, looks at my face and mouth, and shakes his head. "You'll be all right. Lucky the beer can was only half-full." We're both getting tired of patching me up at the scene of the crime, I guess. Next time maybe it'll be too late.

When I wake up again, more clear-headed, the sun is almost down, and the crowd at the park has grown considerably. Now there are other casualties lying around me sleeping it off or nursing hurts. I take my time getting up. I've forgotten about Sonny until I see the flash of his shirt again in the crowd. I wonder if I'll get it from him, too. I'm sure going to confront him. Someone's going to take the blame tonight. I hope Jake is gone, but I figure we'll have it out again later. Why not? Sleeping it off hasn't changed anything. I feel worse, in fact. Married to a murderer. Clinton didn't tell me that, of course, but Jake's response makes him seem guilty. My face feels like he used his fists instead of a beer can. I try to recall exactly what I said to him. About Clinton. The murder. Clinton's always getting me in trouble. But I can't blame him. He's just lonely, being dead and all. When I get there, I sure as hell have no intention of bothering with these jerks.

I'm trying to remember how it all got started and why I have such a rotten headache. Then it comes back about Jasper and the champagne. I ran away, as usual, and he didn't follow. As usual. The men I *should* be with always get fed up, and the ones I shouldn't touch with a ten-foot pole, I can't park my car for the way they hang around. I'm tired of the whole thing, wishing Twyla were here with me, wishing she hadn't gone.

I don't think it would've made any difference if I'd seen him coming, but it does startle me when Jass says behind me, "You're going around like an accident waiting to happen." When I turn a little too fast, my head gives an extra spasm of pain. I wince and grab the top of it with both hands. It's going to be a long night.

"Shit," I answer him.

"Should've stuck with me. I don't go around beating up women, at least."

I look out of the corner of my eye at his legs stiff as fence posts next to me. "Yeah, well, I'd have been okay if I hadn't had all that champagne to drink."

He bends down so I can see the cool glow of his face. "Well, I sure didn't tell you to put a couple of beers on top of that. Where'd you learn to drink, an eighth-grade slumber party?" He spits over to the other side of us. "Here, let me take a look at you." He gently frames my head with his hands and pulls it around to him.

"Ouch, take it easy. I'm not some horse, you know."

"Yeah, well, don't think I don't wish you were. Then I'd at least know what to do with you." Though his one hand holds me firmly in place, I can feel the gentle way he touches the swelling with his finger, picks up my lip and pulls it out a little to check on the cuts underneath. "Well, you can probably get by without stitches. Lucky. I got something like this a few years ago when a horse kicked me. God, that hurt. Had to have my upper lip put back together. Cut the hell out of it. Bled so much you'd think I was dying." His hands linger on either side of my face. His eyes look so sad. Then he lets go of me.

"Thanks. I needed that. Can't you think of some more stuff to make me sick again?"

He smiles for the first time and reaches behind him. "Sure, here, have a drink."

"Oh, no. Come on, Jass, don't be—" I push the beer can back, but he urges it forward again.

"No, really. Take a drink. This works. It'll keep you from having a hangover. It's probably the only one of those theories about drinking that's true. Sure, the first sip's gonna kill you, but if you can keep that down, you'll be fine. Trust me. Go ahead."

I figure I'm not going to get a chance to turn him down. Besides, I do trust him. Hand on my pants and all. Damn it. So I take a big gulp and almost choke to death fighting it down.

"Take it easy, for chrissakes, do you have to overdo *everything*? I *said* a sip. A sip, goddamn it." For the second time that day Jass is keeping my neck company with his hand while I choke. When the beer hits my empty stomach, it threatens to come right back.

"Fight it, don't let it up," he urges, keeping his hand on my neck as I swallow hard a few more times. "Here." He brings a hamburger wrapped in a grease-soaked napkin from behind him. "Put this in there now. The food will help keep it all down, put it right again." When he sees me looking a little green and skeptical, he says, "Come on, Honey, I wouldn't hurt you."

When the hamburger stays down and my stomach starts to settle, with little sips of beer to keep things in order, I say to him, "Look, I don't want you to come rescuing me all the time. I'm not some little wimp. Cinderella, Sleeping Beauty, whatever it is you think I am. I can take care of myself."

For a moment he looks surprised, then pissed off. "Who ever said you were? You think I want that kind of woman? Say, don't flatter yourself, lady, you're not *that* good-looking. I mean, you're no Raquel Welch or something." He's so mad, he's sputtering. Picking up the can of beer he set down while I ate, he takes a long pull. When he stops I can smell the whiskey he's poured in to jack up the beer. It's going to be some night.

"What's the matter with you? If Twyla came along and helped you, I suppose you'd say the same thing, right? How come you're so bent out of shape about men? I never did anything but be nice to you. Treat you like a woman. I happen to like you. So take this and put it on so you don't look like some asshole who managed to get beat up at the centennial picnic." He throws a white T-shirt at me, gets up, and stalks off, turning so quickly that a bit of the contents of the beer can spills on me.

"Thanks a lot," I call after him, and he gives me the finger behind his receding back. He sure has a cute ass.

"There you go again." Clinton's disgusted voice makes my head ring. "He had some aspirin for your headache, but you pissed him off so much he forgot to give it to you."

"Oh, fuck off."

"Sure, that's easy for you to say." He's beginning to feel sorry for himself.

"Come on, Clinton. Leave me alone. I've got a hangover, I've got half the town's men pissing-in-their-pants mad at me. Just take a hike for a while, will you? I'm trying to clear your name while I have a chance, so give me a break."

I try to get up, and on the second try I make it. Then I stumble over to the john, waiting briefly in line behind two little girls who keep staring at the blood down the front of my shirt with those big, condemning eyes. Just wait till it's your turn, I want to tell them, but the throb in my head makes me afraid to risk opening my mouth.

Once inside, I slip out of the ruined centennial T-shirt, throw it down the hole, then watch it lie there, the pink lettering fluorescent. So much for Bowker's money. Then I take a look at the new T-shirt. On the front, printed in big letters so no one can miss it, is SWEETHEART OF THE RODEO. Below is a picture of a big-breasted cowgirl shoving up her puckered lips to kiss a bronc, whose cartoon eyes have a question in them. That does it. I take a longing look down the hole again. Sure enough, the other shirt is still there. I pull the T-shirt over my head, taking care not to snag it on my swollen lips, then smooth it over my chest. It's a little too small. My braless breasts are perfectly outlined. I'll kill him for this. I really will.

I practically tear the handle off the john pulling it toward me, until I realize that it swings out, and when I jump down, the jar of landing on the hard ground reminds me of the headache, which sends shooting pains through the bone in my jaw and teeth. "Screw it," I say to no one in particular, leaving the little line that has formed outside pulling back, out of the way. Behind me I can hear the word *drunk,* and I put an extra swagger in my stride.

Actually, the beer and hamburger are beginning to help, if I can just find some aspirin. Jass. He has them. I'll have to find him or one of those

women who carry aspirin in their purses for those times. As I approach the main picnic area, it's harder to get through the people, so much is going on. A rock band is swinging along, and some of the younger people are trying to dance in their half-drunk way on the grass and sloping ground. Churning around them are a lot of people who are beginning to have trouble standing up. And everywhere you can see the flash of light against beer cans and hear the high hysterical laugh of people having a good time. Closer to the street, there's a horseshoe contest going on, and in between songs you can hear the ring of a shoe against a stake and the cheers of the older people lining the path the shoe will take.

As I stand there, Boyd Ziekert comes over, a beer in his hand, which he offers me. I hesitate, then take it. What the hell. "Your brother Sonny's looking all over for you." As usual, he seems to take everything in the same casual, almost indifferent way. He isn't going to stroke out like the others. I can feel him probing my face with his eyes, so I take a quick drink of the beer, making a sour expression as it threatens to come back up.

"Face okay?"

I nod.

"Better stay out of his way. He's spoiling for it tonight." I nod again.

Boyd looks around for a moment, at folks yelling and dancing, hugging and eating, and falling down. It looks like some crazy, evil ceremony the way the light from the bonfires and the street lamps casts shadows up into the trees and down along the surface of the Mercy River, which glitters like precious metal tonight. Mama would've said it was the devil's dance and probably made us go home.

"I don't know what's gotten into folks tonight. Look at 'em. Acting like they just got out of jail or something, the way they're whooping it up. There, over there, isn't that Nick Silver from the bank with one of his tellers? Now what's his wife going to say when she catches him? And Buckler from the hardware. I'm a little surprised at some of these people. They put the teenagers to shame. I suppose I'll be up all night scraping them off the highway, too. Damn. I was hoping to get up early and do some work in my garden. 'Full moon, time to work on the things that leaf.' Damn." He spits off to one side and stands beside me with his arms folded, watching the townspeople going a little crazy.

"You growing any herbs, Sheriff?"

He gives me a quick glance and smiles. "Yeah, quite a few. That's what I use for seasoning. Do all my own. Organic. Have to order the seeds from a special organic mail service out of California. There's another in Vermont, but I sometimes get the feeling they don't care as much. One year I bought savory from them, and a bunch of wildflowers came up instead. Now I'm thinking about doing that." He gets that faraway expression a person gets when they're looking at a thing they really care about.

"What?"

"Oh. Planting my whole yard, the front, in wildflowers. I'm sick of mowing and watering. What's the point? Wildflowers, the way it's supposed to be."

He smiles at me, and I smile back, take a sip of beer, letting it trickle down and settle gently in my stomach. I'm starting to feel a lot better. The headache is only a thin line from ear to ear now. "I never thought about it, but you're probably right. I hate mowing the lawn, too."

"Yeah, the only thing is your neighbors go up the wall when they see the lawn turn into a field. Be pretty, though. They got it all figured out for you, the selection. 'Meadowlands' for full sun and 'woods' for shade. You get flowers all season. I'm thinking about it."

"Sounds nice, Boyd. I might try it myself."

He scrutinizes me for a moment. "You figure out about that girl yet?"

"I'm working on it. Since when did it become my job, anyway?"

He smiles his sheriff smile, the one where the lips press together and the corners of his mouth turn up, but you don't know whether it's good or mean, what he's smiling about. "Oh, I figure since you're in the middle, you must know how to get the answer. And I figure you owe me, too. For something . . . I'll figure that out later."

"Great."

"Well, you're probably the only person in town who can find out. The only one I can force into it, that is."

He's smiling again, but I don't know whether to be angry or glad. "You got a mean streak in you." He laughs and slaps me gently on the back.

"Took you this long to find that out? Everyone makes that mistake. They think because I eat vegetables I'm pussy, pardon the expression. Thing is, I don't like just one little mean, I like big general mean. You know, stomping a whole crowd of evil, lawbreaking sons-a-bitches. I don't give out traffic tickets. I take the whole frigging car and shove it into the river."

"What have you been drinking, Boyd? I need some of that."

He chuckles and pats his chest. "No, I'm sober, I just been watching

too many *Kojak* reruns. The only problem with things around here is that I never get much of a chance to be real mean. Gets me a bad reputation, all these good folks who won't break the law large enough for me to come out and hang their hides up. I keep having to send the dumb deputy. And that leaves me with nothing much to do but grow my garden. Oh, well, it could be worse," he sighs.

"Sure. Well, I'll see what I can do to start a crime wave for you. I better go now, though, I have to see some people. Thanks for the beer, it's starting to put me back on my feet."

He waves me off, and I slip over in the direction where I've seen Baby and Leigh Hunt, perched among the huge pillows he's brought in and set up on the ground for them. The Fats are all collected around having a feast that would do credit to Henry VIII. From a distance they resemble a bunch of flabby old bears rummaging a garbage dump. Now that Baby has lost some weight, it isn't as easy to spot her among her friends. She isn't the fattest anymore. Leigh Hunt is working on the title now. When I sort them out, I find her, half reclining among the pillows, looking up into his eyes with that sickly sweet expression, while he drops handfuls of green grapes into her open mouth. She looks like a giant baby owl.

I'm standing there for a minute before she sees me. She heaves herself into a sitting position and smiles. "Hi, Honey. Want something to eat?" She waves her hand over the half-eaten platters of food in front of her.

"Oh, no. Are you having a meeting? I mean, am I interrupting?"

She laughs and motions me closer. When she sees my face, she asks, "What in the world happened to you?" Then she motions me to sit down by her. I drop to my knees, but when she catches sight of the T-shirt, she asks, "Honestly, Honey, is that *yours?* Don't you think it's a little too . . . *small?"* She giggles, only louder this time, and looks at her fiancé to share the joke. He laughs, too, his belly going up and down like it might start making a hole in the ground between his legs if he isn't careful.

"Jake threw a beer can at me, cut my lips, and then the blood, and—"

"No, no. Don't tell us any more. We're eating, can't you see that?" She's still laughing, throwing little looks around the group to catch them all up in the joke. I'm used to it, so I don't even want to belt her.

"Have you seen Sonny?"

She shakes her head. "No, and I don't care if I do."

Under my sunburn, I blush, and my throat tightens up to feel the stares of her crowd on my ridiculous shirt and face. Judging from the way I look, I suppose they think she's right.

I get up. "Well, I got to go now. See you. Not later, I guess, sometime, maybe. Oh, who the hell knows." I just wave them off and leave, draining the last of the beer as I walk and tossing the empty over my shoulder. I hope to hell it hit one of them. It's silly. You can't avoid a whole family in a town our size. It seems like the more you try, the more you run into them. She's going to learn that the hard way—just like I did.

Then I'm in front of the horse tank, grabbing another beer, this one not so cold since they can't keep up with the consumption anymore.

"Hey," he says, and I know the voice without turning around. "Where you been? I been looking all over for you. I have to tell you something, come over here." When I turn, Sonny is standing under a tree behind me, pressed against the trunk like it's holding him up. I know he's been drinking, but somehow he still looks sober. In the half-dark, I can't make it all out clearly. There's something peculiar on his face, something I've been noticing all day but not understanding.

As I get close enough, he grabs my arm roughly and pulls me against the trunk next to him. It reminds me of when we were kids and used to hide from the adults when it was time to go home. We always thought we were invisible, and our parents always found us, pressed up against those tree trunks, standing taller and straighter than normal, like we thought that if we *looked* like trees, then we would be.

"Are you hiding from Rose?" I guess it was the memory of being kids or maybe the smell of the tree bark that makes me feel like I can question him so directly.

"Not exactly," he says in a muffled voice. And then I smell the whiskey and beer sour on his breath and the sweat that rises up from his body. Then there's something else, something I can't place. He frightens me, the way he's pressing himself against the tree bark. It must hurt. I keep thinking that, It must hurt, even as he pulls me over next to him, my body outlining his perfectly like we've been cut out by a giant cookie cutter and dropped off one at a time. Now we fit together, even though he's much taller, and I can feel the ridges of tree trunk like bony fingers pressing uncomfortably against my kidneys and shoulders, and still he drags me closer.

It scares me more because there is something I want to get away from, not the beer cans that came bouncing out of the car window like flying saucers to bang against the metal trailer at night, not the names he screamed at me as his car whirled and spun in the dust of the road, and not those memories of so long ago when I found out things you should never know but always do somewhere deep inside of you. Not even that, not that.

I hear a sound, like a hiccup or a sob caught in the throat as he tries to hold it, and in the dark of the tree that sometimes catches the dancers under the streetlights or the bonfire's castings, I see the metallic thread of tears on his cheeks.

"What is it? What's the matter, what's happened?"

This time he tries to answer, "I can't—I have to . . . do it—Christ!" He almost shouts, and I get more scared.

"What's happened, Sonny? What's going on, tell me, *tell me!*"

His sobs are growing, but he tries to choke it out again, one hand over his eyes now, the tears seeping out from under. "Goddamn it, I didn't shoot her, that girl. I was only driving the car, my gun, but I didn't shoot—I'd never . . . Twyla knew, she believed, and now she's dead, and Ziekert wants to say I did it, but I didn't—it was Clinton, Honey, you got to believe me, Clinton."

I want to run away, I do. Everything in me says, Get the hell out of here, get the hell out, but I can't move a step.

He sobs a great loud wail, which makes people turn and look, but then the music rises up wailing louder, and he says, "Twyla . . . died. She's the only one knew the truth, she's dead. She's dead—"

"Don't. No. Don't say it. I know Twyla's gone. I don't want to hear it, don't tell me any more. You're lying about Clinton, aren't you, you always lied, you were the liar, goddamn you, you're lying now. Aren't you? Tell me you're lying. Oh, God, I hate you, I hate you—"

Sonny Boy tries to grab my arm, but I'm already away, oh, I'm away, and someplace, I can't tell where. It's down by the river, I'm walking and running, and in and out of the water, and crying, yes. Twyla wouldn't leave me here all by myself, no, she'd come back with the baby and set up house with her three men. They'd all be happy, and I'd come visit, oh, Christ, it couldn't be Clinton. And I want to drink the river, I fall down, and I can't reach the water, the hands that grab me, hold on, and it's Sonny Boy again.

"No," he says, "no, you have to come back, here, drink this." It's the real stuff, it burns a hole in me and I fall through it, and the rest of the night comes tumbling after me. Sonny and I sitting on the bank, drinking whiskey and crying for Twyla and Clinton, and then he passes out, just crumples, and I don't have the heart for it, so I get up and go to find something.

The party is getting darker and wilder, the fires heaped higher and the dancers drunker and the kids gone home to bed, and only the parents who want to stay with the shadows in their eyes like so long ago. And I can almost see Mama at the table with her friends, and I'm afraid of the bushes where Daddy will be with some other woman, and afraid of the people I know. Everyone looks like their eyes have been put out, they're so dark and their sweat glows, and around their waists they have the corpses of all their lives, all their loves and sadness tied with ropes, and they drag them slowly around the park. It's a job not to get tangled in that sorrow. Everyone with everyone else. The couples hard to see for the bodies piled up around them, and then Jake, and I call him a murderer and he . . . and then the whiskey bottle I hit him with in the mouth. I remember that contact of glass that makes it red. And he falls down and his sister and his friends and mine, and Jasper is pulling me away, away, and Boyd is trying to stop it, and the howling rises up and swirls around us like a cloud, a cyclone, and I can't tell who the noise is. We're all struggling, contending, and I step back. "They all did it," I shout at Boyd and the others. "They all killed the girl."

We look like boats on Spirit Lake as a storm comes up, and beneath us, I think when I walk on the water, is Clinton sitting in his car, and beside him, rocking a baby with no clothes on, is Twyla, and she's happy, her blond hair flowing out behind her like it's windy, but you know it's just water that makes it wave that way, and the final thing—that it's Clinton and Twyla, with that look of fond parents on their faces, looking down at their child, then out the windshield like they're on the road going someplace, and I start to yell, Wait, wait for me—oh, Christ, don't leave me here, but they can't hear, no one can hear me now, they're too far away, the car fading out of sight in the dark water below, and the water closes up on top of them, and someone—Archie Carlson, I think—is rocking me and saying something in a weird voice, flat sounds that don't belong to this place, but maybe they do because when I look up the moon has gone flat, too, and the sky like a stupid picture some school kid has made on paper, everything flat, and I start laughing because the whole place looks like a school kid's version of the world. Everything drawn inaccurately, no precision, and we all have to live in it, and the kid just walks away, goes on with his life.

"Thanks a lot," I want to say, and when I do, Archie says, "Oh, that's okay." I'm too tired to tell him it's not what he thinks. He half walks and carries me to his car.

The soft leather seats come up around me and let their breath out when I curl down into them, and then we are at Boardman's house. When I don't want to go in because the old man will be cross, Archie says, "He moved, he won't mind."

We go upstairs, and I ask him, "Is everyone dead now? Is that it?"

He gives me this weird look. "Just about," he says, and then he's washing me off in the bathroom like I'm a little girl, pulling down Boardman's old boxer shorts and taking off the silly T-shirt Jass has made me wear and going round and round with the washcloth, so it makes me sleepy, and then we're in bed and whatever he does is okay because I'm just a little girl and the adults do what they want. They always do, and if you think about the story where the kid gets to have a pony and do whatever she wants, then it doesn't matter, nothing matters. And when that gets too cluttered, I think of the moon. Finally I settle on that, and it's funny, because the way the bed is placed near the window I can see the full balloon of it hanging in the upper panes. Painted on, I figure, and try to understand how he got it to stay there, and then it starts getting larger and larger, like the moon's going to come into the room. After a while I realize that it's a head, first Archie's, but then Clinton's, and they're both bobbing up and down on the end of the bed, on the frame. It's funny, so I start laughing, and they all join in. I'm so tired, I think there's not much difference between all of us after all, and fade out. Archie's monotone is in my head somewhere, telling me the story of a giant rat that sells pizza and beer and has video games on the edge of town and a TV screen the size of a wall. It's a funny story, and I smile all night while that stuffed rat dances with Twyla and Clinton. They get more dancing than I do, but that's par for the course, I finally decide, and then Jass jerks me awake.

33

“Sweet Eyes”

“What the hell’s going on, Honey? I was worried to death about you.” Jass drags me out of bed, pausing when he notices I’m naked but taking an old wool bathrobe from the closet next to the bed for me. It’s scratchy, and I want to protest. I follow him obediently down the stairs and into the kitchen, where the garbage bag full of food has collapsed, leaking on the floor.

“What’s all this?” he asks, but answers it himself by snapping out a couple of new bags and dividing and stuffing the old one in them. I stand by in a daze, not wanting to move yet, because I know that when I do, it will all be true. I don’t think I can stand that.

After he gets them tied up, he lifts them both easily and heads for the back door. “Back in a minute,” he calls as he limps down the three steps.

I want to stay frozen there, but I can’t. The robe is so prickly, it makes me start shuffling. There’s a grocery bag shoved among the dirty dishes on the counter. When I peek in, there’s coffee, tea, fresh fruit, eggs, bacon, and bread for toast. What a busybody. Why doesn’t he just want to get laid like the rest of them? The sleeves of the robe keep getting in the way, so I decide to change. I’m just on my way up when Jass comes stumbling too fast up the three stairs and catches me. He doesn’t look happy. “Sonny Boy’s asleep out there. Passed out.”

Then I remember that I left him someplace last night. The riverbank, and Clinton. Jass grabs me as I start to let go, and it isn’t hard to cry into his shoulder. He hugs me and rubs my head. I just feel so bad.

In a few minutes I finish blubbering, and Jass quits rubbing the awful scratchy robe into the tender skin on my back and arms. "I've got to get out of this robe."

When I get back downstairs, I'm wearing one of Boardman's old flannel shirts, just big enough to be comfortable, and a pair of pajama bottoms I've found in a drawer. It isn't a great outfit, but it covers me, and my skin is feeling so tender now. I have to walk carefully because I'm afraid something might give out from under me, like my bones have been shaved down with a knife and are really too thin for my weight.

Jass gives me the once-over, like I need his approval, smiles, and goes back to making breakfast. He pushes a big glass of tomato juice in front of me and doesn't have to order me to drink it. As I sip, I notice it's peppery and strong. He watches me for a moment, then says, "For the hangover, takes the bite out. I'm making tea next." Right on cue the kettle starts to whistle. Even if he's a pissant, it's comforting watching Jass make coffee and tea, like the old days with Clinton and Boardman. I like being at the table again. It's lucky he's there because I feel so clumsy, like a person getting up after an operation. I know there are missing parts and my body will have to settle in again, fill in the holes, though I don't know what it does when your fingers get cut off. Not all of them, just the Clinton ones. It isn't sharp pains anymore. Just the ache that follows as it starts to get better and little twinges when you look down and realize your hands look different now. A regret that you hadn't gotten to know those fingers better.

"Eat this." Jass shoves a plate of toast in front of me, and my stomach flips up like a trout out of water.

I start to shove it back. "No—"

"Yes," he says firmly, and picks up a piece, takes a bite, and starts to put the rest in my mouth. God, a baby-sitter. Just what I need.

"Hey, stop that, damn it! I'm not some fucking horse, you know."

He laughs. "No, my horses take better care of themselves," and goes back to the stove, where he's scrambling eggs, putting dashes of this and that in them.

"Take it easy," I call to him, "you want to kill me?"

He chuckles. "In a way, yes, but not with the eggs. I have to eat these, too, and I'll be damned if I'm going to coddle some drunk."

"Hey wait a minute, you can't—" He's pissing me off, but he interrupts again, adding another dash of Tabasco to the pan of eggs. I wince.

"Yes, I can. You're lucky I'm here at all, the way you went crazy last night. But I'll tell you, that's about the last time I'll put up with that crap."

When I start to protest, he adds, "And don't give me any excuses. It's over and done." He slips a plate of eggs and bacon in front of me that look delicious despite my body wanting to give up the ghost. I'm too tired to argue, so I eat. He's right. One of those know-it-all men. The spicy eggs stir me up and get me rolling again. Watching him shovel in the big mounds of food across the table is good, too. He's eating like a pig, but he is a pretty sweet man. But I've been fooled before, haven't I? His face looks a little swollen, I notice then, and there's a cut on one cheekbone.

"What happened to you?"

He stares at me, then smiles. "You don't remember, do you?"

I shake my head. I'm afraid I might if I think about it much.

"There was a little fight last night. You went after Jake with a whiskey bottle, got him the way he got you, only worse, and by the time we got you pulled off, people were generally letting it fly anyway. It'd been brewing all night. I had to fight a couple of people who thought it'd be good to plant me or you."

"Reiler's men?"

He nods. "Boyd's got it under control now. They won't bother us anymore. Silky Blue and Jonesy made sure of that. Jake's gone for good,

too. He'll be an accessory to that girl's murder if he ever shows his face again. By the time I got done, though, you were gone. I just sacked out then. I was a little under the weather myself."

"Shit," I say as my mouth starts to wake up, and I remember the cut from the beer can. It's stinging like crazy. I'm feeling bruised and lumpy all over as I come more awake.

"Shit yourself," he answers, grinning and rubbing a swollen spot along his jawline.

"God, is this the way men feel after a hard night of drinking? Forget it."

"That and worse." He laughs again in a macho way I'm not sure I like.

Jass takes a swig of his coffee, looks out the kitchen window, then says, "I guess I was lucky when I got beat up last summer. I was used to pain." He fingers a red line of scar along his cheek.

"It didn't hurt your looks. Helps, in fact."

He looks at me, puzzled. "What the hell—"

"No, come on, most women like tough faces. Shows character or something, I guess."

He gives me a long look, not altogether friendly, and says, "You really are crazy, aren't you?"

"No, really, I like you *better* this way. Forget character, well, don't forget it. It makes you look handsome. That's it. Handsome."

For a moment he continues to scowl, then he laughs and shrugs.

We let the silence take us along for a minute. Maybe he is the one. Maybe he is. But then I'll still be in Iowa, won't I. And what about Twyla's advice: "Never trust a man with sweet eyes."

I clear my throat, and when he looks at me, I stare deep into his eyes, blue green today, so startling against his skin like burnished leather and black hair. Yesterday his eyes had yellow flecks in them. Today the smoke. I want to watch them change as we make love. Without Clinton around.

As I think about Twyla, I realize it's the first part of her statement that she always lived by: "Never trust a man . . ." As a result, she couldn't be trusted, could she? I can't see myself being able to take her place, follow her example. I'd rather be alone than deal with the products of her distrust: Tom, Sonny Boy, Wolfgang.

"God, you've got such sweet eyes, Jass."

He smiles. "Really? Does that mean I can come over tonight?"

I nod.

He gives an enthusiastic grin and grimaces.

"Hurts?"

"Yeah, I think that's the one Jake got me with, or Sonny. Christ, that sucker can hit. I got some sore ribs from him, too, I think." He rubs his side carefully, feeling a little sorry for himself in the process.

"Sonny was in the fight?"

"Yeah, but you couldn't tell whose side he was on. He just sort of jumped in and hit at anyone. That's what everyone was doing after a while. You know, Boyd was just standing around letting it happen at first. Not that I blame him. He was just shaking his head, taking little sips out of his coffee cup. Finally, he put down the cup and took out his nightstick and waded in. But it was funny, I kept getting glimpses of him. He sure didn't care if we murdered each other. I think it was late enough so most of the citizens had gone home. Maybe he figured we just needed to work off some energy, like bucking horses or something."

Jass and I are sipping our coffee and tea when we hear steps. I keep hoping it isn't Archie, and I luck out because in comes Sonny, matted with dead leaves and bits of grass and mud, looking for all he's worth like he'd been run over by a cultivator. He's holding his head, shaking it every once in a while like he's trying to clear out debris. When he comes into the kitchen, he mumbles something, but neither of us can understand him. "What?"

"Do ya got any coffee?" he says louder and more painfully, squinting like a mole driven out of its hole. When he pulls the other chair out from the table to sit down, I can see how unsteady he is. Then I notice that Jass isn't getting the coffee. He's just looking out the back way, toward the porch, like Sonny isn't even there. I don't blame him. I get up and pour him a cup and bring the pot over to freshen up Jass's, just to make him feel good.

Sonny tries to mumble something again. It sounds like "Thanks," so I nod my head and sit down. I can tell how hard it is for him to lift his head to talk. He sits there with one hand supporting his head, the other trying not to spill all the coffee while it travels a foot from the table to his mouth. It's pretty iffy, the whole thing.

For some reason, I have this urge to help him. I should know better, the way you always know things against yourself, like there's a little spy and a yes-man inside your head going all the time, yes-yes-yes to whatever the boss says, and the spy looking out for secret things, like wanting to help Sonny. But he does look like he needs something. I reach over and pull an old maple leaf off the shoulder of his shirt. Part of it's so rotted, it sticks to the damp cloth. When Sonny sees me do that, he gets this real pained expression on his face, then he crumples up. Just like that. Like someone has squeezed his whole head together into a fist, he starts bawling and honking to beat the band. It's enough to wake the world.

When I finally get him settled down, I notice that Jass has taken a walk. When he comes back, he has a warm beer and two aspirins, which he shoves in front of Sonny. Sonny turns pretty gray at the sight of the beer, but he opens it and starts gulping. It makes my stomach turn, but by the time he's done, he can talk and his hand's a little steadier. Most of the coffee makes it to his mouth this time.

"When you did that, pulled the leaf off . . ." He sniffles again but catches himself, bracing his back up, like the officer in his head tells him to do.

"You reminded me of Twyla," he sniffles. "She always cleaned me up. Never criticized. Just brushed my clothes off when I wandered in like this. Gave me something to get straight, sent me home after a while so Rose wouldn't get the troops out. She knew what a hard time I had of it. Twyla was such an understanding woman." It sure doesn't sound like the

Twyla I knew, the one who'd make Tom Tooley sleep out in his car half the time because he came home after midnight and she'd warned him.

But as I watch Sonny not even bothering to wipe the tears that have streaked through the dirt on his face, I can see how she'd find him a little more pathetic than Tom. Sonny Boy isn't a fool, at least. He's a man. A bad, crazy man a lot of the time, but he isn't a fool. Even after all he's done, I can't stand to see him so down. I want to brush his clothes off, too, send him home to Rose.

I notice that Jass is watching the porch again, like he expects Robert Redford or Meryl Streep to come strolling in any minute. Like he already lives here. We'll see about that. I get up and get more coffee, noticing that Sonny is getting stronger. Not so shaky.

"God, I miss that woman. Really *miss* her, you know what I mean?" He looks at me for a second. "I'm sorry. 'Course you know what I mean. She was your best friend, wasn't she? Mine, too." He takes a drink of coffee, then continues, "She ever talk about me, you know, tell you how she felt about me and our baby?"

He's watching me, and I try not to give away the surprise. "She kept a lot of that to herself. We discussed men in general most of the time. Not the particulars."

He buys it. That's the good thing about Sonny Boy. He's so vain, he doesn't notice a lot of things. We're all silent until Jass turns and says, "Tell Honey about the shooting."

Sonny shrugs. "Just what I said last night. We were screwing around, taking turns shooting at stuff. Drinking. Smoking pot. There was this girl, colored girl, standing in front of the Trailways sign. Four in the morning. A stranger. Clinton gets weird, says, 'Gimme the gun.' So Jake hands it to him. He was only trying to scare her. He hit her, though. Dead shot. Right in the head. She fluttered down like a piece of clothes off the line. We stopped, checked. She was dead. Clinton started losing it. We all got him back in the car and took off. God, we hated each other after that. Clinton was the worst. He went crazy. That's why he drowned himself." Sonny sips his coffee. "It was an accident. Tolson thought I did it. I had to beat him. Had to keep the others clean. It was an accident. I was driving. Twyla believed me."

I get up to get more coffee, even though Jass is staring holes through me. I think he's going to explode when Sonny looks over at my half-finished plate and says, "You going to eat that?" When I shake my head, he pulls it over and eats the rest.

"Why'd you attack Honey's trailer?" Jass asks.

"Trying to scare her into keeping quiet. I figured Tolson told her, and she'd tell on me. Tell on all of us. Besides, I just never liked her." He shifts his eyes to my face. "Never paid much attention when you were a kid. You were just there, under foot. Gettin' in my way. Then later, I don't know. You just pissed me off. Yeah. I guess I can't say why exactly. Just, well, I just didn't like you much. Then you stood up to Julius—sure changed *my* mind. Made me decide to take a chance and talk to you. Turned out okay, then, huh?"

After the plate's wiped clean with the last sliver of toast, Sonny brightens up more, rubbing his face all over with a paper napkin he finds crumpled up on the table and brushing off his clothes.

"That's it?" I ask.

"I can't go to jail, Honey. It'd kill me. If I lived, Daddy would kill me. You know that. You can't tell."

I look him over carefully. "I believe you, Sonny, but you know since you and Jake are the only two left, you can accuse each other and both go to jail. No one's going to believe you blaming a dead man. Your only safety is keeping on the straight and narrow, or I'm going to Boyd. Stay away from me. Stay away from Jass, you hear? Especially Jass."

Sonny Boy looks at Jass. "That was just having fun. We didn't mean nothing."

Jass nods. "Next time I'll kill you."

"Fair enough." Sonny laughs nervously and scrapes his chair back hard on the old linoleum, catching one leg in a hole that he gouges deeper by continuing to push. "Boy, you need a new floor—" He laughs as he stands up. "Give me a call and I'll come over and lay one if you buy the stuff." Halfway out the back door, he calls, "Thanks for the eats. See you all around," and clumps down the steps and away.

"Nice going, idiot," Jass growls at me. "Now we've inherited him."

"What about the beer and aspirins? And what do you mean 'we'?"

Jass looks hard at his swollen knuckles, then back at me, a little grin on his face. "Well, you know, that's man stuff. Guy could be a real asshole, and you give him his morning beer. I'd do the same for Jack the Ripper. But you don't have to feed the son of a bitch. That's the same as inviting him for good. Man like that, he goes where people'll take care of him. Rottener he is, the more he needs it. And you didn't say a word about not wanting that damn floor done."

I give him a level, neutral look for a moment. "What, *you* want to do the floor? Be my guest." I get up and carry the dirty dishes over to the sink. But the sink is too dirty and full to do dishes in. The sight of its yellow-and-brown puddles sends my stomach into loops, so I sit down at the table again.

"Well, Christ, Honey, I never even got a chance, you know? I'd do the floor. Hell, I'd even pay for the thing. All you have to do is ask." He looks embarrassed but reaches across the table for my fingertips. "It's just that Sonny's such an arrogant bastard. Always was. Treats women like they're dying to have him around. I guess they are. They don't stop him from doing the things he does. He treats you like he's king shit and he can dump it on you whenever he feels like it. Besides that, he's a drunk."

I try to pull my hand away, but he's ready for me. "No, you don't. That's the truth, Honey. He is. He's no better than Mike Jackson. Just that Twyla and Baby and a few others—Rose included—have been picking up after him for a long time. Hell, he's just lucky, I guess. Most of us have to pick up after ourselves. Now I can see him getting ready to move in on you, too. You wait and see. He'll spend half his nights here. If you don't let him sleep it off on the sofa, he'll be in the garage, in his car out front, or like today, in the backyard. I meant it when I said you inherited him. Twyla left him for you. I don't think you should let it happen."

He's right. I've sort of known it all along. The problem is I can't see what to do about it. Besides, Jass irritates me being so cocksure. "Let me
think about it, okay? I mean, too much has been happening. I don't know anything right now. I don't even know what to do about Clinton." It doesn't make sense, but it does. What's happened is sitting like a big mound of dirt I'm supposed to shovel, spread around. I just don't have the energy yet to work on it.

"Take your time, Honey. I've waited a year, guess I can wait a little longer."

It's so hard, partly because I feel like all my life I've been waiting for Sonny Boy, waiting for him to recognize me somehow, show me he cared, like a brother, like family. I used to feel so proud of him when I was a girl. He was big and handsome and strong. A good athlete. Popular. He was everything, and I just kept waiting for him to be something to me, like a big brother, the way they were in books and movies. They took care of you. They beat up kids that bothered you. They got you out of trouble. They helped you with the parents.

The one thing he did was teach me to dance. I remember him in the garage with me when I was thirteen. I was too embarrassed to let Baby or anyone see, and he took me out there and we set up the radio and he taught me to slow-dance. It worked. I remember that first dance in eighth grade when a boy got up nerve to ask me, we did the little square box Sonny Boy taught me. Each of us counting out the numbers under our breath, concentrating. One two three four, one two three four. By the time the music ended, both of us were red and sweaty from working so hard, and we forgot to say a word to each other. Dancing with Sonny was easier. He laughed and made jokes and didn't tease me about my clumsiness. But I remember what ended it, feeling the shadow cross over us, then looking up to see Baby in the doorway, her face flushed and angry, and Sonny pushing me away suddenly and snapping off the radio. "That's all."

I wish I could call Twyla to talk it over. I try to feel something about Twyla's baby, to work up some energy about it. I'd like to be the good friend, the one who takes the kid and raises it herself, but I know I can't. I'm past those times, I'm way past those times. It has to stay with Tom. Homeless already. Like so many of us, I guess. Funny, it has three fathers and no mother. There seems to be a kind of true thing about that, I decide as I sip my tea and watch the day gathering itself together outside. There are always more fathers than you need and not enough mothers. It was true in our family. We could have each one of us used a mother to ourselves. There wasn't ever enough to go around, and yet there was more than plenty with Julius as father. I think of what Clinton told me once: "There's always more."

"Honey?" Jass interrupts. "I have to get going, take care of the horses. Break out a couple of two-year-olds. You going to be all right now? See you later, okay?"

I don't want him to go like that. "Wait a minute." I get up and go over to him. He stands still while I put my arms around his hard body and my face against his chest. When I bend my head back to look at him, he leans down and we kiss. It hurts like hell. Both of us have forgotten about our swollen mouths and faces. "Ow—" We laugh and stumble back, holding our lips regretfully.

"Say, there's not much left for the horses to mash now."

"God, be careful," I admonish him, but he gets that look in his eyes men get when they want to let you know how tough they are.

"Oh, don't worry. It'll take more than an old horse to get me down."

I kiss him lightly on the cheek. He's gone to that place men save for themselves, where they all hang out together, not letting it show. "Sure, you're tough. See you later," I call as he leaves.

Suddenly there is nothing but the slight *whish* of air from the breeze blowing through the windows, a good warm spring to early summer breeze, and the ticking of the clock. I don't know, maybe I would've sat there all day if it wasn't for the phone ringing.

It's Boyd, telling me to meet him at Bob and Shirley's Cafe in twenty minutes. I'm glad Jass has gone home. I hope Sonny is sleeping it off at home, with Rose shushing the kids so he won't be disturbed. Rose. Suddenly I wish I could talk to her. There seem to be so many people I've never gotten to know who might have something to say. I've hardly even begun to know the people of this town; how can I leave and have to start all over with a whole new batch? Maybe there is a possibility here for a new study, I decide as I measure off the bare lengths of kitchen walls. This place might do nicely, it might work out perfectly. And this time I'll do it right. I'll buy poster board in colors, transparent Scotch tape, and a set of twenty-four—no, the whole boat, forty-eight Magic Markers in different colors. That will be a start, at least.

I want to ask Clinton what he thinks, but I remember what he's done. It makes me feel sick and weak. Now that I'm alone, I really am alone. Clinton is gone. I bet Boardman knew. He didn't have the nerve to tell me. Only Jass wanted to take it on. He had to, though. I could never love anyone else as long as Clinton was still alive. Now he's dead. A few hours, yet I don't feel miserable. I feel free. I feel sad—I'll miss him, but I like the silence better. Like I've lost a fifty-pound weight I've
been packing all these years.

Upstairs I kick at my pile of clothes until a fairly clean shirt surfaces and my other pair of jeans. I don't bother with the Obsession in the crotch routine. Let Boyd get a cheap thrill. Raw Honey. I will have to buy a bra first thing Monday. Can't go to work like this, hardly fair to Bowker's hormones.

Outside, it's another beautiful spring day, even though the streets and walks are littered with centennial debris.

34

Ordinary Dreams

It's ten o'clock in the morning when I arrive at Bob and Shirley's, and although it's Sunday, the place has a few people in it. People in for the celebration or people like me with hangovers and cut lips, looking for a little peace from home life. Simpy is behind the counter, smiling and humming to himself, working on a plate of something. When the menu arrives, there's a little typed note paper-clipped to the inside plastic cover. "Our son Simpson, who cooks here, has won a trip to France for best garlic recipe from *Gourmet* magazine. His picture and the cafe's will appear next month, along with the recipe. Another Divinity crown! Good luck, Simpson, love, Shirley and Bob."

When Simpy catches sight of me, he bustles over carrying a concoction on a plate that he shoves in front of me. It's red and white, mounds of cream whipped stiffly with a strawberry in the middle. My stomach rolls over. "Oh, I don't—"

"No, no, try it, just a bite." Simpy stands over me. He winks when I take a bite. "Pretty good, huh? I think it's the touch of Amaretto and nutmeg. Most people put Grand Marnier in. Next time I'm going to try a dash of Russian vodka, what they distill it with should bring up the flavor of those wild strawberries even more."

Suddenly as I watch him and listen to him, I'm struck by how much we are alike, Simpson and me. "Don't you ever get lonely, Simpy?"

He looks at me for a moment. "Sometimes. Then I get in a car and drive someplace. Visit a friend, or just go to a good restaurant. I usually meet people that way. I guess I've given up on the idea of ever finding a

. . . well, a 'soulmate' or something." His voice drops, and he looks away, back to the counter, where Bob and Shirley are working shoulder to shoulder on the morning's orders. For a moment, I wonder what that would be for Simpson. A woman? A man? What could he want? Maybe he doesn't know, maybe he'll never know. Maybe some people don't pursue that question the way I have. It must be lonely with Bob and Shirley, being the smaller piece of pie in between two large slices. In families it never comes out even, no matter how you divide it up. Maybe that's why Simpy took to cooking—at least he gets his share that way.

"What about you?" His question startles me.

"What do you mean?"

"Are you leaving? People were saying yesterday that now you're leaving—something about Marylou going, both of you quitting Bowker, and now with the house and money Boardman gave you . . ."

I shrug it off. "I'm not sure what to do right now." Then I remember Clinton and Twyla. I'm not trying that hard to put them out of my mind. They keep coming back, not in big waves like you'd expect when you lose your best friends, but in neat, razor-sharp jabs that cut clean through to the white bone beneath and leave me gasping. It always starts as a scratch and ends in an amputation. I won't be getting over this so easily.

"I have more of that," Simpy offers, like condolences, gesturing to
the plate.

"No, I'm really full, had a huge breakfast, too. I was just thinking about things." He reaches over and pulls the plate into the center of the table between us. We both look out the window, but nothing much is going on. It's Sunday morning, and folks are either crawling out of bed, holding their heads, in church, working on their farms, or getting ready for the day's celebration.

"Quiet," he remarks. We sit silently, watching the street, where it looks like nothing is going to happen until the hearse from Cramer's Mortuary comes driving slowly by. It seems to hang suspended for a long time in front of us, like one of those gas-filled balloons you get at carnivals that hangs in the air by your bed as you go to sleep at night and when you wake up in the morning is flat and sprawled out of shape when your feet land beside it on the floor.

"Bluegills," I hear Twyla say, and I almost laugh out loud at the code. Monday specials, old ladies.

"I miss her." Simpy's holding his head in his hands.

"What?"

"Twyla. She used to come in here, when she was working, take her break here. Run over for a bite to take back. We'd talk . . ." He looks up and sees the expression on my face. "Oh. No. I mean, I never, no, it was just—I admired her." He says it in that old-fashioned way people had of talking about Eleanor Roosevelt or Ted Williams.

"Besides," he continues, "she appreciated my cooking. I'm going to invent a special dessert for her, name it after her, with everything she used to like in it." He cheers up at the thought. "But don't tell a soul," he cautions.

"Don't worry, I won't."

Suddenly I feel myself looking at it, the table and our conversation, and the town, even, from a great distance. Like I could see it happening on stage, all at once. It isn't painful anymore. Just odd. Living here in Divinity. It isn't unlike anywhere else then. There are all these people with all their secrets, all their plans, all their living that's going on. You're a part of it for a while, and then you aren't. Like sitting at Bob and Shirley's waiting for Boyd, who is late, which is odd, and talking to Simpy, who is odd, and thinking about old-lady hair, which is also odd.

Then Wolfgang Reese's long black car slinks down the street in front of us, humming so low and silent you can almost feel how smooth it must be inside on the cool, good-smelling leather seats, Wolf's big figure of sorrow, silent and cool behind the wheel, fixed into that position by Twyla's death and by me being able to see him, though the windows are that dark glass. He can't name a dessert after her. He can't go sprawling his grief out into the bars and fields around the county. He can't even take the baby and grow up with it. Of all of us in Divinity, he's the one I feel most sorry for. He's the one who can't get out of the car, whose dark form slices through the town as soundlessly and viciously as a shark patrolling the waters.

"You don't understand Wolfie," Twyla used to say. "He's actually very sweet." And we'd both laugh as she raised a glass of champagne he supplied, which we always drank together afterward.

Simpy gets up and walks back to the kitchen.

In a minute the waitress comes over, and I order some water and a cup of tea.

I wait for another hour, but no Boyd. It doesn't matter. I'm just going to tell him it was Clinton. We'll all let it go at that. I wish Boardman had told me years ago, saved me somehow. Maybe it wouldn't have mattered, though.

Outside, the birds are warming up in the sun, the sky is clear, the breeze is blowing the honeysuckle and lilac and cherry blossoms down Highway 11 and out across the fields that are dark as chocolate, already a hint of green lingers over them like a haze you can't be sure of even when you shade your eyes, and the people look like people as they drive slowly to their houses from church, families of them, laughing in their cars, relaxing the stiffness of their dress-up clothes.

I feel a curiosity about them begin in me, about each and every one of them. About what they've felt, about what they've done, about what they are doing and feeling, hour to hour, day to day, year to year. Time. "Dig a musty bone," I once heard a teacher tell her class. "Stay in your own backyard and dig. Put your nose in the dirt, put your eyes to the ground, you'll find it. It's buried there, always right under your feet." When I'd asked Clinton what the hell she was talking about, he'd just shrugged. He didn't know. I figure he was right about something, though. Iowa *is* a state of mind.

So I'll just go home, walk the long way around. Look in the stores and windows. Listen to people's yelling and living coming out of their houses. Wait for Boyd. Take care of my family if they need it. Talk to Larue. Help Tom with the baby. He's going to need help, even if Wolf and Sonny pitch in, and who knows, they might. You can't ever know what's going to happen. Twyla always told me that. You can't predict, no matter what the prognosticators say. I can tell Baby that, but I suppose she'll just say, "I knew you'd say that." It must ruin the surprise for her, and maybe that's why she's been in such a bad mood all these years.

And what about me? I'm not leaving after all. I have places to live, jobs. More important, I have my new search—a family to assemble out of the town. Years later, maybe I'll finally see that this has always been a love story—Clinton's and mine, the family's, Twyla's, and now Jass's. And because it is a love story, it's a story of forgiveness, also. The town's and mine. We all need the waters of the Mercy River. Though they don't run deep, there's usually enough, just enough, for the extravagance of our lives. I wouldn't have it any other way.

Tonight Jasper and I will make love with our eyes open. I'll get to know his scars again, and he can get to know mine. Tomorrow I'll go talk to Boyd, and I'll feel bad, cry, even carry on for a while about losing Clinton. Then things will go on. No one will go to jail for that girl's death. Two of them are dead. Two are in exile. One of them remains here, in the town's custody. Archie Carlson will build his pizza parlor with the giant rat presiding, and parents will complain about their kids dumping all their quarters into the video games. Maybe Jass and I will live together or get married and raise horses, and folks will complain about that, too.

I guess the only thing I regret, I mean really regret, is Jake. I'll never get the chance to straighten it out between us. Who knows, maybe we said it all last night. I guess not everything falls evenly, predictably, into place at the end. There is always the fraying away of things, always the pieces that don't fit into something, no matter how you try. No matter how hard Clinton tried to make what he did not true.

Just when the corn is coming up good, the oats like slender green ribbons in the wind, and the first cutting of hay down drying in the hot afternoon, then the hail comes, the tornado howls up over the horizon from the south, flinging the grasshoppers, the drought, the days and days of flooding rain. And you sit indoors, feet propped against the cool enamel of the stove, wishing it were winter again, and all this just possibility under the snow, waiting to be thawed and plowed and planted again with the ordinary dreams of spring in Divinity.

"Good-bye, Clinton," I whisper, opening the screen door to my house, relieved that the breeze brings no reply.

I'd like to thank Paul McDonough, who worked with me so tirelessly on the manuscript through its many evolutions. Thanks to Lon Otto for friendship and criticism in the right doses. Thanks to Robert Ferguson, Tom Redshaw, and Brad Guy. Thanks to Laurie Gray for her excellent job of producing the typescript from a jumble of notes and scrawls. Finally, thank you to Ned Leavitt for his years of belief in my work. And thank you to Jane von Mehren for her extraordinary efforts to bring this book into being. Her support and criticism throughout the process made it possible.